Herbert Allen Giles, Sung-ling Pu

Strange Stories from a Chinese Studio

Vol. 2

Herbert Allen Giles, Sung-ling Pu

Strange Stories from a Chinese Studio
Vol. 2

ISBN/EAN: 9783337164546

Printed in Europe, USA, Canada, Australia, Japan

Cover: Foto ©Andreas Hilbeck / pixelio.de

More available books at **www.hansebooks.com**

CHINESE STUDIO.

TRANGE STORIES

FROM A

CHINESE STUDIO.

TRANSLATED AND ANNOTATED

BY

HERBERT A. GILES,

Of H.M.'s Consular Service.

IN TWO VOLUMES.

VOL. II.

LONDON:

THOS. DE LA RUE & CO.

110, BUNHILL ROW.

1880.

STRANGE STORIES

FROM A

CHINESE STUDIO.

LXIII.

THE LO-CH'A COUNTRY AND THE SEA-MARKET.[1]

ONCE upon a time there was a young man, named Ma Chün, who was also known as Lung-mei. He was the son of a trader, and a youth of surpassing beauty. His manners were courteous, and he loved nothing better than singing and playing. He used to associate with actors, and with an embroidered handkerchief round his head the effect was that of a beautiful woman. Hence he acquired the sobriquet of the Beauty. At fourteen years of age he graduated and began to make a name for himself; but his father, who was growing old and wished to retire from business, said to him, " My boy, book-

---

[1] The term "sea-market" is generally understood in the sense of *mirage*, or some similar phenomenon.

learning will never fill your belly or put a coat on your back; you had much better stick to the old thing." Accordingly, Ma from that time occupied himself with scales and weights, with principle and interest, and such matters.

He made a voyage across the sea, and was carried away by a typhoon. After being tossed about for many days and nights he arrived at a country where the people were hideously ugly. When these people saw Ma they thought he was a devil and all ran screeching away. Ma was somewhat alarmed at this, but finding that it was they who were frightened at him, he quickly turned their fear to his own advantage. If he came across people eating and drinking he would rush upon them, and when they fled away for fear, he would regale himself upon what they had left. By-and-by he went to a village among the hills, and there the people had at any rate some facial resemblance to ordinary men. But they were all in rags and tatters like beggars. So Ma sat down to rest under a tree, and the villagers, not daring to come near him, contented themselves with looking at him from a distance. They soon found, however, that he did not want to eat them, and by degrees approached a little closer to him. Ma, smiling, began to talk; and although their language was different, yet he was able to make himself tolerably intelligible, and told them whence he had come. The villagers were much pleased, and spread the news that the stranger was not a man-eater. Nevertheless, the very ugliest of all would only take a look and be off again; they would

not come near him. Those who did go up to him were
not very much unlike his own countrymen, the Chinese.
They brought him plenty of food and wine. Ma asked
them what they were afraid of. They replied, "We had
heard from our forefathers that 26,000 *li* to the west
there is a country called China. We had heard that the
people of that land were the most extraordinary in appearance you can possibly imagine. Hitherto it has
been hearsay; we can now believe it." He then asked
them how it was they were so poor. They answered,
"You see, in our country everything depends, not on
literary talent, but on beauty. The most beautiful are
made ministers of state; the next handsomest are made
judges and magistrates; and the third class in looks are
employed in the palace of the king. Thus these are
enabled out of their pay to provide for their wives and
families. But we, from our very birth, are regarded by
our parents as inauspicious, and are left to perish, some
of us being occasionally preserved by more humane
parents to prevent the extinction of the family." Ma
asked the name of their country, and they told him it
was Lo-ch'a. Also that the capital city was some 30 *li*
to the north. He begged them to take him there, and
next day at cock-crow he started thitherwards in their
company, arriving just about dawn. The walls of the
city were made of black stone, as black as ink, and the
city gate-houses were about 100 feet high. Red stones
were used for tiles, and picking up a broken piece Ma
found that it marked his finger-nail like vermilion. They
arrived just when the Court was rising, and saw all the

equipages of the officials. The village people pointed
out one who they said was Prime Minister. His ears
drooped forward in flaps; he had three nostrils, and his
eye-lashes were just like bamboo screens hanging in
front of his eyes. Then several came out on horseback,
and they said these were the privy councillors. So they
went on, telling him the rank of all the ugly uncouth
fellows he saw. The lower they got down in the official
scale the less hideous the officials were. By-and-by Ma
went back, the people in the streets marvelling very
much to see him, and tumbling helter-skelter one over
another as if they had met a goblin. The villagers
shouted out to re-assure them, and then they stood at a
distance to look at him. When he got back, there was
not a man, woman, or child in the whole nation but
knew that there was a strange man at the village; and
the gentry and officials became very desirous to see him.
However, if he went to any of their houses the porter
always slammed the door in his face, and the master,
mistress, and family, in general, would only peep at, and
speak to him through the cracks. Not a single one
dared receive him face to face; but, finally, the village
people, at a loss what to do, bethought themselves of a
man who had been sent by a former king on official
business among strange nations. "He," said they,
"having seen many kinds of men, will not be afraid of
you." So they went to his house, where they were
received in a very friendly way. He seemed to be about
eighty or ninety years of age; his eye-balls protruded,
and his beard curled up like a hedge-hog. He said,

"In my youth I was sent by the king among many nations, but I never went to China. I am now one hundred and twenty years of age, and that I should be permitted to see a native of your country is a fact which it will be my duty to report to the Throne. For ten years and more I have not been to Court, but have remained here in seclusion; yet I will now make an effort on your behalf." Then followed a banquet, and when the wine had already circulated pretty freely, some dozen singing girls came in and sang and danced before them. The girls all wore white embroidered turbans, and long scarlet robes which trailed on the ground. The words they uttered were unintelligible, and the tunes they played perfectly hideous. The host, however, seemed to enjoy it very much, and said to Ma "Have you music in China?" He replied that they had, and the old man asked for a specimen. Ma hummed him a tune, beating time on the table, with which he was very much pleased, declaring that his guest had the voice of a phœnix and the notes of a dragon, such as he had never heard before. The next day he presented a memorial to the Throne, and the king at once commanded Ma to appear before him. Several of the ministers, however, represented that his appearance was so hideous it might frighten His Majesty, and the king accordingly desisted from his intention. The old man returned and told Ma, being quite upset about it. They remained together some time until they had drunk themselves tipsy. Then Ma, seizing a sword, began to attitudinize, smearing his face all over with coal-dust. He acted the part of Chang

Fei,[2] at which his host was so delighted that he begged him to appear before the Prime Minister in the character of Chang Fei. Ma replied "I don't mind a little amateur acting, but how can I play the hypocrite [3] for my own personal advantage?" On being pressed he consented, and the old man prepared a great feast, and asked some of the high officials to be present, telling Ma to paint himself as before. When the guests had arrived, Ma was brought out to see them; whereupon they all exclaimed "Ai-yah! how is it he was so ugly before and is now so beautiful?" By-and-by, when they were all taking wine together, Ma began to sing them a most bewitching song, and they got so excited over it that next day they recommended him to the king. The king sent a special summons for him to appear, and asked him many questions about the government of China, to all of which Ma replied in detail, eliciting sighs of admiration from His Majesty. He was honoured with a banquet in the royal guest-pavilion, and when the king had made himself tipsy he said to him "I hear you are a very skilful musician. Will you be good enough to let me hear you?" Ma then got up and began to attitudinize, singing a plaintive air like the girls with the turbans. The king was charmed, and at once made him a privy councillor, giving him a private banquet, and bestowing other marks of royal favour. As time went on

---

[2] A famous General who played a leading part in the wars of the Three Kingdoms. See No. XCIII., note 8.

[3] A hit at the hypocrisy of the age.

his fellow-officials found out the secret of his painted face,[4] and whenever he was among them they were always whispering together, besides which they avoided being near him as much as possible. Thus Ma was left to himself, and found his position anything but pleasant in consequence. So he memorialized the Throne, asking to be allowed to retire from office, but his request was refused. He then said his health was bad, and got three months' sick leave, during which he packed up his valuables and went back to the village. The villagers on his arrival went down on their knees to him, and he distributed gold and jewels amongst his old friends. They were very glad to see him, and said " Your kindness shall be repaid when we go to the sea-market; we will bring you some pearls and things." Ma asked them where that was. They said it was at the bottom of the sea, where the mermaids [5] kept their treasures, and that as many as twelve nations were accustomed to go thither to trade. Also that it was frequented by spirits, and that to get there it was necessary to pass through red vapours and great waves. " Dear Sir," they said, " do not yourself risk this great danger, but let us take your money and purchase these rare pearls for you. The season is now at hand." Ma asked them how they knew this. They said " Whenever we see red birds flying backwards and forwards over the sea, we know that within seven days the market will open." He asked when they were

---

[4] Shewing that hypocrisy is bad policy in the long run.
[5] The tears of Chinese mermaids are said to be pearls.

going to start, that he might accompany them; but they begged him not to think of doing so. He replied "I am a sailor: how can I be afraid of wind and waves?" Very soon after this people came with merchandise to forward, and so Ma packed up and went on board the vessel that was going.

This vessel held some tens of people, was flat-bottomed with a railing all round, and, rowed by ten men, it cut through the water like an arrow. After a voyage of three days they saw afar off faint outlines of towers and minarets, and crowds of trading vessels. They soon arrived at the city, the walls of which were made of bricks as long as a man's body, the tops of its buildings being lost in the Milky Way.[6] Having made fast their boat they went in, and saw laid out in the market rare pearls and wondrous precious stones of dazzling beauty, such as are quite unknown amongst men. Then they saw a young man come forth riding upon a beautiful steed. The people of the market stood back to let him pass, saying he was the third son of the king; but when the Prince saw Ma, he exclaimed "This is no foreigner," and immediately an attendant drew near and asked his name and country. Ma made a bow, and standing at one side told his name and family. The prince smiled, and said, "For you to have honoured our country thus is no small piece of good luck." He then gave him a horse and begged him to follow. They went out of the city gate and down to the sea-shore, whereupon their

---

[6] See No. XIX., note 1.

horses plunged into the water. Ma was terribly
frightened and screamed out; but the sea opened dry
before them and formed a wall of water on either side.
In a little time they reached the king's palace, the beams
of which were made of tortoise-shell and the tiles of
fishes' scales. The four walls were of crystal, and
dazzled the eye like mirrors. They got down off their
horses and went in, and Ma was introduced to the king.
The young prince said, " Sire, I have been to the
market, and have got a gentleman from China." Whereupon Ma made obeisance before the king, who addressed him as follows:—" Sir, from a talented scholar
like yourself I venture to ask for a few stanzas upon our
sea-market. Pray do not refuse." Ma thereupon made
a *kot'ow*, and undertook the king's command. Using an
ink-slab of crystal, a brush of dragon's beard, paper as
white as snow, and ink scented like the larkspur,[7] Ma
immediately threw off some thousand odd verses, which
he laid at the feet of the king. When His Majesty saw
them, he said, " Sir, your genius does honour to these
marine nations of ours." Then, summoning the members
of the royal family, the king gave a great feast in the
Coloured Cloud pavilion; and, when the wine had
circulated freely, seizing a great goblet in his hand, the
king rose and said before all the guests, " It is a thousand
pities, Sir, that you are not married. What say you to

---

[7] Good ink of the kind miscalled " Indian," is usually very highly
scented ; and from a habit the Chinese have of sucking their
writing-brushes to a fine point, the phrase " to eat ink " has become
a synonym of " to study."

entering the bonds of wedlock?" Ma rose blushing, and stammered out his thanks; upon which the king looking round spoke a few words to the attendants, and in a few moments in came a bevy of court ladies supporting the king's daughter, whose ornaments went tinkle, tinkle, as she walked along. Immediately the nuptial drums and trumpets began to sound forth, and bride and bridegroom worshipped Heaven and Earth together.[8] Stealing a glance Ma saw that the princess was endowed with a fairy-like loveliness. When the ceremony was over she retired, and by-and-by the wine-party broke up. Then came several beautifully-dressed waiting-maids, who with painted candles escorted Ma within. The bridal couch was made of coral adorned with eight kinds of precious stones, and the curtains were thickly hung with pearls as big as acorns. Next day at dawn a crowd of young slave-girls trooped into the room to offer their services; whereupon Ma got up and went off to Court to pay his respects to the king. He was then duly received as royal son-in-law and made an officer of state. The fame of his poetical talents spread far and wide, and the kings of the various seas sent officers to congratulate him, vying with each other in their invitations to him. Ma dressed himself in gorgeous clothes, and went forth riding on a superb steed, with a mounted body-guard all splendidly armed. There were musicians on horseback and musicians in

---

[8] This all-important point in a Chinese marriage ceremony is the equivalent of our own " signing in the vestry."

chariots, and in three days he had visited every one
of the marine kingdoms, making his name known in
all directions. In the palace there was a jade tree,
about as big round as a man could clasp. Its roots
were as clear as glass, and up the middle ran, as it were,
a stick of pale yellow. The branches were the size of
one's arm; the leaves like white jade, as thick as a
copper cash. The foliage was dense, and beneath its
shade the ladies of the palace were wont to sit and sing.
The flowers which covered the tree resembled grapes,
and if a single petal fell to the earth it made a ringing
sound. Taking one up, it would be found to be exactly
like carved cornelian, very bright and pretty to look at.
From time to time a wonderful bird came and sang
there. Its feathers were of a golden hue, and its tail as
long as its body. Its notes were like the tinkling of
jade, very plaintive and touching to listen to. When Ma
heard this bird sing, it called up in him recollections of
his old home, and accordingly he said to the princess,
" I have now been away from my own country for three
years, separated from my father and mother. Thinking
of them my tears flow and the perspiration runs down
my back. Can you return with me ? " His wife replied,
" The way of immortals is not that of men. I am
unable to do what you ask, but I cannot allow the feelings of husband and wife to break the tie of parent and
child. Let us devise some plan." When Ma heard this
he wept bitterly, and the princess sighed and said, " We
cannot both stay or both go." The next day the king
said to him " I hear that you are pining after your old

home. Will to-morrow suit you for taking leave ? " Ma
thanked the king for his great kindness, which he declared he could never forget, and promised to return
very shortly.   That evening the princess and Ma talked
over their wine of their approaching separation. Ma
said they would soon meet again ; but his wife averred
that their married life was at an end. Then he wept
afresh, but the princess said, " Like a filial son you are
going home to your parents. In the meetings and
separations of this life, a hundred years seem but a
single day; why, then, should we give way to tears like
children? I will be true to you ; do you be faithful to
me ; and then, though separated, we shall be united in
spirit, a happy pair. Is it necessary to live side by side in
order to grow old together? If you break our contract
your next marriage will not be a propitious one ; but if
loneliness [9] overtakes you then choose a concubine.
There is one point more of which I would speak, with
reference to our married life. I am about to become a
mother, and I pray you give me a name for your child."
To this Ma replied, " If a girl I would have her called
Lung Kung ; if a boy, then name him Fu-Hai. " [10] The
princess asked for some token of remembrance, and Ma
gave her a pair of jade lilies that he had got during his
stay in the marine kingdom. She added " On the 8th
of the 4th moon, three years hence, when you once

---

[9] Literally, " if you have no one to cook your food."
[10] " Dragon Palace " and " Happy Sea," respectively.

more steer your course for this country, I will give you
up your child." She next packed a leather bag full of
jewels and handed it to Ma, saying, "Take care of this ;
it will be a provision for many generations." When the
day began to break a splendid farewell feast was given him
by the king, and Ma bade them all adieu. The princess,
in a car drawn by snow-white sheep, escorted him to the
boundary of the marine kingdom, where he dismounted
and stepped ashore. "Farewell !" cried the princess, as
her returning car bore her rapidly away, and the sea,
closing over her, snatched her from her husband's sight.
Ma returned to his home across the ocean. Some had
thought him long since dead and gone ; all marvelled at
his story. Happily his father and mother were yet alive,
though his former wife had married another man ; and
so he understood why the princess had pledged him to
constancy, for she already knew that this had taken
place. His father wished him to take another wife, but
he would not. He only took a concubine. Then, after
the three years had passed away, he started across the
sea on his return journey, when lo ! he beheld, riding on
the wave-crests and splashing about the water in playing,
two young children. On going near, one of them seized
hold of him and sprung into his arms ; upon which the
elder cried until he, too, was taken up. They were a boy
and girl, both very lovely, and wearing embroidered caps
adorned with jade lilies. On the back of one of them
was a worked case, in which Ma found the following
letter :—

"I presume my father and mother-in-law are well.

Three years have passed away and destiny still keeps us apart. Across the great ocean, the letter-bird would find no path.[11] I have been with you in my dreams until I am quite worn out. Does the blue sky look down upon any grief like mine? Yet Ch'ang-ngo[12] lives solitary in the moon, and Chih Nü[13] laments that she cannot cross the Silver River. Who am I that I should expect happiness to be mine? Truly this thought turns my tears into joy. Two months after your departure I had twins, who can already prattle away in the language of childhood, at one moment snatching a date, at another a pear. Had they no mother they would still live. These I now send to you, with the jade lilies you gave me in their hats, in token of the sender. When you take them upon your knee, think that I am standing by your side. I know that you have kept your promise to me, and I am happy. I shall take no second husband, even unto death. All thoughts of dress and finery are gone from me; my looking-glass sees no new fashions; my face has long been unpowdered, my eyebrows unblacked. You are my Ulysses, I am your Penelope;[14] though not actually leading a married life, how can it be said that

---

[11] Alluding to an old legend of a letter conveyed by a bird.

[12] See No. V., note 2.

[13] The "Spinning Damsel," or name of a star in Lyra, connected with which there is a celebrated legend of its annual transit across the Milky Way.

[14] These are of course only the equivalents of the Chinese names in the text.

we are not husband and wife. Your father and mother will take their grandchildren upon their knees, though they have never set eyes upon the bride. Alas! there is something wrong in this. Next year your mother will enter upon the long night. I shall be there by the side of the grave as is becoming in her daughter-in-law. From this time forth our daughter will be well; later on she will be able to grasp her mother's hand. Our boy, when he grows up, may possibly be able to come to and fro. Adieu, dear husband, adieu, though I am leaving much unsaid." Ma read the letter over and over again, his tears flowing all the time. His two children clung round his neck, and begged him to take them home. "Ah, my children," said he, "where is your home?" Then they all wept bitterly, and Ma, looking at the great ocean stretching away to meet the sky, lovely and pathless, embraced his children, and proceeded sorrowfully to return. Knowing, too, that his mother could not last long, he prepared everything necessary for the ceremony of interment, and planted a hundred young pine-trees at her grave.[15] The following year the old lady did die, and her coffin was borne to its last resting-place, when lo! there was the princess standing by the side of the grave. The lookers-on were much alarmed, but in a moment there was a flash of lightning, followed by a clap of thunder and a squall of rain, and she was gone.

---

[15] To keep off the much-dreaded wind, which disturbs the rest of the departed.

It was then noticed that many of the young pine-trees which had died were one and all brought to life. Subsequently, Fu Hai went in search of the mother for whom he pined so much, and after some days' absence returned. Lung Kung, being a girl, could not accompany him, but she mourned much in secret. One dark day her mother entered and bid her dry her eyes, saying, " My child, you must get married. Why these tears?" She then gave her a tree of coral eight feet in height, some Baroos camphor,[16] one hundred valuable pearls, and two boxes inlaid with gold and precious stones, as her dowry. Ma having found out she was there, rushed in and seizing her hand began to weep for joy, when suddenly a violent peal of thunder rent the building, and the princess had vanished.

---

[16] For which a very high price is obtained in China.

LXIV.

THE FIGHTING CRICKET.

During the reign of Hsüan Tê,[1] cricket fighting was very much in vogue at court, levies of crickets being exacted from the people as a tax. On one occasion the magistrate of Hua-yin, wishing to make friends with the Governor, presented him with a cricket which, on being set to fight, displayed very remarkable powers; so much so that the Governor commanded the magistrate to supply him regularly with these insects. The latter, in his turn, ordered the beadles of his district to provide him with crickets; and then it became a practice for people who had nothing else to do to catch and rear them for this purpose. Thus the price of crickets rose very high; and when the beadle's[2] runners came to

---

[1] Of the Ming dynasty; reigned A.D. 1426—1436.

[2] These beadles are chosen by the officials from among the respectable and substantial of the people to preside over a small area and be responsible for the general good behaviour of its inhabitants. The post is one of honour and occasional emolument, since all petitions presented to the authorities, all mortgages, transfers of land, &c., should bear the beadle's seal or signature in

exact even a single one, it was enough to ruin several families.

Now in the village of which we are speaking there lived a man named Ch'êng, a student who had often failed for his bachelor's degree; and, being a stupid sort of fellow, his name was sent in for the post of beadle. He did all he could to get out of it, but without success; and by the end of the year his small patrimony was gone. Just then came a call for crickets, and Ch'êng, not daring to make a like call upon his neighbours, was at his wits' end, and in his distress determined to commit suicide. "What's the use of that?" cried his wife. "You'd do better to go out and try to find some." So off went Ch'êng in the early morning, with a bamboo tube and a silk net, not returning till late at night; and he searched about in tumble-down walls, in bushes, under stones, and in holes, but without catching more than two or three, do what he would. Even those he did catch were weak creatures, and of no use at all, which made the magistrate fix a limit of time, the result of which was that in a few days Ch'êng got one hundred blows with the bamboo. This made him so sore that he was quite unable to go after the crickets any more, and,

---

evidence of their *bonâ fide* character. On the other hand, the beadle is punished by fine, and sometimes bambooed, if robberies are too frequent within his jurisdiction, or if he fails to secure the person of any malefactor particularly wanted by his superior officers. And other causes may combine to make the post a dangerous one; but no one is allowed to refuse acceptance of it point-blank.

as he lay tossing and turning on the bed, he determined
once again to put an end to his life.

About that time a hump-backed fortune-teller of great
skill arrived at the village, and Ch'êng's wife, putting together a trifle of money, went off to seek his assistance.
The door was literally blocked up—fair young girls and
white-headed dames crowding in from all quarters. A
room was darkened, and a bamboo screen hung at the
door, an altar being arranged outside at which the
fortune-seekers burnt incense in a brazier, and prostrated
themselves twice, while the soothsayer stood by the side,
and, looking up into vacancy, prayed for a response. His
lips opened and shut, but nobody heard what he said, all
standing there in awe waiting for the answer. In a few
moments a piece of paper was thrown from behind the
screen, and the soothsayer said that the petitioner's desire would be accomplished in the way he wished.
Ch'êng's wife now advanced, and, placing some money
on the altar, burnt her incense and prostrated herself in
a similar manner. In a few moments the screen began
to move, and a piece of paper was thrown down, on
which there were no words, but only a picture. In the
middle was a building like a temple, and behind this a
small hill, at the foot which were a number of curious
stones, with the long, spiky feelers of innumerable
crickets appearing from behind. Hard by was a frog,
which seemed to be engaged in putting itself into various
kinds of attitudes. The good woman had no idea what
it all meant; but she noticed the crickets, and accordingly went off home to tell her husband. "Ah," said

he, "this is to shew me where to hunt for crickets;" and, on looking closely at the picture, he saw that the building very much resembled a temple to the east of their village. So he forced himself to get up, and, leaning on a stick, went out to seek crickets behind the temple. Rounding an old grave, he came upon a place where stones were lying scattered about as in the picture, and then he set himself to watch attentively. He might as well have been looking for a needle or a grain of mustard-seed; and by degrees he became quite exhausted, without finding anything, when suddenly an old frog jumped out. Ch'êng was a little startled, but immediately pursued the frog, which retreated into the bushes. He then saw one of the insects he wanted sitting at the root of a bramble; but on making a grab at it, the cricket ran into a hole, from which he was unable to move it until he poured in some water, when out the little creature came. It was a magnificent specimen, strong and handsome, with a fine tail, green neck, and golden wings; and, putting it in his basket, he returned home in high glee to receive the congratulations of his family. He would not have taken anything for this cricket, and proceeded to feed it up carefully in a bowl. Its belly was the colour of a crab's, its back that of a sweet chestnut; and Ch'êng tended it most lovingly, waiting for the time when the magistrate should call upon him for a cricket.

Meanwhile, a son of Ch'êng's, aged nine, one day took the opportunity of his father being out to open the bowl. Instantaneously the cricket made a spring for-

ward and was gone; and all efforts to catch it again
were unavailing. At length the boy made a grab at it
with his hand, but only succeeded in seizing one of its
legs, which thereupon broke, and the little creature soon
afterwards died. Ch'êng's wife turned deadly pale when
her son, with tears in his eyes, told her what had happened. "Oh! won't you catch it when your father
comes home," said she; at which the boy ran away,
crying bitterly. Soon after Ch'êng arrived, and when he
heard his wife's story he felt as if he had been turned to
ice, and went in search of his son, who, however, was
nowhere to be found, until at length they discovered his
body lying at the bottom of a well. Their anger was
thus turned to grief, and death seemed as though it
would be a pleasant relief to them as they sat facing
each other in silence in their thatched and smokeless[3]
hut. At evening they prepared to bury the boy; but,
on touching the body, lo! he was still breathing. Overjoyed, they placed him upon the bed, and towards the
middle of the night he came round; but a drop of
bitterness was mingled in his parents' cup when they
found that his reason had fled. His father, however,
caught sight of the empty bowl in which he had kept
the cricket, and ceased to think any more about his son,
never once closing his eyes all night; and as day
gradually broke, there he lay stiff and stark, until
suddenly he heard the chirping of a cricket outside

---

[3] A favourite Chinese expression, signifying the absence of food.

the house door. Jumping up in a great hurry to see, there was his lost insect; but, on trying to catch it, away it hopped directly. At last he got it under his hand, though, when he came to close his fingers on it, there was nothing in them. So he went on, chasing it up and down, until finally it hopped into a corner of the wall; and then, looking carefully about, he espied it once more, no longer the same in appearance, but small, and of a dark red colour. Ch'êng stood looking at it, without trying to catch such a worthless specimen, when all of a sudden the little creature hopped into his sleeve; and, on examining it more nearly, he saw that it really was a handsome insect, with well-formed head and neck, and forthwith took it indoors. He was now anxious to try its prowess; and it so happened that a young fellow of the village, who had a fine cricket which used to win every bout it fought, and was so valuable to him that he wanted a high price for it, called on Ch'êng that very day. He laughed heartily at Ch'êng's champion, and, producing his own, placed it side by side, to the great disadvantage of the former. Ch'êng's countenance fell, and he no longer wished to back his cricket; however, the young fellow urged him, and he thought that there was no use in rearing a feeble insect, and that he had better sacrifice it for a laugh; so they put them together in a bowl. The little cricket lay quite still like a piece of wood, at which the young fellow roared again, and louder than ever when it did not move even though tickled with a pig's bristle. By dint of tickling it was roused at last, and then it fell upon its adversary with such fury, that in a moment the young fellow's cricket would have been killed outright had not its master interfered and stopped the fight. The little cricket then stood up and chirped to Ch'êng as a sign of victory; and Ch'êng, overjoyed, was just talking over the battle with the young fellow, when a cock caught sight of the insect, and ran up to eat it. Ch'êng was in a great state of alarm; but the cock luckily missed its aim, and the cricket hopped away, its enemy pursuing at full speed. In another moment it would have been snapped up, when, lo! to his great astonishment, Ch'êng saw his cricket seated on the cock's head, holding firmly on to its comb. He then put it into a cage, and by-and-by sent it to the magistrate, who, seeing what a small one he had provided, was very angry indeed. Ch'êng told the story of the cock, which the magistrate refused to believe, and set it to fight with other crickets, all of which it vanquished without exception. He then tried it with a cock, and as all turned out as Ch'êng had said, he gave him a present, and sent the cricket in to the Governor. The Governor put it into a golden cage, and forwarded it to the palace, accompanied by some remarks on its performances; and when there, it was found that of all the splendid collection of His Imperial Majesty, not one was worthy to be placed alongside of this one. It would dance in time to music, and thus became a great favourite, the Emperor in return bestowing magnificent gifts of horses and silks upon the Governor. The Governor did not forget whence he had obtained the cricket, and the magistrate also well rewarded Ch'êng by excusing him from the duties of beadle, and by instructing the Literary Chancellor to pass him for the first degree. A few months afterwards Ch'êng's son recovered his intellect, and said that he had been a cricket, and had proved himself a very skilful fighter.[4] The Governor, too, rewarded Ch'êng handsomely, and in a few years he was a rich man, with flocks, and herds, and houses, and acres, quite one of the wealthiest of mankind.

---

[4] That is to say, his spirit had entered, during his period of temporary insanity, into the cricket which had allowed itself to be caught by his father, and had animated it to fight with such extraordinary vigour in order to make good the loss occasioned by his carelessness in letting the other escape.

LXV.

TAKING REVENGE.

HSIANG KAO, otherwise called Ch'u-tan, was a T'ai-yüan man, and deeply attached to his half-brother Shêng. Shêng himself was desperately enamoured of a young lady named Po-ssŭ,[1] who was also very fond of him : but the mother wanted too much money for her daughter. Now a rich young fellow named Chuang thought he should like to get Po-ssŭ for himself, and proposed to buy her as a concubine. "No, no," said Po-ssŭ to her mother, "I prefer being Shêng's wife to becoming Chuang's concubine." So her mother consented, and informed Shêng, who had only recently buried his first wife; at which he was delighted and made preparations to take her over to his own house. When Chuang heard this he was infuriated against Shêng for thus depriving him of Po-ssŭ ; and chancing to meet him out one day, set to and abused him

---

[1] This is the term used by the Chinese for " Persia," often put by metonymy for things which come from that country, *sc.* "valuables." Thus, "to be poor in Persia" is to have but few jewels, gold and silver ornaments, and even clothes.

roundly. Shêng answered him back, and then Chuang ordered his attendants to fall upon Shêng and beat him well, which they did, leaving him lifeless on the ground. When Hsiang heard what had taken place he ran out and found his brother lying dead upon the ground. Overcome with grief, he proceeded to the magistrate's, and accused Chuang of murder; but the latter bribed so heavily that nothing came of the accusation. This worked Hsiang to frenzy, and he determined to assassinate Chuang on the high road; with which intent he daily concealed himself, with a sharp knife about him, among the bushes on the hill-side, waiting for Chuang to pass. By degrees, this plan of his became known far and wide, and accordingly Chuang never went out except with a strong body-guard, besides which he engaged at a high price the services of a very skilful archer, named Chiao T'ung, so that Hsiang had no means of carrying out his intention. However, he continued to lie in wait day after day, and on one occasion it began to rain heavily, and in a short time Hsiang was wet through to the skin. Then the wind got up, and a hailstorm followed, and by-and-by Hsiang was quite numbed with the cold. On the top of the hill there was a small temple wherein lived a Taoist priest, whom Hsiang knew from the latter having occasionally begged alms in the village, and to whom he had often given a meal. This priest, seeing how wet he was, gave him some other clothes, and told him to put them on; but no sooner had he done so than he crouched down like a dog, and found that he had been changed into a tiger, and that the priest had vanished. It now occurred to him to seize this opportunity of revenging himself upon his enemy; and away he went to his old ambush, where lo and behold! he found his own body lying stiff and stark. Fearing lest it should become food for birds of prey, he guarded it carefully, until at length one day Chuang passed by. Out rushed the tiger and sprung upon Chuang, biting his head off, and swallowing it upon the spot; at which Chiao T'ung, the archer, turned round and shot the animal through the heart. Just at that moment Hsiang awaked as though from a dream, but it was some time before he could crawl home, where he arrived to the great delight of his family, who didn't know what had become of him. Hsiang said not a word, lying quietly on the bed until some of his people came in to congratulate him on the death of his great enemy Chuang. Hsiang then cried out, "I was that tiger," and proceeded to relate the whole story, which thus got about until it reached the ears of Chuang's son, who immediately set to work to bring his father's murderer to justice. The magistrate, however, did not consider this wild story as sufficient evidence against him, and thereupon dismissed the case.

LXVI.

THE TIPSY TURTLE.

At Lin-t'iao there lived a Mr. Fêng, whose other name the person who told me this story could not remember; he belonged to a good family, though now somewhat falling into decay. Now a certain man, who caught turtles, owed him some money which he could not pay, but whenever he captured any turtles he used to send one to Mr. Fêng. One day he took him an enormous creature, with a white spot on its forehead; but Fêng was so struck with something in its appearance, that he let it go again. A little while afterwards he was returning home from his son-in-law's, and had reached the banks of the river,[1] when in the dusk of the evening he saw a drunken man come rolling along, attended by two or three servants. No

---

[1] The name here used is the *Hêng* or "ceaseless" river, which is applied by the Chinese to the Ganges. A certain number, extending to fifty-three places of figures, is called "Ganges sand," in allusion to a famous remark that "Buddha and the Bôdhisatvas knew of the creation and destruction of every grain of dust in Jambudwipa (the universe); how much more the number of the sand-particles in the river Ganges?"

sooner did he perceive Fêng than he called out, "Who
are you?" to which Fêng replied that he was a traveller. "And haven't you got a name?" shouted out
the drunken man in a rage, "that you must call yourself a traveller?" To this Fêng made no reply, but
tried to pass by; whereupon he found himself seized
by the sleeve and unable to move. His adversary
smelt horribly of wine, and at length Fêng asked him,
saying, "And pray who are you?" "Oh, I am the
late magistrate at Nan-tu," answered he; "what do
you want to know for?" "A nice disgrace to society
you are, too," cried Fêng; "however, I am glad to
hear you are only *late* magistrate, for if you had been
present magistrate there would be bad times in store
for travellers." This made the drunken man furious,
and he was proceeding to use violence, when Fêng
cried out, "My name is So-and-so, and I'm not the
man to stand this sort of thing from anybody." No
sooner had he uttered these words than the drunken
man's rage was turned into joy, and, falling on his
knees before Fêng, he said, "My benefactor! pray
excuse my rudeness." Then getting up, he told his
servants to go on ahead and get something ready;
Fêng at first declining to go with him, but yielding on
being pressed. Taking his hand, the drunken man led
him along a short distance until they reached a village,
where there was a very nice house and grounds, quite
like the establishment of a person of position. As his
friend was now getting sober, Fêng inquired what
might be his name. "Don't be frightened when I tell

you," said the other; "I am the Eighth Prince of the
T'iao river. I have just been out to take wine with
a friend, and somehow I got tipsy; hence my bad behaviour to you, which please forgive." Fêng now knew
that he was not of mortal flesh and blood; but, seeing
how kindly he himself was treated, he was not a bit afraid.
A banquet followed, with plenty of wine, of which the
Eighth Prince drank so freely that Fêng thought he
would soon be worse than ever, and accordingly said
he felt tipsy himself, and asked to be allowed to go to
bed. "Never fear," answered the Prince, who perceived Fêng's thoughts; "many drunkards will tell you
that they cannot remember in the morning the extravagances of the previous night, but I tell you this
is all nonsense, and that in nine cases out of ten
those extravagances are committed wittingly and with
malice prepense.[2] Now, though I am not the same
order of being as yourself, I should never venture to
behave badly in your good presence; so pray do not
leave me thus." Fêng then sat down again and said
to the Prince, " Since you are aware of this, why not
change your ways?" "Ah," replied the Prince, " when
I was a magistrate I drank much more than I do now;
but I got into disgrace with the Emperor and was
banished here, since which time, ten years and more, I

---

[2] Drunkenness is not recognised in China as an extenuating
circumstance; neither, indeed, is insanity,—a lunatic who takes
another man's life being equally liable with ordinary persons to the
forfeiture of his own.

have tried to reform. Now, however, I am drawing near the wood,[3] and being unable to move about much, the old vice has come upon me again ; I have found it impossible to stop myself, but perhaps what you say may do me some good." While they were thus talking, the sound of a distant bell broke upon their ears ; and the Prince, getting up and seizing Fêng's hand, said, "We cannot remain together any longer; but I will give you something by which I may in part requite your kindness to me. It must not be kept for any great length of time; when you have attained your wishes, then I will receive it back again." Thereupon he spit out of his mouth a tiny man, no more than an inch high, and scratching Fêng's arm with his nails until Fêng felt as if the skin was gone, he quickly laid the little man upon the spot. When he let go, the latter had already sunk into the skin, and nothing was to be seen but a cicatrix well healed over. Fêng now asked what it all meant, but the Prince only laughed, and said, " It's time for you to go," and forthwith escorted him to the door. The prince here bade him adieu, and when he looked round, Prince, village, and house had all disappeared together, leaving behind a great turtle which

---

[3] A favourite Chinese figure expressive of old age. It dates back to the celebrated commentary by Tso Ch'iu Ming on Confucius' *Spring and Autumn* (See No. XLI., note 2):—"Hsi is twenty-three and I am twenty-five; and marrying thus we shall approach the wood together;" the "wood" being, of course, that of the coffin.

waddled down into the water, and disappeared likewise. He could now easily account for the Prince's present to him; and from this moment his sight became intensely keen. He could see precious stones lying in the bowels of the earth, and was able to look down as far as Hell itself; besides which he suddenly found that he knew the names of many things of which he had never heard before. From below his own bedroom he dug up many hundred ounces of pure silver, upon which he lived very comfortably; and once when a house was for sale, he perceived that in it lay concealed a vast quantity of gold, so he immediately bought it, and so became immensely rich in all kinds of valuables. He secured a mirror, on the back of which was a phœnix, surrounded by water and clouds, and portraits of the celebrated wives of the Emperor Shun,[4] so beautifully executed that each hair of the head and eyebrows could easily be counted. If any woman's face came upon the mirror, there it remained indelibly fixed and not to be rubbed out; but if the same woman looked into the mirror again, dressed in a different dress, or if some other woman chanced to look in, then the former face would gradually fade away.

Now the third princess in Prince Su's family was very beautiful; and Fêng, who had long heard of her fame, concealed himself on the K'ung-tung hill, when he knew the Princess was going there. He waited until she

---

4 See No. VIII., note 3.

alighted from her chair, and then getting the mirror full upon her, he walked off home. Laying it on the table, he saw therein a lovely girl in the act of raising her handkerchief, and with a sweet smile playing over her face; her lips seemed about to move, and a twinkle was discernible in her eyes.[5] Delighted with this picture, he put the mirror very carefully away; but in about a year his wife had let the story leak out, and the Prince, hearing of it, threw Fêng into prison, and took possession of the mirror. Fêng was to be beheaded; however, he bribed one of the Prince's ladies to tell His Highness that if he would pardon him all the treasures of the earth might easily become his; whereas, on the other hand, his death could not possibly be of any advantage to the Prince. The Prince now thought of confiscating all his goods and banishing him; but the third princess observed, that as he had already seen her, were he to die ten times over it would not give her back her lost face, and that she had much better marry him. The Prince would not hear of this, whereupon his daughter shut herself up and refused all nourishment, at which the ladies of the palace were dreadfully alarmed, and reported it at once to the Prince. Fêng was accordingly liberated, and was informed of the determination of the Princess, which, however, he declined to fall in with,

---

[5] " .... Move these eyes?
.... Here are severed lips."
—*Merchant of Venice*, Act. iii., sc. 2.

saying that he was not going thus to sacrifice the wife of his days of poverty,[6] and would rather die than carry out such an order. He added that if His Highness would consent, he would purchase his liberty at the price of everything he had. The Prince was exceedingly angry at this, and seized Fêng again; and meanwhile one of the concubines got Fêng's wife into the palace, intending to poison her. Fêng's wife, however, brought her a beautiful present of a coral stand for a looking-glass, and was so agreeable in her conversation, that the concubine took a great fancy to her, and presented her to the Princess, who was equally pleased, and forthwith determined that they would both be Fêng's wives.[7] When Fêng heard of this plan, he said to his wife, "With a Prince's daughter there can be no distinctions of first and second wife;" but Mrs. Fêng paid no heed to him, and immediately sent off to the Prince such an enormous quantity of valuables that it took a thousand men to carry them, and the Prince himself had never before heard of such treasures in his life. Fêng was now liberated once more, and solemnized his marriage with the Princess.

One night after this he dreamt that the Eighth Prince came to him and asked him to return his former present, saying that to keep it too long would

---

[6] See No. LIII., note 1.

[7] This method of arranging a matrimonial difficulty is a common one in Chinese fiction, but I should say quite unknown in real life.

be injurious to his chances of life. Fêng asked him to take a drink, but the Eighth Prince said that he had forsworn wine, acting under Fêng's advice, for three years. He then bit Fêng's arm, and the latter waked up with the pain to find that the cicatrix on his arm was no longer there.

LXVII.

THE MAGIC PATH.

In the province of Kuangtung there lived a scholar named Kuo, who was one evening on his way home from a friend's, when he lost his way among the hills. He got into a thick jungle, where, after about an hour's wandering, he suddenly heard the sound of laughing and talking on the top of the hill. Hurrying up in the direction of the sound, he beheld some ten or a dozen persons sitting on the ground engaged in drinking. No sooner had they caught sight of Kuo than they all cried out, "Come along! just room for one more; you're in the nick of time." So Kuo sat down with the company, most of whom, he noticed, belonged to the literati,[1] and began by asking them to direct him on his way home;

---

[1] This term, while really including all literary men, of no matter what rank or standing, is more usually confined to that large section of unemployed scholarship made up of (1) those who are waiting to get started in an official career, (2) those who have taken one or more degrees and are preparing for the next, (3) those who have failed to distinguish themselves at the public examinations, and eke out a small patrimony by taking pupils, and (4) scholars of sufficiently high qualifications who have no taste for official life.

but one of them cried out, "A nice sort of fellow you are, to be bothering about your way home, and paying no attention to the fine moon we have got to-night." The speaker then presented him with a goblet of wine of exquisite bouquet, which Kuo drank off at a draught, and another gentleman filled up again for him at once. Now, Kuo was pretty good in that line, and being very thirsty withal from his long walk, tossed off bumper after bumper, to the great delight of his hosts, who were unanimous in voting him a jolly good fellow. He was, moreover, full of fun, and could imitate exactly the note of any kind of bird ; so all of a sudden he began on the sly to twitter like a swallow, to the great astonishment of the others, who wondered how it was a swallow could be out so late. He then changed his note to that of a cuckoo, sitting there laughing and saying nothing, while his hosts were discussing the extraordinary sounds they had just heard. After a while he imitated a parrot, and cried, "Mr. Kuo is very drunk : you'd better see him home ; " and then the sounds ceased, beginning again by-and-by, when at last the others found out who it was, and all burst out laughing. They screwed up their mouths and tried to whistle like Kuo, but none of them could do so ; and soon one of them observed, "What a pity Madam Ch'ing isn't with us : we must rendezvous here again at mid-autumn, and you, Mr. Kuo, must be sure and come." Kuo said he would, whereupon another of his hosts got up and remarked that, as he had given them such an amusing entertainment, they would try to shew him a few acrobatic feats. They all arose, and one of them planting his feet firmly, a second jumped up on to his shoulders, a third on to the second's shoulders, and a fourth on to his, until it was too high for the rest to jump up, and accordingly they began to climb as though it had been a ladder. When they were all up, and the topmost head seemed to touch the clouds, the whole column bent gradually down until it lay along the ground transformed into a path. Kuo remained for some time in a state of considerable alarm, and then, setting out along this path, ultimately reached his own home. Some days afterwards he revisited the spot, and saw the remains of a feast lying about on the ground, with dense bushes on all sides, but no sign of a path. At mid-autumn he thought of keeping his engagement; however, his friends persuaded him not to go.

LXVIII.

THE FAITHLESS WIDOW.[1]

MR. NIU was a Kiangsi man who traded in piece goods. He married a wife from the Chêng family, by whom he had two children, a boy and a girl. When thirty-three years of age he fell ill and died, his son Chung being then only twelve and his little girl eight or nine. His wife did not remain faithful to his memory, but, selling off all the property, pocketed the proceeds and married another man, leaving her two children almost in a state of destitution with their aunt, Niu's sister-in-law, an old lady of sixty, who had lived with them previously, and had now nowhere to seek a shelter.

---

[1] Unless under exceptional circumstances it is not considered creditable in China for widows to marry again. It may here be mentioned that the honorary tablets conferred from time to time by His Imperial Majesty upon virtuous widows are only given to women who, widowed before the age of thirty, have remained in that state for a period of thirty years. The meaning of this is obvious: temptations are supposed to be fewer and less dangerous after thirty, which is the equivalent of forty with us; and it is wholly improbable that thirty years of virtuous life, at which period the widow would be at least fifty, would be followed by any act that might cast a stain upon the tablet thus bestowed.

A few years later this aunt died, and the family fortunes began to sink even lower than before; Chung, however, was now grown up, and determined to carry on his father's trade, only he had no capital to start with. His sister marrying a rich trader·named Mao, she begged her husband to lend Chung ten ounces of silver, which he did, and Chung immediately started for Nanking. On the road he fell in with some bandits, who robbed him of all he had, and consequently he was unable to return; but one day when he was at a pawnshop he noticed that the master of the shop was wonderfully like his late father, and on going out and making inquiries he found that this pawnbroker bore precisely the same names. In great astonishment, he forthwith proceeded to frequent the place with no other object than to watch this man, who, on the other hand, took no notice of Chung; and by the end of three days, having satisfied himself that he really saw his own father, and yet not daring to disclose his own identity, he made application through one of the assistants, on the score of being himself a Kiangsi man, to be employed in the shop. Accordingly, an indenture was drawn up; and when the master noticed Chung's name and place of residence he started, and asked him whence he came. With tears in his eyes Chung addressed him by his father's name, and then the pawnbroker became lost in a deep reverie, by-and-by asking Chung how his mother was. Now Chung did not like to allude to his father's death, and turned the question by saying, " My father went away on business six years ago, and never came back; my

mother married again and left us, and had it not been
for my aunt our corpses would long ago have been cast
out in the kennel." Then the pawnbroker was much
moved, and cried out, "I am your father!" seizing his
son's hand and leading him within to see his step-mother.
This lady was about twenty-two, and, having no children
of her own, was delighted with Chung, and prepared a
banquet for him in the inner apartments. Mr. Niu himself was, however, somewhat melancholy, and wished to
return to his old home; but his wife, fearing that there
would be no one to manage the business, persuaded him
to remain; so he taught his son the trade, and in three
months was able to leave it all to him. He then prepared for his journey, whereupon Chung informed his
step-mother that his father was really dead, to which she
replied in great consternation that she knew him only as
a trader to the place, and that six years previously he
had married her, which proved conclusively that he
couldn't be dead. He then recounted the whole story,
which was a perfect mystery to both of them; and
twenty-four hours afterwards in walked his father, leading
a woman whose hair was all dishevelled. Chung looked
at her and saw that she was his own mother; and Niu
took her by the ear and began to revile her, saying,
"Why did you desert my children?" to which the
wretched woman made no reply. He then bit her
across the neck, at which she screamed to Chung for
assistance, and he, not being able to bear the sight,
stepped in between them. His father was more than
ever enraged at this, when, lo! Chung's mother had dis-

appeared. While they were still lost in astonishment at this strange scene, Mr. Niu's colour changed; in another moment his empty clothes had dropped upon the ground, and he himself became a black vapour and also vanished from their sight. The step-mother and son were much overcome; they took Niu's clothes and buried them, and after that Chung continued his father's business and soon amassed great wealth. On returning to his native place he found that his mother had actually died on the very day of the above occurrence, and that his father had been seen by the whole family.

LXIX.

THE PRINCESS OF THE TUNG-T'ING LAKE.

CH'EN PI-CHIAO was a Pekingese; and being a poor man he attached himself as secretary to the suite of a high military official named Chia. On one occasion, while anchored on the Tung-t'ing lake, they saw a dolphin[1] floating on the surface of the water; and General Chia took his bow and shot at it, wounding the creature in the back. A fish was hanging on to its tail, and would not let go; so both were pulled out of the water together, and attached to the mast. There

---

[1] Literally, a "pig old-woman dragon." Porpoise (Fr. *porc-poisson*) suggests itself at once; but I think fresh-water dolphin is the best term, especially as the Tung-t'ing lake is many hundred miles inland. The commentator explains it by *t'o*, which would be "alligator" or "cayman," and is of course out of the question. My friend, Mr. L. C. Hopkins, has taken the trouble to make some investigations for me on this subject. He tells me that this fish, also called the "river pig," has first to be surrounded and secured by a strong net. Being too large to be hauled on board a boat, it is then driven ashore, where oil is extracted from the carcase and used for giving a gloss to silk thread, &c.

they lay gasping, the dolphin opening its mouth as if
pleading for life, until at length young Ch'ên begged the
General to let them go again; and then he himself half
jokingly put a piece of plaster upon the dolphin's wound,
and had the two thrown back into the water, where they
were seen for some time afterwards diving and rising
again to the surface. About a year afterwards, Ch'ên
was once more crossing the Tung-t'ing lake on his way
home, when the boat was upset in a squall, and he himself only saved by clinging to a bamboo crate, which
finally, after floating about all night, caught in the over-
hanging branch of a tree, and thus enabled him to
scramble on shore. By-and-by, another body floated in,
and this turned out to be his servant; but on dragging
him out, he found life was already extinct. In great
distress, he sat himself down to rest, and saw beautiful
green hills and waving willows, but not a single human
being of whom he could ask the way. From early dawn
till the morning was far advanced he remained in that
state; and then, thinking he saw his servant's body move,
he stretched out his hand to feel it, and before long
the man threw up several quarts of water and recovered
his consciousness. They now dried their clothes in the
sun, and by noon these were fit to put on; at which
period the pangs of hunger began to assail them, and
accordingly they started over the hills in the hope of
coming upon some habitation of man. As they were
walking along, an arrow whizzed past, and the next
moment two young ladies dashed by on handsome
palfreys. Each had a scarlet band round her head,

with a bunch of pheasant's feathers stuck in her hair, and wore a purple riding-jacket with small sleeves, confined by a green embroidered girdle round the waist. One of them carried a cross-bow for shooting bullets, and the other had on her arm a dark-coloured bow-and-arrow case. Reaching the brow of the hill, Ch'ên beheld a number of riders engaged in beating the surrounding cover, all of whom were beautiful girls and dressed exactly alike. Afraid to advance any further, he inquired of a youth who appeared to be in attendance, and the latter told him that it was a hunting party from the palace; and then, having supplied him with food from his wallet, he bade him retire quickly, adding that if he fell in with them he would assuredly be put to death. Thereupon Ch'ên hurried away; and descending the hill, turned into a copse where there was a building which he thought would in all probability be a monastery. On getting nearer, he saw that the place was surrounded by a wall, and between him and a half-open red-door was a brook spanned by a stone bridge leading up to it. Pulling back the door, he beheld within a number of ornamental buildings circling in the air like so many clouds, and for all the world resembling the Imperial pleasure-grounds; and thinking it must be the park of some official personage, he walked quietly in, enjoying the delicious fragrance of the flowers as he pushed aside the thick vegetation which obstructed his way. After traversing a winding path fenced in by balustrades, Ch'ên reached a second enclosure, wherein were a quantity of tall willow-trees which swept the red eaves of the buildings with their branches. The note of some bird would set the petals of the flowers fluttering in the air, and the least wind would bring the seed-vessels down from the elm-trees above; and the effect upon the eye and heart of the beholder was something quite unknown in the world of mortals. Passing through a small kiosque, Ch'ên and his servant came upon a swing which seemed as though suspended from the clouds, while the ropes hung idly down in the utter stillness that prevailed.[2] Thinking by this that they were approaching the ladies' apartments,[3] Ch'ên would have turned back, but at that moment he heard sounds of horses' feet at the door, and what seemed to be the laughter of a bevy of girls. So he and his servant hid themselves in a bush; and by-and-by, as the sounds came nearer, he heard one of the young ladies say, " We've had but poor sport to-day ; " whereupon another cried out, " If the princess hadn't shot that wild goose, we should have taken all this trouble for nothing." Shortly after this, a number of girls dressed in red came in escorting a young lady, who went and sat down

---

[2] Literally, in the utter absence of anybody.

[3] In passing near to the women's quarters in a friend's house, it is etiquette to cough slightly, that inmates may be warned and withdraw from the doors or windows in time to escape observation. Over and over again at interviews with mandarins of all grades I have heard the rustling of the ladies' dresses from some coigne of vantage, whence every movement of mine was being watched by an inquisitive crowd; and on one occasion I actually saw an eye peering through a small hole in the partition behind me.

under the kiosque. She wore a hunting costume with
tight[4] sleeves, and was about fourteen or fifteen years old.
Her hair looked like a cloud of mist at the back of her
head, and her waist seemed as though a breath of
wind might snap it[5]—incomparable for beauty, even
among the celebrities of old. Just then the attendants
handed her some exquisitely fragrant tea, and stood
glittering round her like a bank of beautiful embroidery. In a few moments the young lady arose and
descended the kiosque; at which one of her attendants
cried out, "Is your Highness too fatigued by riding
to take a turn in the swing?" The princess replied
that she was not; and immediately some supported
her under the shoulders, while others seized her arms,
and others again arranged her petticoats, and brought
her the proper shoes.[6] Thus they helped her into the
swing, she herself stretching out her shining arms, and
putting her feet into a suitable pair of slippers; and
then—away she went, light as a flying-swallow, far up
into the fleecy clouds. As soon as she had had enough,
the attendants helped her out, and one of them ex-

---

[4] Literally, "bald"—*i.e.*, without the usual width and ornamentation of a Chinese lady's sleeve.

[5] Small waists are much admired in China, but any such artificial
aids as stays and tight lacing are quite unknown. A certain Prince
Wei admitted none but the possessors of small waists into his
harem; hence his establishment came to be called the *Palace of
Small Waists*.

[6] Probably of felt or some such material, to prevent the young
lady from slipping as she stood, not sat, in the swing.

claimed, "Truly, your Highness is a perfect angel!" At this the young lady laughed, and walked away, Ch'ên gazing after her in a state of semi-consciousness, until, at length, the voices died away, and he and his servant crept forth. Walking up and down near the swing, he suddenly espied a red handkerchief near the paling, which he knew had been dropped by one of the young ladies; and, thrusting it joyfully into his sleeve, he walked up and entered the kiosque. There, upon a table, lay writing materials, and taking out the handkerchief he indited upon it the following lines :—

> "What form divine was just now sporting nigh ?—
> 'Twas she, I trow of 'golden lily' fame ;
> Her charms the moon's fair denizens might shame,
> Her fairy footsteps bear her to the sky."

Humming this stanza to himself, Ch'ên walked along seeking for the path by which he had entered ; but every door was securely barred, and he knew not what to do. So he went back to the kiosque, when suddenly one of the young ladies appeared, and asked him in astonishment what he did there. "I have lost my way," replied Ch'ên; "I pray you lend me your assistance." "Do you happen to have found a red handkerchief?" said the girl. "I have, indeed," answered Ch'ên, "but I fear I have made it somewhat dirty ; " and, suiting the action to the word, he drew it forth, and handed it to her. "Wretched man !" cried the young lady, "you are undone. This is a handkerchief the princess is constantly using, and you have gone and scribbled all over it ; what will become of

you now?" Ch'ên was in a great fright, and begged the
young lady to intercede for him; to which she replied,
"It was bad enough that you should come here and
spy about; however, being a scholar, and a man of
refinement, I would have done my best for you; but
after this, how am I to help you?" Off she then ran
with the handkerchief, while Ch'ên remained behind
in an agony of suspense, and longing for the wings of a
bird to bear him away from his fate. By-and-by, the
young lady returned and congratulated him, saying,
"There is some hope for you. The Princess read your
verses several times over, and was not at all angry. You
will probably be released; but, meanwhile, wait here,
and don't climb the trees, or try to get through the
walls, or you may not escape after all." Evening was
now drawing on, and Ch'ên knew not, for certain, what
was about to happen; at the same time he was very
empty, and, what with hunger and anxiety, death would
have been almost a happy release. Before long, the
young lady returned with a lamp in her hand, and
followed by a slave-girl bearing wine and food, which
she forthwith presented to Ch'ên. The latter asked if
there was any news about himself; to which the young
lady replied that she had just mentioned his case to
the Princess who, not knowing what to do with him
at that hour of the night, had given orders that he
should at once be provided with food, "which, at any
rate," added she, "is not bad news." The whole night
long Ch'ên walked up and down unable to take rest;
and it was not till late in the morning that the young

lady appeared with more food for him. Imploring her once more to intercede on his behalf, she told him that the Princess had not instructed them either to kill or to release him, and that it would not be fitting for such as herself to be bothering the Princess with suggestions. So there Ch'ên still remained until another day had almost gone, hoping for the welcome moment; and then the young lady rushed hurriedly in, saying, "You are lost! Some one has told the Queen, and she, in a fit of anger, threw the handkerchief on the ground, and made use of very violent language. Oh dear! oh dear! I'm sure something dreadful will happen." Ch'ên threw himself on his knees, his face as pale as ashes, and begged to know what he should do; but at that moment sounds were heard outside, and the young lady waved her hand to him, and ran away. Immediately a crowd came pouring in through the door, with ropes ready to secure the object of their search; and among them was a slave-girl, who looked fixedly at our hero, and cried out, "Why, surely you are Mr. Ch'ên, aren't you?" at the same time stopping the others from binding him until she should have reported to the Queen. In a few minutes she came back, and said the Queen requested him to walk in; and in he went, through a number of doors, trembling all the time with fear, until he reached a hall, the screen before which was ornamented with green jade and silver. A beautiful girl drew aside the bamboo curtain at the door, and announced, " Mr. Ch'ên;" and he himself advanced, and fell down before a lady, who was sitting upon a dais at the other end, knocking his head upon the ground, and crying out, "Thy servant is from a far-off country; spare, oh! spare his life." "Sir!" replied the Queen, rising hastily from her seat, and extending a hand to Ch'ên, "but for you, I should not be here to-day. Pray excuse the rudeness of my maids." Thereupon a splendid repast was served, and wine was poured out in chased goblets, to the no small astonishment of Ch'ên, who could not understand why he was treated thus. "Your kindness," observed the Queen, "in restoring me to life, I am quite unable to repay; however, as you have made my daughter the subject of your verse, the match is clearly ordained by fate, and I shall send her along to be your handmaid." Ch'ên hardly knew what to make of this extraordinary accomplishment of his wishes, but the marriage was solemnized there and then; bands of music struck up wedding-airs, beautiful mats were laid down for them to walk upon, and the whole place was brilliantly lighted with a profusion of coloured lamps. Then Ch'ên said to the Princess, "That a stray and unknown traveller like myself, guilty of spoiling your Highness's handkerchief, should have escaped the fate he deserved, was already more than could be expected; but now to receive you in marriage—this, indeed, far surpasses my wildest expectations." "My mother," replied the Princess, "is married to the King of this lake, and is herself a daughter of the River Prince. Last year, when on her way to visit her parents, she happened to cross the lake, and was wounded by an arrow; but you saved her life, and gave her plaster for the wound. Our family, therefore, is grateful to you, and can never forget your good act. And do not regard me as of another species than yourself; the Dragon King has bestowed upon me the elixir of immortality, and this I will gladly share with you." Then Ch'ên knew that his wife was a spirit, and by-and-by he asked her how the slave-girl had recognised him; to which she replied, that the girl was the small fish which had been found hanging to the dolphin's tail. He then inquired why, as they didn't intend to kill him, he had been kept so long a prisoner. "I was charmed with your literary talent," answered the Princess, "but I did not venture to take the responsibility upon myself; and no one saw how I tossed and turned the livelong night." "Dear friend," said Ch'ên; "but, come, tell me who was it that brought my food." "A trusty waiting-maid of mine," replied the Princess; "her name is A-nien." Ch'ên then asked how he could ever repay her, and the Princess told him there would be plenty of time to think of that; and when he inquired where the king, her father, was, she said he had gone off with the God of War to fight against Ch'ih-yu,[7] and had not returned. A few days passed, and Ch'ên began to think his people at home would be anxious about him; so he sent off his servant with a letter to tell them he was safe and

---

[7] A rebel chieftain of the legendary period of China's history, who took up arms against the Emperor Huang Ti (B.C. 2697–2597), but was subsequently defeated in what was perhaps the first decisive battle of the world.

sound, at which they were all overjoyed, believing him
to have been lost in the wreck of the boat, of which
event news had already reached them. However, they
were unable to send him any reply, and were considerably
distressed as to how he would find his way home again.
Six months afterwards Ch'ên himself appeared, dressed
in fine clothes, and riding on a splendid horse, with
plenty of money, and valuable jewels in his pocket—
evidently a man of wealth. From that time forth he
kept up a magnificent establishment; and in seven or
eight years had become the father of five children.
Every day he kept open house, and if any one asked
him about his adventures, he would readily tell them
without reservation. Now a friend of his, named Liang,
whom he had known since they were boys together, and
who, after holding an appointment for some years in
Nan-fu, was crossing the Tung-t'ing Lake, on his way
home, suddenly beheld an ornamental barge, with carved
wood-work and red windows, passing over the foamy
waves to the sound of music and singing from within.
Just then a beautiful young lady leant out of one of the
windows, which she had pushed open, and by her side
Liang saw a young man sitting, in a *négligé* attitude,
while two nice-looking girls stood by and shampooed[8]

---

[8] This favourite process consists in gently thumping the person
operated upon all over the back with the soft part of the closed fists.
Compare Lane, *Arabian Nights*, Vol. I., p. 551 :—"She then pressed
me to her bosom, and laid me on the bed, and continued gently
kneading my limbs until slumber overcame me."

him. Liang, at first, thought it must be the party of some high official, and wondered at the scarcity of attendants ;[9] but, on looking more closely at the young man, he saw it was no other than his old friend Ch'ên. Thereupon he began almost involuntarily to shout out to him ; and when Ch'ên heard his own name, he stopped the rowers, and walked out towards the figure-head,[10] beckoning Liang to cross over into his boat, where the remains of their feast was quickly cleared away, and fresh supplies of wine, and tea, and all kinds of costly foods spread out by handsome slave-girls. " It's ten years since we met," said Liang, "and what a rich man you have become in the meantime." "Well," replied Ch'ên, "do you think that so very extraordinary for a poor fellow like me ?" Liang then asked him who was the lady with whom he was taking wine, and Ch'ên said she was his wife, which very much astonished Liang, who further inquired whither they were going. "West-wards," answered Ch'ên, and prevented any further ques-tions by giving a signal for the music, which effectually put a stop to all further conversation.[11] By-and-by, Liang found the wine getting into his head, and seized

---

[9] See No. LVI, note 5. A considerable number of the attend-ants there mentioned would accompany any high official, some in the same, the rest in another barge.

[10] Generally known as the "cut-wave God."

[11] At all great banquets in China a theatrical troupe is engaged to perform while the dinner, which may last from four to six hours, drags its slow length along.

the opportunity to ask Ch'ên to make him a present of one of his beautiful slave-girls. "You are drunk,[12] my friend," replied Ch'ên; "however, I will give you the price of one as a pledge of our old friendship." And, turning to a servant, he bade him present Liang with a splendid pearl, saying, "Now you can buy a Green Pearl;[13] you see I am not stingy;" adding forthwith, "but I am pressed for time, and can stay no longer with my old friend." So he escorted Liang back to his boat, and, having let go the rope, proceeded on his way. Now, when Liang reached home, and called at Ch'ên's house, whom should he see but Ch'ên himself drinking with a party of friends. "Why, I saw you only yesterday," crien Liang, "upon the Tung-t'ing. How quickly you have got back!" Ch'ên denied this, and then Liang repeated the whole story, at the conclusion of which, Ch'ên laughed, and said, "You must be mistaken. Do you imagine I can be in two places at once?" The company were all much astonished, and knew not what to make of it; and subsequently when Ch'ên, who died at the age of eighty, was being carried to his grave, the bearers thought the coffin seemed remarkably light, and on opening it to see, found that the body had disappeared.

---

[12] See No. LIV., note 1.

[13] The name of a celebrated beauty.

LXX.

THE PRINCESS LILY.

AT Chiao-chou there lived a man named Tou Hsün, otherwise known as Hsiao-hui. One day he had just dropped off to sleep when he beheld a man in serge clothes standing by the bedside, and apparently anxious to communicate something to him. Tou inquired his errand; to which the man replied that he was the bearer of an invitation from his master. "And who is your master?" asked Tou. "Oh, he doesn't live far off," replied the other; so away they went together, and after some time came to a place where there were innumerable white houses rising one above the other, and shaded by dense groves of lemon-trees. They threaded their way past countless doors, not at all similar to those usually used, and saw a great many official-looking men and women passing and repassing, each of whom called out to the man in serge, "Has Mr. Tou come?" to which he always replied in the affirmative. Here a mandarin met them and escorted Tou into a palace, upon which the latter remarked, "This is really very kind of you; but I haven't the honour of knowing you, and I feel somewhat diffident about going in." "Our Prince," answered his guide, "has long heard of you as a man of good family and excellent principles, and is very anxious to make your acquaintance," "Who is your Prince?" inquired Tou. "You'll see for yourself in a moment," said the other; and just then out came two girls with banners, and guided Tou through a great number of doors until they came to a throne, upon which sat the Prince. His Highness immediately descended to meet him, and made him take the seat of honour; after which ceremony exquisite viands of all kinds were spread out before them. Looking up, Tou noticed a scroll, on which was inscribed, *The Cassia Court*, and he was just beginning to feel puzzled as to what he should say next, when the Prince addressed him as follows :—"The honour of having you for a neighbour is, as it were, a bond of affinity between us. Let us, then, give ourselves up to enjoyment, and put away suspicion and fear." Tou murmured his acquiescence; and when the wine had gone round several times there arose from a distance the sound of pipes and singing, unaccompanied, however, by the usual drum, and very much subdued in volume. Thereupon the Prince looked about him and cried out, "We are about to set a verse for any of you gentlemen to cap; here you are :—'*Genius seeks the Cassia Court.*'" While the courtiers were all engaged in thinking of some fit antithesis,[1] Tou added, "*Refinement loves the Lily flower;*"

---

[1] In this favourite pastime of the literati in China the important point is that each word in the second line should be a due and proper antithesis of the word in the first line to which it corresponds.

upon which the Prince exclaimed, "How strange! Lily is my daughter's name; and, after such a coincidence, she must come in for you to see her." In a few moments the tinkling of her ornaments and a delicious fragrance of musk announced the arrival of the Princess, who was between sixteen and seventeen and endowed with surpassing beauty. The Prince bade her make an obeisance to Tou, at the same time introducing her as his daughter Lily; and as soon as the ceremony was over the young lady moved away. Tou remained in a state of stupefaction, and, when the Prince proposed that they should pledge each other in another bumper, paid not the slightest attention to what he said. Then the Prince, perceiving what had distracted his guest's attention, remarked that he was anxious to find a consort for his daughter, but that unfortunately there was the difficulty of *species*, and he didn't know what to do; but again Tou took no notice of what the Prince was saying, until at length one of the bystanders plucked his sleeve, and asked him if he hadn't seen that the Prince wished to drink with him, and had just been addressing some remarks to him. Thereupon Tou started, and, recovering himself at once, rose from the table and apologized to the Prince for his rudeness, declaring that he had taken so much wine he didn't know what he was doing. "Besides," said he, "your Highness has doubtless business to transact; I will therefore take my leave." "I am extremely pleased to have seen you," replied the Prince, "and only regret that you are in such a hurry to be gone. However, I won't detain you now;

but, if you don't forget all about us, I shall be very glad
to invite you here again." He then gave orders that Tou
should be escorted home; and on the way one of the
courtiers asked the latter why he had said nothing when
the Prince had spoken of a consort for his daughter, as
his Highness had evidently made the remark with an
eye to securing Tou as his son-in-law. The latter was
now sorry that he had missed his opportunity; meanwhile they reached his house, and he himself awoke.
The sun had already set, and there he sat in the gloom
thinking of what had happened. In the evening he put
out his candle, hoping to continue his dream; but, alas!
the thread was broken, and all he could do was to pour
forth his repentance in sighs. One night he was sleeping at a friend's house when suddenly an officer of the
court walked in and summoned him to appear before the
Prince; so up he jumped, and hurried off at once to the
palace, where he prostrated himself before the throne.
The Prince raised him and made him sit down, saying
that since they had last met he had become aware that
Tou would be willing to marry his daughter, and hoped
that he might be allowed to offer her as a handmaid.
Tou rose and thanked the Prince, who thereupon gave
orders for a banquet to be prepared; and when they had
finished their wine it was announced that the Princess
had completed her toilet. Immediately a bevy of young
ladies came in with the Princess in their midst, a red
veil covering her head, and her tiny footsteps sounding
like rippling water as they led her up to be introduced to
Tou. When the ceremonies were concluded, Tou said

to the Princess, "In your presence, Madam, it would be easy to forget even death itself; but, tell me, is not this all a dream?" "And how can it be a dream," asked the Princess, "when you and I are here together?"

Next morning Tou amused himself by helping the Princess to paint her face,[2] and then, seizing a girdle, began to measure the size of her waist[3] and the length of her fingers and feet. "Are you crazy?" cried she, laughing; to which Tou replied, "I have been deceived so often by dreams, that I am now making a careful record. If such it turns out to be, I shall still have something as a souvenir of you." While they were thus chatting a maid rushed into the room, shrieking out, "Alas, alas! a great monster has got into the palace: the Prince has fled into a side chamber: destruction is surely come upon us." Tou was in a great fright when he heard this, and rushed off to see the Prince, who grasped his hand and, with tears in his eyes, begged him not to desert them. "Our relationship," cried he, "was cemented when Heaven sent this calamity upon us ; and now my kingdom will be overthrown. What shall I do?" Tou begged to know what was the matter ; and then the Prince laid a despatch upon the table, telling Tou to open it and make himself acquainted with its contents. This despatch ran as follows :—"The Grand Secretary of State, Black Wings, to His Royal Highness,

---

[2] See No. LXII., note 1.
[3] See No. LXIX., note 5.

announcing the arrival of an extraordinary monster, and
advising the immediate removal of the Court in order to
preserve the vitality of the empire.   A report has just
been received from the officer in charge of the Yellow
Gate stating that, ever since the 6th of the 5th moon, a
huge monster, 10,000 feet in length, has been lying
coiled up outside the entrance to the palace, and that it
has already devoured 13,800 and odd of your Highness's
subjects, and is spreading desolation far and wide.   On
receipt of this information your servant proceeded to
make a reconnaissance, and there beheld a venomous
reptile with a head as big as a mountain and eyes like
vast sheets of water.   Every time it raised its head,
whole buildings disappeared down its throat; and, on
stretching itself out, walls and houses were alike laid in
ruins.   In all antiquity there is no record of such a
scourge.   The fate of our temples and ancestral halls is
now a mere question of hours; we therefore pray your
Royal Highness to depart at once with the Royal Family
and seek somewhere else a happier abode."[4]   When
Tou had read this document his face turned ashy pale;
and just then a messenger rushed in, shrieking out,
" Here is the monster ! " at which the whole Court burst
into lamentations as if their last hour was at hand.   The
Prince was beside himself with fear; all he could do

---

[4] The language in which this fanciful document is couched is
precisely such as would be used by an officer of the Government in
announcing some national calamity; hence the value of these tales,
—models as they are of the purest possible style.

was to beg Tou to look to his own safety without regarding the wife through whom he was involved in their
misfortunes.   The Princess, however, who was standing
by bitterly lamenting the fate that had fallen upon them,
begged Tou not to desert her; and, after a moment's
hesitation, he said he should be only too happy to place
his own poor home at their immediate disposal if they
would only deign to honour him.   "How can we talk of
deigning," cried the Princess, "at such a moment as
this?   I pray you take us there as quickly as possible."
So Tou gave her his arm, and in no time they had arrived at Tou's house, which the Princess at once
pronounced to be a charming place of residence, and
better even than their former kingdom.   "But I must
now ask you," said she to Tou, "to make some arrangement for my father and mother, that the old order of
things may be continued here."   Tou at first offered
objections to this; whereupon the Princess said that a
man who would not help another in his hour of need
was not much of a man, and immediately went off into
a fit of hysterics, from which Tou was trying his best to
recall her, when all of a sudden he awoke and found
that it was all a dream.   However, he still heard a
buzzing in his ears which he knew was not made by any
human being, and, on looking carefully about he discovered two or three bees which had settled on his
pillow.   He was very much astonished at this, and consulted with his friend, who was also greatly amazed at
his strange story; and then the latter pointed out a
number of other bees on various parts of his dress, none

of which would go away even when brushed off. His friend now advised him to get a hive for them, which he did without delay; and immediately it was filled by a whole swarm of bees, which came flying from over the wall in great numbers. On tracing whence they had come, it was found that they belonged to an old gentleman who lived near, and who had kept bees for more than thirty years previously. Tou thereupon went and told him the story; and when the old gentleman examined his hive he found the bees all gone. On breaking it open he discovered a large snake inside of about ten feet in length, which he immediately killed, recognising in it the "huge monster" of Tou's adventure. As for the bees, they remained with Tou, and increased in numbers every year.

LXXI.

THE DONKEY'S REVENGE.

CHUNG CH'ING-YÜ was a scholar of some reputation, who lived in Manchuria. When he went up for his master's degree, he heard that there was a Taoist priest at the capital who would tell people's fortunes, and was very anxious to see him; and at the conclusion of the second part of the examination,[1] he accidentally met him at Pao-t'u-ch'üan.[2] The priest was over sixty years of age, and had the usual white beard, flowing down over his breast. Around him stood a perfect wall of people inquiring their future fortunes, and to each the old man made a brief reply: but when he saw Chung among the crowd, he was overjoyed, and, seizing him by the hand, said, "Sir, your virtuous intentions command my esteem." He then led him up behind a screen, and asked if he did not wish to know what was to come; and when Chung replied in the affirmative, the priest

---

[1] The examination consists of three bouts of three days each, during which periods the candidates remain shut up in their examination cells day and night.

[2] The name of a place.

informed him that his prospects were bad, "You may succeed in passing this examination," continued he, "but on returning covered with honour to your home, I fear that your mother will be no longer there." Now Chung was a very filial son; and as soon as he heard these words, his tears began to flow, and he declared that he would go back without competing any further. The priest observed that if he let this chance slip, he could never hope for success; to which Chung replied that, on the other hand, if his mother were to die he could never hope to have her back again, and that even the rank of Viceroy would not repay him for her loss. "Well," said the priest, "you and I were connected in a former existence, and I must do my best to help you now." So he took out a pill which he gave to Chung, and told him that if he sent it post-haste by some one to his mother, it would prolong her life for seven days, and thus he would be able to see her once again after the examination was over. Chung took the pill, and went off in very low spirits; but be soon reflected that the span of human life is a matter of destiny, and that every day he could spend at home would be one more day devoted to the service of his mother. Accordingly, he got ready to start at once, and, hiring a donkey, actually set out on his way back. When he had gone about half-a-mile, the donkey turned round and ran home; and when he used his whip, the animal threw itself down on the ground. Chung got into a great perspiration, and his servant recommended him to remain where he was; but this he would not hear of, and hired another donkey, which served him exactly the same trick as the other one. The sun was now sinking behind the hills, and his servant advised his master to stay and finish his examination while he himself went back home before him. Chung had no alternative but to assent, and the next day he hurried through with his papers, starting immediately afterwards, and not stopping at all on the way either to eat or to sleep. All night long he went on, and arrived to find his mother in a very critical state; however, when he gave her the pill she so far recovered that he was able to go in and see her. Grasping his hand, she begged him not to weep, telling him that she had just dreamt she had been down to the Infernal Regions, where the King of Hell had informed her with a gracious smile that her record was fairly clean, and that in view of the filial piety of her son she was to have twelve years more of life. Chung was rejoiced at this, and his mother was soon restored to her former health.

Before long the news arrived that Chung had passed his examination; upon which he bade adieu to his mother, and went off to the capital, where he bribed the eunuchs of the palace to communicate with his friend the Taoist priest. The latter was very much pleased, and came out to see him, whereupon Chung prostrated himself at his feet. "Ah," said the priest, "this success of yours, and the prolongation of your good mother's life, is all a reward for your virtuous conduct. What have I done in the matter?" Chung was very much astonished that the priest should already know what had happened; however, he now inquired as to his own future. "You will never rise to high rank," replied the priest, "but you will attain the years of an octogenarian. In a former state of existence you and I were once travelling together, when you threw a stone at a dog, and accidentally killed a frog. Now that frog has re-appeared in life as a donkey, and according to all principles of destiny you ought to suffer for what you did; but your filial piety has touched the Gods, a protecting star-influence has passed into your nativity sheet, and you will come to no harm. On the other hand, there is your wife; in her former state she was not as virtuous as she might have been, and her punishment in this life was to be widowed quite young; you, however, have secured the prolongation of your own term of years, and therefore I fear that before long your wife will pay the penalty of death." Chung was much grieved at hearing this; but after a while he asked the priest where his second wife to be was living. "At Chung-chou," replied the latter; "she is now fourteen years old." The priest then bade him adieu, telling him that if any mischance should befall him he was to hurry off towards the south-east. About a year after this, Chung's wife did die; and his mother then desiring him to go and visit his uncle, who was a magistrate in Kiangsi, on which journey he would have to pass through Chung-chou, it seemed like a fulfilment of the old priest's prophecy. As he went along, he came to a village on the banks of a river, where a large crowd of people was gathered together round a theatrical performance which was going on there. Chung would have passed quietly by, had not a stray donkey followed so close behind him that he turned round and hit it over the ears. This startled the donkey so much that it ran off full gallop, and knocked a rich gentleman's child, who was sitting with its nurse on the bank, right into the water, before any one of the servants could lend a hand to save it. Immediately there was a great outcry against Chung, who gave his mule the rein and dashed away, mindful of the priest's warning, towards the south-east. After riding about seven miles, he reached a mountain village, where he saw an old man standing at the door of a house, and, jumping off his mule, made him a low bow. The old man asked him in, and inquired his name and whence he came; to which Chung replied by telling him the whole adventure. "Never fear," said the old man; "you can stay here, while I send out to learn the position of affairs." By the evening his mes- senger had returned, and then they knew for the first time that the child belonged to a wealthy family. The old man looked grave and said, "Had it been anybody else's child, I might have helped you; as it is I can do nothing." Chung was greatly alarmed at this; however, the old man told him to remain quietly there for the night, and see what turn matters might take. Chung was overwhelmed with anxiety, and did not sleep a wink; and next morning he heard that the constables were after him, and that it was death to any one who should conceal him. The old man changed countenance at this, and went inside, leaving Chung to his own reflections; but towards the middle of the night he came and knocked at Chung's door, and, sitting down, began to ask how old his wife was. Chung replied that he was a widower; at which the old man seemed rather pleased, and declared that in such case help would be forthcoming; "for," said he, "my sister's husband has taken the vows and become a priest,[3] and my sister herself has died, leaving an orphan girl who has now no home; and if you would only marry her. . . . ." Chung was delighted, more especially as this would be both the fulfilment of the Taoist priest's prophecy, and a means of extricating himself from his present difficulty; at the same time, he declared he should be sorry to implicate his future father-in-law. "Never fear about that," replied the old man; "my sister's husband is pretty skilful in the black art. He has not mixed much with the world of late; but when you are married, you can discuss the matter with my niece." So Chung married the young lady, who was sixteen years of age, and very beautiful; but whenever he looked at her he took occasion to sigh. At last she said, "I may be ugly; but you needn't be in such a hurry to let me

---

[3] This interesting ceremony is performed by placing little conical pastilles on a certain number of spots, varying from three to twelve, on the candidate's head. These are then lighted and allowed to burn down into the flesh, while the surrounding parts are vigorously rubbed by attendant priests in order to lessen the pain. The whole thing lasts about twenty minutes, and is always performed on the eve of Shâkyamuni Buddha's birthday. The above was well described by Mr. S. L. Baldwin in the *Foochow Herald*.

know it;" whereupon Chung begged her pardon, and said he felt himself only too lucky to have met with such a divine creature; adding that he sighed because he feared some misfortune was coming on them which would separate them for ever. He then told her his story, and the young lady was very angry that she should have been drawn into such a difficulty without a word of warning. Chung fell on his knees, and said he had already consulted with her uncle, who was unable him-self to do anything, much as he wished it. He con-tinued that he was aware of her power; and then, pointing out that his alliance was not altogether beneath her, made all kinds of promises if she would only help him out of this trouble. The young lady was no longer able to refuse, but informed him that to apply to her father would entail certain disagreeable conse-quences, as he had retired from the world, and did not any more recognise her as his daughter. That night they did not attempt to sleep, spending the in-terval in padding their knees with thick felt concealed beneath their clothes ; and then they got into chairs and were carried off to the hills. After journeying some distance, they were compelled by the nature of the road to alight and walk; and it was only by a great effort that Chung succeeded at last in getting his wife to the top. At the door of the temple they sat down to rest, the powder and paint on the young lady's face having all mixed with the perspiration trickling down; but when Chung began to apologize for bringing her to this pass, she replied that it was a mere trifle compared with what

was to come. By-and-by, they went inside; and
threading their way to the wall beyond, found the
young lady's father sitting in contemplation,[4] his eyes
closed, and a servant-boy standing by with a chowry.[5]
Everything was beautifully clean and nice, but before
the dais were sharp stones scattered about as thick as
the stars in the sky. The young lady did not venture
to select a favourable spot; she fell on her knees at once,
and Chung did likewise behind her. Then her father
opened his eyes, shutting them again almost instantaneously; whereupon the young lady said, "For a long
time I have not paid my respects to you. I am now
married, and I have brought my husband to see you."
A long time passed away, and then her father opened
his eyes and said, "You're giving a great deal of
trouble," immediately relapsing into silence again.
There the husband and wife remained until the stones
seemed to pierce into their very bones; but after a
while the father cried out, "Have you brought the
donkey?" His daughter replied that they had not;
whereupon they were told to go and fetch it at once,
which they did, not knowing what the meaning of this
order was. After a few more days' kneeling, they
suddenly heard that the murderer of the child had been
caught and beheaded, and were just congratulating each

---

[4] There is a room in most Buddhist temples specially devoted
to this purpose.

[5] The Buddhist emblem of cleanliness; generally a yak's tail, and
commonly used as a fly-brush.

other on the success of their scheme, when a servant came in with a stick in his hand, the top of which had been chopped off. "This stick," said the servant, "died instead of you. Bury it reverently, that the wrong done to the tree may be somewhat atoned for."[6] Then Chung saw that at the place where the top of the stick had been chopped off there were traces of blood; he therefore buried it with the usual ceremony, and immediately set off with his wife, and returned to his own home.

---

[6] Tree-worship can hardly be said to exist in China at the present day; though at a comparatively recent epoch this phase of religious sentiment must have been widely spread. See *The Flower Nymphs* and *Mr. Willow*.

LXXII.

THE WOLF DREAM.

Mr. Pai was a native of Chi-li, and his eldest son was called Chia. The latter had been some two years holding an appointment[1] as magistrate in the south; but because of the great distance between them, his family had heard nothing of him. One day a distant connection, named Ting, called at the house; and Mr. Pai, not having seen this gentleman for a long time, treated him with much cordiality. Now Ting was one of those persons who are occasionally employed by the Judge of the Infernal Regions to make arrests on earth;[2] and, as they were chatting together, Mr. Pai questioned him about the realms below. Ting told him all kinds of strange things, but Pai did not believe them, answering only by a smile. Some days afterwards, he had just lain

---

[1] Literally, "had been allotted the post of Nan-fu magistrate," such appointments being always determined by drawing lots.

[2] Such is one common explanation of catalepsy (see No. I., note 5), it being further averred that the proper lictors of the Infernal regions are unable to·remain long in the *light* of the upper world.

down to sleep when Ting walked in and asked him to go for a stroll; so they went off together, and by-and-by reached the city. "There," said Ting, pointing to a door, "lives your nephew," alluding to a son of Mr. Pai's elder sister, who was a magistrate in Honan; and when Pai expressed his doubts as to the accuracy of this statement, Ting led him in, when, lo and behold! there was his nephew, sitting in his court dressed in his official robes. Around him stood the guard, and it was impossible to get near him; but Ting remarked that his son's residence was not far off, and asked Pai if he would not like to see him too. The latter assenting, they walked along till they came to a large building, which Ting said was the place. However, there was a fierce wolf at the entrance,[3] and Mr. Pai was afraid to go in. Ting bade him enter, and accordingly they walked in, when they found that all the employés of the place, some of whom were standing about and others lying down to sleep, were all wolves. The central pathway was piled up with whitening bones, and Mr. Pai began to feel horribly alarmed; but Ting kept close to him all the time, and at length they got safely in. Pai's son, Chia, was just coming out; and when he saw his father accompanied by Ting, he was overjoyed, and, asking them to sit

---

[3] Upon a wall at the entrance to every official residence is painted a huge fabulous animal, called *Greed*, in such a position that the resident mandarin must see it every time he goes out of his front gates. It is to warn him against greed and the crimes that are sure to flow from it.

down, bade the attendants serve some refreshment.
Thereupon a great big wolf brought in in his mouth
the carcase of a dead man, and set it before them, at
which Mr. Pai rose up in consternation, and asked his
son what this meant. "It's only a little refreshment for
you, father," replied Chia; but this did not calm Mr.
Pai's agitation, who would have retired precipitately, had
it not been for the crowd of wolves which barred the
path. Just as he was at a loss what to do, there was a
general stampede among the animals which scurried
away, some under the couches and some under the
tables and chairs; and while he was wondering what the
cause of this could be, in marched two knights in golden
armour, who looked sternly at Chia, and, producing a
black rope, proceeded to bind him hand and foot. Chia
fell down before them, and was changed into a tiger with
horrid fangs; and then one of the knights drew a glittering sword and would have cut off its head, had not
the other cried out, "Not yet! not yet! that is for the
fourth month next year. Let us now only take out its
teeth." Immediately that knight produced a huge
mallet, and, with a few blows, scattered the tiger's teeth
all over the floor, the tiger roaring so loudly with pain as
to shake the very hills, and frightening all the wits out of
Mr. Pai—who woke up with a start. He found he had
been dreaming, and at once sent off to invite Ting to
come and see him; but Ting sent back to say he must
beg to be excused. Then Mr. Pai, pondering on what
he had seen in his dream, despatched his second son
with a letter to Chia, full of warnings and good advice;

and lo! when his son arrived, he found that his elder brother had lost all his front teeth, these having been knocked out, as he averred, by a fall he had had from his horse when tipsy; and, on comparing dates, the day of that fall was found to coincide with the day of his father's dream. The younger brother was greatly amazed at this, and took out their father's letter, which he gave to Chia to read. The latter changed colour, but immediately asked his brother what there was to be astonished at in the coincidence of a dream. And just at that time he was busily engaged in bribing his superiors to put him first on the list for promotion, so that he soon forgot all about the circumstance; while the younger, observing what harpies Chia's subordinates were, taking presents from one man and using their influence for another, in one unbroken stream of corruption, sought out his elder brother, and, with tears in his eyes, implored him to put some check upon their rapacity. "My brother," replied Chia, "your life has been passed in an obscure village; you know nothing of our official routine. We are promoted or degraded at the will of our superiors, and not by the voice of the people. He, therefore, who gratifies his superiors is marked out for success;[4] whereas he who consults the wishes of the people is unable to gratify his superiors as well." Chia's brother saw that his advice was thrown away; he accordingly returned home and told his father all that had taken place. The old man

---

[4] Such, indeed, is the case at the present day in China, and elsewhere.

was much affected, but there was nothing that he could do in the matter, so he devoted himself to assisting the poor, and such acts of charity, daily praying the Gods that the wicked son alone might suffer for his crimes, and not entail misery on his innocent wife and children. The next year it was reported that Chia had been recommended for a post in the Board of Civil Office,[5] and friends crowded the father's door, offering their congratulations upon the happy event. But the old man sighed and took to his bed, pretending he was too unwell to receive visitors. Before long another message came, informing them that Chia had fallen in with bandits while on his way home, and that he and all his retinue had been killed. Then his father arose and said, "Verily the Gods are good unto me, for they have visited his sins upon himself alone ;" and he immediately proceeded to burn incense and return thanks. Some of his friends would have persuaded him that the report was probably untrue ; but the old man had no doubts as to its correctness, and made haste to get ready his son's grave. But Chia was not yet dead. In the fatal fourth moon he had started on his journey and had fallen in with bandits, to whom he had offered all his money and valuables ; upon which the latter cried out, "We have come to avenge the cruel wrongs of many hundreds of victims ; do you imagine we want only *that?*" They then cut off his head, and the head of his wicked secretary, and the heads of several of his servants who had

---

[5] See No. VII., note 1.

- been foremost in carrying out his shameful orders, and were now accompanying him to the capital. They then divided the booty between them, and made off with all speed. Chia's soul remained near his body for some time, until at length a high mandarin passing by asked who it was that was lying there dead. One of his servants replied that he had been a magistrate at such and such a place, and that his name was Pai. " What ! " said the mandarin, " the son of old Mr. Pai? It is hard that his father should live to see such sorrow as this. Put his head on again."[6] Then a man stepped forward and placed Chia's head upon his shoulders again, when the mandarin interrupted him, saying, " A crooked-minded man should not have a straight body: put his head on sideways." By-and-by Chia's soul returned to its tenement; and when his wife and children arrived to take away the corpse, they found that he was still breathing. Carrying him home, they poured some nourishment down his throat, which he was able to swallow; but there he was at an out-of-the-way place, without the means of continuing his journey. It was some six months before his father heard the real state of the case, and then he sent off the second son to bring his brother home. Chia had indeed come to life again, but he was able to see down his own back, and was regarded ever afterwards

---

[6] The great sorrow of decapitation as opposed to strangulation is that the body will appear in the realms below without a head. The family of any condemned man who may have sufficient means always bribe the executioner to sew it on again.

more as a monstrosity than as a man. Subsequently the nephew, whom old Mr. Pai had seen sitting in state surrounded by officials, actually became an Imperial Censor, so that every detail of the dream was thus strangely realised.[7]

---

[7] This story is an admirable *exposé* of Chinese official corruption, as rampant at the present day as ever in the long history of China.

LXXIII.

THE UNJUST SENTENCE.

MR. CHU was a native of Yang-ku, and, as a young man, was much given to playing tricks and talking in a loose kind of way. Having lost his wife, he went off to ask a certain old woman to arrange another match for him; and on the way, he chanced to fall in with a neighbour's wife who took his fancy very much. So he said in joke to the old woman, "Get me that stylish-looking, handsome lady, and I shall be quite satisfied." "I'll see what I can do," replied the old woman, also joking, "if you will manage to kill her present hus-band;" upon which Chu laughed and said he certainly would do so. Now about a month afterwards, the said husband, who had gone out to collect some money due to him, was actually killed in a lonely spot; and the magistrate of the district immediately summoned the neighbours and beadle[1] and held the usual inquest, but was unable to find any clue to the murderer. However, the old woman told the story of her conversation with Chu, and suspicion at once fell upon him. The con-

---

[1] See No. LXIV, note 2.

stables came and arrested him; but he stoutly denied the charge; and the magistrate now began to suspect the wife of the murdered man. Accordingly, she was severely beaten and tortured in several ways until her strength failed her, and she falsely acknowledged her guilt.[2] Chu was then examined, and he said, "This

---

[2] Such has, doubtless, been the occasional result of torture in China; but the singular keenness of the mandarins, as a body, in recognising the innocent and detecting the guilty,—that is, when their own avaricious interests are not involved,—makes this contingency so rare as to be almost unknown. A good instance came under my own notice at Swatow in 1876. For years a Chinese servant had been employed at the foreign Custom House to carry a certain sum of money every week to the bank, and at length his honesty was above suspicion. On the occasion to which I allude he had been sent as usual with the bag of dollars, but after a short absence he rushed back with a frightful gash on his right arm, evidently inflicted by a heavy chopper, and laying the bone bare. The money was gone. He said he had been invited into a teahouse by a couple of soldiers whom he could point out; that they had tried to wrest the bag from him, and that at length one of them seized a chopper and inflicted so severe a wound on his arm, that in his agony he dropped the money, and the soldiers made off with it. The latter were promptly arrested and confronted with their accuser; but, with almost indecent haste, the police magistrate dismissed the case against them, and declared that he believed the man had made away with the money and inflicted the wound on himself. And so it turned out to be, under overwhelming evidence. This servant of proved fidelity had given way to a rash hope of making a little money at the gaming-table; had hurried into one of these hells and lost everything in three stakes; had wounded himself on the right arm (he was a left-handed man), and had concocted the story of the soldiers, all within the space of about twenty-five minutes. When he saw that he was detected, he confessed everything, without having received a single blow of the bamboo; but up to the moment of his confession the foreign feeling against that police-magistrate was undeniably strong.

delicate woman could not bear the agony of your tortures; what she has stated is untrue; and, even should
her wrong escape the notice of the Gods, for her to die
in this way with a stain upon her name is more than I
can endure. I will tell the whole truth. I killed the
husband that I might secure the wife : she knew nothing
at all about it." And when the magistrate asked for
some proof, Chu said his bloody clothes would be
evidence enough; but when they sent to search his
house, no bloody clothes were forthcoming. He was
then beaten till he fainted; yet when he came round he
still stuck to what he had said. "It is my mother,"
cried he, "who will not sign the death-warrant of her
son. Let me go myself and I will get the clothes." So
he was escorted by a guard to his home, and there he
explained to his mother that whether she gave up or
withheld the clothes, it was all the same; that in either
case he would have to die, and it was better to die early
than late. Thereupon his mother wept bitterly, and
going into the bedroom, brought out, after a short delay,
the required clothes, which were taken at once to the
magistrate's. There was now no doubt as to the truth of
Chu's story; and as nothing occurred to change the
magistrate's opinion, Chu was thrown into prison to
await the day for his execution. Meanwhile, as the
magistrate was one day inspecting his gaol, suddenly a
man appeared in the hall, who glared at him fiercely and
roared out, " Dull-headed fool ! unfit to be the guardian
of the people's interests !"—whereupon the crowd of servants standing round rushed forward to seize him, but with

one sweep of his arms he laid them all flat on the ground. The magistrate was frightened out of his wits, and tried to escape, but the man cried out to him, " I am one of Kuan Ti's [3] lieutenants. If you move an inch you are lost." So the magistrate stood there, shaking from head to foot with fear, while his visitor continued, " The murderer is Kung Piao: Chu had nothing to do with it."

The lieutenant then fell down on the ground, and was to all appearance lifeless; however, after a while he recovered, his face having quite changed, and when they asked him his name, lo ! it was Kung Piao. Under the application of the bamboo he confessed his guilt. Always an unprincipled man, he had heard that the murdered man was going out to collect money, and thinking he would be sure to bring it back with him, he had killed him, but had found nothing. Then when he learnt that Chu had acknowledged the crime as his own doing, he had rejoiced in secret at such a stroke of luck. How he had got into the magistrate's hall he was quite unable to say. The magistrate now called for some ex- planation of Chu's bloody clothes, which Chu himself was unable to give; but his mother, who was at once sent for, stated that she had cut her own arm to stain them, and when they examined her they found on her left arm the scar of a recent wound. The magistrate was lost in amazement at all this; unfortunately for him

---

[3] See No. I., note 3.

the reversal of his sentence cost him his appointment, and he died in poverty, unable to find his way home. As for Chu, the widow of the murdered man married him [4] in the following year, out of gratitude for his noble behaviour.

---

[4] See No. LXVIII., note 1. The circumstances which led to this marriage would certainly be considered "exceptional."

LXXIV.

A RIP VAN WINKLE.[1]

[THE story runs that a Mr. Chia, after obtaining, with the assistance of a mysterious friend, his master's degree, became alive to the vanity of mere earthly honours, and determined to devote himself to the practice of Taoism, in the hope of obtaining the elixir of immortality.[2]]

So early one morning Chia and his friend, whose name was Lang, stole away together, without letting Chia's family know anything about it; and by-and-by they found themselves among the hills, in a vast cave where there was another world and another sky. An old man was sitting there in great state, and Lang presented Chia to him as his future master. "Why have you come so soon?" asked the old man; to which Lang replied, " My friend's determination is firmly fixed: I pray you receive him amongst you." "Since you have come," said the old man, turning to Chia, "you must begin by

---

[1] This being a long and tedious story, I have given only such part of it as is remarkable for its similarity to Washington Irving's famous narrative.

[2] See No. IV., note 1.

putting away from you your earthly body." Chia murmured his assent, and was then escorted by Lang to a
sleeping-chamber where he was provided with food,
after which Lang went away. The room was beautifully
clean:[3] the doors had no panels and the windows no
lattices; and all the furniture was one table and one
couch. Chia took off his shoes and lay down, with the
moon shining brightly into the room; and beginning
soon to feel hungry, he tried one of the cakes on the
table, which he found sweet and very satisfying. He
thought Lang would be sure to come back, but there he
remained hour after hour by himself, never hearing a
sound. He noticed, however, that the room was fragrant
with a delicious perfume; his viscera seemed to be removed from his body, by which his intellectual faculties
were much increased; and every one of his veins and
arteries could be easily counted. Then suddenly he
heard a sound like that of a cat scratching itself; and,
looking out of the window, he beheld a tiger sitting under
the verandah. He was horribly frightened for the
moment, but immediately recalling the admonition of
the old man, he collected himself and sat quietly down
again. The tiger seemed to know that there was a man
inside, for it entered the room directly afterwards, and
walking straight up to the couch sniffed at Chia's feet.
Whereupon there was a noise outside, as if a fowl were
having its legs tied, and the tiger ran away. Shortly

---

[3] Borrowed from Buddhism.

afterwards a beautiful young girl came in, suffusing an exquisite fragrance around; and going up to the couch where Chia was, she bent over him and whispered, "Here I am." Her breath was like the sweet odour of perfumes; but as Chia did not move, she whispered again, "Are you sleeping?" The voice sounded to Chia remarkably like that of his wife; however, he reflected that these were all probably nothing more than tests of his determination, so he closed his eyes firmly for a while. But by-and-by the young lady called him by his pet name, and then he opened his eyes wide to discover that she was no other than his own wife. On asking her how she had come there, she replied that Mr. Lang was afraid her husband would be lonely, and had sent an old woman to guide her to him. Just then they heard the old man outside in a towering rage, and Chia's wife, not knowing where to conceal herself, jumped over a low wall near by and disappeared. In came the old man, and gave Lang a severe beating before Chia's face, bidding him at once to get rid of his visitor; so Lang led Chia away over the low wall, saying, "I knew how anxious you were to consummate your immortality, and accordingly I tried to hurry things on a bit; but now I see that your time has not yet come: hence this beating I have had. Good-by: we shall meet again some day." He then shewed Chia the way to his home, and waving his hand bade him farewell. Chia looked down—for he was in the moon—and beheld the old familiar village; and recollecting that his wife was not a good walker and would not have got very far, hurried on to overtake her. Before long he was at his own door, but he noticed that the place was all tumbledown and in ruins, and not as it was when he went away. As for the people he saw, old and young alike, he did not recognise one of them; and recollecting the story of how Liu and Yüan came back from heaven,[4] he was afraid to go in at the door. So he sat down and rested outside; and after a while an old man leaning on a staff came out, whereupon Chia asked him which was the house of Mr. Chia. "This is it," replied the old man; "you probably wish to hear the extraordinary story connected with the family? I know all about it. They say that Mr. Chia ran away just after he had taken his master's degree, when his son was only seven or eight years old; and that about seven years afterwards the child's mother went into a deep sleep from which she did not awake. As long as her son was alive he changed his mother's clothes for her according to the seasons, but when he died, her grandsons fell into poverty, and had nothing but an old shanty to put the sleeping lady into. Last month she awaked, having been asleep for over a hundred years. People from far and near have been coming in great numbers to hear the strange story; of

---

[4] Alluding to a similar story, related in the *Record of the Immortals*, of how these two friends lost their way while gathering simples on the hills, and were met and entertained by two lovely young damsels for the space of half-a-year. When, however, they subsequently returned home, they found that ten generations had passed away.

late, however, there have been rather fewer." Chia was
amazed when he heard all this, and, turning to the old
man, said, "I am Chia Fêng-chih." This astonished the
old man very much, and off he went to make the an-
nouncement to Chia's family. The eldest grandson was
dead; and the second, a man of about fifty, refused to
believe that such a young-looking man was really his
grandfather; but in a few moments out came Chia's
wife, and she recognised her husband at once. They
then fell upon each other's necks and mingled their tears
together.

[After which the story is drawn out to a considerable
length, but is quite devoid of interest.]⁵

---

⁵ Besides the above, there is the story of a man named Wang,
who, wandering one day in the mountains, came upon some old
men playing a game of *wei-ch'i* (see *Appendix*); and after watching
them for some time, he found that the handle of an axe he had
with him had mouldered away into dust. Seven generations of
men had passed away in the interval. Also, a similar legend of a
horseman, who, when riding over the hills, saw several old men
playing a game with rushes, and tied his horse to a tree while he
himself approached to observe them. A few minutes afterwards he
turned to depart, but found only the skeleton of his horse and the
rotten remnants of the saddle and bridle. He then sought his
home, but that was gone too; and so he laid himself down upon
the ground and died of a broken heart.

LXXV.

THE THREE STATES OF EXISTENCE.

A CERTAIN man of the province of Hunan could recall what had happened to him in three previous lives. In the first, he was a magistrate; and, on one occasion, when he had been nominated Assistant-Examiner,[1] a candidate, named Hsing, was unsuccessful. Hsing went home dreadfully mortified, and soon after died; but his spirit appeared before the King of Purgatory, and read aloud the rejected essay, whereupon thousands of other shades, all of whom had suffered in a similar way, thronged around, and unanimously elected Hsing as their chief. The Examiner was immediately summoned to take his trial, and when he arrived the King asked him, saying, " As you are appointed to examine the various essays, how is it that you throw out the able and admit the worthless ? " " Sire," replied he, "the ultimate decision rests with the Grand Examiner; I only pass them on to him." The King then issued a warrant for the apprehension of the Grand Examiner,

---

[1] See *Appendix* A.

and, as soon as he appeared, he was told what had just now been said against him; to which he answered, "I am only able to make a general estimate of the merits of the candidates. Valuable essays may be kept back from me by my Associate-Examiners, in which case I am powerless."[2] But the King cried out, " It's all very well for you two thus to throw the blame on each other; you are both guilty, and both of you must be bambooed according to law." This sentence was about to be carried into effect, when Hsing, who was not at all satisfied with its lack of severity, set up such a fearful screeching and howling, in which he was well supported by all the other hundreds and thousands of shades, that the King stopped short, and inquired what was the

---

[2] If there is one institution in the Chinese empire which is jealously guarded and honestly administered, it is the great system of competitive examinations which has obtained in China now for many centuries.   And yet frauds do take place, in spite of the exceptionally heavy penalties incurred upon detection.   Friends are occasionally smuggled through by the aid of marked essays ; and dishonest candidates avail themselves of "sleeve editions," as they are called, of the books in which they are to be examined.   On the whole, the result is a successful one.   As a rule the best candidates pull through ; while, in exceptional cases, unquestionably good men are rejected.   Of the latter class, the author of this work is a most striking instance.   Excelling in literary attainments of the highest order, he failed' more than once to obtain his master's degree, and finally threw up in disgust.   Thenceforward he became the enemy of the mandarinate ; and how he has lashed the corruption of his age may be read in such stories as *The Wolf Dream*, and many others, while the policy that he himself would have adopted, had he been fortunate enough to succeed, must remain for ever a matter of doubt and speculation.

matter. Thereupon Hsing informed His Majesty that the sentence was too light, and that the Examiners should both have their eyes gouged out, so as not to be able to read essays any more. The King would not consent to this, explaining to the noisy rabble that the Examiners did not purposely reject good essays, but only because they themselves were naturally wanting in capacity. The shades then begged that, at any rate, their hearts might be cut out, and to this the King was obliged to yield; so the Examiners were seized by the attendants, their garments stripped off, and their bodies ripped open with sharp knives. The blood poured out on the ground, and the victims screamed with pain; at which all the shades rejoiced exceedingly, and said, "Here we have been pent up, with no one to redress our wrongs ; but now Mr. Hsing has come, our injuries are washed away." They then dispersed with great noise and hubbub. As for our Associate-Examiner, after his heart had been cut out, he came to life again as the son of a poor man in Shensi; and when he was twenty years old he fell into the hands of the rebels, who were at that time giving great trouble to the country. By-and-by, a certain official was sent at the head of some soldiers to put down the insurrection, and he succeeded in capturing a large number of the rebels, among whom was our hero. The latter reflected that he himself was no rebel, and he was hoping that he would be able to obtain his release in consequence, when he noticed that the officer in charge was also a man of his own age, and, on looking more closely, he saw that it was his old enemy, Hsing. "Alas!" cried he, "such is destiny;" and so indeed it turned out, for all the other prisoners were forthwith released, and he alone was beheaded. Once more his spirit stood before the King of Purgatory, this time with an accusation against Hsing. The King, however, would not summon Hsing at once, but said he should be allowed to complete his term of official life on earth; and it was not till thirty years afterwards that Hsing appeared to answer to the charge. Then, because he had made light of the lives of his people, he was condemned to be born again as a brute-beast; and our hero, too, inasmuch as he had been known to beat his father and mother, was sentenced to a similar fate. The latter, fearing the future vengeance of Hsing, persuaded the King to give him the advantage of size; and, accordingly, orders were issued that he was to be born again as a big, and Hsing as a little, dog. The big dog came to life in a shop in Shun-t'ien Fu, and was one day lying down in the street, when a trader from the south arrived, bringing with him a little golden-haired dog, about the size of a wild cat, which, lo and behold! turned out to be Hsing. The other, thinking Hsing's size would render him an easy prey, seized him at once; but the little one caught him from underneath by the throat, and hung there firmly, like a bell. The big dog tried hard to shake him off, and the people of the shop did their best to separate them, but all was of no avail, and in a few moments both dogs were dead. Upon their spirits presenting themselves, as usual, before the King, each with its grievance against the other, the King cried out, " When will ye have done with your wrongs and your animosities ? I will now settle the matter finally for you;" and immediately commanded that Hsing should become the other's son-in-law in the next world. The latter was then born at Ch'ing-yün, and when he was twenty-eight years of age took his master's degree. He had one daughter, a very pretty girl, whom many of his wealthy neighbours would have been glad to get for their sons; but he would not accept any of their offers. On one occasion, he happened to pass through the prefectural city just as the examination for bachelor's degree was over ; and the candidate who had come out at the top of the list, though named Li, was no other than Mr. Hsing. So he led this man away, and took him to an inn, where he treated him with the utmost cordiality, finally arranging that, as Mr. Li was still unmarried, he should marry his pretty daughter. Every-one, of course, thought that this was done in admiration of Li's talents, ignorant that destiny had already decreed the union of the young couple. No sooner were they married than Li, proud of his own literary achievements, began to slight his father-in-law, and often passed many months without going near him; all of which the father-in-law bore very patiently, and when, at length, Li had repeatedly failed to get on any farther in his career, he even went so far as to set to work, by all manner of means, to secure his success ; after which they lived happily together as father and son.

LXXVI.

IN THE INFERNAL REGIONS.

Hsi Fang-p'ing was a native of Tung-an. His father's name was Hsi-Lien—a hasty-tempered man, who had quarrelled with a neighbour named Yang. By-and-by Yang died : and some years afterwards when Lien was on his death-bed, he cried out that Yang was bribing the devils in hell to torture him. His body then swelled up and turned red, and in a few moments he had breathed his last. His son wept bitterly, and refused all food, saying, "Alas! my poor father is now being maltreated by cruel devils; I must go down and help to redress his wrongs." Thereupon he ceased speaking, and sat for a long time like one dazed, his soul having already quitted its tenement of clay. To himself he appeared to be outside the house, not knowing in what direction to go, so he inquired from one of the passers-by which was the way to the district city.[1] Before long he found himself there, and, direct-

---

[1] The Infernal Regions are supposed to be pretty much a counterpart of the world above, excepting in the matter of light.

ing his steps towards the prison, found his father lying outside[2] in a very shocking state. When the latter beheld his son, he burst into tears, and declared that the gaolers had been bribed to beat him, which they did both day and night, until they had reduced him to his present sorry plight. Then Fang-p'ing turned round in a great rage, and began to curse the gaolers. "Out upon you!" cried he; "if my father is guilty he should be punished according to law, and not at the will of a set of scoundrels like you." Thereupon he hurried away, and prepared a petition, which he took with him to present at the morning session of the City God; but his enemy, Yang, had meanwhile set to work, and bribed so effectually, that the City God dismissed his petition for want of corroborative evidence.[3] Fang-p'ing was furious, but could do nothing; so he started at once for the prefectural city, where he managed to get his plaint received, though it was nearly a month before it came on for hearing, and then all he got was a reference back to the district city, where he was severely tortured, and escorted back to the door of his own home, for fear he should give further trouble. How-

---

[2] The visitor to Canton cannot fail to observe batches of prisoners with chains on them sitting in the street outside the prisons, many of them engaged in plying their particular trades.

[3] The judge in a Chinese court is necessarily very much dependent on his secretaries; and, except in special cases, he takes his cue almost entirely from them. They take theirs from whichever party to the case knows best how to "cross the palm."

ever, he did not go in, but stole away and proceeded to lay his complaint before one of the ten Judges of Purgatory; whereupon the two mandarins who had previously ill-used him, came forward and secretly offered him a thousand ounces of silver if he would withdraw the charge. This he positively refused to do; and some days subsequently the landlord of the inn, where he was staying, told him he had been a fool for his pains, and that he would now get neither money nor justice, the Judge himself having already been tampered with. Fang-p'ing thought this was mere gossip, and would not believe it; but, when his case was called, the Judge utterly refused to hear the charge, and ordered him twenty blows with the bamboo, which were administered in spite of all his protestations. He then cried out, "Ah! it's all because I have no money to give you;" which so incensed the Judge, that he told the lictors to throw Fang-p'ing on the fire-bed. This was a great iron couch, with a roaring fire underneath, which made it red-hot; and upon that the devils cast Fang-p'ing, having first stripped off his clothes, pressing him down on it, until the fire ate into his very bones, though in spite of that he could not die. After a while the devils said he had had enough, and made him get off the iron bed, and put his clothes on again. He was just able to walk, and when he went back into court, the Judge asked him if he wanted to make any further complaints. "Alas!" cried he, "my wrongs are still unredressed, and I should only be lying were I to say I would complain no more." The Judge then inquired what he had to complain of; to which Fang-p'ing replied that it was of the injustice of his recent punishment. This enraged the Judge so much that he ordered his attendants to saw Fang-p'ing in two. He was then led away by devils, to a place where he was thrust in between a couple of wooden boards, the ground on all sides being wet and sticky with blood. Just at that moment he was summoned to return before the Judge, who asked him if he was still of the same mind; and, on his replying in the affirmative, he was taken back again, and bound between the two boards. The saw was then applied, and as it went through his brain he experienced the most cruel agonies, which, however, he managed to endure without uttering a cry. "He's a tough customer," said one of the devils, as the saw made its way gradually through his chest; to which the other replied, "Truly, this is filial piety; and, as the poor fellow has done nothing, let us turn the saw a little out of the direct line, so as to avoid injuring his heart." Fang-p'ing then felt the saw make a curve inside him, which caused him even more pain than before; and, in a few moments, he was cut through right down to the ground, and the two halves of his body fell apart, along with the boards to which they were tied, one on either side. The devils went back to report progress, and were then ordered to join Fang-p'ing together again, and bring him in. This they accordingly did,—the cut all down Fang-p'ing's body hurting him dreadfully, and feeling as if it would re-open every minute. But, as Fang-p'ing was unable to walk, one of the devils took out a cord and tied it round his waist, as a reward, he said, for his filial piety. The pain immediately ceased, and Fang-p'ing appeared once more before the Judge, this time promising that he would make no more complaints. The Judge now gave orders that he should be sent up to earth, and the devils, escorting him out of the north gate of the city, shewed him his way home, and went away. Fang-p'ing now saw that there was even less chance of securing justice in the Infernal Regions than upon the earth above; and, having no means of getting at the Great King to plead his case, he bethought himself of a certain upright and benevolent God, called Erh Lang, who was a relative of the Great King's, and him he determined to seek. So he turned about and took his way southwards, but was immediately seized by some devils, sent out by the Judge to watch that he really went back to his home. These devils hurried him again into the Judge's presence, where he was received, contrary to his expectation, with great affability; the Judge himself praising his filial piety, but declaring that he need trouble no further in the matter, as his father had already been born again in a wealthy and illustrious family. " And upon you," added the Judge, " I now bestow a present of one thousand ounces of silver to take home with you, as well as the old age of a centenarian, with which I hope you will be satisfied." He then shewed Fang-p'ing the stamped record of this, and sent him away in charge of the devils. The latter now began to abuse him for giving them so much trouble, but Fang-p'ing turned

sharply upon them, and threatened to take them back
before the Judge. They were then silent, and marched
along for about half-a-day, until at length they reached a
village, where the devils invited Fang-p'ing into a house,
the door of which was standing half-open. Fang-p'ing
was just going in, when suddenly the devils gave him a
shove from behind, and . . . . there he was, born
again on earth as a little girl. For three days he pined
and cried, without taking any food, and then he died.
But his spirit did not forget Erh Lang, and set out at
once in search of that God. He had not gone far when
he fell in with the retinue of some high personage,
and one of the attendants seized him for getting in the
way, and hurried him before his master. He was taken
to a chariot, where he saw a handsome young man,
sitting in great state; and thinking that now was his
chance, he told the young man, who he imagined to be
a high mandarin, all his sad story from beginning to
end. His bonds were then loosed, and he went along
with the young man until they reached a place where
several officials came out to receive them ; and to one
of these he confided Fang-p'ing, who now learnt that
the young man was no other than God himself, the
officials being the nine princes of heaven, and the one
to whose care he was entrusted no other than Erh Lang.
This last was very tall, and had a long white beard, not
at all like the popular representation of a God; and
when the other princes had gone, he took Fang-p'ing
into a court-room, where he saw his father and their old
enemy, Yang, besides all the lictors and others who had

been mixed up in the case. By-and-by, some criminals were brought in in cages, and these turned out to be the Judge, Prefect, and Magistrate. The trial was then commenced, the three wicked officers trembling and shaking in their shoes; and when he had heard the evidence, Erh Lang proceeded to pass sentence upon the prisoners, each of whom he sentenced, after enlarging upon the enormity of their several crimes, to be roasted, boiled, and otherwise put to most excruciating tortures. As for Fang-p'ing, he accorded him three extra decades of life, as a reward for his filial piety, and a copy of the sentence was put in his pocket. Father and son journeyed along together, and at length reached their home; that is to say, Fang-p'ing was the first to recover consciousness, and then bade the servants open his father's coffin, which they immediately did, and the old man at once came back to life. But when Fang-p'ing looked for his copy of the sentence, lo! it had disappeared. As for the Yang family, poverty soon overtook them, and all their lands passed into Fang-p'ing's hands; for as sure as any one else bought them, they became sterile forthwith, and would produce nothing; but Fang-p'ing and his father lived on happily, both reaching the age of ninety and odd years.[4]

---

[4] The whole story is of course simply a satire upon the venality and injustice of the ruling classes in China.

LXXVII.

SINGULAR CASE OF OPHTHALMIA.

A Mr. Ku, of Chiang-nan, was stopping in an inn at Chi-hsia, when he was attacked by a very severe inflammation of the eyes. Day and night he lay on his bed groaning, no medicines being of any avail; and when he did get a little better, his recovery was accompanied by a singular phenomenon. Every time he closed his eyes, he beheld in front of him a number of large buildings, with all their doors wide open, and people passing and repassing in the background, none of whom he recognised by sight. One day he had just sat down to have a good look, when, all of a sudden, he felt himself passing through the open doors. He went on through three court-yards without meeting any one; but, on looking into some rooms on either side, he saw a great number of young girls sitting, lying, and kneeling about on a red carpet, which was spread on the ground. Just then a man came out from behind the building, and, seeing Ku, said to him, " Ah, the Prince said there was a stranger at the door; I suppose you are the person he meant." He then asked Ku to walk

in, which the latter was at first unwilling to do ; however, he yielded to the man's instances, and accompanied him in, asking whose palace it was. His
guide told him it belonged to the son of the Ninth
Prince, and that he had arrived at the nick of time,
for a number of friends and relatives had chosen this
very day to come and congratulate the young gentleman
on his recent recovery from a severe illness. Meanwhile
another person had come out to hurry them on, and they
soon reached a spot where there was a pavilion facing
the north, with an ornamental terrace and red balus·
trades, supported by nine pillars. Ascending the
steps, they found the place full of visitors, and then
espied a young man seated with his face to the north,[1]
whom they at once knew to be the Prince's son, and
thereupon they prostrated themselves before him, the
whole company rising as they did so. The young
Prince made Ku sit down to the east of him, and
caused wine to be served ; after which some singing-
girls came in and performed the Hua-fêng-chu.[2] They
had got to about the third scene, when, all of a sudden,
Ku heard the landlord of the inn and his servant
shouting out to him that dinner was ready, and was

---

[1] In Book V. of Mencius' works we read that Shun, the perfect
man, stood with his face to the south, while the Emperor Yao (see
No. VIII., note 3) and his nobles faced the north. This arrangement is said to have been adopted in deference to Shun's virtue ;
for in modern times the Emperor always sits facing the south.

[2] Name of a celebrated play.

dreadfully afraid that the young Prince, too, had heard. No one, however, seemed to have noticed anything, so Ku begged to be excused a moment, as he wished to change his clothes, and immediately ran out. He then looked up, and saw the sun low in the west, and his servant standing by his bedside, whereupon he knew that he had never left the inn. He was much chagrined at this, and wished to go back as fast as he could; he, therefore, dismissed his servant, and on shutting his eyes once more, he found everything just as he had left it, except that where, on the first occasion, he had observed the young girls, there were none now to be seen, but only some dishevelled humpbacked creatures, who cried out at him, and asked him what he meant by spying about there. Ku didn't dare reply, but hurried past them as quickly as he could, and on to the pavilion of the young Prince. There he found him still sitting, but with a black beard over a foot in length; and the Prince was anxious to know where he had been, saying that seven scenes of the play were already over. He then seized a big goblet of wine, and made Ku drink it as a penalty, by which time the play was finished, and the list was handed up for a further selection, The "Marriage of P'êng Tsu" was selected, and then the singing-girls began to hand round the wine in cocoa-nuts big enough to hold about five quarts, which Ku declined, on the ground that he was suffering from weak eyes, and was consequently afraid to drink too much. "If your eyes are bad," cried the young Prince, "the Court physician is at hand,

and can attend to you." Thereupon, one of the guests sitting to the east came forward, and opening Ku's eyes with his fingers, touched them with some white ointment, which he applied from the end of a jade pin. He then bade Ku close his eyes, and take a short nap; so the Prince had him conducted into a sleeping-room, where he found the bed so soft, and surrounded by such delicious perfume, that he soon fell into a deep slumber. By-and-by he was awaked by what appeared to be the clashing of cymbals, and fancied that the play was still going on; but on opening his eyes, he saw that it was only the inn-dog, which was licking an oilman's gong.[3] His ophthalmia, however, was quite cured; and when he shut his eyes again he could see nothing.

---

[3] These are about as big as a cheese-plate and attached to a short stick, from which hangs suspended a small button of metal in such a manner as to clash against the face of the gong at every turn of the hand. The names and descriptions of various instruments employed by costermongers in China would fill a good-sized volume.

LXXVIII.

CHOU K'O-CH'ANG AND HIS GHOST.

AT Huai-shang there lived a graduate named Chou
T'ien-i, who, though fifty years of age, had but one son,
called K'o-ch'ang, whom he loved very dearly.   This
boy, when about thirteen or fourteen, was a handsome,
well-favoured fellow, strangely averse to study, and often
playing truant from school, sometimes for the whole day,
without any remonstrance on the part of his father.   One
day he went away and did not come back in the evening; neither, after a diligent search, could any traces of
him be discovered.   His father and mother were in
despair, and hardly cared to live; but after a year and
more had passed away, lo and behold! Ko-ch'ang returned, saying that he had been beguiled away by a
Taoist priest, who, however, had not done him any
harm, and that he had seized a moment while the priest
was absent to escape and find his way home again.   His
father was delighted, and asked him no more questions,
but set to work to give him an education; and K'o-ch'ang
was so much cleverer and more intelligent than he had
been before, that by the following year he had taken his

bachelor's degree and had made quite a name for himself. Immediately all the good families of the neighbourhood wanted to secure him as a son-in-law. Among
others proposed there was an extremely nice girl, the
daughter of a gentleman named Chao, who had taken
his doctor's degree, and K'o-ch'ang's father was very
anxious that he should marry the young lady. The
youth himself would not hear of it, but stuck to his
books and took his master's degree, quite refusing to en-
tertain any thought of marriage; and this so exasperated
his mother that one day the good lady began to rate him
soundly. K'o-ch'ang got up in a great rage and cried
out, "I have long been wanting to get away, and have
only remained for your sakes. I shall now say farewell,
and leave Miss Chao for any one that likes to marry her."
At this his mother tried to detain him, but in a moment
he had fallen forwards on the ground, and there was
nothing left of him but his hat and clothes. They were
all dreadfully frightened, thinking that it must have been
K'o-ch'ang's ghost who had been with them, and gave
themselves up to weeping and lamentation; however, the
very next day K'o-ch'ang arrived, accompanied by a
retinue of horses and servants, his story being that he
had formerly been kidnapped[1] and sold to a wealthy
trader, who, being then childless, had adopted him, but
who, when he subsequently had a son born to him by his
own wife, sent K'o-ch'ang back to his old home. And

---

[1] See No. XXIII., note 10.

as soon as his father began to question him as to his studies, his utter dulness and want of knowledge soon made it clear that he was the real K'o-ch'ang of old; but he was already known as a man who had got his master's degree, (that is, the ghost of him had got it,) so it was determined in the family to keep the whole affair secret. This K'o-ch'ang was only too ready to espouse Miss Chao; and before a year had passed over their heads his wife had presented the old people with the much longed-for grandson.

LXXIX.

THE SPIRITS OF THE PO-YANG LAKE.

An official, named Chai, was appointed to a post at Jao-chou, and on his way thither crossed the Po-yang lake. Happening to visit the shrine of the local spirits, he noticed a carved image of the patriotic Ting P'u-lang,[1] and another of a namesake of his own, the latter occupying a very inferior position. "Come! come!" said Chai, "my patron saint shan't be put in the background like that;" so he moved the image into a more honourable place, and then went back on board his boat again. Soon after, a great wind struck the vessel, and carried away the mast and sails; at which the sailors, in great alarm, set to work to howl and cry. However, in a few moments they saw a small skiff come cutting through the waves, and before long they were all safely on board. The man who rowed it was strangely like the image in the shrine, the position of which Chai had changed; but they were hardly out of danger when the squall had passed over, and skiff and man had both vanished.

---

[1] A famous official who lived in the reign of Hung Wu, first Emperor of the Ming dynasty (A.D. 1368-1399). I have not been able to discover what was the particular act for which he has been celebrated as "loyal to the death."

LXXX.

THE STREAM OF CASH.

A CERTAIN gentleman's servant was one day in his master's garden, when he beheld a stream of cash[1] flowing by, two or three feet in breadth and of about the same depth. He immediately seized two large handfuls, and then threw himself down on the top of the stream in order to try and secure the rest. However, when he got up he found that it had all flowed away from under him, none being left except what he had got in his two hands.

["Ah !" says the commentator, " money is properly a circulating medium, and is not intended for a man to lie upon and keep all to himself."][2]

---

[1] See No. II., note 2.

[2] The Chinese, fond as they are of introducing water, under the form of miniature lakes, into their gardens and pleasure-grounds, do not approve of a running stream near the dwelling-house, I myself knew a case of a man, provided with a pretty little house, rent free, alongside of which ran a mountain-rill, who left the place and paid for lodgings out of his own pocket rather than live so close to a stream which he averred *carried all his good luck away*. Yet this man was a fair scholar and a graduate to boot.

LXXXI.

THE INJUSTICE OF HEAVEN.

MR. HSU was a magistrate at Shantung. A certain upper chamber of his house was used as a store-room; but some creature managed so frequently to get in and make havoc among the stores, for which the servants were always being scolded, that at length some of the latter determined to keep watch. By-and-by they saw a huge spider as big as a peck measure, and hurried off to tell their master, who thought it so strange that he gave orders to the servants to feed the insect with cakes. It thus became very tame, and would always come forth when hungry, returning as soon as it had taken enough to eat.[1] Years passed away, and one day Mr. Hsü was consulting his archives, when suddenly the spider appeared and ran under the table. Thinking it was hungry, he bade his servants give it a cake; but the next moment he noticed two snakes, of about the thickness of a chop-stick, lying one on each side. The spider

---

[1] That Chinaman thinks his a hard lot who cannot "eat till he is full." It may be noticed here that the Chinese seem not so much to enjoy the process of eating as the subsequent state of repletion. As a rule, they bolt their food, and get their enjoyment out of it afterwards.

drew in its legs as if in mortal fear, and the snakes began
to swell out until they were as big round as an egg; at
which Mr. Hsü was greatly alarmed, and would have
hurried away, when crash! went a peal of thunder,
killing every person in the house.   Mr. Hsü himself recovered consciousness after a little while, but only to see
his wife and servants, seven persons in all, lying dead;
and after a month's illness he, too, departed this life.
Now Mr. Hsü was an upright, honourable man, who
really had the interests of the people at heart.   A subscription was accordingly raised to pay his funeral
expenses, and on the day of his burial the air was rent
for miles round with cries of weeping and lamentation.

[Hereon the commentator, I Shih-shih, makes the
following remark :—" That dragons play with pearls² I
have always regarded as an old woman's tale.   Is it
possible, then, that the story is a fact?   I have heard,
too, that the thunder strikes only the guilty man;³ and,
if so, how could a virtuous official be visited with this
dire calamity?"]

---

¹ The full explanation and origin of this saying I have failed to
elucidate.   Dragons are often represented with pearls before their
mouths; and these they are supposed to spit out or swallow as
fancy may take them.   The pearl, too, is said to be the essence of
the dragon's nature, without which it would be powerless; but this
is all I know about the subject.

³ Such is the common belief in China at the present day.   There
is a God of Thunder who punishes wicked people; the lightning is
merely a mirror, by the aid of which he singles out his victims.

LXXXII.

THE SEA-SERPENT.

A TRADER named Chia was voyaging on the south seas, when one night it suddenly became as light as day on board his ship. Jumping up to see what was the matter, he beheld a huge creature with its body half out of the water, towering up like a hill. Its eyes resembled two suns, and threw a light far and wide; and when the trader asked the boatmen what it was, there was not one who could say. They all crouched down and watched it; and by-and-by the monster gradually disappeared in the water again, leaving everything in darkness as before. And when they reached port, they found all the people talking about a strange phenomenon of a great light that had appeared in the night, the time of which coincided exactly with the strange scene they themselves had wit-nessed.[1]

---

[1] The "sea-serpent" in this case was probably nothing more or less than some meteoric phenomenon.

LXXXIII.

THE MAGIC MIRROR.[1]

" . . . . BUT if you would really like to have some-thing that has belonged to me," said she, " you shall." Whereupon she took out a mirror and· gave it to him, saying, " Whenever you want to see me, you must' look for me in your books; otherwise I shall not be visible ;" —and in a moment she had vanished. Liu went home very melancholy at heart; but when he looked in the mirror, there was Fêng-hsien, standing with her back to him, gazing, as it were, at some one who was going away, and about a hundred paces from her. He then be-thought himself of her injunctions, and settled down to his studies, refusing to receive any visitors; and a few days subsequently, when he happened to look in the mirror, there was Fêng-hsien, with her face turned to-wards him, and smiling in every feature. After this, he was always taking out the mirror to look at her; how-ever, in about a month his good resolutions began to disappear, and he once more went out to enjoy himself

---

[1] The following is merely a single episode taken from a long and otherwise uninteresting story. Miss Fêng-hsien was a fox; hence her power to bestow such a singular present as the mirror here described, the object of which was to incite her lover to success— the condition of their future union.

and waste his time as before. When he returned home and looked in the mirror, Fêng-hsien seemed to be crying bitterly; and the day after, when he looked at her again, she had her back turned towards him as on the day he received the mirror. He now knew that it was because he had neglected his studies, and forthwith set to work again with all diligence, until in a month's time she had turned round once again. Henceforward, whenever anything interrupted his progress, Fêng-hsien's countenance became sad; but whenever he was getting on well, her sadness was changed to smiles. Night and morning Liu would look at the mirror, regarding it quite in the light of a revered preceptor; and in three years' time he took his degree in triumph. "Now," cried he, "I shall be able to look Fêng-hsien in the face." And there, sure enough, she was, with her delicately-pencilled arched eye-brows, and her teeth just showing between her lips, as happy-looking as she could be, when, all of a sudden, she seemed to speak, and Liu heard her say, "A pretty pair we make, I must allow"—and the next moment Fêng-hsien stood by his side.

LXXXIV.

COURAGE TESTED.

MR. TUNG was a Hsü-chou man, very fond of playing broad-sword, and a light-hearted, devil-may-care fellow, who was often involving himself in trouble. One day he fell in with a traveller who was riding on a mule and going the same way as himself; whereupon they entered into conversation, and began to talk to each other about feats of strength and so on. The traveller said his name was T'ung,[1] and that he belonged to Liao-yang; that he had been twenty years away from home, and had just returned from beyond the sea. "And I venture to say," cried Tung, "that in your wanderings on the Four Seas[2]

---

[1] Besides the all-important aspirate, this name is pronounced in a different *tone* from the first-mentioned "Tung;" and is moreover expressed in writing by a totally different character. To a Chinese ear, the two words are as unlikely to be confounded as Brown and Jones.

[2] The Four Seas are supposed by the Chinese to bound the habitable portions of the earth, which, by the way, they further believe to be square. In the centre of all is China, extending far and wide in every direction,—the eye of the universe, the Middle Kingdom. Away at a distance from her shores lie a number of small islands, wherein dwell such barbarous nations as the English, French, Dutch, etc.

you have seen a great many people; but have you seen
any supernaturally clever ones?" T'ung asked him to
what he alluded; and then Tung explained what his own
particular hobby was, adding how much he would like to
learn from them any tricks in the art of broad-sword.
"Supernaturals," replied the traveller, "are to be found
everywhere. It needs but that a man should be a loyal
subject and a filial son for him to know all that the
supernaturals know." "Right you are, indeed!" cried
Tung, as he drew a short sword from his belt, and,
tapping the blade with his fingers, began to accompany
it with a song. He then cut down a tree that was by
the wayside, to shew T'ung how sharp it was; at which
T'ung smoothed his beard and smiled, begging to be
allowed to have a look at the weapon. Tung handed it
to him, and, when he had turned it over two or three
times, he said, "This is a very inferior piece of steel;
now, though I know nothing about broad-sword myself,
I have a weapon which is really of some use." He then
drew from beneath his coat a sword of a foot or so in
length, and with it he began to pare pieces off Tung's
sword, which seemed as soft as a melon, and which he
cut quite away like a horse's hoof. Tung was greatly
astonished, and borrowed the other's sword to examine
it, returning it after carefully wiping the blade. He then
invited T'ung to his house, and made him stay the night;
and, after begging him to explain the mystery of his
sword, began to nurse his leg and sit listening respectfully without saying a word. It was already pretty late,
when suddenly there was a sound of scuffling next door,

where Tung's father lived; and, on putting his ear to the
wall, he heard an angry voice saying, "Tell your son to
come here at once, and then I will spare you." This
was followed by other sounds of beating and a continued
groaning, in a voice which Tung knew to be his father's.
He therefore seized a spear, and was about to rush forth,
but T'ung held him back, saying, "You'll be killed for a
certainty if you go. Let us think of some other plan."
Tung asked what plan he could suggest; to which the
other replied, "The robbers are killing your father:
there is no help for you; but as you have no brothers,
just go and tell your wife and children what your last
wishes are, while I try and rouse the servants." Tung
agreed to this, and ran in to tell his wife, who clung to
him and implored him not to go, until at length all his
courage had ebbed away, and he went upstairs with her
to get his bow and arrows ready to resist the robbers
attack. At that juncture he heard the voice of his friend
T'ung, outside on the eaves of the house, saying, with a
laugh, "All right; the robbers have gone;" but on
lighting a candle, he could see nothing of him. He
then stole out to the front door, where he met his father
with a lantern in his hand, coming in from a party at a
neighbour's house; and the whole court-yard was covered
with the ashes of burnt grass, whereby he knew that
T'ung the traveller was himself a supernatural.[3]

---

[3] The commentator, I Shih-shih, adds a note to this story which
might be summed up in our own—

"The [wo]man that deliberates is lost."

LXXXV.

THE DISEMBODIED FRIEND.

MR. CH'EN, M.A., of Shun-t'ien Fu, when a boy of sixteen, went to school at a Buddhist temple.[1] There were a great many scholars besides himself, and, among others, one named Ch'u, who said he came from Shan-tung. This Ch'u was a very hard-working fellow; he never seemed to be idle, and actually slept in the school-room, not going home at all. Ch'ên became much attached to him, and one day asked him why he never went away. "Well, you see," replied Ch'u, "my people are very poor, and can hardly afford to pay for my schooling; but, by dint of working half the night, two of my days are equal to three of anybody else's." Thereupon Ch'ên said he would bring his own bed to the school, and that they would sleep there together; to which Ch'u replied that the teaching they got wasn't worth much, and that they would do better by putting

---

[1] Buddhist priests not unusually increase the revenue of their monastery by taking pupils; and it is only fair to them to add that the curriculum is strictly secular, the boys learning precisely what they would at an ordinary school and nothing else.

themselves under a certain old scholar named Lü. This they were easily able to do, as the arrangement at the temple was monthly, and at the end of each month any- one was free to go or to come. So off they went to this Mr. Lü, a man of considerable literary attainments, who had found himself in Shun-t'ien Fu without a cash in his pocket, and was accordingly obliged to take pupils. He was delighted at getting two additions to his number; and, Ch'u showing himself an apt scholar, the two soon became very great friends, sleeping in the same room and eating at the same table. At the end of the month Ch'u asked for leave of absence, and, to the astonishment of all, ten days elapsed without anything being heard of him. It then chanced that Ch'ên went to the T'ien-ning temple, and there he saw Ch'u under one of the veran- dahs, occupied in cutting wood for lucifer-matches.[2] The latter was much disconcerted by the arrival of Ch'ên, who asked him why he had given up his studies; so the latter took him aside, and explained that he was so poor as to be obliged to work half a month to scrape together funds enough for his next month's schooling.

---

[2] These consist simply of thin slips of wood dipped in brimstone, and resemble those used in England as late as the first quarter of the present century. They are said to have been invented by the people of Hang-chou, the capital of Chekiang; but it is quite possible that the hint may have first reached China from the west. They were called *yin kuang* "bring light," (*cf. lucifer*), *fa chu* "give forth illumination," and other names. Lucifer matches are now generally spoken of as *tzŭ lai huo* "self-come fire," and are almost universally employed, except in remote parts where the flint and steel still hold sway.

" You come along back with me," cried Ch'ên, on hearing
this, " I will arrange for the payment," which Ch'u immediately consented to do on condition that Ch'ên would
keep the whole thing a profound secret. Now Ch'ên's
father was a wealthy tradesman, and from his till Ch'ên
abstracted money wherewith to pay for Ch'u; and by-
and-by, when his father found him out, he confessed why
he had done so. Thereupon Ch'ên's father called him a
fool, and would not let him resume his studies; at which
Ch'u was much hurt, and would have left the school too,
but that old Mr. Lü discovered what had taken place, and
gave him the money to return to Ch'ên's father, keeping
him still at the school, and treating him quite like his
own son. So Ch'ên studied no more, but whenever he
met Ch'u he always asked him to join in some refreshment at a restaurant, Ch'u invariably refusing, but
yielding at length to his entreaties, being himself loth to
break off their old acquaintanceship.

Thus two years passed away, when Ch'ên's father died,
and Ch'ên went back to his books under the guidance of
old Mr. Lü, who was very glad to see such determination. Of course Ch'ên was now far behind Ch'u;
and in about six months Lü's son arrived, having begged
his way in search of his father, so Mr. Lü gave up his
school and returned home with a purse which his pupils
had made up for him, Ch'u adding nothing thereto but
his tears. At parting, Mr. Lü advised Ch'ên to take
Ch'u as his tutor, and this he did, establishing him comfortably in the house with him. The examination was
very shortly to commence, and Ch'ên felt convinced that

he should not get through; but Ch'u said he thought he should be able to manage the matter for him. On the appointed day he introduced Ch'ên to a gentleman who he said was a cousin of his, named Liu, and asked Ch'ên to accompany this cousin, which Ch'ên was just proceeding to do when Ch'u pulled him back from behind,[3] and he would have fallen down but that the cousin pulled him up again, and then, after having scrutinized his appearance, carried him off to his own house. There being no ladies there, Ch'ên was put into the inner apartments; and a few days afterwards Liu said to him, "A great many people will be at the gardens to-day; let us go and amuse ourselves awhile, and afterwards I will send you home again." He then gave orders that a servant should proceed on ahead with tea and wine, and by-and-by they themselves went, and were soon in the thick of the fête. Crossing over a bridge, they saw beneath an old willow tree a little painted skiff, and were soon on board, engaged in freely passing round the wine. However, finding this a little dull, Liu bade his servant go and see if Miss Li, the famous singing-girl, was at home; and in a few minutes the servant returned bringing Miss Li with him. Ch'ên had met her before, and so they at once exchanged greetings, while Liu begged her to be good enough to favour them with a song. Miss Li, who seemed labouring under a fit of melancholy, forthwith began a funeral dirge; at which

---

[3] The whole point of the story hinges on this.

Ch'ên was not much pleased, and observed that such a theme was hardly suitable to the occasion. With a forced smile, Miss Li changed her key, and gave them a love-song; whereupon Ch'ên seized her hand, and said, "There's that song of the Huan-sha river,[4] which you sang once before; I have read it over several times, but have quite forgotten the words." Then Miss Li began—

" Eyes overflowing with tears, she sits gazing into her glass,
Lifting the bamboo screen, one of her comrades approaches;
She bends her head and seems intent on her bow-like slippers,
And forces her eyebrows to arch themselves into a smile.
With her scarlet sleeve she wipes the tears from her perfumed cheek,
In fear and trembling lest they should guess the thoughts that o'erwhelm her."[5]

Ch'ên repeated this over several times, until at length the skiff stopped, and they passed through a long verandah, where a great many verses had been inscribed on the walls,[6] to which Ch'ên at once proceeded to add a stanza of his own. Evening was now coming on, and Liu remarked that the candidates would be just about

---

[4] Beside which lived Hsi Shih, the famous beauty of the fifth century after Christ.

[5] I fear that the translation of this "Singing-girl's Lament" falls so considerably below the pathetic original as to give but a poor idea of the real merit of the latter as a lyric gem.

[6] The Chinese have precisely the same mania as our Browns, Joneses, and Robinsons, for scribbling and carving their names and compositions all over the available parts of any place of public resort. The literature of inn walls alone would fill many ponderous tomes.

leaving the examination-hall ;[7] so he escorted him back
to his own home, and there left him. The room was
dark, and there was no one with him; but by-and-by the
servants ushered in some one whom at first he took to
be Ch'u. However, he soon saw that it was not Ch'u,
and in another moment the stranger had fallen against
him and knocked him down. "Master's fainted!"
cried the servants, as they ran to pick him up; and then
Ch'ên discovered that the one who had fallen down was
really no other than himself.[8] On getting up, he saw
Ch'u standing by his side; and when they had sent away
the servants the latter said, "Don't be alarmed: I am
nothing more than a disembodied spirit. My time for
re-appearing on earth[9] is long overdue, but I could not
forget your great kindness to me, and accordingly I have
remained under this form in order to assist in the accomplishment of your wishes. The three bouts[10] are over, and
your ambition will be gratified." Ch'ên then inquired if
Ch'u could assist him in like manner for his doctor's
degree; to which the latter replied, "Alas! the luck
descending to you from your ancestors is not equal to
that.[11] They were a niggardly lot, and unfit for the

---

[7] The examination, which lasts nine days, has been going on all
this time.

[8] That is, his own body, into which Ch'u's spirit had temporarily
passed, his own occupying, meanwhile, the body of his friend.

[9] That is, for being born again, the sole hope and ambition of a
disembodied shade.

[10] See No. LXXI., note 1.

[11] See No. LXI., note 3.

posthumous honours you would thus confer on them."
Ch'ên next asked him whither he was going; and Ch'u
replied that he hoped, through the agency of his cousin,
who was a clerk in Purgatory, to be born again in old
Mr. Lü's family. They then bade each other adieu;
and, when morning came, Ch'ên set off to call on Miss
Li, the singing-girl; but on reaching her house he found
that she had been dead some days.[12] He walked on to
the gardens, and there he saw traces of verses that had
been written on the walls, and evidently rubbed out, so
as to be hardly decipherable. In a moment it flashed
across him that the verses and their composers
belonged to the other world. Towards evening Ch'u
re-appeared in high spirits, saying that he had succeeded
in his design, and had come to wish Ch'ên a long farewell. Holding out his open palms, he requested Ch'ên
to write the word *Ch'u* on each; and then, after refusing
to take a parting cup, he went away, telling Ch'ên that
the examination-list would soon be out, and that they
would meet again before long. Ch'ên brushed away his
tears and escorted him to the door, where a man, who
had been waiting for him, laid his hand on Ch'u's head
and pressed it downwards until Ch'u was perfectly flat.
The man then put him in a sack and carried him off on
his back. A few days afterwards the list came out,
and, to his great joy, Ch'ên found his name among the
successful candidates; whereupon he immediately started

---

[12] His own spirit in Ch'u's body had met her in a disembodied
state.

off to visit his old tutor, Mr. Lü.[13]   Now Mr. Lü's wife
had had no children for ten years, being about fifty years
of age, when suddenly she gave birth to a son, who was
born with both fists doubled up so that no one could
open them.   On his arrival Ch'ên begged to see the
child, and declared that inside its hands would be found
written the word Ch'u.   Old Mr. Lü laughed at this ;
but no sooner had the child set eyes on Ch'ên than both
its fists opened spontaneously, and there was the word as
Ch'ên had said.   The story was soon told, and Ch'ên
went home, after making a handsome present to the
family ; and later on, when Mr. Lü went up for his
doctor's degree[14] and stayed at Ch'ên's house, his son
was thirteen years old, and had already matriculated as a
candidate for literary honours.

---

[13] Such is the invariable custom.   Large presents are usually
made by those who can afford the outlay, and the tutor's name
has ever afterwards an honourable place in the family records.

[14] See No. XLVIII., note 1.

LXXXVI.

THE CLOTH MERCHANT.

A CERTAIN cloth merchant went to Ch'ing-chou, where he happened to stroll into an old temple, all tumble-down and in ruins. He was lamenting over this sad state of things, when a priest who stood by observed that a devout believer like himself could hardly do better than put the place into repair, and thus obtain favour in the eyes of Buddha. This the merchant consented to do; whereupon the priest invited him to walk into the private quarters of the temple, and treated him with much courtesy; but he went on to propose that our friend the merchant should also undertake the general ornamentation of the place both inside and out.[1] The

---

[1] The elaborate gilding and wood-work of an ordinary Chinese temple form a very serious item in the expense of restoration. Public subscriptions are usually the means employed for raising sufficient funds, the names of subscribers and amount given by each being published in some conspicuous position. Occasionally devout priests—black swans, indeed, in China—shut themselves up in boxes studded with nails, one of which they pull out every time a certain donation is given, and there they remain until every nail is withdrawn. But after all it is difficult to say whether they endure

latter declared he could not afford the expense, and the priest began to get very angry, and urged him so strongly that at last the merchant, in terror, promised to give all the money he had. After this he was preparing to go away, but the priest detained him, saying, "You haven't given the money of your own free will, and consequently you'll be owing me a grudge: I can't do better than make an end of you at once." Thereupon he seized a knife, and refused to listen to all the cloth merchant's entreaties, until at length the latter asked to be allowed to hang himself, to which the priest consented; and, showing him into a dark room, told him to make haste about it.

At this juncture, a Tartar-General[2] happened to pass by the temple; and from a distance, through a breach in the old wall, he saw a damsel in a red dress pass into the priest's quarters. This roused his suspicions,[3] and dismounting from his horse, he entered the temple and searched high and low, but without discovering anything. The dark room above-mentioned was locked and double-

---

these trials so much for the faith's sake as for the funds from which they derive more of the luxuries of life, and the temporary notoriety gained by thus coming before the public. A Chinese proverb says, "The image-maker doesn't worship Buddha. He knows too much about the idol;" and the application of this saying may safely be extended to the majority of Buddhist priests in China.

[2] This is the title generally applied to the Manchu commanders of Manchu garrisons, who are stationed at certain of the most important points of the Chinese Empire, and whose presence is intended as a check upon the action of the civil authorities.

[3] See No. VI., note 2.

barred, and the priest refused to open it, saying the place was haunted.   The General in a rage burst open the door, and there beheld the cloth merchant hanging from a beam.   He cut him down at once, and in a short time he was brought round and told the General the whole story.   They then searched for the damsel, but she was nowhere to be found, having been nothing more than a divine manifestation.   The General cut off the priest's head and restored the cloth merchant's property to him, after which the latter put the temple in thorough repair and kept it well supplied with lights and incense ever afterwards.

Mr. Chao, M.A., told me this story with all its details.[4]

---

[4] The moral being, of course, that Buddha protects those who look after his interests on earth.

LXXXVII.

A STRANGE COMPANION.

HAN KUNG-FU, of Yü-ch'êng, told me that he was one day travelling along a road with a man of his village, named P'eng, when all of a sudden the latter disappeared, leaving his mule to jog along with an empty saddle. At the same moment, Mr. Han heard his voice calling for assistance, and apparently proceeding from inside one of the panniers strapped across the mule's back; and on looking closely, there indeed he was in one of the panniers, which, however, did not seem to be at all displaced by his weight. On trying to get him out the mouth of the pannier closed itself tightly; and it was only when he cut it open with a knife that he saw P'êng curled up in it like a dog. He then helped him out, and asked him how he managed to get in; but this he was unable to say. It further appeared that his family was under fox influence, many strange things of this kind having happened before.

LXXXVIII.

SPIRITUALISTIC SÉANCES.

IT is customary in Shantung, when any one is sick, for the womenfolk to engage an old sorceress or medium, who strums on a tambourine and performs certain mysterious antics. This custom obtains even more in the capital, where young ladies of the best families frequently organize such *séances* among themselves. On a table in the hall they spread out a profusion of wine and meat, and burn huge candles which make the place as light as day. Then the sorceress, shortening her skirts, stands on one leg and performs the *shang-yang*,[1] while two of the others support her, one on each side. All this time she is chattering unintelligible sentences,[2] some-

---

[1] It is related in the *Family Sayings*, an apocryphal work which professes to give conversations of Confucius, that a number of one-legged birds having suddenly appeared in Ch'i, the Duke of Ch'i sent off to ask the Sage what was the meaning of this strange phenomenon. Confucius replied, "The bird is the *shang-yang*, and portends beneficial rain." And formerly the boys and girls in Shantung would hop about on one leg, crying, "The *shang-yang* has come;" after which rain would be sure to follow.

[2] Speaking in the unknown tongue, like the Irvingites and others.

thing between a song and a prayer, the words being confused but uttered in a sort of tune; while the hall re-
sounds with the thunder of drums, enough to stun a
person, with which her vaticinations are mixed up and
lost. By-and-by her head begins to droop, and her eyes
to look aslant; and but for her two supporters she would
inevitably fall to the ground. Suddenly she stretches
forth her neck and bounds several feet into the air, upon
which the other women regard her in terror, saying,
"The spirits have come to eat;" and immediately all
the candles are blown out and everything is in total
darkness. Thus they remain for about a quarter of an
hour, afraid to speak a word, which in any case would
not be heard through the din, until at length the
sorceress calls out the personal name of the head of the
family[3] and some others; whereupon they immediately
relight the candles and hurry up to ask if the reply of
the spirits is favourable or otherwise. They then see
that every scrap of the food and every drop of the wine
has disappeared. Meanwhile, they watch the old
woman's expression, whereby they can tell if the spirits
are well disposed; and each one asks her some question, to which she as promptly replies. Should there be
any unbelievers among the party, the spirits are at once
aware of their presence; and the old sorceress, pointing

---

[3] This is a clever hit. The "personal" name of a man may not
be uttered except by his father or mother, grandfather, grandmother, uncles, etc. Thus, the mere use of the personal name of
the *head of a family* proves conclusively that the spirit of some
one of his ancestors must be present.

her finger at such a one, cries out, "Disrespectful
mocker! where are your trousers?" upon which the
mocker alluded to looks down, and lo! her trousers are
gone—gone to the top of a tree in the court-yard, where
they will subsequently be found.[4]

Manchu women and girls, especially, are firm believers
in spiritualism. On the slightest provocation they consult their medium, who comes into the room gorgeously
dressed, and riding on an imitation horse or tiger.[5] In
her hand she holds a long spear, with which she mounts
the couch[6] and postures in an extraordinary manner,
the animal she rides snorting or roaring fiercely all the
time. Some call her Kuan Ti,[7] others Chang Fei, and
others again Chou Kung, from her terribly martial

---

[4] I consider the whole of the above a curious story to be found
in a Chinese work exactly 200 years old, but no part of it more so
than the forcible removal of some part of the clothing, which has
been so prominent a feature in the *séances* of our own day. It
may be added that in many a court-yard in Peking will be found
one or more trees, which cause the view from the city wall to
be very pleasing to the eye, in spite of the filth and ruins which a
closer inspection reveals.

[5] The arrangement being that of the hobby-horse of by-gone
days.

[6] The couches of the north of China are brick beds, heated by a
stove underneath, and covered with a mat. Upon one of these is
generally a dwarf table and a couple of pillows; and here it is that
the Chinaman loves to recline, his wine-kettle, opium-pipe, or tea-
pot within reach, and a friend at his side, with whom he may converse far into the night.

[7] See No. LXXIII., note 3. Chang Fei was the bosom-friend of
the last, and was his associate-commander in the wars of the Three
Kingdoms. Chou Kung was the first Emperor of the Chou

aspect, which strikes fear into all beholders. And should any daring fellow try to peep in while the *séance* is going on, out of the window darts the spear, transfixes his hat, and draws it off his head into the room, while women and girls, young and old, hop round one after the other like geese, on one leg, without seeming to get the least fatigued.

---

dynasty, and a pattern of wisdom and virtue. He is said by the Chinese to have invented the mariner's compass; but the legend will not bear investigation.

LXXXIX.

THE MYSTERIOUS HEAD.

SEVERAL traders who were lodging at an inn in Peking, occupied a room which was divided from the adjoining apartment by a partition of boards from which a piece was missing, leaving an aperture about as big as a basin. Suddenly a girl's head appeared through the opening, with very pretty features and nicely dressed hair; and the next moment an arm, as white as polished jade. The traders were much alarmed, and, thinking it was the work of devils, tried to seize the head, which, however, was quickly drawn in again out of their reach. This happened a second time, and then, as they could see no body belonging to the head, one of them took a knife in his hand and crept up against the partition underneath the hole. In a little while the head reappeared, when he made a chop at it and cut it off, the blood spurting out all over the floor and wall. The traders hurried off to tell the landlord, who immediately reported the matter to the authorities, taking the head with him, and the traders were forthwith arrested and examined ; but the magistrate could make nothing of the case, and, as no one appeared for the prosecution, the accused, after about six months' incarceration, were accordingly released, and orders were given for the girl's head to be buried.

XC.

THE SPIRIT OF THE HILLS.

A MAN named Li, of I-tu, was once crossing the hills when he came upon a number of persons sitting on the ground engaged in drinking. As soon as they saw Li they begged him to join them, and vied with each other in filling his cup. Meanwhile, he looked about him and noticed that the various trays and dishes contained all kinds of costly food; the wine only seemed to him a little rough on the palate. In the middle of their fun up came a stranger with a face about three feet long and a very tall hat; whereupon the others were very much alarmed, and cried out, "The hill spirit! the hill spirit!" running away in all directions as fast as they could go. Li hid himself in a hole in the ground; and when by-and-by he peeped out to see what had happened, the wine and food had disappeared, and there was nothing there but a few dirty potsherds and some pieces of broken tiles with efts and lizards crawling over them.[1]

---

[1] Mr. Li had, doubtless, taken a "drop too much" before he started on his mountain walk.

XCI.

INGRATITUDE PUNISHED.

K'u Ta-Yu was a native of the Yang district, and managed to get a military appointment under the command of Tsu Shu-shun.[1] The latter treated him most kindly, and finally sent him as Major-General of some troops by which he was then trying to establish the dynasty of the usurping Chows. K'u soon perceived that the game was lost, and immediately turned his forces upon Tsu Shu-shun, whom he succeeded in capturing, after Tsu had been wounded in the hand, and whom he at once forwarded as a prisoner to headquarters. That night he dreamed that the Judge of Purgatory appeared to him, and, reproaching him with his base ingratitude, bade the devil-lictors seize him and scald his feet in a cauldron of boiling oil. K'u then woke up with a start, and found that his feet were very sore and painful; and in a short time they swelled up, and his toes dropped off. Fever set in, and in his agony he shrieked out, " Ungrateful wretch that I was indeed," and fell back and expired.

---

[1] Of whom I can learn nothing.

XCII.

SMELLING ESSAYS.[1]

Now as they wandered about the temple they came upon an old blind priest sitting under the verandah, engaged in selling medicines and prescribing for patients. "Ah!" cried Sung, "there is an extraordinary man who is well versed in the arts of composition;" and immediately he sent back to get the essay they had just been reading, in order to obtain the old priest's opinion as to its merits. At the same moment up came their friend from Yü-hang, and all three went along together. Wang began by addressing him as "Professor;" whereupon the priest, who thought the stranger had come to consult him as a doctor, inquired what might be the disease from which he was suffering. Wang then explained what his mission was; upon which the priest smiled and said, "Who's been telling you this nonsense? How can a man with no eyes discuss with you the merits

---

[1] The following extract from a long and otherwise tedious story tells its own tale. Wang is the modest man, and the young man from Yü-hang the braggart. Sung is merely a friend of Wang's.

of your compositions?" Wang replied by asking him to
let his ears do duty for his eyes; but the priest answered
that he would hardly have patience to sit out Wang's
three sections, amounting perhaps to some two thousand
and more words. "However," added he, "if you like
to burn it, I'll try what I can do with my nose." Wang
complied, and burnt the first section there and then; and
the old priest, snuffing up the smoke, declared that it
wasn't such a bad effort, and finally gave it as his
opinion that Wang would probably succeed at the
examination. The young scholar from Yü-hang didn't
believe that the old priest could really tell anything by
these means, and forthwith proceeded to burn an essay
by one of the old masters; but the priest no sooner
smelt the smoke than he cried out, "Beautiful indeed!
beautiful indeed! I do enjoy this. The light of genius
and truth is evident here." The Yü-hang scholar was
greatly astonished at this, and began to burn an essay of
his own; whereupon the priest said, "I had had but a
taste of that one; why change so soon to another?"
"The first paragraph," replied the young man, "was by
a friend; the rest is my own composition." No sooner
had he uttered these words than the old priest began to
retch violently, and begged that he might have no more,
as he was sure it would make him sick. The Yü-hang
scholar was much abashed at this, and went away; but
in a few days the list came out and his name was among
the successful ones, while Wang's was not. He at once
hurried off to tell the old priest, who, when he heard the
news, sighed and said, "I may be blind with my eyes

but I am not so with my nose, which I fear is the case with the examiners. Besides," added he, " I was talking to you about composition : I said nothing about *destiny*."[2]

---

[2] This is one of our author's favourite shafts—a sneer at examiners in general, and those who rejected him in particular.

XCIII.

HIS FATHER'S GHOST.

A MAN named T'ien Tzŭ-ch'êng, of Chiang-ning, was crossing the Tung-t'ing lake, when the boat was capsized, and he was drowned. His son, Liang-ssŭ, who, towards the close of the Ming dynasty, took the highest degree, was then a baby in arms; and his wife, hearing the bad news, swallowed poison forthwith,[1] and left the child to the care of his grandmother. When Liang-ssŭ grew up, he was appointed magistrate in Hu-pei, where he remained about a year. He was then transferred to Hu-nan, on military service ; but, on reaching the Tung-t'ing lake, his feelings overpowered him, and he returned to plead inability as an excuse for not taking up his post. Accordingly, he was degraded to the rank of Assistant-Magistrate, which he at first declined, but was finally compelled to accept; and thenceforward gave himself up to roaming about on the lakes and

---

[1] This would be regarded as a very meritorious act by the Chinese.

streams of the surrounding country, without paying
much attention to his official duties.

One night he had anchored his boat alongside the
bank of a river, when suddenly the cadence of a
sweetly-played flageolet broke upon his ear; so he
strolled along by the light of the moon in the direction
of the music, until, after a few minutes' walking, he
reached a cottage standing by itself, with a few citron-
trees round it, and brilliantly-lighted inside. Approaching a window, he peeped in, and saw three persons
sitting at a table, engaged in drinking. In the place
of honour was a graduate of about thirty years of age;
an old man played the host, and at the side sat a
much younger man playing on the flageolet. When
he had finished, the old man clapped his hands in
admiration; but the graduate turned away with a sigh,
as if he had not heard a note. "Come now, Mr. Lu,"
cried the old man, addressing the latter, "kindly
favour us with one of your songs, which, I know, must
be worth hearing." The graduate then began to sing as
follows :—

> " Over the river the wind blows cold on lonely me :
>   Each flow'ret trampled under foot, all verdure gone.
> At home a thousand *li* away, I cannot be ;
>   So towards the Bridge my spirit nightly wanders on."

The above was given in such melancholy tones that
the old man smiled and said, "Mr. Lu, these must be
experiences of your own," and, immediately filling a
goblet, added, "I can do nothing like that; but if you
will let me, I will give you a song to help us on with

our wine." He then sung a verse from "Li T'ai-poh,"[2] and put them all in a lively humour again; after which the young man said he would just go outside and see how high the moon was, which he did, and observing Liang-ssŭ outside, clapped his hands, and cried out to his companions, "There is a man at the window, who has seen all we have been doing." He then led Liang-ssŭ in; whereupon the other two rose, and begged him to be seated, and to join them in their wine. The wine, however, was cold,[3] and he therefore declined; but the young man at once perceived his reason, and proceeded to warm some for him. Liang-ssŭ now ordered his servant to go and buy some more, but this his host would not permit him to do. They next inquired Liang-ssŭ's name, and whence he came, and then the old man said, "Why, then, you are the father and mother[4] of the district in which I live. My name is River: I am an old resident here. This young man is a Mr. Tu, of Kiang-si; and this gentleman," added he, pointing to the graduate, "is Mr. Rushten,[5] a fellow-provincial of yours." Mr.

---

[2] The Byron of China.

[3] Chinese wine—or, more correctly, *spirits*—is always taken hot; hence the term wine-kettle, which frequently occurs in these pages.

[4] The Magistrate; who is supposed to be towards the people what a father is to his children.

[5] This singularly un-Chinese surname is employed to keep up a certain play upon words which exists in the original, and which is important to the *denôuement* of the story. "River" is the simple translation of a name actually in use.

Rushten looked at Liang-ssŭ in rather a contemptuous way, and without taking much notice of him; whereupon Liang-ssŭ asked him whereabouts he lived in Chiang-ning, observing that it was strange he himself should never have heard of such an accomplished gentleman. "Alas!" replied Rushten, "it is many a long day since I left my home, and I know nothing even of my own family. Alas, indeed!" These words were uttered in so mournful a tone of voice that the old man broke in with, "Come, come, now! talking like this, instead of drinking when we're all so jolly together; this will never do." He then drained a bumper himself, and said, "I propose a game of forfeits. We'll throw with three dice; and whoever throws so that the spots on one die[6] equal those on the other two shall give us a verse with a corresponding classical allusion in it." He then threw himself, and turned up an ace, a two, and a three; whereupon he sung the following lines :—

"An ace and a deuce on one side, just equal a three on the other :
For Fan a chicken was boiled, though three years had passed, by Chang's mother.[7]
    Thus friends love to meet!"

---

[6] Chinese dice are the exact counterpart of our own, except that the ace and the four are coloured red : the ace because the combination of black and white would be unlucky, and the four because this number once turned up in response to the call of an Emperor of the T'ang dynasty, who particularly wanted a four to win him the *partie*. All letters, despatches, and such documents, have invariably something *red* about them, this being the lucky colour, and to the Chinese, emblematic of prosperity and joy.

[7] Alluding to an ancient story of a promise by a Mr. Fan that he

Then the young musician threw, and turned up two twos and a four; whereupon he exclaimed, " Don't laugh at the feeble allusion of an unlearned fellow like me:—

' Two deuces are equal to a four :
Four men united their valour in the old city.[8]
Thus brothers love to meet ! ' "

Mr. Rushten followed with two aces and a two, and recited these lines :—

" Two aces are equal to a two :
Lu-hsiang stretched out his two arms and embraced his father.[9]
Thus father and son love to meet ! "

Liang then threw, and turned up the same as Mr. Rushten; whereupon he said :—

" Two aces are equal to a two :
Mao-jung regaled Lin-tsung with two baskets.[10]
Thus host and guest love to meet ! "

---

would be at his friend Chang's house that day three years. When the time drew near, Chang's mother ridiculed the notion of a man keeping a three years' appointment; but, acceding to her son's instances, prepared a boiled chicken, which was barely ready when Fan arrived to eat of it.

[8] Alluding to the celebrated oath of confederation sworn in the peach garden between Kuan Yü, or Kuan Ti (see No. I., note 3), Chang Fei (see No. LXIII., note 2), Liu Pei, who subsequently proclaimed himself Emperor, A.D. 221, and Chu-ko Liang, his celebrated minister, to whose sage counsels most of the success of the undertaking was due. The whole story is one of the best known of Chinese historical romances, bringing about, as it did, the downfall of the famous Han dynasty, which had endured for over 400 years.

[9] Alluding to the story of a young man who went in search of his missing father.

[10] Lin-tsung saw his host kill a chicken which he thought was destined for himself. However, Mao-jung served up the dainty

When the *partie* was over Liang-ssŭ rose to go, but Mr. Rushten said, " Dear me ! why are you in such a hurry ; we haven't had a moment to speak of the old place. Please stay : I was just going to ask you a few questions." So Liang-ssŭ sat down again, and Mr. Rushten proceeded. "I had an old friend," said he, "who was drowned in the Tung-t'ing lake. He bore the same name as yourself; was he a relative ? " " He was my father," replied Liang-ssŭ ; " how did you know him ? " " We were friends as boys together ; and when he was drowned, I recovered and buried his body by the river-side "[11] Liang-ssŭ here burst into tears, and thanked Mr. Rushten very warmly, begging him to point out his father's grave. " Come again to-morrow," said Mr. Rushten, "and I will shew it to you. You could easily find it yourself. It is close by here, and has ten stalks of water-rush growing on it." Liang-ssŭ now took his leave, and went back to his boat, but he could not sleep for thinking of what Mr. Rushten had told him ; and at length, without waiting for the dawn, he set out to look for the grave. To his great astonishment, the house where he had spent the previous evening had disappeared ; but hunting about in the direction indicated

morsel to his mother, while he and his guest regaled themselves with two baskets of common vegetables. At this instance of filial piety, Lin-tsung bad the good sense to be charmed.

[11] The Chinese recognise no act more worthy a virtuous man than that of burying stray bones, covering up exposed coffins, and so forth. By such means the favour of the Gods is most surely obtained, to say nothing of the golden opinions of the living.

by Mr. Rushten, he found a grave with ten water-rushes growing on it, precisely as Mr. Rushten had described. It then·flashed across him that Mr. Rushten's name had a special meaning, and that he had been holding converse with none other than the disembodied spirit of his own father. And, on inquiring of the people of the place, he learnt that twenty years before a benevolent old gentleman, named Kao, had been in the habit of collecting the bodies of persons found drowned, and burying them in that spot. Liang then opened the grave, and carried off his father's remains to his own home, where his grandmother, to whom he described Mr. Rushten's appearance, confirmed the suspicion he himself had formed. It also turned out that the young musician was a cousin of his, who had been drowned when nineteen years of age; and then he recollected that the boy's father had subsequently gone to Kiang-si, and that his mother had died there, and had been buried at the Bamboo Bridge, to which Mr. Rushten had alluded in his song. But he did not know who the old man was.[12]

---

[12] This is merely our author's way of putting the question of the old man's identity. He was the Spirit of the Waters—his name, it will be recollected, was River—just, in fact, as we say Old Father Thames.

XCIV.

THE BOAT-GIRL BRIDE.

WANG KULI-NGAN was a young man of good family. It happened once when he was travelling southwards, and had moored his boat to the bank, that he saw in another boat close by a young boat-girl embroidering shoes. He was much struck by her beauty, and continued gazing at her for some time, though she took not the slightest notice of him. By-and-by he began singing—

> " The Lo-yang lady lives over the way :
> [Fifteen years is her age I should say "] [1]

to attract her attention, and then she seemed to perceive that he was addressing himself to her; but, after just raising her head and glancing at him, she resumed her embroidery as before. Wang then threw a piece of silver towards her, which fell on her skirt; however she merely picked it up, and flung it on to the bank, as if she had not seen what it was, so Wang

---

[1] From a poem by Wang Wei, a noted poet of the T'ang dynasty. The second line is not given in the text.

put it back in his pocket again. He followed up by throwing her a gold bracelet, to which she paid no attention whatever, never taking her eyes off her work. A few minutes after her father appeared, much to the dismay of Wang, who was afraid he would see the bracelet; but the young girl quietly placed her feet over it, and concealed it from his sight. The boatman let go the painter, and away they went down stream, leaving Wang sitting there, not knowing what to do next. And, having recently lost his wife, he regretted that he had not seized this opportunity to make another match ; the more so, as when he came to ask the other boat-people of the place, no one knew anything about them. So Wang got into his own boat, and started off in pursuit; but evening came on, and, as he could see nothing of them, he was obliged to turn back and proceed in the direction where business was taking him. When he had finished that, he returned, making inquiries all the way along, but without hearing anything about the object of his search. On arriving at home, he was unable either to eat or to sleep, so much did this affair occupy his mind ; and about a year afterwards he went south again, bought a boat, and lived in it as his home, watching carefully every single vessel that passed either up or down, until at last there was hardly one he didn't know by sight. But all this time the boat he was looking for never reappeared.

Some six months passed away thus, and then, having exhausted all his funds, he was obliged to go home, where he remained in a state of general inaptitude for

anything.   One night he dreamed that he entered a
village on the river-bank, and that, after passing several
houses, he saw one with a door towards the south,
and a palisade of bamboos inside.   Thinking it was a
garden, he walked in and beheld a beautiful magnolia,
covered with blossoms, which reminded him of the
line—

"And Judas-tree in flower before her door."[2]

A few steps farther on was a neat bamboo hedge, on
the other side of which, towards the north, he found
a small house, with three columns, the door of which
was locked; and another, towards the south, with its
window shaded by the broad leaves of a plaintain-tree.
The door was barred by a clothes-horse,[3] on which

---

[2] From a poem by P'an T'ang-shên, which runs :—

"Her rustic home stands by the Tung-t'ing lake.
Ye who would there a pure libation pour,
Look for mud walls—a roof of rushy make—
And Judas-tree in flower before the door."

The Chinese believe that the Judas-tree will only bloom where fraternal love prevails.

[3] I have already observed that men and women should not let their hands touch when passing things to each other (see No. XL., note 3); neither is it considered proper for persons of different sexes to hang their clothes on the same clothes-horse. (See *Appendix*, note 42.)

With regard to shaking hands, I have omitted to mention how hateful this custom is in the eyes of the Chinese, as in vogue among foreigners, without reference to sex.   They believe that a bad man might easily secrete some noxious drug in the palm of his hand, and so convey it into the system of any woman, who would then be at his mercy.

was hanging an embroidered petticoat; and, on seeing this, Wang stepped back, knowing that he had got to the ladies' quarters; but his presence had already been noticed inside, and, in another moment, out came his heroine of the boat. Overjoyed at seeing her, he was on the point of grasping her hand, when suddenly the girl's father arrived, and, in his consternation, Wang waked up, and found that it was all a dream. Every incident of it, however, remained clear and distinct in his mind, and he took care to say nothing about it to anybody, for fear of destroying its reality.

Another year passed away, and he went again to Chinkiang, where lived an official, named Hsü, who was an old friend of the family, and who invited Wang to come and take a cup of wine with him. On his way thither, Wang lost his way, but at length reached a village which seemed familiar to him, and which he soon found, by the door with the magnolia inside, to be identical, in every particular, with the village of his dream. He went in through the doorway, and there was everything as he had seen it in his dream, even to the boat-girl herself. She jumped up on his arrival, and, shutting the door in his face, asked what his business was there. Wang inquired if she had forgotten about the bracelet, and went on to tell her how long he had been searching for her, and how, at last, she had been revealed to him in a dream. The girl then begged to know his name and family; and when she heard who he was, she asked what a gentleman like himself could want with a poor boat-girl like her, as he must have a wife of his own. "But for you," replied Wang, "I should, indeed, have been married long ago." Upon which the girl told him if that was really the case, he had better apply to her parents, · "although," added she, "they have already refused a great many offers for me. The bracelet you gave me is here, but my father and mother are just now away from home; they will be back shortly. You go away now and engage a match-maker, when I dare say it will be all right if the proper formalities are observed." Wang then retired, the girl calling after him to remember that. her name was Mêng Yün, and her father's Mêng Chiang-li. He proceeded at once on his way to Mr. Hsü's, and after that sought out his intended father-in-law, telling him who he was, and offering him at the same time one hundred ounces of silver, as betrothal-money for his daughter. "She is already promised," replied the old man; upon which Wang declared he had been making careful inquiries, and had heard, on all sides, that the young lady was not engaged, winding up by begging to know what objection there was to his suit. "I have just promised her," answered her father, "and I cannot possibly break my word;" so Wang went away, deeply mortified, not knowing whether to believe it or not. That night he tossed about a good deal; and next morning, braving the ridicule with which he imagined his friend would view his wished-for alliance with a boat-girl, he went off to Mr. Hsü, and told him all about it. "Why didn't you consult me before?" cried Mr. Hsü; "her

father is a connection of mine." Wang then went on
to give fuller particulars, which his friend interrupted
by saying, "Chang-li is indeed poor, but he has never
been a boatman. Are you sure you are not making
a mistake?" He then sent off his elder son to make
inquiries; and to him the girl's father said, "Poor I
am, but I don't *sell* my daughter.[4] Your friend imagined
that I should be tempted by the sight of his money
to forego the usual ceremonies, and so I won't have
anything to do with him. But if your father desires
this match, and everything is in proper order, I will
just go in and consult with my daughter, and see if she
is willing." He then retired for a few minutes, and
when he came back he raised his hands in congratu-
lation, saying, "Everything is as you wish;" whereupon
a day was fixed, and the young man went home to
report to his father. Wang now sent off betrothal
presents, with the usual formalities, and took up his
abode with his friend, Mr. Hsü, until the marriage
was solemnized, three days after which he bade adieu
to his father-in-law, and started on his way northwards.
In the evening, as they were sitting on the boat together, Wang said to his wife, "When I first met you
near this spot, I fancied you were not of the ordinary
boating-class. Where were you then going?" "I was
going to visit my uncle," she replied. "We are not a

---

[4] Alluding to Wang's breach of etiquette in visiting the father
himself, instead of sending a go-between, who would have offered
the same sum in due form as the usual dowry or present to the
bride's family.

wealthy family, you know, but we don't want anything through an improper channel; and I couldn't help smiling at the great eyes you were making at me, all the time trying to tempt me with money. But when I heard you speak, I knew at once you were a man of refinement, though I guessed you were a bit of a rake; and so I hid your bracelet, and saved you from the wrath of my father." "And yet," replied Wang, "you have fallen into my snare after all;" adding, after a little pressure, "for I can't conceal from you much longer the fact that I have already a wife, belonging to a high official family." This she did not believe, until he began to affirm it seriously; and then she jumped up and ran out of the cabin. Wang followed at once, but, before he could reach her, she was already in the river; whereupon he shouted out to boats to come to their assistance, causing quite a commotion all round about; but nothing was to be seen in the river, save only the reflection of the stars shining brightly on the water. All night long Wang went sorrowfully up and down, and offered a high reward for the body, which, however, was not forthcoming. So he went home in despair, and then, fearing lest his father-in-law should come to visit his daughter, he started on a visit to a connection of his, who had an appointment in Honan. In the course of a year or two, when on his homeward journey, he chanced to be detained by bad weather at a roadside inn of rather cleaner appearance than usual. Within he saw an old woman playing with a child, which, as soon as he entered, held out its arms to him to be taken. Wang took the child on his knee, and there it remained, refusing to go back to its nurse; and, when the rain had stopped, and Wang was getting ready to go, the child cried out, "Pa-pa gone!" The nurse told it to hold its tongue, and, at the same moment, out from behind the screen came Wang's long-lost wife. "You bad fellow," said she, "what am I to do with this?" pointing to the child; and then Wang knew that the boy was his own son. He was much affected, and swore by the sun[5] that the words he had uttered had been uttered in jest, and by-and-by his wife's anger was soothed. She then explained how she had been picked up by a passing boat, the occupant of which was the owner of the house they were in, a man of sixty years of age, who had no children of his own, and who kindly adopted her.[6] She

---

[5] Witnesses in a Chinese court of justice take no oath, in our sense of the term. Their written depositions, however, are always ended with the words "the above evidence is the truth!" In ordinary life people call heaven and earth to witness, or, as in this case, the sun; or they declare themselves willing to forfeit their lives; and so on, if their statements are not true. "Saucer-breaking" is one of those pleasant inductions from probably a single instance, which may have been the fancy of a moment; at any rate, it is quite unknown in China as a national custom. "Cock-killing" usually has reference to the ceremonies of initiation performed by the members of the numerous secret societies which exist over the length and breadth of the Empire, in spite of Government prohibitions, and the penalty of death incurred upon detection.

[6] Adoption is common all over China, and is regulated by law. For instance, an adopted son excludes all the daughters of the family. A man is not allowed to marry a girl whom he has adopted until he shall have given her away to be adopted in a family of a *different surname from his own;* after which fictitious ceremony, his

also told him how she had had several offers of marriage, all of which she had refused, and how her child was born, and that she had called him Chi-shêng, and that he was then a year old. Wang now unpacked his baggage again, and went in to see the old gentleman and his wife, whom he treated as if they had actually been his wife's parents. A few days afterwards they set off together towards Wang's home, where they found his wife's real father awaiting them. He had been there more than two months, and had been considerably disconcerted by the mysterious remarks of Wang's servants; but the arrival of his daughter and her husband made things all smooth again, and when they told him what had happened, he understood the demeanour of the servants which had seemed, so strange to him at first.

---

marriage with her becomes legal (see No. XV., note 3); for the child adopted takes the same surname as that of the family into which he is adopted, and is so far cut off from his own. relations, that he would not venture even to put on mourning for his real parents without first obtaining the consent of those who had adopted him. A son or daughter may be sold, but an adopted child may not ; neither may the adopted child be given away in adoption to any one else without the specific consent of his real parents. The general object in adopting children is to leave some one behind at death to look after the duties of ancestral worship. For this boys are preferred ; but the *Fortunate Union* gives an instance in which these rites were very creditably performed by the heroine of the tale.

XCV.

THE TWO BRIDES.

Now Chi-shêng, or Wang Sun, was one of the cleverest young fellows in the district; and his father and mother, who had foreseen his ability from the time when, as a baby in long clothes, he distinguished them from other people, loved him very dearly. He grew up into a handsome lad; at eight or nine he could compose elegantly, and by fourteen he had already entered his name as a candidate for the first degree, after which his marriage became a question for consideration. Now his father's younger sister, Erh-niang, had married a gentleman named Chêng Tzŭ-ch'iao, and they had a daughter called Kuei-hsiu, who was extremely pretty, and with whom Chi-shêng fell deeply in love, being soon unable either to eat or to sleep. His parents became extremely uneasy about him, and inquired what it was that ailed him; and when he told them, they at once sent off a match-maker to Mr. Chêng. The latter, however, was rather a stickler for the proprieties, and replied that the near relationship precluded him from accepting the

---

¹ This story is a sequel to the last.

offer.[2] Thereupon Chi-shêng became dangerously ill, and his mother, not knowing what to do, secretly tried to persuade Erh-niang to let her daughter come over to their house ; but Mr. Chêng heard of it, and was so angry that Chi-shêng's father and mother gave up all hope of arranging the match.

At that time there was a gentleman named Chang living near by, who had five daughters, all very pretty, but the youngest, called Wu-k'o, was singularly beautiful, far surpassing her four sisters. She was not betrothed to any one, when one day, as she was on her way to worship at the family tombs, she chanced to see Chi-shêng, and at her return home spoke about him to her mother. Her mother guessed what her meaning was, and arranged with a match-maker, named Mrs. Yü, to call upon Chi-shêng's parents. This she did precisely at the time when Chi-shêng was so ill, and forthwith told his mother that her son's complaint was one she, Mrs. Yü, was quite competent to cure; going on to tell her about Miss Wu-k'o and the proposed marriage, at which the good lady was delighted, and sent her in to talk about it to Chi-shêng himself. "Alas !" cried he, when he had heard Mrs. Yü's story, "you are bringing me the wrong medicine for my complaint." "All depends upon the efficacy of the medicine," replied Mrs. Yü ; "if the medicine is good, it matters not what is the name of the doctor who administers the draught ; while

---

[2] The surnames would in this case be different, and no obstacle could be offered on that score. See No. XV., note 3.

to set your heart on a particular person, and to lie there
and die because that person doesn't come, is surely
foolish in the extreme." "Ah," rejoined Chi-shêng,
"there's no medicine under heaven that will do me any
good." Mrs. Yü told him his experience was limited,
and proceeded to expatiate by speaking and gesticulating
on the beauty and liveliness of Wu-k'o. But all Chi-
shêng said was that she was not what he wanted, and,
turning round his face to the wall, would listen to no
more about her. So Mrs. Yü was obliged to go away,
and Chi-shêng became worse and worse every day, until
suddenly one of the maids came in and informed him
that the young lady herself was at the door. Immediately he jumped up and ran out, and lo! there before
him stood a beautiful girl, whom, however, he soon discovered not to be Kuei-hsiu. She wore a light yellow
robe with a fine silk jacket and an embroidered petticoat,
from beneath which her two little feet peeped out; and
altogether she more resembled a fairy than anything else.
Chi-shêng inquired her name; to which she replied that
it was Wu-k'o, adding that she couldn't understand his
devoted attachment to Kuei-hsiu, as if there was nobody
else in the world. Chi-shêng apologized, saying that he
had never before seen any one so beautiful as Kuei-hsiu,
but that he was now aware of his mistake. He then
swore everlasting fidelity to her, and was just grasping
her hand, when he awoke and found his mother rubbing
him. It was a dream, but so accurately defined in all
its details that he began to think if Wu-k'o was really
such as he had seen her, there would be no further need

to try for his impracticable cousin. So he communicated his dream to his mother; and she, only too
delighted to notice this change of feeling, offered to go
to Wu-k'o's house herself; but Chi-shêng would not hear
of this, and arranged with an old woman who knew the
family to find some pretext for going there, and to report
to him what Wu-k'o was like. When she arrived Wu-k'o
was ill in bed, and lay with her head propped up by
pillows, looking very pretty indeed. The old woman
approached the couch and asked what was the matter;
to which Wu-k'o made no reply, her fingers fidgetting all
the time with her waistband. "She's been behaving
badly to her father and mother," cried the latter, who
was in the room; "there's many a one has offered to
marry her, but she says she'll have none but Chi-shêng:
and then when I scold her a bit, she takes on and won't
touch her food for days." "Madam," said the old
woman, "if you could get that young man for your
daughter they would make a truly pretty pair; and as for
him, if he could only see Miss Wu-k'o, I'm afraid it
would be too much for him. What do you think of my
going there and getting them to make proposals?" "No,
thank you," replied Wu-k'o; "I would rather not risk
his refusal;" upon which the old woman declared she
would succeed, and hurried off to tell Chi-shêng, who
was delighted to find from her report that Wu-k'o was
exactly as he had seen her in his dream, though he
didn't trust implicitly in all the old woman said. By-
and-by, when he began to get a little better, he consulted
with the old woman as to how he could see Wu-k'o with

his own eyes; and, after some little difficulty, it was arranged that Chi-shêng should hide himself in a room from which he would be able to see her as she crossed the yard supported by a maid, which she did every day at a certain hour. This Chi-shêng proceeded to do, and in a little while out she came, accompanied by the old woman as well, who instantly drew her attention either to the clouds or the trees, in order that she should walk more leisurely. Thus Chi-shêng had a good look at her, and saw that she was truly the young lady of his dream. He could hardly contain himself for joy; and when the old woman arrived and asked if she would do instead of Kuei-hsiu, he thanked her very warmly and returned to his own home. There he told his father and mother, who sent off a match-maker to arrange the preliminaries; but the latter came back and told them that Wu-k'o was already betrothed. This was a terrible blow for Chi-shêng, who was soon as ill as ever, and offered no reply to his father and mother when they charged him with having made a mistake. For several months he ate nothing but a bowl of rice-gruel a-day, and he became as emaciated as a fowl, when all of a sudden the old woman walked in and asked him what was the matter. " Foolish boy," said she, when he had told her all; " before you wouldn't have her, and do you imagine she is bound to have you now? But I'll see if I can't help you; for were she the Emperor's own daughter, I should still find some way of getting her." Chi-shêng asked what he should do, and she then told him to send a servant with a letter next day to Wu-k'o's house, to which his father

at first objected for fear of another repulse ; but the old
woman assured him that Wu-k'o's parents had since re-
pented, besides which no written contract had as yet
been made ; "and you know the proverb," added she,
"that those who are first at the fire will get their dinner
first." So Chi-shêng's father agreed, and two servants
were accordingly sent, their mission proving a complete
success. Chi-shêng now rapidly recovered his health,
and thought no more of Kuei-hsiu, who, when she heard
of the intended match, became in her turn very seriously
ill, to the great anger of her father, who said she might
die for all he cared, but to the great sorrow of her
mother, who was extremely fond of her daughter. The
latter even went so far as to propose to Mr. Chang that
Kuei-hsiu should go as second wife, at which he was so
enraged that he declared he would wash his hands of the
girl altogether. The mother then found out when Chi-
shêng's wedding was to take place ; and, borrowing a
chair and attendants from her brother under pretence of
going to visit him, put Kuei-hsui inside and sent her off
to her uncle's house. As she arrived at the door, the
servants spread a carpet for her to walk on, and the
band struck up the wedding march. Chi-shêng went out
to see what it was all about, and there met a young lady
in a bridal veil, from whom he would have escaped had
not her servants surrounded them, and, before he knew
what he was doing, he was making her the usual salutation of a bridegroom. They then went in together, and,
to his further astonishment, he found that the young
lady was Kuei-hsiu ; and, being now unable to go and

meet Wu-k'o, a message was sent to her father, telling him what had occurred. He, too, got into a great rage, and vowed he would break off the match; but Wu-k'o herself said she would go all the same, her rival having only got the start of her in point of time. And go she did; and the two wives, instead of quarrelling, as was expected, lived very happily together like sisters, and wore each other's clothes and shoes without distinction, Kuei-hsiu taking the place of an elder sister as being somewhat older than Wu-k'o.[3] One day, after these events, Chi-shêng asked Wu-k'o why she had refused his offer; to which she replied that it was merely to pay him out for having previously refused her father's proposal. "Before you had seen me, your head was full of Kuei-hsiu; but after you had seen me, your thoughts were somewhat divided; and I wanted to know how I compared with her, and whether you would fall ill on my account as you had on hers, that we mightn't quarrel about our looks." "It was a cruel revenge," said Chi-shêng; "but how should I ever have got a sight of you had it not been for the old woman?" "What had she to do with it?" replied Wu-k'o; "I knew you were behind the door all the time. When I was ill I dreamt that I went to your house and saw you, but I looked upon it only as a dream until I heard that you had dreamt that I had actually been there, and then I knew

---

[3] The *dénoûement* of the *Yü-chiao-li*, a small novel which was translated into French by Rémusat, and again by Julien under the title of *Les Deux Cousines*, is effected by the hero of the tale marrying both the heroines.

that my spirit must have been with you." Chi-shêng now related to her the particulars of his vision, which coincided exactly with her own ; and thus, strangely enough, had the matrimonial alliances of both father and son been brought about by dreams.

XCVI.

A SUPERNATURAL WIFE.

A CERTAIN Mr. Chao, of Ch'ang-shan, lodged in a family of the name of T'ai. He was very badly off, and, falling sick, was brought almost to death's door. One day they moved him into the verandah, that it might be cooler for him; and, when he awoke from a nap, lo ! a beautiful girl was standing by his side. " I am come to be your wife," said the girl, in answer to his question as to who she was ; to which he replied that a poor fellow like himself did not look for such luck as that ; adding that, being then on his death-bed, he would not have much occasion for the services of a wife. The girl said she could cure him ; but he told her he very much doubted that ; "And even," continued he, "should you have any good prescription, I have not the means of getting it made up." " I don't want medicine to cure you with," rejoined the girl, proceeding at once to rub his back and sides with her hand, which seemed to him like a ball of fire. He soon began to feel much better, and asked the young lady what her name was, in order, as he said, that he might remember her in his prayers. " I am a spirit," replied she ; " and you, when alive

under the Han dynasty as Ch'u Sui-liang, were a benefactor of my family. Your kindness being engraven on my
heart, I have at length succeeded in my search for you,
and am able in some measure to requite you. Chao was
dreadfully ashamed of his poverty-stricken state, and
afraid that his dirty room would spoil the young lady's
dress; but she made him show her in, and accordingly
he took her into his apartment, where there were neither
chairs to sit upon, nor signs of anything to eat, saying, "You
might, indeed, be able to put up with all this; but you
see my larder is empty, and I have absolutely no means
of supporting a wife." "Don't be alarmed about that,"
cried she; and in another moment he saw a couch
covered with costly robes, the walls papered with a
silver-flecked paper, and chairs and tables appear, the
latter laden with all kinds of wine and exquisite viands.
They then began to enjoy themselves, and lived together
as husband and wife, many people coming to witness
these strange things, and being all cordially received by
the young lady, who in her turn always accompanied
Mr. Chao when he went out to dinner anywhere.[1] One
day there was an unprincipled young graduate among
the company, which she seemed immediately to become

---

[1] The sexes do not dine together. On the occasion of a dinner-
party, private or official, the ladies give a separate entertainment to
the wives of the various guests in the "inner" or women's apartments, as an adjunct to which a theatrical troupe is often engaged,
precisely as in the case of the opposite sex. Singing-girls are,
however, present at and share in the banquets of the *roués* of
China.

aware of; and, after calling him several bad names, she struck him on the side of the head, causing his head to fly out of the window while his body remained inside; and there he was, stuck fast, unable to move either way, until the others interceded for him and he was released. After some time visitors became too numerous, and if she refused to see them they turned their anger against her husband. At length, as they were sitting tegether drinking with some friends at the Tuan-yang festival,[2] a white rabbit ran in, whereupon the girl jumped up and said, "The doctor[3] has come for me;" then, turning to the rabbit, she added, "You go on: I'll follow you." So the rabbit went away, and then she ordered them to get a ladder and place it against a high tree in the back yard, the top of the ladder overtopping the tree. The young lady went up first and Chao close behind her; after which she called out to anybody who wished to join them to make haste up. None ventured to do so with the exception of a serving-boy belonging to the house,

---

[2] This occurs on the 5th of the 5th moon, and is commonly known as the Dragon-Boat Festival, from a practice of racing on that day in long, narrow boats. It is said to have been instituted in memory of a patriotic statesman, whose identity, however, is not settled, some writers giving Wu Yun (see *The Middle Kingdom*, Vol. II., p. 82), others Ch'ü Yüan (see *The Chinese Reader's Manual*, p. 107), as the hero of the day.

[3] A hare or rabbit is believed to sit at the foot of the cassia-tree in the moon, pounding the drugs out of which is concocted the elixir of immortality. An allusion to this occurs in the poems of Tu Fu, one of the celebrated bards of the T'ang dynasty:—

"The frog is not drowned in the river;
The medicine hare lives for ever."

who followed after Chao; and thus they went up, up, up, up, until they disappeared in the clouds and were seen no more. However, when the bystanders came to look at the ladder, they found it was only an old door-frame with the panels knocked out; and when they went into Mr. Chao's room, it was the same old, dirty, unfurnished room as before. So they determined to find out all about it from the serving-boy when he came back; but this he never did.

XCVII.

BRIBERY AND CORRUPTION.

At Pao-ting Fu there lived a young man, who having purchased the lowest[1] degree was about to proceed to Peking, in the hope of obtaining, by the aid of a little bribery, an appointment as District Magistrate. His boxes were all ready packed, when he was taken suddenly ill and was confined to his bed for more than a month. One day the servant entered and announced a visitor; whereupon our sick man jumped up and ran to the door as if there was nothing the matter with him. The visitor was elegantly dressed like a man of some position in society; and, after bowing thrice, he walked into the house, explaining that he was Kung-sun Hsia,[2] tutor to the Eleventh Prince, and that he had heard our Mr. So-and-so wished to arrange for the purchase of a magistracy. "If that is really so," added he, "would you not do better to buy a prefecture?" So-and-so thanked him warmly, but said his funds would

---

[1] By which he would become eligible for Government employ. The sale of degrees has been extensively carried on under the present dynasty, as a means of replenishing an empty Treasury.

[2] Kung-sun is an example of a Chinese double surname.

not be sufficient; upon which Mr. Kung-sun declared he should be delighted to assist him with half the purchase-money, which he could repay after taking up the post.[3] He went on to say that being on intimate terms with the various provincial Governors the thing could be easily managed for about five thousand taels; and also that at that very moment Chên-ting Fu being vacant, it would be as well to make an early effort to get the appointment. So-and-so pointed out that this place was in his native province;[4] but Kung-sun only laughed at his objection, and reminded him that money[5] could obliterate all distinctions of that kind. This did not seem quite satisfactory; however, Kung-sun told him not to be alarmed, as the post of which he was speaking was below in the infernal regions. "The fact is," said he, "that your

---

[3] Such is the common system of repaying the loan, by means of which an indigent nominee is enabled to defray the expenses of his journey to the post to which he has been appointed, and other calls upon his purse. These loans are generally provided by some "western" merchant, which term is an ellipsis for a "Shansi" banker, Shansi being literally "west of the mountains." Some one accompanies the newly-made official to his post, and holds his commission in pawn until the amount is repaid; which settlement is easily effected by the issue of some well-understood proclamation, calling, for instance, upon the people to close all gambling-houses within a given period. Immediately the owners of these hells forward presents of money to the incoming official, the Shansi banker gets his principal with interest, perhaps at the rate of 2 per cent. *per month*, the gambling-houses carry on as usual, and everybody is perfectly satisfied.

[4] Which fact would disqualify him from taking the post.

[5] Literally, "Square hole." A common name for the Chinese cash. See No. II, note 2.

term of life has expired, and that your name is already on the death list; by these means you will take your place in the world below as a man of official position. Farewell! in three days we shall meet again." He then went to the door and mounted his horse and rode away. So-and-so now opened his eyes and spoke a few parting words to his wife and children, bidding them take money from his strong-room [6] and go buy large quantities of paper ingots,[7] which they immediately did, quite exhausting all the shops. This was piled in the court-yard with paper images of men, devils, horses, &c., and burning went on day and night until the ashes formed quite a hill. In three days Kung-sun returned, bringing with him the money; upon which So-and-so hurried off to the Board of Civil Office,[8] where he had an interview with the high officials, who, after asking his name, warned him to be a pure and upright officer, and then calling him up to the table handed him his letter of appointment. So-and-so bowed and took his leave; but recollecting at once that his purchased degree would not

---

[6] In the case of wealthy families these strong rooms often contain, in addition to bullion, jewels to a very great amount belonging to the ladies of the house; and, as a rule, the door may not be opened unless in the presence of a certain number of the male representatives of the house.

[7] Pieces of silver and gold paper made up to represent the ordinary Chinese "shoes" of bullion (See No. XVIII., note 4), and burnt for the use of the dead. Generally known to foreigners in China as "joss-paper."

[8] See No. VII., note 1. In this case the reference is to a similar Board in the Infernal Regions.

carry much weight with it in the eyes of his subordinates,[9] he sent off to buy elaborate chairs and a
number of horses for his retinue, at the same time
despatching several devil lictors to fetch his favourite
wife in a beautifully adorned sedan-chair. All arrangements were just completed when some of the Chên-ting
staff came to meet the new Prefect,[10] others awaiting
him all along the line of road, about half a mile in
length. He was immensely gratified at this reception,
when all of a sudden the gongs before him ceased to
sound and the banners were lowered to the ground. He
had hardly time to ask what was the matter before he
saw those of his servants who were on horseback jump
hastily to the ground and dwindle down to about a foot
in height, while their horses shrunk to the size of foxes
or racoons. One of the attendants near his chariot
cried out in alarm, "Here's Kuan Ti!"[11] and then he,
too, jumped out in a fright, and saw in the distance Kuan
Ti himself slowly approaching them, followed by four or
five retainers on horseback. His great beard covered
the lower half of his face, quite unlike ordinary mortals;
his aspect was terrible to behold, and his eyes reached
nearly to his ears. "Who is this?" roared he to his
servants; and they immediately informed him that it
was the new Prefect of Chên-ting. "What!" cried he;

---

[9] These would be sure to sneer at him behind his back.

[10] A compliment usually paid to an in-coming official.

[11] See No. I., note 3.

"a petty fellow like that to have a retinue like this?"[12]
Whereupon So-and-so's flesh began to creep with fear,
and in a few moments he found that he too had shrunk
to the size of a little boy of six or seven. Kuan Ti
bade his attendants bring the new Prefect with them,
and went into a building at the roadside, where he took
up his seat facing the south[13] and calling for writing
materials told So-and-so to write down his name and
address. When this was handed to him he flew into a
towering passion, and said, "The scribbly scrawl of a
placeman, indeed![14] Can such a one be entrusted with
the welfare of the people? Look me up the record of
his good works." A man then advanced, and whispered
something in a low tone; upon which Kuan Ti exclaimed
in a loud voice, "The crime of the briber is comparatively trifling; the heavy guilt lies with those who sell
official posts for money." So-and-so was now seized by
angels in golden armour, and two of them tore off his
cap and robes, and administered to him fifty blows with
the bamboo until hardly any flesh remained on his
bones. He was then thrust outside the door, and lo!
his carriages and horses had disappeared, and he himself
was lying, unable to walk for pain, at no great distance
from his own house. However, his body seemed as light

---

[12] The retinue of a Mandarin should be in accordance with his
rank. I have given elsewhere (See No. LVI, note 5) what would
be that of an official of the highest rank.

[13] See No. LXXVII., note 1.

[14] Good writing holds a much higher place in the estimation of
the Chinese than among western nations. The very nature of their
characters raises calligraphy almost to the rank of an art.

as a leaf, and in a day and a night he managed to crawl home. When he arrived, he awoke as it were from a dream, and found himself groaning upon the bed; and to the inquiries of his family he only replied that he felt dreadfully sore. Now he really had been dead for seven days; and when he came round thus, he immediately asked for A-lien, which was the name of his favourite wife. But the very day before, while chatting with the other members of the family, A-lien had suddenly cried out that her husband was made Prefect of Chên-ting, and that his lictors had come to escort her thither. Accordingly she retired to dress herself in her best clothes, and, when ready to start, she fell back and expired. Hearing this sad story, So-and-so began to mourn and beat his breast, and he would not allow her to be buried at once, in the hope that she might yet come round; but this she never did. Meanwhile So-and-so got slowly better, and by the end of six months was able to walk again. He would often exclaim, "The ruin of my career and the punishment I received—all this I could have endured; but the loss of my dear A-lien is more than I can bear."[15]

---

[15] The commentator here adds a somewhat similar case, which actually occurred in the reign of K'ang Hsi, of a Viceroy modestly attended falling in with the gorgeous retinue of a Magistrate, and being somewhat rudely treated by the servants of the latter. On arriving at his destination, the Viceroy sent for that Magistrate, and sternly bade him retire from office, remarking that no simple magistrate could afford to keep such a retinue of attendants unless by illegal exactions from the suffering people committed to his charge.

XCVIII.
A CHINESE JONAH.

A MAN named Sun Pi-chên was crossing the river[1] when a great thunder-squall broke upon the vessel and caused her to toss about fearfully, to the great terror of all the passengers. Just then, an angel in golden armour appeared standing upon the clouds above them, holding in his hand a scroll inscribed with certain characters, also written in gold, which the people on the vessel easily made out to be three in number, namely *Sun Pi chên.* So, turning at once to their fellow-traveller, they said to him, "You have evidently in-curred the displeasure of Heaven; get into a boat by yourself, and do not involve us in your punishment." And without giving him time to reply whether he would do so or not, they hurried him over the side into a small boat and set him adrift; but when Sun Pi-chên looked back, lo! the vessel itself had capsized.[2]

---

[1] The Yang-tsze: sometimes spoken of as the Long River.

[2] The full point of this story can hardly be conveyed in tran-slation. The man's surname was Sun, and his prænomen, Pi-chên, (which in Chinese *follows* the nomen) might be rendered "Must-be-saved." However, there is another word meaning "struck," precisely similar in sound and tone, though written differently, to the above *chên;* and, as far as the ear alone is concerned, our hero's name might have been either *Sun Must-be-saved* or *Sun Must-be-struck.* That the merchants mistook the character *chên,* "saved," for *chên,* "struck," is evident from the catastrophe which overtook their vessel, while Mr. Sun's little boat rode safely through the storm.

XCIX.

CHANG PU-LIANG.

A CERTAIN trader who was travelling in the province of Chih-li, being overtaken by a storm of rain and hail, took shelter among some standing crops by the way-side. There he heard a voice from heaven, saying, "These are Chang Pu-liang's fields; do not injure his crops." The trader began to wonder who this Chang Pu-liang could be, and how, if he was *pu liang* (not virtuous), he came to be under divine protection; so when the storm was over and he had reached the neighbouring village, he made enquiries on the subject, and told the people there what he had heard. The villagers then informed him that Chang Pu-liang was a very wealthy farmer, who was accustomed every spring to make loans of grain to the poor of the district, and who was not too particular about getting back the exact amount he had lent,—taking, in fact, whatever they brought him without discussion; hence the sobriquet of *pu liang* "no measure" (*i.e.*, the man who doesn't measure the repayments of his loans).[1]

---

[1] Here again we have a play upon words similar to that in the last story.

After that, they all proceeded in a body to the fields, where it was discovered that vast damage had been done to the crops generally, with the exception of Chang Pu-liang's, which had escaped uninjured.

C.

THE DUTCH CARPET.

FORMERLY, when the Dutch [1] were permitted to trade
with China, the officer in command of the coast defences
would not allow them, on account of their great numbers,
to come ashore. The Dutch begged very hard for the
grant of a piece of land such as a carpet would cover;
and the officer above-mentioned, thinking that this could
not be very large, acceded to their request. A carpet
was accordingly laid down, big enough for about two
people to stand on; but by dint of stretching, it was
soon enough for four or five; and so they went on,
stretching and stretching, until at last it covered about

---

[1] We read in the *History of Amoy:*—"In the year 1622 the
red-haired barbarians seized the Pescadores and attacked Amoy."
From the Pescadores they finally retired, on a promise that trade
would be permitted, to Formosa, whence they were expelled by
the famous Koxinga in 1662. "Red-haired barbarians," a term
now commonly applied to all foreigners, was first used in the
records of the Ming dynasty to designate the Dutch.

N 2

an acre, and by-and-by, with the help of their knives, they had filched a piece of ground several miles in extent.[2]

---

[2] Our author would here seem to have heard of the famous bull's hide which is mentioned in the first book of the *Æneid*. In any case, the substitution of "stretching" is no improvement on the celebrated device by which the bull's hide was made to enclose so large a space.

CI.

CARRYING A CORPSE.

A WOODSMAN who had been to market was returning home with his pole across his shoulder,[1] when suddenly he felt it become very heavy at the end behind him, and looking round he saw attached tc it the headless trunk of a man. In great alarm, he got his pole quit of the burden and struck about him right and left, whereupon the body disappeared. He then hurried on to the next village, and when he arrived there in the dusk of the evening, he found several men holding lights to the ground as if looking for something. On asking what was the matter, they told him that while sitting together a man's head had fallen from the sky into their midst; that they had noticed the hair and beard were all draggled, but in a moment the head had vanished. The woodsman then related what had happened to himself; and thus one whole man was accounted for, though no

---

[1] The common method of porterage in China is by a bamboo pole over the shoulder with well-balanced burdens hanging from each end. I have often seen children carried thus, sitting in wicker baskets; sometimes for long journeys.

one could tell whence he came. Subsequently, another man was carrying a basket when some one saw a man's head in it, and called out to him ; whereupon he dropped the basket in a fright, and the head rolled away and disappeared.

CII.

A TAOIST DEVOTEE.

CHÜ YAO-JU was a Ch'ing-chou man, who, when his wife died left his home and became a priest.[1] Some years afterwards he returned, dressed in the Taoist garb, and carrying his praying-mat[2] over his shoulder; and after staying one night he wanted to go away again. His friends, however, would not give him back his cassock and staff; so at length he pretended to take a stroll outside the village, and when there, his clothes and other belongings came flying out of the house after him, and he got safely away.

---

[1] It would be more usual to "renew the guitar string," as the Chinese idiom runs. In the paraphrase of the first maxim of the *Sacred Edict* we are told that "The closest of all ties is that of husband and wife; but suppose your wife dies, why, you can marry another. But if your brother were to die," &c., &c.

[2] This, as well as the staff mentioned below, belongs to Buddhism. See No. IV., note 1.

CIII.

JUSTICE FOR REBELS.

During the reign of Shun Chih,[1] of the people of T'êng-i, seven in ten were opposed to the Manchu dynasty. The officials dared not touch them; and subsequently, when the country became more settled, the magistrates used to distinguish them from the others by always deciding any cases in their favour: for they feared lest these men should revert to their old opposition. And thus it came about that one litigant would begin by declaring himself to have been a "rebel," while his adversary would follow up by shewing such statement to be false; so that before any case could be heard on its actual merits, it was necessary to determine the status both of plaintiff and defendant, whereby infinite labour was entailed upon the Registrars.

Now it chanced that the yamên of one of the officials was haunted by a fox, and the official's daughter was

---

[1] The first Manchu ruler of the empire of China. He came to the throne in A.D. 1644.

bewitched by it. Her father, therefore, engaged the services of a magician, who succeeded in capturing the animal and putting it into a bottle ; but just as he was going to commit it to the flames, the fox cried out from inside the bottle, " I'm a rebel !" at which the by-standers were unable to suppress their laughter.

CIV.

THEFT OF THE PEACH.

WHEN I was a little boy I went one day to the prefectural city.[1]   It was the time of the Spring festival,[2]
and the custom was that on the day before, all the
merchants of the place should proceed with banners and
drums to the judge's yamên : this was called "bringing
in the Spring." I went with a friend to see the fun ; the
crowd was immense, and there sat the officials in
crimson robes arranged right and left in the hall; but I
was small and didn't know who they were, my attention
being attracted chiefly by the hum of voices and the
noise of the drums.   In the middle of it all, a man
leading a boy with his hair unplaited and hanging down
his back, walked up to the dais.   He carried a pole on
his shoulder, and appeared to be saying something which
I couldn't hear for the noise ; I only saw the officials
smile, and immediately afterwards an attendant came

---

[1] It is worth noting that the author professes actually to have
witnessed the following extraordinary scene.

[2] The vernal equinox, which would fall on or about the 20th of
March.

down, and in a loud voice ordered the man to give a performance. "What shall it be?" asked the man in reply; whereupon, after some consultation between the officials on the dais, the attendant inquired what he could do best. The man said he could invert the order of nature; and then, after another pause, he was instructed to produce some peaches; to this he assented; and taking off his coat, laid it on his box, at the same time observing that they had set him a hard task, the winter frost not having broken up, and adding that he was afraid the gentlemen would be angry with him, &c., &c. His son here reminded him that he had agreed to the task and couldn't well get out of it; so, after fretting and grumbling awhile, he cried out, "I have it! with snow on the ground we shall never get peaches here; but I guess there are some up in heaven in the Royal Mother's garden,[3] and there we must try." "How are we to get up, father?" asked the boy; whereupon the man said, "I have the means," and immediately proceeded to take from his box a cord some tens of feet in length. This he carefully arranged, and then threw one end of it high up into the air where it remained as if caught by something. He now paid out the rope which kept going up higher and higher until the end he had thrown up disappeared in the clouds and only a short piece was left in his hands. Calling his son, he then ex-

---

[3] A fabulous lady, said to reside at the summit of the K'un-lun mountain, where, on the border of the Gem Lake, grows the peach-tree of the angels, the fruit of which confers immortality on him who eats it.

plained that he himself was too heavy, and, handing him
the end of the rope, bid him go up at once. The boy,
however, made some difficulty, objecting that the rope
was too thin to bear his weight up to such a height, and
that he would surely fall down and be killed; upon
which his father said that his promise had been given
and that repentance was now too late, adding that if the
peaches were obtained they would surely be rewarded
with a hundred ounces of silver, which should be set
aside to get the boy a pretty wife. So his son seized the
rope and swarmed up, like a spider running up a thread
of its web; and in a few moments he was out of sight in
the clouds. By-and-by down fell a peach as large as a
basin, which the delighted father handed up to his
patrons on the dais who were some time coming to a
conclusion whether it was real or imitation. But just
then down came the rope with a run, and the affrighted
father shrieked out, "Alas! alas! some one has cut the
rope: what will my boy do now?" and in another
minute down fell something else, which was found on
examination to be his son's head. "Ah me!" said he,
weeping bitterly and shewing the head; "the gardener
has caught him, and my boy is no more." After that, his
arms, and legs, and body, all came down in like manner;
and the father, gathering them up, put them in the box
and said, "This was my only son, who accompanied me
everywhere; and now what a cruel fate is his. I must
away and bury him." He then approached the dais and
said, "Your peach, gentlemen, was obtained at the cost
of my boy's life; help me now to pay his funeral ex-

penses, and I will be ever grateful to you." The officials who had been watching the scene in horror and amazement, forthwith collected a good purse for him; and when he had received the money, he rapped on his box and said, "Pa-pa'rh! why don't you come out and thank the gentlemen?" Thereupon, there was a thump on the box from the inside and up came the boy himself, who jumped out and bowed to the assembled company. I have never forgotten this strange trick, which I subsequently heard could be done by the White Lily sect,[4] who probably got it from this source.[5]

---

[4] One of the most celebrated of the numerous secret societies of China, the origin of which dates back to about A.D. 1350. Its members have always been credited with a knowledge of the black art.

[5] Of Chinese jugglers, Ibu Batuta writes as follows:—"They produced a chain fifty cubits in length, and in my presence threw one end of it towards the sky, where it remained, as if fastened to something in the air. A dog was then brought forward, and, being placed at the lower end of the chain, immediately ran up, and reaching the other end immediately disappeared in the air. In the same manner a hog, a panther, a lion, and a tiger were alternately sent up the chain, and all equally disappeared at the upper end of it. At last they took down the chain, and put it into a bag, no one ever discerning in what way the different animals were made to vanish into the air in the mysterious manner above described. This, I may venture to affirm, was beyond measure strange and surprising."

Apropos of which passage, Mr. Maskelyne, the prince of all black-artists, ancient or modern, says:—"These apparent effects were, doubtless, due to the aid of concave mirrors, the use of which was known to the ancients, especially in the East, but they could not have been produced in the open air."

CV.

KILLING A SERPENT.

At Ku-chi island in the eastern sea, there were camellias of all colours which bloomed throughout the year. No one, however, lived there, and very few people ever visited the spot. One day, a young man of Têng-chou, named Chang, who was fond of hunting and adventure, hearing of the beauties of the place, put together some wine and food, and rowed himself across in a small open boat. The flowers were just then even finer than usual, and their perfume was diffused for a mile or so around; while many of the trees he saw were several armfuls in circumference. So he roamed about and gave himself up to enjoyment of the scene; and by-and-by he opened a flask of wine, regretting very much that he had no companion to share it with him, when all of a sudden a most beautiful young girl, with extremely bright eyes and dressed in red, stepped down from one of the camellias before him.[1] " Dear me ! " said she on seeing Mr. Chang; "I expected to be alone here, and

---

[1] See No. LXXI., note 6.

was not aware that the place was already occupied."
Chang was somewhat alarmed at this apparition, and
asked the young lady whence she came; to which she
replied that her name was Chiao-ch'ang, and that
she had accompanied thither a Mr. Hai, who had
gone off for a stroll and had left her to await his return.
Thereupon Chang begged her to join him in a cup of
wine, which she very willingly did, and they were just
beginning to enjoy themselves when a sound of rushing
wind was heard and the trees and plants bent beneath it.
"Here's Mr. Hai!" cried the young lady; and jumping
quickly up, disappeared in a moment. The horrified
Chang now beheld a huge serpent coming out of the
bushes near by, and immediately ran behind a large tree
for shelter, hoping the reptile would not see him. But
the serpent advanced and enveloped both Chang and the
tree in its great folds, binding Chang's arms down to his
sides so as to prevent him from moving them; and then
raising its head, darted out its tongue and bit the poor
man's nose, causing the blood to flow freely out. This
blood it was quietly sucking up, when Chang, who
thought that his last hour had come, remembered that
he had in his pocket some fox poison; and managing to
insert a couple of fingers, he drew out the packet, broke
the paper, and let the powder lie in the palm of his
hand. He next leaned his hand over the serpent's coils
in such a way that the blood from his nose dripped into
his hand, and when it was nearly full the serpent actually
did begin to drink it. And in a few moments the grip
was relaxed; the serpent struck the ground heavily with

its tail, and dashed away up against another tree, which was broken in half, and then stretched itself out and died. Chang was a long time unable to rise, but at length he got up and carried the serpent off with him. He was very ill for more than a month afterwards, and even suspected the young lady of being a serpent, too, in disguise.

CVI.

THE RESUSCITATED CORPSE.

A CERTAIN old man lived at Ts'ai-tien, in the Yang-hsin district. The village was some miles from the district city, and he and his son kept a roadside inn where travellers could pass the night. One day, as it was getting dusk, four strangers presented themselves and asked for a night's lodging; to which the landlord replied that every bed was already occupied. The four men declared it was impossible for them to go back, and urged him to take them in somehow; and at length the landlord said he could give them a place to sleep in if they were not too particular,—which the strangers imme-diately assured him they were not. The fact was that the old man's daughter-in-law had just died, and that her body was lying in the women's quarters, waiting for the coffin, which his son had gone away to buy. So the landlord led them round thither, and walking in, placed a lamp on the table. At the further end of the room lay the corpse, decked out with paper robes, &c., in the usual way; and in the foremost section were sleeping-couches for four people. The travellers were tired, and, throwing themselves on the beds, were soon snoring loudly, with the exception of one of them, who was not quite off when suddenly he heard a creaking of the trestles on which the dead body was laid out, and, opening his eyes, he saw by the light of the lamp in front of the corpse that the girl was raising the coverings from her and preparing to get down. In another moment she was on the floor and advancing towards the sleepers. Her face was of a light yellow hue, and she had a silk kerchief round her head; and when she reached the beds she blew on the other three travellers, whereupon the fourth, in a great fright, stealthily drew up the bedclothes over his face, and held his breath to listen. He heard her breathe on him as she had done on the others, and then heard her go back again and get under the paper robes, which rustled distinctly as she did so. He now put out his head to take a peep, and saw that she was lying down as before; whereupon, not daring to make any noise, he stretched forth his foot and kicked his companions, who, however, shewed no signs of moving. He now determined to put on his clothes and make a bolt for it; but he had hardly begun to do so before he heard the creaking sound again, which sent him back under the bed-clothes as fast as he could go. Again the girl came to him, and breathing several times on him, went away to lie down as before, as he could tell by the noise of the trestles. He then put his hand very gently out of bed, and, seizing his trousers, got quickly into them, jumped up with a bound, and rushed out of the place as fast as his legs would carry him. The corpse, too, jumped up; but by this time the traveller had already drawn the bolt, and was outside the door, running along and shrieking at the top of his voice, with the corpse following close behind. No one seemed to hear him, and he was afraid to knock at the door of the inn for fear they should not let him in in time; so he made for the highway to the city, and after awhile he saw a monastery by the roadside, and, hearing the "wooden fish,"[1] he ran up and thumped with all his might at the gate. The priest, however, did not know what to make of it, and would not open to him; and as the corpse was only a few yards off, he could do nothing but run behind a tree which stood close by, and there shelter himself, dodging to the right as the corpse dodged to the left, and so on. This infuriated the dead girl to madness; and at length, as tired and panting they stood watching each other on opposite sides of the tree, the corpse made a rush forward with one arm on each side in the hope of thus grabbing its victim. The traveller, however, fell backwards and escaped, while the corpse remained rigidly embracing the tree. By-and-by the priest, who had been listening from the inside, hearing no sounds for some time, came out and found the traveller lying senseless on the ground; whereupon he had him carried into the monastery, and by morning

---

[1] This instrument, used by Buddhist priests in the musical accompaniment to their liturgies, is said to be so called because a fish never closes its eyes, and is therefore a fit model of vigilance to him who would walk in the paths of holiness and virtue.

they had got him round again. After giving him a little broth to drink, he related the whole story; and then in the early dawn they went out to examine the tree, where they found the girl fixed tightly to the tree. The news being sent to the magistrate, that functionary attended at once in person,[2] and gave orders to remove the body; but this they were at first unable to do, the girl's fingers having penetrated into the bark so far that her nails were not to be seen. At length they got her away, and then a messenger was despatched to the inn, already in a state of great commotion over the three travellers, who had been found dead in their beds. The old man accordingly sent to fetch his daughter-in-law; and the surviving traveller petitioned the magistrate, saying, "Four of us left home, but only one will go back. Give me something that I may show to my fellow-townsmen." So the magistrate gave him a certificate and sent him home again.[3]

---

[2] The duties of Coroner belong to the office of a District Magistrate in China.

[3] Without such certificate he would be liable to be involved in trouble and annoyance at the will of any unfriendly neighbour.

CVII.

THE FISHERMAN AND HIS FRIEND.

In the northern parts of Tzŭ-chou there lived a man named Hsü, a fisherman by trade. Every night when he went to fish he would carry some wine with him, and drink and fish by turns, always taking care to pour out a libation on the ground, accompanied by the following invocation—"Drink too, ye drowned spirits of the river!" Such was his regular custom; and it was also noticeable that, even on occasions when the other fishermen caught nothing, he always got a full basket. One night, as he was sitting drinking by himself, a young man suddenly appeared and began walking up and down near him. Hsü offered him a cup of wine, which was readily accepted, and they remained chatting together throughout the night, Hsü meanwhile not catching a single fish. However, just as he was giving up all hope of doing anything, the young man rose and said he would go a little way down the stream and beat them up towards Hsü, which he accordingly did, returning in a few minutes and warning him to be on the look-out. Hsü now heard a noise like that of a shoal coming up the stream, and, casting his net, made a splendid haul,—all that he caught being over a foot in length. Greatly delighted, he now prepared to go home, first offering his companion a share of the fish, which the latter declined, saying that he had often received kindnesses from Mr. Hsü, and that he would he only too happy to help him regularly in the same manner if Mr. Hsü would accept his assistance. The latter replied that he did not recollect ever meeting him before, and that he should be much obliged for any aid the young man might choose to afford him; regretting, at the same time, his inability to make him any adequate return. He then asked the young man his name and surname; and the young man said his surname was Wang, adding that Hsü might address him when they met as Wang Liu-lang, he having no other name. Thereupon they parted, and the next day Hsü sold his fish and bought some more wine, with which he repaired as usual to the river bank. There he found his companion already awaiting him, and they spent the night together in precisely the same way as the preceding one, the young man beating up the fish for him as before. This went on for some months, until at length one evening the young man, with many expressions of his thanks and his regrets, told Hsü that they were about to part for ever. Much alarmed by the melancholy tone in which his friend had communicated this news, Hsü was on the point of asking for an explanation, when the young man stopped him, and himself proceeded as follows :—" The friendship that has grown up between us is truly surprising; and, now that we shall meet no more, there is no harm in telling you the whole truth. I am a disembodied spirit—the soul of one who

was drowned in this river when tipsy. I have been here
many years, and your former success in fishing was due
to the fact that I used secretly to beat up the fish towards you, in return for the libations you were accustomed to pour out. To-morrow my time is up: my
substitute will arrive, and I shall be born again in the
world of mortals.[1] We have but this one evening left,
and I therefore take advantage of it to express my feelings to you." On hearing these words, Hsü was at
first very much alarmed; however, he had grown so
accustomed to his friend's society, that his fears soon
passed away; and, filling up a goblet, he said, with a
sigh, " Liu-lang, old fellow, drink this up, and away with
melancholy. It's hard to lose you; but I'm glad enough
for your sake, and won't think of my own sorrow." He
then inquired of Liu-lang who was to be his substitute;
to which the latter replied, " Come to the river-bank
to-morrow afternoon and you'll see a woman drowned:
she is the one." Just then the village cocks began to
crow, and, with tears in their eyes, the two friends bade
each other farewell.

Next day Hsü waited on the river bank to see if anything would happen, and lo! a woman carrying a child
in her arms came along. When close to the edge of the
river, she stumbled and fell into the water, managing,
however, to throw the child safely on to the bank, where
it lay kicking and sprawling and crying at the top of its

---

[1] See No. XLV., note 8.

voice. The woman herself sank and rose several times, until at last she succeeded in clutching hold of the bank and pulled herself, dripping, out ; and then, after resting awhile, she picked up the child and went on her way. All this time Hsü had been in a great state of excitement, and was on the point of running to help the woman out of the water ; but he remembered that she was to be the substitute of his friend, and accordingly restrained himself from doing so.[2] Then when he saw the woman get out by herself, he began to suspect that Liu-lang's words had not been fulfilled. That night he

---

[2] We have in this story the keynote to the notorious and much-to-be-deprecated dislike of the Chinese people to assist in saving the lives of drowning strangers. Some of our readers may, perhaps, not be aware that the Government of Hong-Kong has found it necessary to insert a clause on the junk-clearances issued in that colony, by which the junkmen are bound to assist to the utmost in saving life. The apparent apathy of the Chinese in this respect comes before us, however, in quite a different light when coupled with the superstition that disembodied spirits of persons who have met a violent death may return to the world of mortals if only fortunate enough to secure a substitute. For among the crowd of shades, anxious all to revisit their "sweet sons," may perchance be some dear relative or friend of the man who stands calmly by while another is drowning; and it may be that to assist the drowning stranger would be to take the longed-for chance away from one's own kith or kin. Therefore, the superstition-ridden Chinaman turns away, often perhaps, as in the story before us, with feelings of pity and remorse. And yet this belief has not prevented the establishment, especially on the river Yang-tsze, of institutions provided with life-boats, for the express purpose of saving life in those dangerous waters; so true is it that when the Chinese people wish to move *en masse* in any given direction, the fragile barrier of superstition is trampled down and scattered to the winds.

went to fish as usual, and before long the young man arrived and said, "We meet once again : there is no need now to speak of separation." Hsü asked him how it was so; to which he replied, "The woman you saw had already taken my place, but I could not bear to hear the child cry, and I saw that my one life would be purchased at the expense of their two lives, wherefore I let her go, and now I cannot say when I shall have another chance.[3]   The union of our destinies may not yet be worked out."   "Alas !" sighed Hsü, "this noble conduct of yours is enough to move God Almighty."

After this the two friends went on much as they had done before, until one day Liu-lang again said he had come to bid Hsü farewell. Hsü thought he had found another substitute, but Liu-lang told him that his former behaviour had so pleased Almighty Heaven, that he had been appointed guardian angel of Wu-chên, in the Chao-yüan district, and that on the following morning he would start for his new post. "And if you do not forget the days of our friendship," added he, "I pray you come and see me, in spite of the long journey."   "Truly," replied Hsü, "you well deserved to be made a God ; but the paths of Gods and

---

[3] As there are good and bad foxes, so may devils be beneficent or malicious according to circumstances; and Chinese apologists for the discourtesy of the term "foreign devils," as applied to Europeans and Americans alike, have gone so far as to declare that in this particular instance the allusion is to the more virtuous among the denizens of the Infernal Regions.

men lie in different directions, and even if the distance
were nothing, how should I manage to meet you
again?" "Don't be afraid on that score," said Liu-
lang, "but come;" and then he went away, and Hsü
returned home. The latter immediately began to prepare for the journey, which caused his wife to laugh at
him and say, "Supposing you do find such a place at
the end of that long journey, you won't be able to hold
a conversation with a clay image." Hsü, however, paid
no attention to her remarks, and travelled straight to
Chao-yüan, where he learned from the inhabitants that
there really was a village called Wu-chên, whither he
forthwith proceeded and took up his abode at an inn.
He then inquired of the landlord where the village
temple was; to which the latter replied by asking him
somewhat hurriedly if he was speaking to Mr. Hsü.
Hsü informed him that his name was Hsü, asking in
reply how he came to know it; whereupon the landlord
further inquired if his native place was not Tzŭ-chou.
Hsü told him it was, and again asked him how he knew
all this; to which the landlord made no answer, but
rushed out of the room; and in a few moments the
place was crowded with old and young, men, women,
and children, all come to visit Hsü. They then told
him that a few nights before they had seen their guardian
deity in a vision, and he had informed them that Mr. Hsü
would shortly arrive, and had bidden them to provide
him with travelling expenses, &c. Hsü was very much
astonished at this, and went off at once to the shrine,
where he invoked his friend as follows:—"Ever since we

parted I have had you daily and nightly in my thoughts ; and now that I have fulfilled my promise of coming to see you, I have to thank you for the orders you have issued to the people of the place. As for me, I have nothing to offer you but a cup of wine, which I pray you accept as though we were drinking together on the river-bank" He then burnt a quantity of paper money,[4] when lo ! a wind suddenly arose, which, after whirling round and round behind the shrine, soon dropped, and all was still. That night Hsü dreamed that his friend came to him, dressed in his official cap and robes, and very different in appearance from what he used to be, and thanked him, saying, " It is truly kind of you to visit me thus : I only regret that my position makes me unable to meet you face to face, and that though near we are still so far. The people here will give you a trifle, which pray accept for my sake ; and when you go away, I will see you a short way on your journey." A few days afterwards Hsü prepared to start, in spite of the numerous invitations to stay which poured in upon him from all sides ; and then the inhabitants loaded him with presents of all kinds, and escorted him out of the village. There a whirlwind arose and accompanied him several miles, when he turned round and invoked his friend thus :—" Liu-lang, take care of your valued person. Do not trouble yourself to come any farther.[5]

---

[4] See No. XCVII., note 7.

[5] A phrase constantly repeated, in other terms, by a guest to a host who is politely escorting him to the door.

Your noble heart will ensure happiness to this district, and there is no occasion for me to give a word of advice to my old friend." By-and-by the whirlwind ceased, and the villagers, who were much astonished, returned to their own homes. Hsü, too, travelled homewards, and being now a man of some means, ceased to work any more as a fisherman. And whenever he met a Chao-yüan man he would ask him about that guardian angel, being always informed in reply that he was a most beneficent God. Some say the place was Shih-k'êng-chuang, in Chang-ch'in: I can't say which it was myself.

CVIII.

THE PRIEST'S WARNING.

A MAN named Chang died suddenly, and was escorted at once by devil-lictors[1] into the presence of the King of Purgatory. His Majesty turned to Chang's record of good and evil, and then, in great anger, told the lictors they had brought the wrong man, and bade them take him back again. As they left the judgment-hall, Chang persuaded his escort to let him have a look at Purgatory; and, accordingly, the devils conducted him through the nine sections,[2] pointing out to him the Knife Hill,[3] the Sword Tree, and other objects of interest. By-and-by, they reached a place where there was a Buddhist priest, hanging suspended in the air head downwards, by a rope through a hole in his leg.

---

[1] The spiritual lictors who are supposed to arrest the souls of dying persons, are also believed to be armed with warrants signed and sealed in due form as in the world above.

[2] Literally, the "nine dark places," which will remind readers of Dante of the nine "bolgie" of the *Inferno*.

[3] This is a cliff over which sinners are hurled, to alight upon the upright points of knives below. The branches of the Sword Tree are sharp blades which cut and hack all who pass within reach.

He was shrieking with pain, and longing for death ; and when Chang approached, lo ! he saw that it was his own brother. In great distress, he asked his guides the reason of this punishment; and they informed him that the priest was suffering thus for collecting subscriptions on behalf of his order, and then privately squandering the proceeds in gambling and debauchery.[4] " Nor," added they, " will he escape this torment unless he repents him of his misdeeds." When Chang came round,[5] he thought his brother was already dead, and hurried off to the Hsing-fu monastery, to which the latter belonged. As he went in at the door, he heard a loud shrieking ; and, on proceeding to his brother's room, he found him laid up with a very bad abscess in his leg, the leg itself being tied up above him to the wall, this being, as his brother informed him, the only bearable position in which he could lie. Chang now told him what he had seen in Purgatory, at which the priest was so terrified, that he at once gave up taking wine and meat,[6] and devoted himself entirely to religious exercises. In a fortnight he was well, and was known ever afterwards as a most exemplary priest.

---

[4] A crime by no means unknown to the clergy of China.

[5] That is, when the lictors had returned his soul to its tenement.

[6] See No. VI., note 2.

CIX.

METEMPSYCHOSIS.

MR. LIN, who took his master's degree in the same year as the late Mr. Wên Pi,[1] could remember what had happened to him in his previous state of existence, and once told the whole story, as follows :—I was originally of a good family, but, after leading a very dissolute life, I died at the age of sixty-two. On being conducted into the presence of the King of Purgatory, he received me civilly, bade me be seated, and offered me a cup of tea. I noticed, however, that the tea in His Majesty's cup was clear and limpid, while that in my own was muddy, like the lees of wine. It then flashed across me that this was the potion which was given to all dis-embodied spirits to render them oblivious of the past:[2]

---

[1] In A.D. 1621.

[2] According to the *Yü-li-ch'ao*, this potion is administered by an old beldame, named Mother Mêng, who sits upon the Terrace of Oblivion. "Whether they swallow much or little it matters not; but sometimes there are perverse devils who altogether refuse to drink. Then beneath their feet sharp blades start up, and a copper tube is forced down their throats, by which means they are com-pelled to swallow some."

and, according, when the King was looking the other way, I seized the opportunity of pouring it under the table, pretending afterwards that I had drunk it all up. My record of good and evil was now presented for inspection, and when the King saw what it was, he flew into a great passion, and ordered the attendant devils to drag me away, and send me back to earth as a horse. I was immediately seized and bound, and the devils carried me off to a house, the door-sill of which was so high I could not step over it. While I was trying to do so, the devils behind lashed me with all their might, causing me such pain that I made a great spring, and—lo and behold! I was a horse in a stable. "The mare has got a nice colt," I then heard a man call out; but, although I was perfectly aware of all that was passing, I could say nothing myself. Hunger now came upon me, and I was glad to be suckled by the mare ; and by the end of four or five years I had grown into a fine strong horse, dreadfully afraid of the whip, and running away at the very sight of it. When my master rode me, it was always with a saddle-cloth, and at a leisurely pace, which was bearable enough ; but when the servants mounted me barebacked, and dug their heels into me, the pain struck into my vitals; and at length I refused all food, and in three days I died. Reappearing before the King of Purgatory, His Majesty was enraged to find that I had thus tried to shirk working out my time ; and, flaying me forthwith, condemned me to go back again as a dog. And when I did not move, the devils came behind me and lashed me until I ran away from them into the open country, where, thinking I had better die right off, I jumped over a cliff, and lay at the bottom unable to move. I then saw that I was among a litter of puppies, and that an old bitch was licking and suckling me by turns; whereby I knew that I was once more among mortals. In this hateful form I continued for some time, longing to ' kill myself, and yet fearing to incur the penalty of shirking. At length, I purposely bit my master in the leg, and tore him badly; whereupon he had me destroyed, and I was taken again into the presence of the King, who was so displeased with my vicious behaviour that he condemned me to become a snake, and shut me up in a dark room, where I could see nothing. After a while I managed to climb up the wall, bore a hole in the roof, and escape ; and immediately I found myself lying in the grass, a veritable snake. Then I registered a vow that I would harm no living thing, and I lived for some years, feeding upon berries and such like, ever remembering neither to take my own life, nor by injuring any one to incite them to take it, but longing all the while for the happy release, which did not come to me. One day, as I was sleeping in the grass, I heard the noise of a passing cart, and, on trying to get across the road out of its way, I was caught by the wheel, and cut in two. The King was astonished to see me back so soon, but I humbly told my story, and, in pity for the innocent creature that loses its life, he pardoned me, and permitted me to be born again at my appointed time as a human being.

Such was Mr. Lin's story.   He could speak as soon as he came into the world; and could repeat anything he had once read.   In the year 1621 he took his master's degree, and was never tired of telling people to put saddle-cloths on their horses, and recollect that the pain of being gripped by the knees is even worse than the lash itself.

CX.

THE FORTY STRINGS OF CASH.

MR. JUSTICE WANG had a steward, who was possessed of considerable means. One night the latter dreamt that a man rushed in and said to him, "To-day you must repay me those forty strings of cash." The steward asked who he was; to which the man made no answer, but hurried past him into the women's apartments. When the steward awoke, he found that his wife had been delivered of a son; and, knowing at once that retribution was at hand, he set aside forty strings of cash to be spent solely in food, clothes, medicines, and so on, for the baby. By the time the child was between three and four years old, the steward found that of the forty strings only about seven hundred cash remained; and when the wet-nurse, who happened to be standing by, brought the child and dandled it in her arms before him, he looked at it and said, "The forty strings are all but repaid; it is time you were off again." Thereupon the child changed colour; its head fell back, and its eyes stared fixedly, and, when they tried to revive it, lo! respiration had already ceased. The father then took the balance of the forty strings, and with it defrayed the child's funeral expenses—truly a warning to people to be sure and pay their debts.

Formerly, an old childless man consulted a great many Buddhist priests on the subject. One of them said to him, "If you owe no one anything, and no one owes you anything, how can you expect to have children? A good son is the repayment of a former debt; a bad son is a dunning creditor, at whose birth there is no rejoicing, at whose death no lamentations."[1]

---

[1] And such is actually the prevalent belief in China to this day.

CXI.

SAVING LIFE.

A CERTAIN gentleman of Shên-yu, who had taken the highest degree, could remember himself in a previous state of existence. He said he had formerly been a scholar, and had died in middle life; and that when he appeared before the Judge of Purgatory, there stood the cauldrons, the boiling oil, and other apparatus of torture, exactly as we read about them on earth. In the eastern corner of the hall were a number of frames from which hung the skins of sheep, dogs, oxen, horses, etc.; and when anybody was condemned to reappear in life under any one of these forms, his skin was stripped off and a skin was taken from the proper frame and fixed on to his body. The gentleman of whom I am writing heard himself sentenced to become a sheep; and the attendant devils had already clothed him in a sheep's-skin in the manner above described, when the clerk of the record informed the Judge that the criminal before him had once saved another man's life. The Judge consulted his books, and forthwith cried out, " I pardon him ; for although his sins have been many, this one act has redeemed them all."[1] The devils then tried to take off the sheep's-skin, but it was so tightly stuck on him that they couldn't move it. However, after great efforts, and causing the gentleman most excruciating agony, they managed to tear it off bit by bit, though not quite so cleanly as one might have wished. In fact, a piece as big as the palm of a man's hand was left near his shoulder; and when he was born again into the world, there was a great patch of hair on his back, which grew again as fast as it was cut off.

---

[1] Note 2 to No. CVII. should be read here. To save life is indeed the bounden duty of every good Buddhist, for which he will be proportionately rewarded in the world to come.

CXII.

THE SALT SMUGGLER.

WANG SHIH, of Kao-wan, a petty salt huckster, was inordinately fond of gambling. One night he was arrested by two men, whom he took for lictors of the Salt Gabelle; and, flinging down what salt he had with him, he tried to make his escape.[1] He found, however, that his legs would not move with him, and he was

---

[1] Salt is a Government monopoly in China, and its sale is only permitted to licensed dealers. It is a contraband article of commerce, whether for import or export, to foreign nations trading with China. In an account of a journey from Swatow to Canton in March-April, 1877, I wrote :—"*Apropos* of salt, we came across a good-sized bunker of it when stowing away our things in the space below the deck. The boatmen could not resist the temptation of doing a little smuggling on the way up. . . . . . . At a secluded point in a bamboo-shaded bend of the river, they ran the boat alongside the bank, and were instantly met by a number of suspicious-looking gentlemen with baskets, who soon relieved them of the smuggled salt and separated in different directions." Thus do the people of China seek to lighten the grievous pressure of this tax. A curious custom exists in Canton. Certain blind old men and women are allowed to hawk salt about the streets, and earn a scanty living from the profits they are able to make.

It may interest some to know that in the cities of the north of China *ice* and *coal* may only be retailed by licensed dealers, who retain such authority on the condition of supplying the yamêns of the local mandarins with these two necessaries, free of all charge.

forthwith seized and bound. "We are not sent by the Salt Commissioner," cried his captors, in reply to an entreaty to set him free; "we are the devil-constables of Purgatory." Wang was horribly frightened at this, and begged the devils to let him bid farewell to his wife and children; but this they refused to do, saying, "You aren't going to die; you are only wanted for a little job there is down below." Wang asked what the job was; to which the devils replied, "A new Judge has come into office, and, finding the river[2] and the eighteen hells choked up with the bodies of sinners, he has determined to employ three classes of mortals to clean them out. These are thieves, unlicensed founders,[3] and unlicensed

---

[2] The Styx.

[3] These words require some explanation. Ordinarily they would be taken in the sense of casting *cash* of a base description; but they might equally well signify the casting of iron articles of any kind, and thereby hang some curious details. Iron foundries in China may only be opened under license from the local officials, and the articles there made, consisting chiefly of cooking utensils, may only be sold within a given area, each district having its own particular foundries from which alone the supplies of the neighbourhood may be derived. Free trade in iron is much feared by the authorities, as thereby pirates and rebels would be enabled to supply themselves with arms. At the framing of the Treaty of Tientsin, with its accompanying tariff and rules, iron was not specified among other prohibited articles of commerce. Consequently, British merchants would appear to have a full right to purchase iron in the interior and convey it to any of the open ports under Transit-pass. But the Chinese officials steadily refuse to acknowledge, or permit the exercise of, this right, putting forward their own time-honoured custom with regard to iron, and enumerating the disadvantages to China were such an innovation to be brought about.

dealers in salt, and, for the dirtiest work of all, he is going to take musicians."[4]

Wang accompanied the devils until at length they reached a city, where he was brought before the Judge, who was sitting in his Judgment-hall. On turning up his record in the books, one of the devils explained that the prisoner had been arrested for unlicensed trading; whereupon the Judge became very angry, and said, "Those who drive an illicit trade in salt, not only defraud the State of its proper revenue, but also prey upon the livelihood of the people. Those, however, whom the greedy officials and corrupt traders of to-day denounce as unlicensed traders, are among the most virtuous of mankind—needy unfortunates who struggle to save a few cash in the purchase of their pint of salt.[5] Are they your unlicensed traders?" The Judge then bade the lictors buy four pecks of salt, and send it to Wang's house for him, together with that which had been found upon him; and, at the same time, he gave Wang an iron scourge, and told him to superintend the works at the river. So Wang followed the devils, and found the river swarming with people like ants in an ant-hill. The water was turbid and red, the stench from it being almost unbearable, while those who were employed in cleaning it out were working

---

[4] The allusion is to women, of a not very respectable class.

[5] No Chinese magistrate would be found to pass sentence upon a man who stole food under stress of hunger.

there naked. Sometimes they would sink down in the horrid mass of decaying bodies : sometimes they would get lazy, and then the iron scourge was applied to their backs. The assistant-superintendents had small scented balls, which they held in their mouths. Wang himself approached the bank, and saw the licensed salt-merchant of Kao-wan[6] in the midst of it all, and thrashed him well with his scourge, until he was afraid he would never come up again. This went on for three days and three nights, by which time half the workmen were dead, and the work completed; whereupon the same two devils escorted him home again, and then he waked up.

As a matter of fact, Wang had gone out to sell some salt, and had not come back. Next morning, when his wife opened the house door, she found two bags of salt in the court-yard ; and, as her husband did not return, she sent off some people to search for him, and they discovered him lying senseless by the wayside. He was immediately conveyed home, where, after a little time, he recovered consciousness, and related what had taken place. Strange to say, the licensed salt-merchant had fallen down in a fit on the previous evening, and had only just recovered ; and Wang, hearing that his body was covered with sores—the result of the beating with the iron scourge—went off to his house to see him ; however, directly the wretched man set eyes on Wang, he

---

[6] His own village.

hastily covered himself up with the bed-clothes, forgetting that they were no longer at the infernal river.
He did not recover from his injuries for a year, after
which he retired from trade.[7]

---

[7] The whole story is meant as a satire upon the iniquity of the
Salt Gabelle.

CXIII.

COLLECTING SUBSCRIPTIONS.

THE Frog-God frequently employs a magician to deliver its oracles to those who have faith. Should the magician declare that the God is pleased, happiness is sure to follow; but if he says the God is angry, women and children[1] sit sorrowfully about, and neglect even their meals. Such is the customary belief, and it is probably not altogether devoid of foundation.

There was a certain wealthy merchant, named Chou, who was a very stingy man. Once, when some repairs were necessary to the temple of the God of War,[2] and rich and poor were subscribing as much as each could afford, he alone gave nothing.[3] By-and-by the works

---

[1] The chief supporters of superstition in China.

[2] See No. I., note 3.

[3] Such is one of the most common causes of hostile demonstration against Chinese Christians. The latter, acting under the orders of the missionaries, frequently refuse to subscribe to the various local celebrations and processions, the great annual festivities, and ceremonies of all kinds, on the grounds that these are idolatrous and forbidden by the Christian faith. Hence bad feeling, high words, blows, and sometimes bloodshed. I say "frequently,"

wcre stopped for want of funds, and the committee of management were at a loss what to do next. It happened that just then there was a festival in honour of the Frog-God, at which the magician suddenly cried out, "General Chou [4] has given orders for a further subscription. Bring forth the books." The people all shouting assent to this, the magician went on to say, "Those who have already subscribed will not be compelled to do so again; those who have not subscribed must give according to their means." Thereupon various persons began to put down their names, and

---

because I have discovered several cases in which converts have quietly subscribed like other people rather than risk an *émeute*.

An amusing incident came under my own special notice not very long ago. A missionary appeared before me one day to complain that a certain convert of his had been posted in his own village, and cut off from his civic rights for two years, merely because he had agreed to let a room of his house to be used as a missionary *dépôt*. I took a copy of the placard which was handed to me in proof of this statement, and found it to run thus :—"In consequence of —— having entered into an agreement with a barbarian pastor, to lease to the said barbarian pastor a room in his house to be used as a missionary chapel, we, the elders of this village, do hereby debar —— from the privilege of worshipping in our ancestral hall for the space of two years." It is needless, of course, to mention that Ancestral Worship is prohibited by all sects of missionaries in China alike ; or that, when I pointed this out to the individual in question. who could not have understood the import of the Chinese placard, the charge was promptly withdrawn.

[4] An historical character who was formerly among the ranks of the Yellow Turban rebels, but subsequently entered the service of Kuan Yü (see No. I., note 3), and was canonized by an Emperor of the last dynasty.

when this was finished, the magician examined the books. He then asked if Mr. Chou was present; and the latter, who was skulking behind, in dread lest he should be detected by the God, had no alternative but to come to the front. "Put yourself down for one hundred taels," said the magician to him; and when Chou hesitated, he cried out to him in anger, "You could give two hundred for your own bad purposes: how much more should you do so in a good cause?" alluding to a scandalous intrigue of Chou's, the consequences of which he had averted by payment of the sum mentioned. This put our friend to the blush, and he was obliged to enter his name for one hundred taels, at which his wife was very angry, and said the magician was a rogue, and whenever he came to collect the money he was put off with some excuse.

Shortly afterwards, Chou was one day going to sleep, when he heard a noise outside his house, like the blowing of an ox, and beheld a huge frog walking leisurely through the front door, which was just big enough to let it pass. Once inside, the creature laid itself down to sleep, with its head on the threshold, to the great horror of all the inmates; upon which Chou observed that it had probably come to collect his subscription, and burning some incense, he vowed that he would pay down thirty taels on the spot, and send the balance later on. The frog, however, did not move, so Chou promised fifty, and then there was a slight decrease in the frog's size. Another twenty brought it down to the size of a peck measure; and when Chou said the

full amount should be paid on the spot, the frog became
suddenly no larger than one's fist, and disappeared
through a hole in the wall.   Chou immediately sent off
fifty taels, at which all the other subscribers were much
astonished, not knowing what had taken place.   A few
days afterwards the magician said Chou still owed fifty
taels, and that he had better send it in soon ; so Chou
forwarded ten more, hoping now to have done with
the matter.   However, as he and his wife were one day
sitting down to dinner, the frog reappeared, and glaring
with anger, took up a position on the bed, which creaked
under it, as though unable to bear the weight.   Putting
its head on the pillow, the frog went off to sleep, its
body gradually swelling up until it was as big as a
buffalo, and nearly filled the room, causing Chou to send
off the balance of his subscription without a moment's
delay.   There was now no diminution in the size of the
frog's body ; and by-and-by crowds of small frogs came
hopping in, boring through the walls, jumping on the
bed, catching flies on the cooking-stove, and dying in
the saucepans, until the place was quite unbearable.
Three days passed thus, and then Chou sought out the
magician, and asked him what was to be done.   The
latter said he could manage it, and began by vowing on
behalf of Chou twenty more taels' subscription.   At
this the frog raised its head, and a further increase
caused it to move one foot ; and by the time a hundred
taels was reached, the frog was walking out of the door.
At the door, however, it stopped, and lay down once
more, which the magician explained by saying, that

immediate payment was required; so Chou handed over the amount at once, and the frog, shrinking down to its usual size, mingled with its companions, and departed with them.

The repairs to the temple were accordingly completed, but for "lighting the eyes,"[5] and the attendant festivities, some further subscriptions were wanted. Suddenly, the magician, pointing at the managers, cried out, " There is money short; of fifteen men, two of you are defaulters." At this, all declared they had given what they could afford; but the magician went on to say, " It is not a question of what you can afford; you have misappropriated the funds[6] that should not have

---

[5] This curious ceremony is the final touch to a newly-built or newly-restored temple, and consists in giving expression to the eyes of the freshly-painted idols, which have been purposely left blank by the painter. Up to that time these blocks of clay or wood are not supposed to have been animated by the spiritual presence of the deity in question; but no sooner are the eyes lighted than the gratified God smiles down upon the handsome decorations thus provided by devout and trusting suppliants.

There is a cognate custom belonging to the ceremonies of ancestral worship, of great importance in the eyes of the Chinese. On a certain day after the death of a parent, the surviving head of the family proceeds with much solemnity to dab a spot of ink upon the memorial tablet of the deceased. This is believed to give to the departed spirit the power of remaining near to, and watching over the fortunes of, those left behind.

[6] Such indeed is the fate of a per-centage of all public subscriptions raised and handled by Chinese of no matter what class. A year or two ago an application was made to me for a donation to a native foundling hospital at Swatow, on the ground that I was known as a " read (Chinese) book man," and that consequently other persons, both Chinese and foreigners, might be induced to

been touched, and misfortune would come upon you, but that, in return for your exertions, I shall endeavour to avert it from you. The magician himself is not without taint.[7] Let him set you a good example." Thereupon, the magician rushed into his house, and brought out all the money he had, saying, "I stole eight taels myself, which I will now refund." He then weighed what silver he had, and finding that it only amounted to a little over six taels, he made one of the bystanders take a note of the difference. Then the others came forward and paid up, each what he had misappropriated from the public fund. All this time the magician had been in a divine ecstasy, not knowing what he was saying; and when he came round, and was told what had happened, his shame knew no bounds, so he pawned some of his clothes, and paid in the balance of his own debt. As to the two defaulters who did not pay, one of them was ill for a month and more; while the other had a bad attack of boils.

---

follow my example. On my declining to do so, the manager of the concern informed me that if I would only put down my name for fifty dollars, say £10, no call should be made upon me for the money! Even in the matter of the funds collected for the famine-stricken people of 1878, it is whispered that peculation has been rife.

[7] The reader must recollect that these are the words of the God, speaking from the magician's body.

CXIV.

TAOIST MIRACLES.

At Chi-nan Fu there lived a certain priest: I cannot say whence he came, or what was his name. Winter and summer alike he wore but one unlined robe, and a yellow girdle about his waist, with neither shirt nor trousers. He combed his hair with a broken comb, holding the ends in his mouth, like the strings of a hat. By day he wandered about the market-place; at night he slept in the street, and to a distance of several feet round where he lay, the ice and snow would melt. When he first arrived at Chi-nan he used to perform miracles, and the people vied with each other in making him presents. One day a disreputable young fellow gave him a quantity of wine, and begged him in return to divulge the secret of his power; and when the priest refused, the young man watched him get into the river to bathe, and then ran off with his clothes. The priest called out to him to bring them back, promising that he would do as the young man required; but the latter, distrusting the priest's good faith, refused to do so; whereupon the priest's girdle was forthwith changed into a snake, several spans in circumference, which coiled itself round its master's head, and glared and hissed terribly. The young man now fell on his knees, and humbly prayed the priest to save his life; at which the priest put his girdle on again, and a snake that had appeared to be his girdle, wriggled away and disappeared. The priest's fame was thus firmly established, and the gentry and officials of the place were constantly inviting him to join them in their festive parties. By-and-by the priest said he was going to invite his entertainers to a return feast; [1] and at the appointed time each one of them found on his table a formal invitation to a banquet at the Water Pavilion, but no one knew who had brought the letters. However, they all went, and were met at the door by the priest, in his usual garb; and when they got inside, the place was all desolate and bare, with no banquet ready. "I'm afraid I shall be obliged to ask you gentlemen to let me use your attendants," said the priest to his guests; "I am a poor man, and keep no servants myself." To this all readily consented; whereupon the priest drew a double door upon the wall, and rapped upon it with his knuckles. Somebody answered from within, and immediately the door was thrown open, and a splendid array of handsome chairs, and tables

---

[1] It is considered a serious breach of Chinese etiquette to accept invitations without returning the compliment at an early date.

loaded with exquisite viands and costly wines, burst upon the gaze of the astonished guests. The priest bade the attendants receive all these things from the door, and bring them outside, cautioning them on no account to speak with the people inside; and thus a most luxurious entertainment was provided to the great amazement of all present.

Now this Pavilion stood upon the bank of a small lake, and every year, at the proper season, it was literally covered with lilies; but, at the time of this feast, the weather was cold, and the surface of the lake was of a smoky green colour. "It's a pity," said one of the guests, "that the lilies are not out"——a sentiment in which the others very cordially agreed, when suddenly a servant came running in to say that, at that moment, the lake was a perfect mass of lilies. Every one jumped up directly, and ran to look out of the window, and, lo! it was so; and in another minute the fragrant perfume of the flowers was borne towards them by the breeze. Hardly knowing what to make of this strange sight, they sent off some servants, in a boat, to gather a few of the lilies, but they soon returned empty-handed, saying, that the flowers seemed to shift their position as fast as they rowed towards them; at which the priest laughed, and said, "These are but the lilies of your imagination, and have no real existence." And later on, when the wine was finished, the flowers began to droop and fade; and by-and-by a breeze from the north carried off every sign of them, leaving the lake as it had been before.

A certain Taot'ai,[2] at Chi'nan, was much taken with this priest, and gave him rooms at his yamên. One day, he had some friends to dinner, and set before them some very choice old wine that he had, and of which he only brought out a small quantity at a time, not wishing to get through it too rapidly. The guests, however, liked it so much that they asked for more; upon which the Taot'ai said, "he was very sorry, but it was all finished." The priest smiled at this, and said, "I can give the gentlemen some, if they will oblige me by accepting it;" and immediately inserted the wine-kettle [3] in his sleeve, bringing it out again directly, and pouring out for the guests. This wine tasted exactly like the choice wine they had just been drinking, and the priest gave them all as much of it as they wanted, which made the Taot'ai suspect that something was wrong; so, after the dinner, he went into his cellar to look at his own stock, when he found the jars closely tied down, with unbroken seals, but one and all empty. In a great rage, he caused the priest to be arrested for sorcery, and proceeded to have him bambooed; but no sooner had the bamboo touched the priest than the Taot'ai himself felt a sting of pain, which increased at every blow; and, in a few moments, there was the

---

[2] A high Chinese official, known to foreigners as Intendant of Circuit; the circuit being a circuit of Prefectures, over which he has full control, subject only to the approval of the highest provincial authorities. It is with this functionary that foreign Consuls rank.

[3] See No. XCIII., note 3.

priest writhing and shrieking under every cut,[4] while the Taot'ai was sitting in a pool of blood. Accordingly, the punishment was soon stopped, and the priest was commanded to leave Chi-nan, which he did, and I know not whither he went. He was subsequently seen at Nanking, dressed precisely as of old; but on being spoken to, he only smiled and made no reply.

---

[4] Of course only pretending to be hurt, the pain of the blows being transferred by his magical art to the back of the Taot'ai.

CXV.

ARRIVAL OF BUDDHIST PRIESTS.

Two Buddhist priests having arrived from the West,[1] one went to the Wu-t'ai hill, while the other hung up his staff[2] at T'ai-shan. Their clothes, complexions, language, and features, were very different from those of our country. They further said they had crossed the Fiery Mountains, from the peaks of which smoke was always issuing as from the chimney of a furnace; that they could only travel after rain, and that excessive caution was necessary to avoid displacing any stone and thus giving a vent to the flames. They also stated that they had passed through the River of Sand, in the middle of which was a crystal hill with perpendicular sides and perfectly transparent; and that there was a defile just broad enough to admit a single cart, its entrance guarded by two dragons with crossed horns. Those who wished to pass prostrated themselves before these dragons, and on receiving permission to enter, the horns

---

[1] That is, missionaries from India.
[2] See No. LVI., note 10.

opened and let them through. The dragons were of a white colour, and their scales and bristles seemed to be of crystal. Eighteen winters and summers these priests had been on the road; and of twelve who started from the west together, only two reached China.[3] These two said that in their country four of our mountains are held in great esteem, namely, T'ai, Hua, Wu-ta'i, and Lo-chia. The people there also think that China[4] is paved with yellow gold, that Kuan-yin and Wên-shu[5] are still alive, and that they have only come here to be sure of their Buddhahood and of immortal life. Hearing these words it struck me that this was precisely what our own people say and think about the West; and that if travellers from each country could only meet half way and tell each other the true state of affairs, there would be some hearty laughter on both sides, and a saving of much unnecessary trouble.

---

[3] Much of the above recalls Fa Hsien's narrative of his celebrated journey from China to India in the early years of the fifth century of our era, with which our author was evidently well acquainted. That courageous traveller complained that of those who had set out with him some had stopped on the way and others had died, leaving him only his own shadow as a companion.

[4] This may almost be said to have been the belief of the Arabs at the date of the composition of " The Arabian Nights."

[5] For Kuan-yin, see No. XXXIII., note 7. Wên-shu, or Manjusiri, is the God of Wisdom, and is generally represented as riding on a lion, in attendance, together with P'u-hsien, the God of Action, who rides an elephant, upon Shâkyamuni Buddha.

CXVI.

THE STOLEN EYES.

WHEN His Excellency Mr. T'ang, of our village, was quite a child, a relative of his took him to a temple to see the usual theatrical performances.[1] He was a clever little fellow, afraid of nothing and nobody; and when he saw one of the clay images in the vestibule staring at him with its great glass[2] eyes, the temptation was irresistible; and, secretly gouging them out with his finger, he carried them off with him. When they reached home, his relative was taken suddenly ill and remained for a long time speechless; at length, jumping up he cried out several times in a voice of thunder, "Why did you gouge out my eyes?" His family did not know what to make of this, until little T'ang told them what he had done; they then immediately began to pray to the possessed man, saying, "A mere child, unconscious

---

[1] See No. XLVIII., note 4.

[2] The term here used stands for a vitreous composition that has long been prepared by the Chinese. Glass, properly so called, is said to have been introduced into China from the west, by a eunuch, during the Ming dynasty.

of the wickedness of his act, took away in his fun thy sacred eyes. They shall be reverently replaced." Thereupon the voice exclaimed, "In that case, I shall go away;" and he had hardly spoken before T'ang's relative fell flat upon the ground and lay there in a state of insensibility for some time. When he recovered, they asked him concerning what he had said; but he remembered nothing of it. The eyes were then forthwith restored to their original sockets.

CXVII.

THE INVISIBLE PRIEST.

MR. HAN was a gentleman of good family, on very intimate terms with a skilful Taoist priest and magician named Tan, who, when sitting amongst other guests, would suddenly become invisible. Mr. Han was extremely anxious to learn this art, but Tan refused all his entreaties, "Not," as he said, "because I want to keep the secret for myself, but simply as a matter of principle. To teach the superior man[1] would be well enough; others, however, would avail themselves of such knowledge to plunder their neighbours. There is no fear that you would do this, though even you might be tempted in certain ways." Mr. Han, finding all his efforts unavailing, flew into a great passion, and secretly arranged with his servants that they should give the magician a sound beating; and, in order to prevent his escape through the power of making himself invisible, he had

---

[1] The perfect man, according to the Confucian standard.

his threshing-floor[2] covered with a fine ash-dust, so that at any rate his footsteps would be seen and the servants could strike just above them.[3] He then inveigled Tan to the appointed spot, which he had no sooner reached than Han's servants began to belabour him on all sides with leathern thongs. Tan immediately became invisible, but his footprints were clearly seen as he moved about hither and thither to avoid the blows, and the servants went on striking above them until finally he succeeded in getting away. Mr. Han then went home, and subsequently Tan reappeared and told the servants that he could stay there no longer, adding that before he went he intended to give them all a feast in return for many things they had done for him. And diving into his sleeve he brought forth a quantity of delicious meats and wines which he spread out upon the table, begging them to sit down and enjoy themselves. The servants did so, and one and all of them got drunk and insensible; upon which Tan picked each of them up and stowed them away in his sleeve. When Mr. Han heard of this, he begged Tan to perform some other trick; so Tan drew upon the wall a city, and knocking at the gate with his hand it was instantly thrown open. He then put in-

---

[2] A large, smooth, area of concrete, to be seen outside all country houses of any size, and used for preparing the various kinds of grain.

[3] Compare—"The not uncommon practice of strewing ashes to show the footprints of ghosts or demons takes for granted that they are substantial bodies." — Tylor's *Primitive Culture*, Vol. I., p. 455.

side it his wallet and clothes, and stepping through the gateway himself, waved his hand and bade Mr. Han farewell.   The city gates were now closed, and Tan vanished from their sight.   It was said that he appeared again in Ch'ing-chou, where he taught little boys to paint a circle on their hands, and, by dabbing this on to another person's face or clothes, to imprint the circle on the place thus struck without a trace of it being left behind upon the hand.

CXVIII.

THE CENSOR IN PURGATORY.

Just beyond Fêng-tu[1] there is a fathomless cave which is reputed to be the entrance to Purgatory. All the implements of torture employed therein are of human manufacture; old, worn-out gyves and fetters being occasionally found at the mouth of the cave, and as regularly replaced by new ones, which disappear the same night, and for which the magistrate of the district makes a formal charge[2] in his accounts.

Under the Ming dynasty, there was a certain Censor,[3]

---

[1] Fêng-tu is a district city in the province of Szechuen, and near it are said to be fire-wells (see Williams' *Syllabic Dictionary*, s.v.), otherwise known as the entrance to Purgatory, the capital city of which is also called Fêng-tu.

[2] To the Imperial Treasury. From what I know of the barefacedness of similar official impostures, I should say that this statement is quite within the bounds of truth. For instance, at Amoy one per cent. is collected by the local mandarins on all imports, ostensibly for the purpose of providing the Imperial table with a delicious kind of bird's-nest said to be found in the neighbourhood! Seven-tenths of the sum thus collected is pocketed by the various officials of the place, and with the remaining three-tenths a certain quantity of the ordinary article of commerce is imported from the Straits and forwarded to Peking.

[3] See No. XXXII., note 4.

named Hua, whose duties brought him to this place;
and hearing the story of the cave, he said he did not
believe it, but would penetrate into it and see for himself.
People tried to dissuade him from such an enterprise;
however, he paid no heed to their remonstrances, and
entered the cave with a lighted candle in his hand,
followed by two attendants.   They had proceeded about
half a mile, when suddenly the candle was violently ex-
tinguished, and Mr. Hua saw before him a broad flight
of steps leading up to the Ten Courts, or Judgment-halls,
in each of which a judge was sitting with his robes and
tablets all complete.   On the eastern side there was one
vacant place; and when the judges saw Mr. Hua, they
hastened down the steps to meet him, and each one
cried out, " So you have come at last have you ? I hope
you have been quite well since last we met."   Mr. Hua
asked what the place was ; to which they replied that it
was the Court of Purgatory, and then Mr. Hua in a
great fright was about to take his leave, when the judges
stopped him, saying, "No, no, Sir ! that is your seat
there ; how can you imagine you are to go back again?"
Thereupon Mr. Hua was overwhelmed with fear, and
begged and implored the judges to forgive him ; but the
latter declared they could not interfere with the decrees
of fate, and taking down the register of Life and Death
they showed him that it had been ordained that on such
a day of such a month his living body would pass into
the realms of darkness.   When Mr. Hua read these
words he shivered and shook as if iced water was being
poured down his back, and thinking of his old mother

and his young children, his tears began to flow. At that juncture an angel in golden armour appeared, holding in his hand a document written on yellow silk,[4] before which the judges all performed a respectful obeisance. They then unfolded and read the document, which was nothing more or less than a general pardon from the Almighty for the suffering sinners in Purgatory, by virtue of which Mr. Hua's fate would be set aside, and he would be enabled to return once more to the light of day. Thereupon the judges congratulated him upon his release, and started him on his way home; but he had not got more than a few steps of the way before he found himself plunged in total darkness. He was just beginning to despair, when forth from the gloom came a God with a red face and a long beard, rays of light shooting out from his body and illuminating the darkness around. Mr. Hua made up to him at once, and begged to know how he could get out of the cave; to which the God curtly replied, "Repeat the *sûtras* of Buddha!" and vanished instantly from his sight. Now Mr. Hua had forgotten almost all the *sûtras* he had ever known; however, he remembered a little of the diamond *sûtra*, and, clasping his hands in an attitude of prayer, he began to repeat it aloud. No sooner had he done this than a faint streak of light glimmered through the darkness, and revealed to him the direction of the path; but the

---

[4] An Imperial mandate is always written on yellow silk, and the ceremony of opening and perusing it is accompanied by prostrations and other acts of reverential submission.

next moment he was at a loss how to go on and the light forthwith disappeared. He then set himself to think hard what the next verse was, and as fast as he recollected and could go on repeating, so fast did the light reappear to guide him on his way, until at length he emerged once more from the mouth of the cave. As to the fate of the two servants who accompanied him it is needless to inquire.

·

CXIX.

MR. WILLOW AND THE LOCUSTS.

DURING the Ming dynasty a plague of locusts [1] visited Ch'ing-yen, and was advancing rapidly towards the I district, when the magistrate of that place, in great tribulation at the pending disaster, retired one day to sleep behind the screen in his office. There he dreamt that a young graduate, named Willow, wearing a tall hat and a green robe, and of very commanding stature, came to see him, and declared that he could tell the magistrate how to get rid of the locusts. "To-morrow," said he, "on the south-west road, you will see a woman riding [2] on a large jennet: she is the Spirit of the Locusts; ask her, and she will help you." The magistrate thought this strange advice; however, he got everything ready, and waited, as he had been told, at

---

[1] Innumerable pamphlets have been published in China on the best methods of getting rid of these destructive insects, but none to my knowledge contain much sound or practical advice.

[2] See No. LII., note 1. The mules of the north of China are marvels of beauty and strength; and the price of a fine animal often goes as high as £100.

the roadside. By-and-by, along came a woman with her hair tied up in a knot, and a serge cape over her shoulders, riding slowly northwards on an old mule ; whereupon the magistrate burned some sticks of incense, and, seizing the mule's bridle, humbly presented a goblet of wine. The woman asked him what he wanted; to which he replied, "Lady, I implore you to save my small magistracy from the dreadful ravages of your locusts." "Oho !" said the woman, "that scoundrel, Willow, has been letting the cat out of the bag, has he? He shall suffer for it : I won't touch your crops." She then drank three cups of wine, and vanished out of sight. Subsequently, when the locusts did come, they flew high in the air, and did not settle on the crops; but they stripped the leaves off every willow-tree far and wide; and then the magistrate awaked to the fact that the graduate of his dream was the Spirit of the Willows. Some said that this happy result was owing to the magistrate's care for the welfare of his people.

CXX.

MR. TUNG, OR VIRTUE REWARDED.

At Ch'ing-chow there lived a Mr. Tung, President of one of the Six Boards, whose domestic regulations were so strict that the men and women servants were not allowed to speak to each other.[1] One day he caught a slave-girl laughing and talking with one of his attendants, and gave them both a sound rating. That night he retired to sleep, accompanied by his *valet-de-chambre*, in his library, the door of which, as it was very hot weather, was left wide open. When the night was far advanced, the valet was awaked by a noise at his master's bed : and, opening his eyes, he saw, by the light of the moon, the attendant above-mentioned pass out of the door with something in his hand. Recognizing the man as one of the family, he thought nothing of the occurrence, but turned round and went to sleep again. Soon after, however, he was again aroused by the noise of footsteps tramping heavily across the room, and, looking up, he beheld a huge being with a red face and a long beard, very like the

---

[1] See No. XL., note 3, and No. XCIV., note 3.

God of War,[2] carrying a man's head. Horribly frightened, he crawled under the bed, and then he heard sounds above him as of clothes being shaken out, and as if some one was being shampooed.[3] In a few moments, the boots tramped once more across the room and went away; and then he gradually put out his head, and, seeing the dawn beginning to peep through the window, he stretched out his hand to reach his clothes. These he found to be soaked through and through, and, on applying his hand to his nose, he smelt the smell of blood. He now called out loudly to his master, who jumped up at once ; and, by the light of a candle, they saw that the bed clothes and pillows were alike steeped in blood. Just then some constables knocked at the door, and when Mr. Tung went out to see who it was, the constables were all astonishment ; "for," said they, "a few minutes ago a man rushed wildly up to our yamên, and said he had killed his master; and, as he himself was covered with blood, he was arrested, and turned out to be a servant of yours. He also declared that he had buried your head alongside the temple of the God of War ; and when we went to look, there, indeed, was a freshly-dug hole, but the head was gone." Mr. Tung was amazed at all this story, and, on proceeding to the magistrate's yamên, he discovered that the man in charge was the attendant whom he had scolded the day before. Thereupon, the

---

[2] See No. I., note 3.
[3] See No. LXIX., note 8.

criminal was severely bambooed and released; and then Mr. Tung, who was unwilling to make an enemy of a man of this stamp, gave him the girl to wife. However, a few nights afterwards the people who lived next door to the newly-married couple heard a terrific crash in their house, and, rushing in to see what was the matter, found that husband and wife, and the bedstead as well, had been cut clean in two as if by a sword. The ways of the God are many, indeed, but few more extraordinary than this.[4]

---

[4] It was the God of War who replaced Mr. Tung's head after it had actually been cut off and buried.

CXXI.

THE DEAD PRIEST.

A CERTAIN Taoist priest, overtaken in his wanderings by the shades of evening, sought refuge in a small Buddhist monastery. The monk's apartment was, however, locked; so he threw his mat down in the vestibule of the shrine, and seated himself upon it. In the middle of the night, when all was still, he heard a sound of some one opening the door behind him; and looking round, he saw a Buddhist priest, covered with blood from head to foot, who did not seem to notice that anybody else was present. Accordingly, he himself pretended not to be aware of what was going on; and then he saw the other priest enter the shrine, mount the altar, and remain there some time embracing Buddha's head, and laughing by turns. When morning came, he found the monk's room still locked; and, suspecting something was wrong, he walked to a neighbouring village, where he told the people what he had seen. Thereupon the villagers went back with him, and broke open the door, and there before them lay the priest weltering in his blood, having evidently been killed by robbers, who had stripped the place bare. Anxious now to find out what had made the disembodied spirit of the priest laugh in the way it had been seen to do, they proceeded to inspect the head of the Buddha on the altar ; and, at the back of it, they noticed a small mark, scraping through which they discovered a sum of over thirty ounces of silver. This sum was forthwith used for defraying the funeral expenses of the murdered man.

CXXII.

THE FLYING COW.

A CERTAIN man, who had bought a fine cow, dreamt the same night that wings grew out of the animal's back, and that it had flown away. Regarding this as an omen of some pending misfortune, he led the cow off to market again, and sold it at a ruinous loss. Wrapping up in a cloth the silver he received, he slung it over his back, and was half way home, when he saw a falcon eating part of a hare.[1] Approaching the bird, he found it was quite tame, and accordingly tied it by the leg to one of the corners of the cloth, in which his money was. The falcon fluttered about a good deal, trying to escape; and, by-and-by, the man's hold being for a moment relaxed, away went the bird, cloth, money, and all. "It was destiny," said the man every time he told the story; ignorant as

---

[1] See No. VI., note 1.

he was, first, that no faith should be put in dreams;[2] and, secondly, that people shouldn't take things they see by the wayside.[3]   Quadrupeds don't usually fly.

---

[2] The highly educated Confucianist rises above the superstition that darkens the lives of his less fortunate fellow countrymen. Had such a dream as the above received an inauspicious interpretation at the hands of some local soothsayer, the owner of the animal would in nine cases out of ten have taken an early opportunity of getting rid of it.

[3] The Chinese love to refer to the "good old time" of their forefathers, when a man who dropped anything on the highway would have no cause to hurry back for fear of its being carried off by a stranger.

CXXIII.

THE "MIRROR AND LISTEN" TRICK.

AT I-tu there lived a family of the name of Chêng. The two sons were both distinguished scholars, but the elder was early known to fame, and, consequently, the favourite with his parents, who also extended their preference to his wife. The younger brother was a trifle wild, which displeased his father and mother very much, and made them regard his wife, too, with anything but a friendly eye. The latter reproached her husband for being the cause of this, and asked him why he, being a man like his brother, could not vindicate the slights that were put upon her. This piqued him; and, setting to work in good earnest, he soon gained a fair reputation, though still not equal to his brother's. That year the two went up for the highest degree; and, on New Year's Eve, the wife of the younger, very anxious for the success of her husband, secretly tried the "mirror and listen" trick.[1] She saw

---

[1] One method is to wrap an old mirror (formerly a polished metal disc) in a handkerchief, and then, no one being present, to bow seven times towards the Spirit of the Hearth: after which the first words heard spoken by any one will give a clue to the issue under

two men pushing each other in jest, and heard them say, "You go and get cool," which remark she was quite unable to interpret for good or for bad, so she thought no more about the matter. After the examination, the two brothers returned home; and one day, when the weather was extremely hot, and their two wives were hard at work in the cook-house, preparing food for their field-labourers, a messenger rode up in hot haste[2] to announce that the elder brother had passed. Thereupon his mother went into the cook-house, and, calling to her daughter-in-law, said, "Your husband has passed; *you go and get cool.*" Rage and grief now filled the breast of the second son's wife, who, with tears in her eyes, continued her task of cooking, when suddenly another messenger rushed in to say, that the second son had passed, too. At this, his wife flung down her frying-pan, and cried out, "Now I'll *go and get cool;*" and as in the heat of her excitement she uttered these words, the recollection of her trial of the "mirror and listen" trick flashed upon her, and she knew that the words of that evening had been fulfilled.

---

investigation. Another method is to close the eyes and take seven paces, opening them at the seventh and getting some hint from the objects first seen in a mirror held in the hand, coupled with the words first spoken within the experimenter's hearing. ·

[2] In former days, these messengers of good tidings to candidates whose homes were in distant parts used to earn handsome sums if first to announce the news; but now, at any rate along the coast, steamers and the telegraph have taken their occupation from them.

CXXIV.

THE CATTLE PLAGUE.

CH'ÊN HUA-FÊNG, of Mêng-shan, overpowered by the great heat, went and lay down under a tree, when suddenly up came a man with a thick comforter round his neck, who also sat down on a stone in the shade, and began fanning himself as hard as he could, the perspiration all the time running off him like a water-fall. Ch'ên rose and said to him with a smile, "If Sir, you were to remove that comforter, you would be cool enough without the help of a fan." "It would be easy enough," replied the stranger, "to take off my comforter; but the difficulty would be in getting it on again." He then went on to converse generally upon other matters, in a manner which betokened consider-able refinement; and by-and-by he exclaimed, "What I should like now is just a draught of iced wine to cool the twelve joints of my œsophagus."[1] "Come along,

---

[1] Accurate anatomical descriptions must not be looked for in Chinese literature. "Man has three hundred and sixty-five bones, corresponding to the number of days it takes the heavens to re-volve." From the *Hsi-yüan-lu*, or *Instructions to Coroners*, Book I., ch. 12. [See No. XIV., note 8.]

then," cried Ch'ên, "my house is close by, and I shall be happy to give you what you want." So off they went together; and Ch'ên set before them some capital wine, which he produced from a cave, cold enough to numb their teeth. The stranger was delighted, and remained there drinking until late in the evening, when, all at once, it began to rain. Ch'ên lighted a lamp; and he and his guest, who now took off the comforter, sat talking together in *dishabille*. Every now and again the former thought he saw a light coming from the back of the stranger's head; and when at length he had gone off into a tipsy sleep, Ch'ên took the light to examine more closely. He found behind the ears a large cavity, partitioned by a number of membranes, and looking like a lattice, with a thin skin hanging down in front of each, the spaces being apparently empty. In great astonishment Ch'ên took a hair-pin, and inserted it into one of these places, when pff! out flew something like a tiny cow, which broke through the window,[2] and was gone. This frightened Ch'êng, and he determined to play no more tricks; just then, however, the stranger waked up. "Alas!" cried he, "you have been at my head, and have let out the Cattle Plague. What is to be done, now?" Ch'ên asked what he meant: upon which the stranger said, "There is no object in further concealment. I will tell you all. I am the Angel of Pesti-

---

[2] See No. X., note 7.

lence for the six kinds of domestic animals. That form which you have let out attacks oxen, and I fear that, for miles round, few will escape alive." Now Ch'êng, himself was a cattle-farmer, and when he heard this was dreadfully alarmed, and implored the stranger to tell him what to do. "What to do!" replied he "why I shall not escape punishment myself; how can I tell you what to do. However, you will find powdered *K'u-ts'an*[3] an efficacious remedy, that is if you don't keep it a secret for your private use."[4] The stranger then departed, first of all piling up a quantity of earth in a niche in the wall, a handful of which, he told Ch'ên, given to each animal, might prove of some avail. Before long the plague did break out; and Ch'ên, who was desirous of making a little money by it, told the remedy to no one, with the exception of his younger brother. The latter tried it on his own beasts with great success; while, on the other hand, those belonging to Ch'ên himself died off, to the number of fifty head,[5] leaving him only four or five old cows, which shewed every sign of soon sharing the same fate. In his distress, Ch'ên suddenly bethought himself of the earth in the niche; and, as a last

---

[3] *Radix robiniæ amaræ.*

[4] As the Chinese invariably do whenever they get hold of a useful prescription or remedy. Master workmen also invariably try to withhold something of their art from the apprentices they engage to teach.

[5] The text has "of two hundred hoofs."

resource, gave some to the sick animals. By the next morning they were quite well, and then he knew that his secrecy about the remedy had caused it to have no effect. From that moment his stock went on increasing, and in a few years he had as many as ever.

CXXV.

THE MARRIAGE OF THE VIRGIN GODDESS.

AT Kuei-chi there is a shrine to the Plum Virgin, who was formerly a young lady named Ma, and lived at Tung-wan. Her betrothed husband dying before the wedding, she swore she would never marry, and at thirty years of age she died. Her kinsfolk built a shrine to her memory, and gave her the title of the Plum Virgin. Some years afterwards, a Mr. Chin, on his way to the examination, happened to pass by the shrine; and entering in, he walked up and down thinking very much of the young lady in whose honour it had been erected. That night he dreamt that a servant came to summon him into the presence of the Goddess; and that, in obedience to her command, he went and found her waiting for him just outside the shrine. "I am deeply grateful to you, Sir," said the Goddess, on his approach, "for giving me so large a share of your thoughts; and I intend to repay you by becoming your humble hand-maid." Mr. Chin bowed an assent; and then the Goddess escorted him back, saying, "When your place is ready, I will come and fetch you." On waking in the morning, Mr. Chin was not over pleased with his new team; however that very night every one of the villagers dreamt that the Goddess appeared and said she was having to marry Mr. Chin, bidding them at once prepare an image of him. This the village elders, out of respect for their Goddess, positively refused to do; until at length they all began to fall ill, and then they made a clay image of Mr. Chin, and placed it on the left of the Goddess. Mr. Chin now told his wife that the Plum Virgin had come for him; and, putting on his official cap and robes, he straightway died. Thereupon his wife was very angry; and, going to the shrine, she first abused the Goddess, and then, getting on the altar, slapped her face well. The Goddess is now called Chin's virgin wife.

CXXVI.

THE WINE INSECT.

A Mr. Lin of Ch'ang-shan was extremely fat, and
so fond of wine[1] that he would often finish a pitcher
by himself. However, he owned about fifty acres of
and, half of which was covered with millet, and being
well off, he did not consider that his drinking would
ring him into trouble. One day a foreign Buddhist
riest saw him, and remarked that he appeared to be
iffering from some extraordinary complaint. Mr. Lin
said nothing was the matter with him ; whereupon the
priest asked him if he often got drunk. Lin acknowledged that he did ; and the priest told him that he was
afflicted by the wine insect. " Dear me ! " cried Lin, in
great alarm, " do you think you could cure me ? " The
priest declared there would be no difficulty in doing so ;
but when Lin asked him what drugs he intended to
use, the priest said he should not use any at all. He
then made Lin lie down in the sun ; and tying his hands
and feet together, he placed a stoup of good wine about

---

[1] The ordinary "wine" of China is a spirit distilled from rice.
See No. XCIII., note 3.

half a foot from his head. By-and-by, Lin felt a deadly thirst coming on; and the flavour of the wine passing through his nostrils, seemed to set his vitals on fire. Just then he experienced a tickling sensation in his throat, and something ran out of his mouth and jumped into the wine. On being released from his bonds, he saw that it was an insect about three inches in length, which wriggled about in the wine like a tadpole, and had mouth and eyes all complete. Lin was overjoyed, and offered money to the priest, who refused to take it, saying, all he wanted was the insect, which he explained to Lin was the essence of wine, and which, on being stirred up in water, would turn it into wine. Lin tried this, and found it was so; and ever afterwards he detested the sight of wine. He subsequently became very thin, and so poor that he had hardly enough to eat and drink.[2]

---

[2] The commentator would have us believe that Mr. Lin's fondness for wine was to him an element of health and happiness rather than a disease to be cured, and that the priest was wrong in meddling with the natural bent of his constitution.

CXXVII.

THE FAITHFUL DOG.

A CERTAIN man of Lu-ngan, whose father had been cast into prison, and was brought almost to death's door,[1] scraped together one hundred ounces of silver, and set out for the city to try and arrange for his parent's release. Jumping on a mule, he saw that a black dog, belonging to the family, was following him. He tried in vain to make the dog remain at home; and when, after travelling for some miles, he got off his mule to rest awhile, he picked up a large stone and threw it at the dog, which then ran off. However, he was no sooner on the road again, than up came the dog, and tried to stop the mule by holding on to its tail. His master beat it off with the whip; whereupon the dog

---

[1] In an entry on torture (see No. LXXIII., note 2), which occurs in my *Glossary of Reference* I made the following state-ment:—"The real tortures of a Chinese prison are the filthy dens in which the unfortunate victims are confined, the stench in which they have to draw breath, the fetters and manacles by which they are secured, the absolute insufficiency even of the disgusting rations doled out to them, and above all the mental agony which must ensue in a country with no *Habeas corpus* to protect the lives and fortunes of its citizens."

ran barking loudly in front of the mule, and seemed to be using every means in its power to cause his master to stop. The latter thought this a very inauspicious omen, and turning upon the animal in a rage, drove it away out of sight. He now went on to the city; but when, in the dusk of the evening, he arrived there, he found that about half his money was gone. In a terrible state of mind he tossed about all night; then, all of a sudden, it flashed across him that the strange behaviour of the dog might possibly have some meaning; so getting up very early, he left the city as soon as the gates were open,[2] and though, from the number of passers-by, he never expected to find his money again, he went on until he reached the spot where he had got off his mule the day before. There he saw his dog lying dead upon the ground, its hair having apparently been wetted through with perspiration;[3] and, lifting up the body by one of its ears, he found his lost silver. Full of gratitude, he bought a coffin and buried the dead animal; and the people now call the place the Grave of the Faithful Dog.

---

[2] For a small bribe, the soldiers at the gates of a Chinese city will usually pass people in and out by means of a ladder placed against the wall at some convenient spot.

[3] I believe it is with us only a recently determined fact that dogs perspire through the skin.

CXXVIII.

AN EARTHQUAKE.

IN 1668 there was a very severe earthquake.[1] I myself was staying at Chi-hsia, and happened to be that night sitting over a kettle of wine with my cousin Li Tu. All of a sudden we heard a noise like thunder, travelling from the south-east in a north-westerly direction. We were much astonished at this, and quite unable to account for the noise; in another moment the table began to rock, and the wine-cups were upset; the beams and supports of the house snapped here and there with a crash, and we looked at each other in fear and trembling. By-and-by we knew that it was an earthquake; and, rushing out, we saw houses and other buildings, as it were, fall down and get up again; and, amidst the sounds of crushing walls, we heard the shrieks of women and children, the whole mass being like a great seething cauldron. Men were giddy and could not stand, but rolled about on the ground; the river overflowed its banks;

[1] The exact date is given,—the 17th of the 6th moon, which would probably fall towards the end of June.

cocks crowed, and dogs barked from one end of the city to the other. In a little while the quaking began to subside; and then might be seen men and women running half naked about the streets, all anxious to tell their own experiences, and forgetting that they had on little or no clothing. I subsequently heard that a well was closed up and rendered useless by this earthquake; that a house was turned completely round, so as to face the opposite direction; that the Ch'i-hsia hill was riven open, and that the waters of the I river flowed in and made a lake of an acre and more. Truly such an earthquake as this is of rare occurrence.

CXXIX.

MAKING ANIMALS.

THE tricks for bewitching people are many. Sometimes drugs are put in their food, and when they eat
they become dazed, and follow the person who has
bewitched them. This is commonly called *ta hsü pa;*
in Kiang-nan it is known as *ch'ê hsü.* Little children
are most frequently bewitched in this way. There is
also what is called "making animals," which is better
known on the south side of the River.[1]

One day a man arrived at an inn in Yang-chow,
leading with him five donkeys. Tying them up near
the stable, he told the landlord he would be back in a
few minutes, and bade him give his donkeys no water.
He had not been gone long before the donkeys, which
were standing out in the glare of the sun, began to kick
about, and make a noise; whereupon the landlord
untied them, and was going to put them in the shade,
when suddenly they espied water, and made a rush to
get at it. So the landlord let them drink; and no
sooner had the water touched their lips than they rolled

---

[1] See No. XCVIII., note I.

on the ground, and changed into women. In great astonishment, the landlord asked them whence they came; but their tongues were tied, and they could not answer, so he hid them in his private apartments, and at that moment their owner returned, bringing with him five sheep. The latter immediately asked the landlord where his donkeys were; to which the landlord replied by offering him some wine, saying, the donkeys would be brought to him directly. He then went out and gave the sheep some water, on drinking which they were all changed into boys. Accordingly, he communicated with the authorities, and the stranger was arrested and forthwith beheaded.

CXXX.

CRUELTY AVENGED.

A CERTAIN magistrate caused a petty oil-vendor, who was brought before him for some trifling misdemeanour, and whose statements were very confused, to be bambooed to death. The former subsequently rose to high rank; and having amassed considerable wealth, set about building himself a fine house.   On the day when the great beam was to be fixed in its place,[1] among the friends and relatives who arrived to offer their congratulations, he was horrified to see the oilman walk in. At the same instant one of the servants came rushing up to announce to him the birth of a son; whereupon, he mournfully remarked, "The house not yet finished, and its destroyer already here."   The bystanders thought he was joking, for they had not seen what he had seen.[2] However, when that boy grew up, by his frivolity and extravagance he quite ruined his father.   He was finally obliged himself to go into service; and spent all his earnings in oil, which he swallowed in large quantities.

---

[1] This corresponds to our ceremony of laying the foundation stone, except that one commemorates the beginning, the other the completion, of a new building.

[2] That is, the disembodied spirit of the oilman.

CXXXI.

THE WEI-CH'I DEVIL.

A CERTAIN general, who had resigned his command, and had retired to his own home, was very fond of roaming about and amusing himself with wine and *wei-ch'i*.[1] One day—it was the 9th of the 9th moon, when everybody goes up high[2]—as he was playing with some friends, a stranger walked up, and watched the game intently for some time without going away. He was a miserable-looking creature, with a very ragged

---

[1] A most abstruse and complicated game of skill, for which the Chinese claim an antiquity of four thousand years, and which I was the first to introduce to a European public through an article in *Temple Bar Magazine* for January, 1877. *Apropos* of which, an accomplished American lady, Miss A. M. Fielde, of Swatow, wrote as follows:—"The game seems to me the peer of chess. . . . . . It is a game for the slow, persistent, astute, multitudinous Chinese; while chess, by the picturesque appearance of the board, the variety and prominent individuality of the men, and the erratic combination of the attack,—is for the Anglo-Saxon."

[2] On this day, annually dedicated to kite-flying, picnics, and good cheer, everybody tries to get up to as great an elevation as possible, in the hope, as some say, of thereby prolonging life. It was this day—4th October, 1878—which was fixed for the total extermination of foreigners in Foochow.

coat, but nevertheless possessed of a refined and courteous air. The general begged him to be seated, an offer which he accepted, being all the time extremely deferential in his manner. "I suppose you are pretty good at this," said the general, pointing to the board; "try a bout with one of my friends here." The stranger made a great many apologies in reply, but finally accepted, and played a game in which, apparently to his great disappointment, he was beaten. He played another with the same result; and now, refusing all offers of wine, he seemed to think of nothing but how to get some one to play with him. Thus he went on until the afternoon was well advanced; when suddenly, just as he was in the middle of a most exciting game, which depended on a single place, he rushed forward, and throwing himself at the feet of the general, loudly implored his protection. The general did not know what to make of this; however, he raised him up, and said, "It's only a game: why get so excited?" To this the stranger replied by begging the general not to let his gardener seize him; and when the general asked what gardener he meant, he said the man's name was Ma-ch'êng. Now this Ma-ch'êng was often employed as a lictor by the Ruler of Purgatory, and would sometimes remain away as much as ten days, serving the warrants of death; accordingly, the general sent off to inquire about him, and found that he had been in a trance for two days.[3] His master cried out that he had

---

[3] See No. XXVI., note 3.

better not behave rudely to his guest, but at that very moment the stranger sunk down to the ground, and was gone. The general was lost in astonishment; however, he now knew that the man was a disembodied spirit, and on the next day, when Ma-ch'êng came round, he asked him for full particulars. "The gentleman was a native of Hu-hsiang," replied the gardener, "who was passion-ately addicted to *wei-ch'i*, and had lost a great deal of money by it. His father, being much grieved at his behaviour, confined him to the house; but he was always getting out, and indulging the fatal passion, and at last his father died of a broken heart. In con-sequence of this, the Ruler of Purgatory curtailed his term of life, and condemned him to become a hungry devil,[4] in which state he has already passed seven years. And now that the Phœnix Tower[5] is com-pleted, an order has been issued for the literati to pre-sent themselves, and compose an inscription to be cut on stone, as a memorial thereof, by which means they would secure their own salvation as a reward. Many of the shades failing to arrive at the appointed time, God was very angry with the Ruler of Purgatory, and the latter sent off me, and others who are employed in the same way, to hunt up the defaulters. But as you, Sir, bade me treat the gentleman with respect, I did not

---

[4] One of the *prêtas*, or the fourth of the six paths (gâti) of existence; the other five being (1) angels), (2) men, (3) demons, (5) brute beasts, and (6) sinners in hell. The term is often used colloquially for a self-invited guest.

[5] An imaginary building in the Infernal Regions.

venture to bind him." The general inquired what had become of the stranger ; to which the gardener replied, "He is now a mere menial in Purgatory, and can never be born again." "Alas !" cried his master, "thus it is that men are ruined by any inordinate passion."[6]

---

[6] Mencius reckoned "to play *wei-ch'i* for money". among the five unfilial acts.

CXXXII.

THE FORTUNE-HUNTER PUNISHED.

A CERTAIN man's uncle had no children, and the nephew, with an eye to his uncle's property, volunteered to become his adopted son.[1] When the uncle died all the property passed accordingly to his nephew, who thereupon broke faith as to his part of the contract.[2] He did the same with another uncle, and thus united three properties in his own person, whereby he became the richest man of the neighbourhood. Suddenly he fell ill, and seemed to go out of his mind; for he cried out, "So you wish to live in wealth, do you?" and immediately seizing a sharp knife, he began hacking away at his own body until he had strewed the floor with pieces of flesh. He then exclaimed, "You cut off other people's posterity and expect to have posterity yourself, do you?" and forthwith he ripped himself open and died. Shortly afterwards his son, too, died, and the property fell into the hands of strangers. Is not this a retribution to be dreaded?

---

[1] See No. LV., note 9; and No. XCIV., note 6.

[2] That is, in carrying out the obligations he had entered into, such as conducting the ceremonies of ancestral worship, repairing the family tombs, &c.

CXXXIII.

LIFE PROLONGED.

A CERTAIN cloth merchant of Ch'ang-ch'ing was stopping at T'ai-ngan, when he heard of a magician who was said to be very skilled in casting nativities. So he went off at once to consult him; but the magician would not undertake the task, saying, "Your destiny is bad : you had better hurry home." At this the merchant was dreadfully frightened, and, packing up his wares, set off towards Ch'ang-ch'ing. On the way he fell in with a man in short clothes,[1] like a constable; and the two soon struck up a friendly intimacy, taking their meals together. By-and-by the merchant asked the stranger what his business was ; and the latter told him he was going to Ch'ang-ch'ing to serve summonses, pro-ducing at the same time a document and showing it to the merchant, who, on looking closely, saw a list of

---

[1] The long flowing robe is a sign of respectability which all but the very poorest classes love to affect in public. At the port of Haiphong, *shoes* are the criterion of social standing; but, as a rule, the well-to-do native merchants prefer to go barefoot rather than give the authorities a chance of exacting heavier squeezes, on the strength of such a palpable acknowledgment of wealth.

names, at the head of which was his own. In great astonishment he inquired what he had done that he should be arrested thus; to which his companion replied, "I am not a living being: I am a lictor in the employ of the infernal authorities, and I presume your term of life has expired." The merchant burst into tears and implored the lictor to spare him, which the latter declared was impossible; "But," added he, "there are a great many names down, and it will take me some time to get through them: you go off home and settle up your affairs, and, as a slight return for your friendship, I'll call for you last." A few minutes afterwards they reached a stream where the bridge was in ruins, and people could only cross with great difficulty; at which the lictor remarked, "You are now on the road to death, and not a single cash can you carry away with you. Repair this bridge and benefit the public; and thus from a great outlay you may possibly yourself derive some small advantage." The merchant said he would do so; and when he got home, he bade his wife and children prepare for his coming dissolution, and at the same time set men to work and made the bridge sound and strong again. Some time elapsed, but no lictor arrived; and his suspicions began to be aroused, when one day the latter walked in and said, "I reported that affair of the bridge to the Municipal God,[2] who communicated it to the Ruler of Purgatory; and for that good act your span of life has been lengthened, and your name struck

---

[2] See No. I., note I.

out of the list. I have now come to announce this to you." The merchant was profuse in his thanks; and the next time he went to T'ai-ngan, he burnt a quantity of paper ingots,[3] and made offerings and libations to the lictor, out of gratitude for what he had done. Suddenly the lictor himself appeared, and cried out, "Do you wish to ruin me? Happily my new master has only just taken up his post, and he has not noticed this, or where should I be?"[4] The lictor then escorted the merchant some distance; and, at parting, bade him never return by that road, but, if he had any business at T'ai-ngan, to go thither by a roundabout way.

---

[3] See No. LVI., note 7; and No. XCVII., note 7.

[4] The lictor had no right to divulge his errand when he first met the cloth merchant, or to remove the latter's name from the top to the bottom of the list.

CXXXIV.

THE CLAY IMAGE.

ON the river I there lived a man named Ma, who married a wife from the Wang family, with whom he was very happy in his domestic life. Ma, however, died young; and his wife's parents were unwilling that their daughter should remain a widow, but she resisted all their importunities, and declared firmly she would never marry again. "It is a noble resolve of yours, I allow," argued her mother; "but you are still a mere girl, and you have no children. Besides, I notice that people who start with such rigid determinations always end by doing something discreditable, and therefore you had better get married as soon as you can, which is no more than is done every day." The girl swore she would rather die than consent, and accordingly her mother had no alternative but to let her alone. She then ordered a clay image to be made, exactly resembling her late husband;[1] and whenever she took her own meals, she

---

[1] The clay image makers of Tientsin are wonderfully clever in taking likenesses by these means. Some of the most skilful will even manipulate the clay behind their backs, and then, adding the proper colours, will succeed in producing an exceedingly good resemblance. They find, however, more difficulty with foreign faces, to which they are less accustomed in the trade.

would set meat and wine before it, precisely as if her husband had been there. One night she was on the point of retiring to rest, when suddenly she saw the clay image stretch itself and step down from the table, increasing all the while in height, until it was as tall as a man, and neither more nor less than her own husband. In great alarm she called out to her mother, but the image stopped her, saying, "Don't do that! I am but shewing my gratitude for your affectionate care of me, and it is chill and uncomfortable in the realms below. Such devotion as yours casts its light back on generations gone by; and now I, who was cut off in my prime because my father did evil, and was condemned to be without an heir, have been permitted, in consequence of your virtuous conduct, to visit you once again, that our ancestral line may yet remain unbroken."[2] Every morning at cock-crow her husband resumed his usual form and size as the clay image; and after a time he told her that their hour of separation had come, upon which husband and wife bade each other an eternal farewell. By-and-by the widow, to the great astonishment of her mother, bore a son, which caused no small amusement among the neighbours who heard the story; and, as the girl herself had no proof of what she stated to be the case, a certain beadle[3] of the place, who had an old grudge against her husband, went off and informed the magistrate of what had occurred. After some investi-

---

[2] See No. LXI., note 3.
[3] See No. LXIV., note 2.

gation, the magistrate exclaimed, " I have heard that the children of disembodied spirits have no shadow; and that those who have shadows are not genuine." Thereupon they took Ma's child into the sunshine, and lo! there was but a very faint shadow, like a thin vapour. The magistrate then drew blood from the child, and smeared it on the clay image; upon which the blood at once soaked in and left no stain. Another clay image being produced and the same experiment tried, the blood remained on the surface so that it could be wiped away.[4] The girl's story was thus acknowledged to be true; and when the child grew up, and in every feature was the counterpart of Ma, there was no longer any room for suspicion.

---

[4] Such is the officially authorised method of determining a doubtful relationship between a dead parent and a living child, substituting a bone for the clay image here mentioned.

CXXXV.

DISHONESTY PUNISHED.

At Chiao-chou there lived a man named Liu Hsi-ch'uan, who was steward to His excellency Mr. Fa. When already over forty a son was born to him, whom he loved very dearly, and quite spoilt by always letting him have his own way. When the boy grew up he led a dissolute, extravagant life, and ran through all his father's property. By-and-by he fell sick, and then he declared that nothing would cure him but a slice off a fat old favourite mule they had ; upon which his father had another and more worthless animal killed ; but his son found out he was being tricked, and, after abusing his father soundly, his symptoms became more and more alarming. The mule was accordingly killed, and some of it was served up to the sick man ; however, he only just tasted it and sent the rest away. From that time he got gradually worse and worse, and finally died, to the great grief of his father, who would gladly have died too. Three or four years afterwards, as some of the villagers were worshipping on Mount Tai, they saw a man riding on a mule, the very image of Mr. Liu's dead son ; and, on approaching more closely, they saw that it was actually he.[1] Jumping from his mule,[2] he made them a salutation, and then they began to chat with him on various subjects, always carefully avoiding that one of his own death. They asked him what he was doing there; to which he replied that he was only roaming about, and inquired of them in his turn at what inn they were staying; "For," added he, "I have an engagement just now, but I will visit you to-morrow." So they told him the name of the inn, and took their leave, not expecting to see him again. However, the next day he came, and, tying his mule to a post outside, went in to see them. "Your father," observed one of the villagers, "is always thinking about you. Why do you not go and pay him a visit?" The young man asked to whom he was alluding; and, at the mention of his father's name, he changed colour and said, "If he is anxious to see me, kindly tell him that on the 7th of the 4th moon I will await him here." He then went away, and the villagers returned and told Mr. Liu all that had taken place. At the appointed time the latter was very desirous of going to see his son; but his master dissuaded him, saying that he thought from what he knew of his son that the interview might possibly not turn out as he would desire; "Although," added he, "if you are bent

---

[1] "In various savage superstitions the minute resemblance of soul to body is forcibly stated."—*Myths and Myth-makers*, by John Fiske, p. 228.

[2] An important point in Chinese etiquette. It is not considered polite for a person in a sitting position to address an equal who is standing.

upon going, I should be sorry to stand in your way. Let me, however, counsel you to conceal yourself in a cupboard, and thus, by observing what takes place, you will know better how to act, and avoid running into any danger." This he accordingly did, and, when his son came, Mr. Fa received him at the inn as before. "Where's Mr. Liu?" cried the son. "Oh, he hasn't come," replied Mr. Fa. "The old beast! What does he mean by that?" exclaimed his son; whereupon Mr. Fa asked him what *he* meant by cursing his own father. "My father!" shrieked the son; "why he's nothing more to me than a former rascally partner in trade, who cheated me out of all my money, and for which I have since avenged myself on him.[3] What sort of a father is that, I should like to know?" He then went out of the door; and his father crept out of the cupboard from which, with the perspiration streaming down him and hardly daring to breathe, he had heard all that had passed, and sorrowfully wended his way home again.

---

[3] By becoming his son and behaving badly to him. See No. CX., note 1, and the text to which it refers.

CXXXVI.

THE MAD PRIEST.

A CERTAIN mad priest, whose name I do not know, lived in a temple on the hills. He would sing and cry by turns, without any apparent reason; and once somebody saw him boiling a stone for his dinner. At the autumn festival of the 9th day of the 9th moon,[1] an official of the district went up in that direction for the usual picnic, taking with him his chair and his red umbrellas. After luncheon he was passing by the temple, and had hardly reached the door, when out rushed the priest, barefooted and ragged, and himself opening a yellow umbrella, cried out as the attendants of a mandarin do when ordering the people to stand back. He then approached the official, and made as though he were jesting at him; at which the latter was extremely indignant, and bade his servants drive the priest away. The priest moved off with the servants after him, and in another moment had thrown down his yellow umbrella, which split into a number of pieces, each piece changing immediately into a falcon, and flying about in all directions. The umbrella handle became a huge serpent,

---

[1] See No. CXXXI., note 2.

with red scales and glaring eyes; and then the party
would have turned and fled, but that one of them declared it was only an optical delusion, and that the
creature couldn't do any hurt. The speaker accordingly
seized a knife and rushed at the serpent, which forthwith
opened its mouth and swallowed its assailant whole. In
a terrible fright the servants crowded round their master
and hurried him away, not stopping to draw breath until
they were fully a mile off. By-and-by several of them
stealthily returned to see what was going on; and, on
entering the temple, they found that both priest and
serpent had disappeared. But from an old ash-tree hard
by they heard a sound proceeding,—a sound, as it were,
of a donkey panting; and at first they were afraid to go
near, though after a while they ventured to peep through
a hole in the tree, which was an old hollow trunk; and
there, jammed hard and fast with his head downwards,
was the rash assailant of the serpent. It being quite
impossible to drag him out, they began at once to cut
the tree away; but by the time they had set him free he
was already perfectly unconscious. However, he ultimately came round and was carried home; but from
this day the priest was never seen again.[2]

---

[2] The story is intended as a satire on those puffed-up dignitaries
who cannot even go to a picnic without all the retinue belonging to
their particular rank. See No. LVI., note 5.

CXXXVII.

FEASTING THE RULER OF PURGATORY.

At Ching-hai there lived a young man, named Shao, whose family was very poor. On the occasion of his mother completing her cycle,[1] he arranged a quantity of meat-offerings and wine on a table in the court-yard, and proceeded to invoke the Gods in the usual manner; but when he rose from his knees, lo and behold! all the meat and wine had disappeared. His mother thought this was a bad omen, and that she was not destined to enjoy a long life; however, she said nothing on the subject to her son, who was himself quite at a loss to account for what had happened. A short time afterwards the Literary Chancellor[2] arrived; and young Chao, scraping together what funds he could, went off to present himself as a candidate. On the road he met with a man who gave him such a cordial invitation to his house that he willingly accepted; and the stranger led him to a stately mansion, with towers and terraces

---

[1] See No. XXIII., note 8.

[2] The examiner for the bachelor's, or lowest, degree.

rising one above the other as far as the eye could reach. In one of the apartments was a king, sitting upon a throne, who received Shao in a very friendly manner; and, after regaling him with an excellent banquet, said, "I have to thank you for the food and drink you gave my servants that day we passed your house." Shao was greatly astonished at this remark, when the King proceeded, "I am the Ruler of Purgatory. Don't you recollect sacrificing on your mother's birthday?" The King then bestowed on Shao a packet of silver, saying, "Pray accept this in return for your kindness." Shao thanked him and retired; and in another moment the palace and its occupants had one and all vanished from his sight, leaving him alone in the midst of some tall trees. On opening his packet he found it to contain five ounces of pure gold; and, after defraying the expenses of his examination, half was still left, which he carried home and gave to his mother.

CXXXVIII.

THE PICTURE HORSE.

A CERTAIN Mr. Ts'ui, of Lin-ch'ing, was too poor to keep his garden walls in repair, and used often to find a strange horse lying down on the grass inside. It was a black horse marked with white, and having a scrubby tail, which looked as if the end had been burnt off;[1] and, though always driven away, would still return to the same spot. Now Mr. Ts'ui had a friend, who was holding an appointment in Shansi; and though he had frequently felt desirous of paying him a visit, he had no means of travelling so far. Accordingly, he one day caught the strange horse and, putting a saddle on its back, rode away, telling his servants that if the owner of the horse should appear, he was to inform him where the animal was to be found. The horse started off at a very rapid pace, and, in a short time, they were thirty or forty miles from home; but at night it did not seem to care for its food, so the next day Mr. Ts'ui, who thought perhaps illness might be the cause, held the

---

[1] The Chinese never cut the tails of their horses or mules.

horse in, and would not let it gallop so fast. However, the animal did not seem to approve of this, and
kicked and foamed until at length Mr. Ts'ui let it go at
the same old pace ; and by mid-day he had reached his
destination. As he rode into the town, the people
were astonished to hear of the marvellous journey just
accomplished, and the Prince[2] sent to say he should
like to buy the horse. Mr. Ts'ui, fearing that the real
owner might come forward, was compelled to refuse this
offer ; but when, after six months had elapsed, no inquiries had been made, he agreed to accept eight
hundred ounces of silver, and handed over the horse to
the Prince. He then bought himself a good mule, and
returned home. Subsequently, the Prince had occasion
to use the horse for some important business at Lin-
ch'ing ; and when there it took the opportunity to run
away. The officer in charge pursued it right up to the
house of a Mr. Tsêng, who lived next door to a Mr.
Ts'ui, and saw it run in and disappear. Thereupon he
called upon Mr. Tsêng to restore it to him ; and, on
the latter declaring he had never even seen the animal,
the officer walked into his private apartments, where he
found, hanging on the wall, a picture of a horse, by
Tzŭ-ang,[3] exactly like the one he was in search of, and
with part of the tail burnt away by a joss-stick. It
was now clear that the Prince's horse was a supernatural creature ; but the officer, being afraid to go back

---

[2] One of the feudal Governors of by-gone days.
[3] A Chinese Landseer.

without it, would have prosecuted Mr. Tsêng, had not Ts'ui, whose eight hundred ounces of silver had since increased to something like ten thousand, stepped in and paid back the original purchase-money. Mr. Tsêng was exceedingly grateful to him for this act of kindness, ignorant, as he was, of the previous sale of the horse by Ts'ui to the Prince.

CXXXIX.

THE BUTTERFLY'S REVENGE.

MR. WANG, of Ch'ang-shan, was in the habit, when a District Magistrate, of commuting the fines and penalties of the Penal Code, inflicted on the various prisoners, for a corresponding number of butterflies. These he would let go all at once in the court, rejoicing to see them fluttering hither and thither, like so many tinsel snippings borne about by the breeze. One night he dreamt that a young lady, dressed in gay-coloured clothes, appeared to him and said, "Your cruel practice has brought many of my sisters to an untimely end, and now you shall pay the penalty of thus gratifying your tastes." The young lady then changed into a butterfly and flew away. Next day, the magistrate was sitting alone, over a cup of wine, when it was announced to him that the censor was at the door; and out he ran at once to receive His Excellency, with a white flower, that some of his women had put in his official hat, still sticking there. His Excellency was very angry at what he deemed a piece of disrespect to himself; and, after severely censuring Mr. Wang, turned round and went away. Thenceforward no more penalties were commuted for butterflies.

.

CXL.

THE DOCTOR.

A CERTAIN poor man, named Chang, who lived at I,
fell in one day with a Taoist priest. The latter was
highly skilled in the science of physiognomy;[1] and,
after looking at Chang's features, said to him, "You
would make your fortune as a doctor." "Alas!"
replied Chang, "I can barely read and write; how
then could I follow such a calling as that." "And
where, you simple fellow," asked the priest, "is the
necessity for a doctor to be a scholar? You just try,
that's all." Thereupon Chang returned home; and,
being very poor, he simply collected a few of the com-
monest prescriptions, and set up a small stall with a
handful of fishes' teeth and some dry honeycomb from
a wasp's nest,[2] hoping thus to earn, by his tongue,
enough to keep body and soul together, to which, how-

---

[1] Advertisements of these professors of physiognomy are to be
seen in every Chinese city.
[2] In order to make some show for the public eye.

'

ever, no one paid any particular attention. Now it chanced that just then the Governor of Ch'ing-chou was suffering from a bad cough, and had given orders to his subordinates to send to him the most skilful doctors in their respective districts; and the magistrate of I, which was an out-of-the-way mountainous district, being unable to lay his hands on any one whom he could send in, gave orders to the beadle[3] to do the best he could under the circumstances. Accordingly, Chang was nominated by the people, and the magistrate put his name down to go in to the Governor. When Chang heard of his appointment, he happened to be suffering himself from a bad attack of bronchitis, which he was quite unable to cure, and he begged, therefore, to be excused; but the magistrate would not hear of this, and forwarded him at once in charge of some constables. While crossing the hills, he became very thirsty, and went into a village to ask for a drink of water; but water there was worth its weight in jade, and no one would give him any. By-and-by he saw an old woman washing a quantity of vegetables in a scanty supply of water which was, consequently, very thick and muddy; and, being unable to bear his thirst any longer, he obtained this and drank it up. Shortly afterwards he found that his cough was quite cured, and then it occurred to him that he had hit upon a capital remedy. When he reached the city, he learned that a great many doctors had already tried their hand upon the patient,

---

[3] See No. LXIV., note 2.

U 2

but without success; so asking for a private room in which to prepare his medicines, he obtained from the town some bunches of bishop-wort, and proceeded to wash them as the old woman had done. He then took the dirty water, and gave a dose of it to the Governor, who was immediately and permanently relieved. The patient was overjoyed; and, besides making Chang a handsome present, gave him a certificate written in golden characters, in consequence of which his fame spread far and wide;[4] and of the numerous cases he subsequently undertook, in not a single instance did he fail to effect a cure. One day, however, a patient came to him, complaining of a violent chill; and Chang, who happened to be tipsy at the time, treated him by mistake for remittent fever. When he got sober, he became aware of what he had done; but he said nothing to anybody about it, and three days afterwards the same patient waited upon him with all kinds of presents to thank him for a rapid recovery. Such cases as this were by no means rare with him; and soon he got so rich

---

[4] A doctor of any repute generally has large numbers of such certificates, generally engraved on wood, hanging before and about his front door. When I was stationed at Swatow, the writer at Her Majesty's Consulate presented one to Dr. E. J. Scott, the resident medical practitioner, who had cured him of opium smoking. It bore two principal characters, "Miraculous Indeed!" accompanied by a few remarks, in a smaller sized character, laudatory of Dr. Scott's professional skill. Banners, with graceful inscriptions written upon them, are frequently presented by Chinese passengers to the captains of coasting steamers who may have brought them safely through bad weather.

that he would not attend when summoned to visit a sick
person, unless the summons was accompanied by a
heavy fee and a comfortable chair to ride in.[5]

---

[5] The story is intended as a satire upon Chinese doctors
generally, whose ranks are recruited from the swarms of half-
educated candidates who have been rejected at the great competitive examinations, medical diplomas being quite unknown in
China. Doctors' fees are, by a pleasant fiction, called "horse-
money;" and all prescriptions are made up by the local apothecary,
never by the physician himself.

CXLI.

SNOW IN SUMMER.

On the 6th day of the 7th moon[1] of the year Ting-Hai (1647) there was a heavy fall of snow at Soochow. The people were in a great state of consternation at this, and went off to the temple of the Great Prince[2] to pray. Then the spirit moved one of them to say, "You now address me as *Your Honour*. Make it *Your Excellency*, and, though I am but a lesser deity, it may be well worth your while to do so." Thereupon the people began to use the latter term, and the snow stopped at once; from which I infer that flattery is just as pleasant to divine as to mortal ears.[3]

---

[1] This would be exactly at the hottest season.

[2] The *Jupiter Pluvius* of the neighbourhood.

[3] A sneer at the superstitious custom of praying for good or bad weather, which obtains in China from the Son of Heaven himself down to the lowest agriculturist whose interests are involved. Droughts, floods, famines, and pestilences, are alike set down to the anger of Heaven, to be appeased only by prayer and repentance.

CXLII.

PLANCHETTE.[1]

AT Ch'ang-shan there lived a man, named Wang Jui-t'ing, who understood the art of planchette. He

---

[1] Planchette was in full swing in China at the date of the composition of these stories, more than 200 years ago, and remains so at the present day. The character *chi*, used here and elsewhere for Planchette, is defined in the *Shuo Wên*, a Chinese dictionary, published A.D. 100, "to inquire by divination on doubtful topics," no mention being made of the particular manner in which responses are obtained. For the purpose of writing from personal experience, I recently attended a *séance* at a temple in Amoy, and witnessed the whole performance. After much delay, I was requested to write on a slip of paper " any question I might have to put to the God ; " and, accordingly, I took a pencil and wrote down, "A humble suppliant ventures to inquire if he will win the Manila lottery." This question was then placed upon the altar, at the feet of the God ; and shortly afterwards two respectable-looking Chinamen, not priests, approached a small table covered with sand, and each seized one arm of a forked piece of wood, at the fork of which was a stumpy end, at right angles to the plane of the arms. Immediately the attendants began burning quantities of joss-paper, while the two performers whirled the instrument round and round at a rapid rate, its vertical point being all the time pressed down upon the table of sand. All of a sudden the whirling movement stopped, and the point of the instrument rapidly traced a character in the sand, which was at once identified by several of the bystanders, and

called himself a disciple of Lü Tung-pin,[2] and some one said he was probably that worthy's crane. At his *séances* the subjects were always literary—essays, poetry, and so on. The well-known scholar, Li Chih, thought very highly of him, and availed himself of his aid on more than one occasion ; so that by degrees the literati generally also patronized him. His responses to questions of doubt or difficulty were remarkable for their reasonableness ; matters of mere good or bad fortune he did not care to enter into. In 1631, just after the examination at Chi-nan, a number of the candidates requested Mr. Wang to tell them how they would stand on the list ; and, after having examined their essays, he proceeded to

---

forthwith copied down by a clerk in attendance. The whirling movement was then continued until a similar pause was made and another character appeared ; and so on, until I had four lines of correctly-rhymed Chinese verse, each line consisting of seven characters. The following is an almost word-for-word translation :—

"The pulse of human nature throbs from England to Cathay,
And gambling mortals ever love to swell their gains by play;
For gold in this vile world of ours is everywhere a prize—
A thousand taels shall meet the prayer that on this altar lies."

As the question is not concealed from view, all that is necessary for such a hollow deception is a quick-witted versifier who can put together a poetical response *stans pede in uno*. But in such matters the unlettered masses of China are easily outwitted, and are a profitable source of income to the more astute of their fellow-countrymen.

[2] An official who flourished in the eighth century of our era, and who, for his devotion to the Taoist religion, was subsequently canonized as one of the Eight Immortals. He is generally represented as riding on a crane.

pass his opinion on their merits.[3]   Among the rest there
happened to be one who was very intimate with another
candidate, not present, whose name was Li Pien ; and
who, being an enthusiastic student and a deep thinker,
was confidently expected to appear among the successful
few.   Accordingly, the friend submitted Mr. Li's essay
for inspection ; and in a few minutes two characters
appeared on the sand—namely, " Number one." After
a short interval this sentence followed :—" The decision
given just now had reference to Mr. Li's essay simply as
an essay.   Mr. Li's destiny is darkly obscured, and he
will suffer accordingly.   It is strange, indeed, that a man's
literary powers and his destiny should thus be out of
harmony.[4]   Surely the Examiner will judge of him by his
essay ;—but stay : I will go and see how matters stand."
Another pause ensued, and then these words were written
down :—" I have been over to the Examiner's yamên,
and have found a pretty state of things going on ; instead of reading the candidates' papers himself, he has
handed them over to his clerks, some half-dozen illite-
rate fellows who purchased their own degrees, and who,
in their previous existence, had no status whatever,—
' hungry devils '[5] begging their bread in all directions ;
and who, after eight hundred years passed in the murky
gloom of the infernal regions, have lost all discrimi-

---

[3] That is, by means of the planchette-table.
[4] Our author was here evidently thinking of his own unlucky
fate.
[5] See No. CXXXI., note 4.

nation, like men long buried in a cave and suddenly transferred to the light of day. Among them may be one or two who have risen above their former selves, but the odds are against an essay falling into the hands of one of these." The young men then begged to know if there was any method by which such an evil might be counteracted ; to which the planchette replied that there was, but, as it was universally understood, there was no occasion for asking the question. Thereupon they went off and told Mr. Li, who was so much distressed at the prediction that he submitted his essay to His Excellency Sun Tzŭ-mei, one of the finest scholars of the day. This gentleman examined it, and was so pleased with its literary merit that he told Li he was quite sure to pass, and the latter thought no more about the planchette prophecy. However, when the list came out, there he was down in the fourth class ; and this so much disconcerted His Excellency Mr. Sun, that he went carefully through the essay again for fear lest any blemishes might have escaped his attention. Then he cried out, " Well, I have always thought this Examiner to be a scholar ; he can never have made such a mistake as this ; it must be the fault of some of his drunken assistants, who don't know the mere rudiments of composition." This fulfilment of the prophecy raised Mr. Wang very high in the estimation of the candidates, who forthwith went and burned incense and invoked the spirit of the planchette, which at once replied in the following terms :—" Let not Mr. Li be disheartened by temporary failure. Let him rather strive to improve himself still further, and next year he may be among the first on the list." Li carried out these injunctions ; and after a time the story reached the ears of the Examiner, who gratified Li by making a public acknowledgment that there had been some miscarriage of justice at the examination ; and the following year he was passed high up on the list.[6]

---

[6] See No. LXXV., note 2.

CXLIII.

FRIENDSHIP WITH FOXES.

A CERTAIN man had an enormous stack of straw, as big as a hill, in which his servants, taking what was daily required for use, had made quite a hole. In this hole a fox fixed his abode, and would often shew himself to the master of the house under the form of an old man. One day the latter invited the master to walk into the cave, which he at first declined, but accepted on being pressed by the fox; and when he got inside, lo! he saw a long suite of handsome apartments. They then sat down, and exquisitely perfumed tea and wine were brought; but the place was so gloomy that there was no difference between night and day. By-and-by, the entertainment being over, the guest took his leave; and on looking back the beautiful rooms and their contents had all disappeared. The old man himself was in the habit of going away in the evening and returning with the first streaks of morning; and as no one was able to follow him, the master of the house asked him one day whither he went. To this he replied that a friend invited him to take wine; and then the master begged to be allowed to accompany him, a proposal to which the old man very reluctantly consented. However, he seized the master by the arm, and away they went as though riding on the wings of the wind; and, in about the time it takes to cook a pot of millet, they reached a city, and walked into a restaurant, where there were a number of people drinking together and making a great noise. The old man led his companion to a gallery above, from which they could look down on the feasters below; and he himself went down and brought away from the tables all kinds of nice food and wine, without appearing to be seen or noticed by any of the company. After awhile a man dressed in red garments came forward and laid upon the table some dishes of cumquats;[1] and the master at once requested the old man to go down and get him some of these. "Ah," replied the latter, "that is an upright man: I cannot approach him." Thereupon the master said to himself, "By thus seeking the companionship of a fox, I then am deflected from the true course. Henceforth I, too, will be an upright man." No sooner had he formed this resolution, than he suddenly lost all control over his body, and fell from the gallery down among the revellers below. These gentlemen were much astonished by his unexpected descent; and he himself, looking up, saw there was no

---

[1] Literally, "golden oranges." These are skilfully preserved by the Cantonese, and form a delicious sweetmeat for dessert.

gallery to the house, but only a large beam upon which he had been sitting. He now detailed the whole of the circumstances, and those present made up a purse for him to pay his travelling expenses; for he was at Yü-t'ai —one thousand *li* from home.

CXLIV.

THE GREAT RAT.

DURING the reign of the Emperor Wan Li,[1] the palace was troubled by the presence of a huge rat, quite as big as a cat, which ate up all the cats that were set to catch it. Just then it chanced that among the tribute offerings sent by some foreign State was a lion-cat, as white as snow. This cat was accordingly put into the room where the rat usually appeared; and, the door being closely shut, a secret watch was kept. By-and-by the rat came out of its hole and rushed at the cat, which turned and fled, finally jumping up on the table. The rat followed, upon which the cat jumped down; and thus they went on up and down for some time. Those who were watching said the cat was afraid and of no use; however, in a little while the rat began to jump less briskly, and soon after squatted down out of breath. Then the cat rushed at it, and, seizing the rat by the back of the neck, shook and shook while its victim squeaked and

---

[1] A.D. 1573–1620, the epoch of the most celebrated "blue china."

squeaked, until life was extinct. Thus they knew that the cat was not afraid, but merely waited for its adversary to be fatigued, fleeing when pursued and itself pursuing the fleeing rat. Truly, many a bad swordsman may be compared with that rat!

CXLV.

WOLVES.

I.—A CERTAIN village butcher, who had bought some meat at market and was returning home in the evening, suddenly came across a wolf, which followed him closely, its mouth watering at the sight of what he was carrying. The butcher drew his knife and drove the animal off; and then reflecting that his meat was the attraction, he determined to hang it up in a tree and fetch it the next morning. This he accordingly did, and the wolf followed him no further; but when he went at daylight to recover his property, he saw something hanging up in the tree resembling a human corpse. It turned out to be the wolf, which, in its efforts to get· at the meat, had been caught on the meat-hook like a fish; and as the skin of a wolf was just then worth ten ounces of silver, the butcher found himself possessed of quite a little capital. Here we have a laughable instance of the result of "climbing trees to catch fish." [1]

II.—A butcher, while travelling along at night, was sore pressed by a wolf, and took refuge in an old mat

---

[1] A satirical remark of Mencius (Book I.), used by the sage when combating the visionary projects of a monarch of antiquity.

shed which had been put up for the watchman of the crops. There he lay, while the wolf sniffed at him from outside, and at length thrust in one of its paws from underneath. This the butcher seized hold of at once, and held it firmly, so that the wolf couldn't stir; and then, having no other weapon at hand, he took a small knife he had with him and slit the skin underneath the wolf's paw. He now proceeded to blow into it, as butchers blow into pork;[2] and after vigorously blowing for some time, he found that the wolf had ceased to struggle; upon which he went outside and saw the animal lying on the ground, swelled up to the size of a cow, and unable to bend its legs or close its open mouth. Thereupon he threw it across his shoulders and carried it off home. However, such a feat as this could only be accomplished by a butcher.

[2] This disgusting process is too frequently performed by native butchers at the present day, in order to give their meat a more tempting appearance. Water is also blown in through a tube, to make it heavier; and inexperienced housekeepers are often astonished to find how light ducks and geese become after being cooked, not knowing that the fraudulent poulterer had previously stuffed their throats as full as possible of sand.

CXLVI.

SINGULAR VERDICT.

A SERVANT in the employ of a Mr. Sun was sleeping alone one night, when all on a sudden he was arrested and carried before the tribunal of the Ruler of Purgatory. "This is not the right man," cried his Majesty, and immediately sent him back. However, after this the servant was afraid to sleep on that bed again, and took up his quarters elsewhere. But another servant, named Kuo Ngan, seeing the vacant place, went and occupied it. A third servant, named Li Lu, who had an old standing grudge against the first, stole up to the bed that same night with a knife in his hand, and killed Kuo Ngan[1] in mistake for his enemy. Kuo's father at once brought the case before the magistrate of the place, pleading that the murdered man was his only son on whom he depended for his living; and the magistrate decided that Kuo was to take Li Lu in the place of his dead son, much to the discomfiture of the old man. Truly the descent of the first servant into Purgatory was not so marvellous as the magistrate's decision!

---

[1] This was the man whose destiny it was really to die just then, and appear before the Ruler of Purgatory.

CXLVII.

THE GRATEFUL DOG.

A CERTAIN trader who had been doing business at Wu-hu and was returning home with the large profits he had made, saw on the river bank a butcher tying up a dog.[1] He bought the animal for much more than its value, and carried it along with him in his boat. Now the boatman had formerly been a bandit; and, tempted by his passenger's wealth, ran the boat among the rushes, and, drawing a knife, prepared to slay him. The trader begged the man to leave him a whole skin;[2] so the boatman wrapped him up in a carpet and threw him into the river. The dog, on seeing what was done, whined piteously, and jumping into the river, seized the bundle with his teeth and did its best to keep the trader above water until at length a shallow spot was reached. The animal then succeeded by continuous barking in attracting the attention of some people on the bank, and

---

[1] The city of Canton boasts several "cat and dog" restaurants; but the consumption of this kind of food is much less universal than is generally supposed.

[2] Not in our sense of the term. It was not death, but decapitation, or even mutilation, from which the trader begged to be spared. See No. LXXII., note 5.

they hauled the bundle out of the river, and released the trader who was still alive. The latter asked to be taken back to Wu-hu where he might look out for the robber boatman; but just as he was about to start, lo! the dog was missing. The trader was much distressed at this; and after spending some days at Wu-hu without being able to find, among the forest of masts collected there, the particular boat he wanted, he was on the point of returning home with a friend, when suddenly the dog reappeared and seemed by its barking to invite its master to follow in a certain direction. This the trader did, until at length the dog jumped on a boat and seized one of the boatmen by the leg. No beating could make the animal let go; and on looking closely at the man, the trader saw he was the identical boatman who had robbed and tried to murder him. He had changed his clothes and also his boat, so that at first he was not recognisable; he was now, however, arrested, and the whole of the money was found in his boat. To think that a dog could show gratitude like that! Truly there are not a few persons who would be put to shame by that faithful animal.[3]

---

[3] The Chinese dog is usually an ill-fed, barking cur, without one redeeming trait in its character. Valued as a guardian of house and property, this animal does not hold the same social position as with us; its very name is a by-word of reproach; and the people of Tonquin explain their filthy custom of blackening the teeth on the ground that a dog's teeth are white.

CXLVIII.

THE GREAT TEST.

BEFORE Mr. Yang Ta-hung[1] was known to fame, he had already acquired some reputation as a scholar in his own part of the country, and felt convinced himself that his was to be no mean destiny. When the list of successful candidates at the examination was brought to where he lived, he was in the middle of dinner, and rushed out with his mouth full to ask if his name was there or not; and on hearing that it was not, he experienced such a revulsion of feeling that what he then swallowed stuck fast like a lump in his chest and made him very ill. His friends tried to appease him by advising him to try at the further examination of the rejected, and when he urged that he had no money,

---

[1] A celebrated scholar and statesman, who flourished towards the close of the Ming dynasty, and distinguished himself by his impeachment of the powerful eunuch, Wei Chung-hsien,—a dangerous step to take in those eunuch-ridden times.

they subscribed ten ounces of silver and started him on
his way.

That night he dreamt that a man appeared to him
and said, "Ahead of you there is one who can cure your
complaint: beseech him to aid you." The man then
added—

"A tune on the flute 'neath the riverside willow:
Oh, show no regret when 'tis cast to the billow!"

Next day, Mr. Yang actually met a Taoist priest sitting
beneath a willow tree; and, making him a bow, asked
him to prescribe for his malady. "You have come to the
wrong person," replied the priest, smiling; "I cannot cure
diseases; but had you asked me for a tune on the flute,
I could have possibly helped you." Then Mr. Yang
knew that his dream was being fulfilled; and going down
on his knees offered the priest all the money he had.
The priest took it, but immediately threw it into the
river, at which Mr. Yang, thinking how hardly he had
come by this money, was moved to express his regret.
"Aha!" cried the priest at this; "so you are not
indifferent, eh? You'll find your money all safe on
the bank." There indeed Mr. Yang found it, at which
he was so much astonished that he addressed the priest
as though he had been an angel. "I am no angel,"
said the priest, "but here comes one;" whereupon Mr.
Yang looked behind him, and the priest seized the op·
portunity to give him a slap on the back, crying out at
the same time, "You worldly-minded fellow!" This

blow brought up the lump of food that had stuck in his chest, and he felt better at once ; but when he looked round the priest had disappeared.[2]

---

[2] Mr. Yang was a man of tried virtue, and had he been able to tolerate *oculo irretorto*, the loss of his money, the priest would have given him, not merely a cure for the bodily ailment under which he was suffering, but a knowledge of those means by which he might have obtained the salvation of his soul, and have enrolled himself among the ranks of the Taoist Immortals. " To those, however," remarks the commentator, "who lament that Mr. Yang was too worldly-minded to secure this great prize, I reply, ' Better one more good man on earth, than an extra angel in heaven.' "

CXLIX.

THE ALCHEMIST.[1]

AT Ch'ang-ngan there lived a scholar named Chia T'zŭ-lung, who one day noticed a very refined-looking stranger; and, on making inquiries about him, learnt that he was a Mr. Chên, who had taken lodgings hard by. Accordingly, next day Chia called and sent in his card, but did not see Chên, who happened to be out at the time. The same thing occurred thrice; and at length Chia engaged some one to watch and let him know when Mr. Chên was at home. However, even then the latter would not come forth to receive his guest, and Chia had to go in and rout him out. The two now entered into conversation, and soon became mutually charmed with each other; and by-and-by Chia sent off a servant to bring wine from a neighbouring wine-shop. Mr. Chên proved himself a pleasant boon companion, and when the wine was nearly finished, he went to a box, and took from it some wine-cups and a large and beautiful jade

---

[1] Alchemy was widely cultivated in China during the Han dynasty by priests of the Taoist religion, but all traces of it have now long since disappeared.

tankard, into the latter of which he poured a single cup of wine, and lo! it was filled to the brim. They then proceeded to help themselves from the tankard; but however much they took out, the contents never seemed to diminish. Chia was astonished at this, and begged Mr. Chên to tell him how it was done. "Ah," replied Mr. Chên, "I tried to avoid making your acquaintance solely because of your one bad quality—avarice. The art I practise is a secret known to the Immortals only: how can I divulge it to you?" "You do me wrong," rejoined Chia, "in thus attributing avarice to me. The avaricious, indeed, are always poor." Mr. Chên laughed, and they separated for that day; but from that time they were constantly together, and all ceremony was laid aside between them. Whenever Chia wanted money, Mr. Chên would bring out a black stone, and, muttering a charm, would rub it on a tile or a brick, which was forthwith changed into a lump of silver. This silver he would give to Chia, and it was always just as much as he actually required, neither more nor less; and if ever the latter asked for more, Mr. Chên would rally him on the subject of avarice. Finally, Chia determined to try and get possession of this stone; and one day, when Mr. Chên was sleeping off the fumes of a drinking-bout, he tried to extract it from his clothes. However, Chên detected him at once, and declared that they could be friends no more, and next day he left the place altogether. About a year afterwards Chia was one day wandering by the river-bank, when he saw a handsome-looking stone, marvellously like that in the possession of

Mr. Chên; and he picked it up at once and carried it home with him. A few days passed away, and suddenly Mr. Chên presented himself at Chia's house, and explained that the stone in question possessed the property of changing anything into gold, and had been bestowed upon him long before by a certain Taoist priest, whom he had followed as a disciple. " Alas ! " added he, " I got tipsy and lost it; but divination told me where it was, and if you will now restore it to me, I shall take care to repay your kindness." "You have divined rightly," replied Chia ; " the stone is with me ; but recollect, if you please, that the indigent Kuan Chung[2] shared the wealth of his friend Pao Shu." At this hint Mr. Chên said he would give Chia one hundred ounces of silver; to which the latter replied that one hundred ounces was a fair offer, but that he would far sooner have Mr. Chên teach him the formula to utter when rubbing the stone on anything, so as just to try the thing once himself. Mr. Chên was afraid to do this; whereupon Chia cried out, "You are an Immortal yourself; you must know well enough that I would never deceive a friend." So Mr. Chên was prevailed upon to teach him the formula, and then Chia would have tried the art upon the immense stone washing-block[3] which was lying near at hand, had not Mr. Chên seized his arm and begged him not to do any thing so outrageous. Chia then picked up half a

---

[2] See No. XXII., note 1.

[3] These are used, together with a heavy wooden *bâton*, by the Chinese washerman, the effect being most disastrous to a European wardrobe.

brick and laid it on the washing-block, saying to Mr. Chên, "This little piece is not too much, surely?" Accordingly, Mr. Chên relaxed his hold and let Chia proceed; which he did by promptly ignoring the half brick and quickly rubbing the stone on the washing-block. Mr. Chên turned pale when he saw him do this, and made a dash forward to get hold of the stone; but it was too late, the washing-block was already a solid mass of silver, and Chia quietly handed him back the stone. "Alas! alas!" cried Mr. Chên, in despair, "what is to be done now? For having thus irregularly conferred wealth upon a mortal,[4] Heaven will surely punish me. Oh, if you would save me, give away one hundred coffins[5] and one hundred suits of wadded clothes." "My friend," replied Chia, "my object in getting money was not to hoard it up like a miser." Mr. Chên was delighted at this; and during the next three years Chia engaged in trade, taking care to be all the time fulfilling his promise to Mr. Chên. At the expiration of that time Mr. Chên himself reappeared, and, grasping Chia's hand, said to him, "Trustworthy and noble friend, when we last parted the Spirit of Happiness impeached me before God,[6] and my name was erased from the list of

---

[4] For thus interfering with the appointments of Destiny.

[5] To provide coffins for poor people has ever been regarded as an act of transcendent merit. The tornado at Canton, in April, 1878, in which several thousand lives were lost, afforded an admirable opportunity for the exercise of this form of charity—an opportunity which was very largely availed of by the benevolent.

[6] For usurping its prerogative by allowing Chia to obtain unauthorized wealth.

angels. But now that you have carried out my request, that sentence has accordingly been rescinded. Go on as you have begun, without ceasing." Chia asked Mr. Chên what office he filled in heaven; to which the latter replied that he was only a fox, who, by a sinless life, had finally attained to that clear perception of the Truth which leads to immortality. Wine was then brought, and the two friends enjoyed themselves together as of old; and even when Chia had passed the age of ninety years, that fox still used to visit him from time to time.

CL.

RAISING THE DEAD.

MR. T'ANG P'ING, who took the highest degree in the year 1661, was suffering from a protracted illness, when suddenly he felt, as it were, a warm glow rising from his extremities upwards. By the time it had reached his knees, his feet were perfectly numb and without sensation; and before long his knees and the lower part of his body were similarly affected. Gradually this glow worked its way up until it attacked the heart,[1] and then some painful moments ensued. Every single incident of Mr. T'ang's life from his boyhood upwards, no matter how trivial, seemed to surge through his mind, borne along on the tide of his heart's blood. At the revival of any virtuous act of his, he experienced a delicious feeling of peace and calm; but when any wicked deed passed before his mind, a painful disturbance took place within him, like oil boiling and fretting in a cauldron. He was quite unable to describe the pangs he suffered; however, he mentioned that he could recollect having stolen, when only seven or eight years

---

[1] See No. XIV., note 5.

old, some young birds from their nest, and having killed them; and for this alone, he said, boiling blood rushed through his heart during the space of an ordinary meal-time. Then when all the acts of his life had passed one after another in panorama before him, the warm glow proceeded up his throat, and, entering the brain, issued out at the top of his head like smoke from a chimney. By-and-by Mr. T'ang's soul escaped from his body by the same aperture, and wandered far away, forgetting all about the tenement it had left behind. Just at that moment a huge giant came along, and, seizing the soul, thrust it into his sleeve, where it remained cramped and confined, huddled up with a crowd of others, until existence was almost unbearable. Suddenly Mr. T'ang reflected that Buddha alone could save him from this horrible state, and forthwith he began to call upon his holy name.[2] At the third or fourth invocation he fell out of the giant's sleeve, whereupon the latter picked him up and put him back; but this happened several times, and at length the giant, wearied of picking him up, let him lie where he was. The soul lay there for some time, not knowing in which direction to proceed; however, it soon recollected that the land of Buddha was in the west, and westwards accordingly it began to shape its course. In a little while the soul came upon a Buddhist priest sitting by the roadside, and, hastening forwards, respectfully inquired of him which was the right way. "The record of life and death for scholars,"

---

[2] See No. LIV., note 2.

replied the priest, "is in the hands of Wên-ch'ang[3] and
Confucius; any application must receive the consent of
both." The priest then directed Mr. T'ang on his way,
and the latter journeyed along until he reached a
Confucian temple, in which the Sage was sitting with
his face to the south.[4] On hearing his business, Confucius referred him on to Wên-ch'ang; and, proceeding
onwards in the direction indicated, Mr. T'ang by-and-by
arrived at what seemed to be the palace of a king,
within which sat Wên-ch'ang, precisely as we depict him
on earth. "You are an upright man," replied the God,
in reply to Mr. T'ang's prayer, "and are certainly
entitled to a longer span of life; but by this time
your mortal body has become decomposed, and unless
you can secure the assistance of P'u-sa,[5] I can give you
no aid." So Mr. T'ang set off, once more, and hurried
along until he came to a magnificent shrine standing in a
thick grove of tall bamboos; and, entering in, he stood
in the presence of the God, on whose head was the
ushnisha,[6] whose golden face was round like the full
moon, and at whose side was a green willow-branch
bending gracefully over the lip of a vase. Humbly Mr.
T'ang prostrated himself on the ground, and repeated
what Wên-ch'ang had said to him; but P'u-sa seemed to
think it would be impossible to grant his request, until

---

[3] The God of Literature.

[4] See No. LXXVII., note 1.

[5] See No. XXVI., note 5.

[6] A fleshy protuberance on the head, which is the distinguishing
mark of a Buddha.

one of the Lohans[7] who stood by cried out, "O God, Thou canst perform this miracle: take earth and make his flesh; take a sprig of willow and make his bones." Thereupon P'u-sa broke off a piece from the willow-branch in the vase beside him; and, pouring a little of the water upon the ground, he made clay, and, casting the whole over Mr. T'ang's soul, bade an attendant lead the body back to the place where his coffin was. At that instant Mr. T'ang's family heard a groan proceeding from within his coffin, and, on rushing to it and helping out the lately-deceased man, they found he had quite recovered. He had then been dead seven days.

---

[7] The eighteen personal disciples of Shâkyamuni Buddha. Sixteen of these are Hindoos, which number was subsequently increased by the addition of two Chinese Buddhists.

CLI.

FENG-SHUI.[1]

AT I-chow there lived a high official named Sung, whose family were all ardent supporters of Fêng-Shui; so much so, that even the women-folk read books[2] on the subject, and understood the principles of the science. When Mr. Sung died, his two sons set up separate establishments,[3] and each invited to his own house geomancers from far and near, who had any reputation

[1] Literally, "wind and water," or that which cannot be seen and that which cannot be grasped. I have explained the term in my *Chinese Sketches*, p. 143, as "a system of geomancy, by the *science* of which it is possible to determine the desirability of sites,—whether of tombs, houses, or cities, from the configuration of such natural objects as rivers, trees, and hills, and to foretell with certainty the fortunes of any family, community, or individual, according to the spot selected; by the *art* of which it is in the power of the geomancer to counteract evil influences by good ones, to transform straight and noxious outlines into undulating and propitious curves, and rescue whole districts from the devastations of flood or pestilence."

[2] As a rule, only the daughters of wealthy families receive any education to speak of.

[3] A reprehensible proceeding in the eyes of all respectable Chinese, both from a moral and a practical point of view; "for when brothers fall out," says the proverb, "strangers get an advantage over them."

in their art, to select a spot for the dead man's grave.
By degrees, they had collected together as many as a
hundred a-piece, and every day they would scour the
country round, each at the head of his own particular
regiment. After about a month of this work, both sides
had fixed upon a suitable position for the grave; and
the geomancers engaged by one brother, declared that
if their spot was selected he would certainly some day
be made a marquis, while the other brother was similarly
informed, by his geomancers, that by adopting their
choice he would infallibly rise to the rank of Secretary
of State. Thus, neither brother would give way to the
other, but each set about making the grave in his own
particular place,—pitching marquees, and arranging
banners, and making all necessary preparations for the
funeral. Then when the coffin arrived at the point where
roads branched off to the two graves, the two brothers,
each leading on his own little army of geomancers, bore
down upon it with a view to gaining possession of the
corpse. From morn till dewy eve the battle raged; and
as neither gained any advantage over the other, the
mourners and friends, who had come to witness the
ceremony of burial, stole away one by one; and the
coolies, who were carrying the coffin, after changing the
poles from one shoulder to another until they were
quite worn out, put the body down by the roadside, and
went off home. It then became necessary to make
some protection for the coffin against the wind and rain;
whereupon the elder brother immediately set about
building a hut close by, in which he purposed leaving

some of his attendants to keep guard ; but he had no
sooner begun than the younger brother followed his
example ; and when the elder built a second and third,
the younger also built a second and third ; and as this
went on for the space of three whole years, by the end of
that time the place had become quite a little village.
By-and-by, both brothers died, one directly after the
other ; and then their two wives determined to cast
to the winds the decision of each party of geomancers.
Accordingly, they went together to the two spots in
question ; and after inspecting them carefully, declared
that neither was suitable.   The next step was to jointly
engage another set of geomancers, who submitted for
their approval several different spots, and ten days had
hardly passed away before the two women had agreed
upon the position for their father-in-law's grave, which,
as the wife of the younger brother prophesied, would
surely give to the family a high military degree.   So the
body was buried, and within three years Mr. Sung's
eldest grandson, who had entered as a military cadet,
actually took the corresponding degree to a literary
master of arts.

[" Fêng-Shui," adds the great commentator I Shih-shih, "may
or may not be based upon sound principles; at any rate, to indulge
a morbid belief in it is utter folly; and thus to join issue and fight
while a coffin is relegated to the roadside, is hardly in accordance
with the doctrines of filial piety or fraternal love.   Can people
believe that mere position will improve the fortunes of their family?
At any rate, that two women should have thus quietly settled the
matter is certainly worthy of record."]

CLII.

THE LINGERING DEATH.

THERE was a man in our village who led an exceedingly disreputable life. One morning when he got up rather early, two men appeared, and led him away to the market-place, where he saw a butcher hanging up half a pig. As they approached, the two men shoved him with all their might against the dead animal, and lo! his own flesh began to blend with the pork before him, while his conductors hurried off in an opposite direction. By-and-by the butcher wanted to sell a piece of his meat; and seizing a knife, began to cut off the quantity required. At every touch of the blade our disreputable friend experienced a severe pang, which penetrated into his very marrow; and when, at length, an old man came and haggled over the weight given him, crying out for a little bit more fat, or an extra portion of lean,[1] then, as the butcher sliced away the

---

[1] Chinese tradesmen invariably begin by giving short weight in such transactions as these, partly in order to be in a position to gratify the customer by throwing in a trifle more and thus acquire a reputation for fair dealing.

pork ounce by ounce, the pain was unendurable in the extreme. By about nine o'clock the pork was all sold, and our hero went home, whereupon his family asked him what he meant by staying in bed so late.[2] He then narrated all that had taken place, and on making inquiries, they found that the pork-butcher had only just come home; besides which our friend was able to tell him every pound of meat he had sold, and every slice he had cut off. Fancy a man being put to the lingering death [3] like this before breakfast!

---

[2] It was only his soul that had left the house.
[3] See No. LVI., note 12.

CLIII.

DREAMING HONOURS.

WANG TZŬ-NGAN was a Tung-ch'ang man, and a scholar of some repute, but unfortunate at the public examinations. On one occasion, after having been up for his master's degree, his anxiety was very great; and when the time for the publication of the list drew near, he drank himself gloriously tipsy, and went and lay down on the bed. In a few moments a man rushed in, and cried out, "Sir! you have passed!" whereupon Wang jumped up, and said, "Give him ten strings of cash." [1] Wang's wife, seeing he was drunk, and wishing to keep him quiet, replied, "You go on sleeping: I've given him the money." So Wang lay down again, but before long in came another man who informed Wang that his name was among the successful candidates for the highest degree. "Why, I haven't been up for it yet;" said Wang, "how can I have passed?" "What! you don't mean to say you have forgotten the examination?" answered the man; and then Wang got up once more, and gave orders to present the informant with ten

---

[1] See No. CXXIII. note 2

strings of cash. "All right," replied his wife; "you go on sleeping: I've given him the money." Another short interval, and in burst a third messenger to say that Wang had been elected a member of the National Academy, and that two official servants had come to escort him thither. Sure enough there were the two servants bowing at the bedside, and accordingly Wang directed that they should be served with wine and meat, which his wife, smiling at his drunken nonsense, declared had been already done. Wang now bethought him that he should go out and receive the congratulations of the neighbours, and roared out several times to his official servants; but without receiving any answer. "Go to sleep," said his wife, "and wait till I have fetched them;" and after awhile the servants actually came in; whereupon Wang stamped and swore at them for being such idiots as to go away. "What! you wretched scoundrel," cried the servants, "are you cursing us in earnest, when we are only joking with you!" At this Wang's rage knew no bounds, and he set upon the men, and gave them a sound beating, knocking the hat of one off on to the ground. In the *mêlée*, he himself tumbled over, and his wife ran in to pick him up, saying, "Shame upon you, for getting so drunk as this!" "I was only punishing the servants as they deserved," replied Wang; "why do you call me drunk?" "Do you mean the old woman who cooks our rice and boils the water for your foot-bath," asked his wife, smiling, "that you talk of servants to wait upon your poverty-stricken carcase?" At this sally all the women burst out in a roar of laughter; and Wang, who was just beginning to get sober, waked up as if from _a dream,_ and knew that there was no reality in all that had taken place. However, he recollected the spot where the servant's hat had fallen off, and on going thither to look for it, lo! he beheld a tiny official hat, no larger than a wine-cup, lying there behind the door. They were all much astonished at this, and Wang himself cried out, " Formerly people were thus tricked by devils; and now foxes are playing the fool with me ! " [2]

---

[2] A common saying is "Foxes in the north; devils in the south," as illustrative of the folk-lore of these two great divisions of China.

CLIV.

THE SHE-WOLF AND THE HERD-BOYS.

Two herd-boys went up among the hills and found a wolf's lair with two little wolves in it. Seizing each of them one, they forthwith climbed two trees which stood there, at a distance of forty or fifty paces apart. Before long the old wolf came back, and, finding her cubs gone, was in a great state of distress. Just then, one of the herd-boys pinched his cub and made it squeak; whereupon the mother ran angrily towards the tree whence the sound proceeded, and tried to climb up it. At this juncture, the boy in the other tree pinched the other cub, and thereby diverted the wolf's attention in that direction. But no sooner had she reached the foot of the second tree, than the boy who had first pinched his cub did so again, and away ran the old wolf back to the tree in which her other young one was. Thus they went on time after time, until the mother was dead tired, and lay down exhausted on the ground. Then, when after some time she shewed no signs of moving, the herd-boys crept stealthily down, and found that the wolf was already stiff and cold. And truly, it is better to meet a blustering foe with his hand upon his sword-hilt, by retiring within doors, and leaving him to fret his violence away unopposed; for such is but the behaviour of brute beasts, of which men thus take advantage.

CLV.

ADULTERATION[1] PUNISHED.

At Chin-ling there lived a seller of spirits, who was in the habit of adulterating his liquor with water and a certain drug, the effect of which was that even a few cups would make the strongest-headed man as drunk as a jelly-fish.[2]   Thus his shop acquired a reputation for having a good article on sale, and by degrees he became a rich man.   One morning, on getting up, he found a fox lying drunk alongside of the spirit vat; and tying its legs together, he was about to fetch a knife, when suddenly the fox waked up, and began pleading for its life, promising in return to do anything the spirit-merchant might require.   The latter then released the animal, which instantly changed into the form of a human being.   Now, at that very time, the wife of a

---

[1] In no country in the world is adulteration more extensively practised than in China, the only formal check upon it being a religious one—the dread of punishment in the world below.

[2] The text has here a word (literally, "mud") explained to be the name of a boneless aquatic creature, which on being removed from the water lies motionless like a lump of mud.   The common term for a jelly-fish is *shui-mu,* "water-mother."

neighbour was suffering under fox influence, and this recently-transformed animal confessed to the spirit-merchant that it was he who had been troubling her. Thereupon the spirit-merchant, who knew the lady in question to be a celebrated beauty, begged his fox friend to secretly introduce him to her. After raising some objections, the fox at length consented, and conducted the spirit-merchant to a cave, where he gave him a suit of serge clothes, which he said had belonged to his late brother, and in which he told him he could easily go. The merchant put them on, and returned home, when to his great delight he observed that no one could see him, but that if he changed into his ordinary clothes everybody could see him as before. Accordingly he set off with the fox for his neighbour's house; and, when they arrived, the first thing they beheld was a charm on the wall, like a great wriggling dragon. At this the fox was greatly alarmed, and said, " That scoundrel of a priest! I can't go any farther." He then ran off home, leaving the spirit-merchant to proceed by himself. The latter walked quietly in to find that the dragon on the wall was a real one, and preparing to fly at him, so he too turned, and ran away as fast as his legs could carry him. The fact was that the family had engaged a priest to drive away the fox influence; and he, not being able to go at the moment himself, gave them this charm to stick up on the wall. The following day the priest himself came, and, arranging an altar, proceeded to exorcise the fox. All the villagers crowded round to see, and among others was the spirit-merchant, who, in the middle of the ceremony, suddenly changed colour, and hurried out of the front door, where he fell on the ground in the shape of a fox, having his clothes still hanging about his arms and legs. The bystanders would have killed him on the spot, but his wife begged them to spare him; and the priest let her take the fox home, where in a few days it died.

CLVI.

A CHINESE SOLOMON.

IN our district there lived two men, named Hu Ch'êng and Fêng Ngan, between whom there existed an old feud. The former, however, was the stronger of the two; and accordingly Fêng disguised his feelings under a specious appearance of friendship, though Hu never placed much faith in his professions. One day they were drinking together, and being both of them rather the worse for liquor, they began to brag of the various exploits they had achieved. "What care I for poverty," cried Hu, "when I can lay a hundred ounces of silver on the table at a moment's notice?" Now Fêng was well aware of the state of Hu's affairs, and did not hesitate to scout such pretensions, until Hu further informed him in perfect seriousness that the day before he had met a merchant travelling with a large sum of money and had tumbled him down a dry well by the wayside; in confirmation of which he produced several hundred ounces of silver, which really belonged to a brother-in-law on whose behalf he was managing some negotiation for the purchase of land. When they separated, Fêng went off and gave information to the magistrate of the place, who summoned Hu to answer to the charge. Hu then told the actual facts of the case, and his brother-in-law and the owner of the land in question corroborated his statement. However, on examining the dry well by letting a man down with a rope round him, lo! there was a headless corpse lying at the bottom. Hu was horrified at this, and called Heaven to witness that he was innocent; whereupon the magistrate ordered him twenty or thirty blows on the mouth for lying in the presence of such irrefragable proof, and cast him into the condemned cell, where he lay loaded with chains. Orders were issued that the corpse was not to be removed, and a notification was made to the people, calling upon the relatives of the deceased to come forward and claim the body. Next day a woman appeared, and said deceased was her husband; that his name was Ho, and that he was proceeding on business with a large sum of money about him when he was killed by Hu. The magistrate observed that possibly the body in the well might not be that of her husband, to which the woman replied that she felt sure it was; and accordingly the corpse was brought up and examined, when the woman's story was found to be correct. She herself did not go near the body, but stood at a little distance making the most doleful lamentations; until at length the magistrate said, "We have got the murderer, but the body is not complete; you go home and wait until the head has been discovered, when life shall be given for life. He then summoned Hu before him, and told him to produce the head

by the next day under penalty of severe torture; but
Hu only wandered about with the guard sent in charge
of him, crying and lamenting his fate, but finding
nothing. The instruments of torture were then produced, and preparations were made as if for torturing
Hu; however, they were not applied,[1] and finally the
magistrate sent him back to prison, saying, "I suppose
that in your hurry you didn't notice where you dropped
the head." The woman was then brought before him
again; and on learning that her relatives consisted only
of one uncle, the magistrate remarked, "A young
woman like you, left alone in the world, will hardly be
able to earn a livelihood. [Here she burst into tears
and implored the magistrate's pity.] The punishment of
the guilty man has been already decided upon, but until
we get the head, the case cannot be closed. As soon as
it is closed, the best thing you can do is to marry again.
A young woman like yourself should not be in and out
of a police-court." The woman thanked the magistrate
and retired; and the latter issued a notice to the people,
calling upon them to make a search for the head. On
the following day, a man named Wang, a fellow villager
of the deceased, reported that he had found the missing
head; and his report proving to be true, he was rewarded with 1,000 *cash*. The magistrate now summoned the woman's uncle above-mentioned, and told
him that the case was complete, but that as it involved
such an important matter as the life of a human being,

---

[1] See No. LXXIII., note 2.

there would necessarily be some delay in closing it for good and all.[2] "Meanwhile," added the magistrate, "your niece is a young woman and has no children; persuade her to marry again and so keep herself out of these troubles, and never mind what people may say."[3] The uncle at first refused to do this; upon which the magistrate was obliged to threaten him until he was ultimately forced to consent. At this, the woman appeared before the magistrate to thank him for what he had done; whereupon the latter gave out that any person who was willing to take the woman to wife was to present himself at his yamên. Immediately afterwards an application was made —— by the very man who had found the head. The magistrate then sent for the woman and asked her if she could say who was the real murderer; to which she replied that Hu Chêng had done the deed. "No!" cried the magistrate; "it was not he. It was you and this man here. [Here both began loudly to protest their innocence.] I have long known this; but, fearing to leave the smallest loophole

---

[2] There is a widespread belief that human life in China is held at a cheap rate. This may be accounted for by the fact that death is the legal punishment for many crimes not considered capital in the West; and by the severe measures that are always taken in cases of rebellion, when the innocent and guilty are often indiscriminately massacred. In times of tranquillity, however, this is not the case; and the execution of a criminal is surrounded by a number of formalities which go far to prevent the shedding of innocent blood. The *Hsi-yüan-lu* (see No. XIV., note 8) opens with the words, "There is nothing more important than human life."

[3] See No. LXVII., note 1.

for escape, I have tarried thus long in elucidating the circumstances. How [to the woman], before the corpse was removed from the well, were you so certain that it was your husband's body? *Because you already knew he was dead.* And does a trader who has several hundred ounces of silver about him dress as shabbily as your husband was dressed? And you, [to the man], how did you manage to find the head so readily? *Because you were in a hurry to marry the woman.*" The two culprits stood there as pale as death, unable to utter a word in their defence; and on the application of torture both confessed the crime. For this man, the woman's paramour, had killed her husband, curiously enough, about the time of Hu Chêng's braggart joke. Hu was accordingly released, but Fêng suffered the penalty of a false accuser; he was severely bambooed, and banished for three years. The case was thus brought to a close without the wrongful punishment of a single person.

CLVII.

THE ROC.

Two herons built their nests under one of the ornaments on the roof of a temple at Tientsin. The
accumulated dust of years in the shrine below concealed
a huge serpent, having the diameter of a washing-basin;
and whenever the heron's young were ready to fly, the
reptile proceeded to the nest and swallowed every one of
them, to the great distress of the bereaved parents. This
took place three years consecutively, and people thought
the birds would build there no more. However, the
following year they came again; and when the time was
drawing nigh for their young ones to take wing, away
they flew, and remained absent for nearly three days.
On their return, they went straight to the nest, and began
amidst much noisy chattering to feed their young ones
as usual. Just then the serpent crawled up to reach his
prey; and as he was nearing the nest the parent-birds
flew out and screamed loudly in mid-air. Immediately,
there was heard a mighty flapping of wings, and darkness
came over the face of the earth, which the astonished
spectators now perceived to be caused by a huge bird
obscuring the light of the sun. Down it swooped with

the speed of wind or falling rain, and, striking the serpent with its talons, tore its head off at a blow, bringing down at the same time several feet of the masonry of the temple. Then it flew away, the herons accompanying it as though escorting a guest. The nest too had come down, and of the two young birds one was killed by the fall; the other was taken by the priests and put in the bell tower, whither the old birds returned to feed it until thoroughly fledged, when it spread its wings and was gone.[1]

[1] This story is inserted chiefly in illustration of the fact that all countries have a record of some enormous bird such as the *roc* of the "Arabian Nights."

CLVIII

THE FAITHFUL GANDER.[1]

A SPORTSMAN of Tientsin, having snared a wild goose, was followed to his home by the gander, which flew round and round him in great distress, and only went away at nightfall. Next day, when the sportsman went out, there was the bird again; and at length it alighted quite close to his feet. He was on the point of seizing it when suddenly it stretched out its neck and disgorged a piece of pure gold; whereupon, the sportsman, understanding what the bird meant, cried out, "I see! this is to ransom your mate, eh?" Accordingly, he at once released the goose, and the two birds flew away with many expressions of their mutual joy, leaving to the sportsman nearly three ounces of pure gold. Can, then, mere birds have such feelings as these? Of all sorrows there is no sorrow like separation from those we love; and it seems that the same holds good even of dumb animals.

---

[1] See No. XXXV., note 3.

CLIX.

THE ELEPHANTS AND THE LION.

A HUNTSMAN of Kuang-si, who was out on the hills
with his bow and arrows, lay down to rest awhile, and
unwittingly fell fast asleep. As he was slumbering, an
elephant came up, and, coiling his trunk around the
man, carried him off. The latter gave himself up for
dead; but before long the elephant had deposited him
at the foot of a tall tree, and had summoned a whole
herd of comrades, who crowded about the huntsman as
though asking his assistance. The elephant who had
brought him went and lay down under the tree, and first
looked up into its branches and then looked down at the
man, apparently requesting him to get up into the tree.
So the latter jumped on the elephant's back and then
clambered up to the topmost branch, not knowing what
he was expected to do next. By-and-by a lion[1] arrived,

---

[1] The term here used refers to a creature which partakes rather
of the fabulous than of the real. The *Kuang-yün* says it is "a
kind of lion;" but other authorities describe it as a horse. Its
favourite food is tiger-flesh. Incense-burners are often made after
the "lion" pattern and called by this name, the smoke of the
incense issuing from the mouth of the animal, like our own gar-
goyles.

and from among the frightened herd chose out a fat
elephant, which he seemed as though about to devour.
The others remained there trembling, not daring to
run away, but looking wistfully up into the tree. Thereupon the huntsman drew an arrow from his quiver and
shot the lion dead, at which all the elephants below
made him a grateful obeisance. He then descended,
when the elephant lay down again and invited him to
mount by pulling at his clothes with its trunk. This he
did, and was carried to a place where the animal
scratched the ground with its foot, and revealed to him
a vast number of old tusks. He jumped down and
collected them in a bundle, after which the elephant
conveyed him to a spot whence he easily found his way
home.

CLX.

THE HIDDEN TREASURE.

LI YÜEH-SHÊNG was the second son of a rich old man who used to bury his money, and who was known to his fellow-townsmen as "Old Crocks." One day the father fell sick, and summoned his sons to divide the property between them.[1] He gave four-fifths to the elder and only one-fifth to the younger, saying to the latter, "It is not that I love your brother more than I love you : I have other money stored away, and when you are alone I will hand that over to you." A few days afterwards the old man grew worse, and Yüeh-shêng, afraid that his father might die at any moment, seized an opportunity of seeing him alone to ask about the money that he himself was to receive. "Ah," replied the dying

---

[1] The Law of Inheritance, as it obtains in China, has been ably illustrated by Mr. Chal. Alabaster in Vols. v. and vi. of the *China Review*. This writer states that "there seems to be no absolutely fixed law in regard either of inheritance or testamentary dispositions of property, but certain general principles are recognised which the court will not allow to be disregarded without sufficient cause." As a rule the sons, whether by wife or concubine, share equally, and in preference to daughters, even though there should be a written will in favour of the latter.

man, "the sum of our joys and of our sorrows is determined by fate. You are now happy in the possession of
a virtuous wife, and have no right to an increase of
wealth." For, as a matter of fact, this second son was
married to a lady from the Ch'ê family whose virtue
equalled that of any of the heroines of history: hence
his father's remark. Yüeh-shêng, however, was not satisfied, and implored to be allowed to have the money;
and at length the old man got angry and said, "You are
only just turned twenty; you have known none of the
trials of life, and were I to give a thousand ounces of
gold, it would soon be all spent. Go! and, until you
have drunk the cup of bitterness to its dregs, expect no
money from me." Now Yüeh-shêng was a filial son, and
when his father spoke thus he did not venture to say any
more, and hoped for his speedy recovery that he might
have a chance of coaxing him to comply with his request. But the old man got worse and worse, and at
length died; whereupon the elder brother took no
trouble about the funeral ceremonies, leaving it all to
the younger, who, being an open-handed fellow, made no
difficulties about the expense. The latter was also fond
of seeing a great deal of company at his house, and his
wife often had to get three or four meals a-day ready for
guests; and, as her husband did very little towards
looking after his affairs, and was further sponged upon
by all the needy ones of the neighbourhood, they were
soon reduced to a state of poverty. The elder brother
helped them to keep body and soul together, but he died
shortly afterwards, and this resource was cut off from

them. Then, by dint of borrowing in the spring and repaying in the autumn,[2] they still managed to exist, until at last it came to parting with their land, and they were left actually destitute. At that juncture their eldest son died, followed soon after by his mother; and Yüeh-shêng was left almost by himself in the world. He now married the widow of a sheep-dealer, who had a little capital; and she was very strict with him, and wouldn't let him waste time and money with his friends. One night his father appeared to him and said, " My son, you have drained your cup of bitterness to the dregs. You shall now have the money. I will bring it to you." When Yüeh-shêng woke up, he thought it was merely a poor man's dream; but the next day, while laying the foundations of a wall, he did come upon a quantity of gold. And then he knew what his father had meant by "when you are alone;" for of those about him at that time, more than half were gone.

---

[2] This has reference to the "seed-time and harvest."

CLXI.

THE BOATMEN OF LAO-LUNG.

WHEN His Excellency Chu was Viceroy of Kuang-tung, there were constant complaints from the traders of mysterious disappearances; sometimes as many as three or four of them disappearing at once and never being seen or heard of again. At length the number of such cases, filed of course against some person or persons unknown, multiplied to such an extent that they were simply put on record, and but little notice was further taken of them by the local officials. Thus, when His Excellency entered upon his duties, he found more than a hundred plaints of the kind, besides innumerable cases in which the missing man's relatives lived at a distance and had not instituted proceedings. The mystery so preyed upon the new Viceroy's mind that he lost all appetite for food; and when, finally, all the inquiries he had set on foot resulted in no clue to an elucidation of these strange disappearances, then His Excellency proceeded to wash and purify himself, and, having notified the Municipal God,[1] he took to fasting

---

[1] See No. I., note I.

and sleeping in his study alone. While he was in ecstasy, lo! an official entered, holding a tablet in his hand, and said that he had come from the Municipal temple with the following instructions to the Viceroy:—

> " Snow on the whiskers descending :
> Live clouds falling from heaven :
> Wood in water buoyed up :
> In the wall an opening effected."

The official then retired, and the Viceroy waked up; but it was only after a night of tossing and turning that he hit upon what seemed to him the solution of the enigma. " The first line," argued he, "must signify *old* (*lao* in Chinese); the second refers to the *dragon*[2] (*lung* in Chinese); the third is clearly a *boat;* and the fourth a *door* here taken in its secondary sense—*man*)." Now, to the east of the province, not far from the pass by which traders from the north connect their line of trade with the southern seas, there was actually a ferry known as the Old Dragon (Lao-lung); and thither the Viceroy immediately despatched a force to arrest those employed in carrying people backwards and forwards. More than fifty men were caught, and they all confessed at once without the application of torture. In fact, they were bandits under the guise of boatmen;[3] and after beguiling passengers on board, they would either drug them or

---

[2] Clouds being naturally connected in every Chinaman's mind with these fabulous creatures, the origin of which has been traced by some to waterspouts. See No. LXXXI., note 2.

[3] " Boat-men " is the solution of the last two lines of the enigma.

burn stupefying incense until they were senseless, finally cutting them open and putting a large stone inside to make the body sink. Such was the horrible story, the discovery of which brought throngs to the Viceroy's door to serenade him in terms of gratitude and praise.[4]

---

[4] The commentator actually supplies a list of the persons who signed a congratulatory petition to the Viceroy on the arrest and punishment of the criminals.

CLXII.

THE PIOUS SURGEON.

A CERTAIN veterinary surgeon, named Hou, was carrying food to his field labourers, when suddenly a whirlwind arose in his path. Hou seized a spoon and poured out a libation of gruel, whereupon the wind immediately dropped. On another occasion, he was wandering about the municipal temple when he noticed an image of Liu-ch'üan presenting the melon,[1] in whose eye was a great splotch of dirt. "Dear me, Sir Liu!" cried Hou, "who has been ill-using you like this?" He then scraped away the dirt with his finger-nail, and passed on. Some years afterwards, as he was lying down very ill, two lictors walked in and carried him off to a

---

[1] When the soul of the Emperor T'ai Tsung of the T'ang dynasty was in the infernal regions, it promised to send Yen-lo (the Chinese *Yama* or Pluto) a melon ; and when His Majesty recovered from the trance into which he had been plunged, he gave orders that his promise was to be fulfilled. Just then a man, named Liu Ch'üan, observed a priest with a hairpin belonging to his wife, and misconstruing the manner in which possession of it had been obtained, abused his wife so severely that she committed suicide. Liu Ch'üan himself then determined to follow her example, and convey the melon to Yen-lo ; for which act he was subsequently deified. See the *Hsi-yu-chi*, Section XI.

yamên, where they insisted on his bribing them heavily.
Hou was at his wits' end what to do; but just at that
moment a personage dressed in green robes came forth,
who was greatly astonished at seeing him there, and
asked what it all meant. Our hero at once explained;
whereupon the man in green turned upon the lictors and
abused them for not shewing proper respect to Mr. Hou.
Meanwhile a drum sounded like the roll of thunder, and
the man in green told Hou that it was for the morning
session, and that he would have to attend. Leading
Hou within he put him in his proper place, and, promising to inquire into the charge against him, went forward and whispered a few words to one of the clerks.
"Oh," said the latter, advancing and making a bow to
the veterinary surgeon, "yours is a trifling matter. We
shall merely have to confront you with a horse, and then
you can go home again." Shortly afterwards, Hou's
case was called; upon which he went forward and knelt
down, as did also a horse which was prosecuting him.
The judge now informed Hou that he was accused by
the horse of having caused its death by medicines, and
asked him if he pleaded guilty or not guilty. "My
lord," replied Hou, "the prosecutor was attacked by the
cattle-plague, for which I treated him accordingly; and
he actually recovered from the disease, though he died
on the following day. Am I to be held responsible for
that?" The horse now proceeded to tell his story; and
after the usual cross-examination and cries for justice,
the judge gave orders to look up the horse's term of life
in the Book of Fate. Therein it appeared that the

animal's destiny had doomed it to death on the very day on which it had died; whereupon the judge cried out, "Your term of years had already expired; why bring this false charge? Away with you!" and turning to Hou, the judge added, "You are a worthy man, and may be permitted to live." The lictors were accordingly instructed to escort him back, and with them went out both the clerk and the man in green clothes, who bade the lictors take every possible care of Hou by the way. "You gentlemen are very kind," said Hou, "but I haven't the honour of your acquaintance, and should be glad to know to whom I am so much indebted." "Three years ago," replied the man in green, "I was travelling in your neighbourhood, and was suffering very much from thirst, which you relieved for me by a few spoonfuls of gruel. I have not forgotten that act." "And my name," observed the other, "is Liu-ch'üan. You once took a splotch of dirt out of my eye that was troubling me very much. I am only sorry that the wine and food we have down here is unsuitable to offer you. Farewell." Hou now understood all that had happened, and went off home with the two lictors where he would have regaled them with some refreshment, but they refused to take even a cup of tea. He then waked up and found that he had been dead for two days. From this time forth he led a more virtuous life than ever, always pouring out libations to Liu-ch'üan at all the festivals of the year. Thus he reached the age of eighty, a hale and hearty man, still able to sit in the saddle; until one day he met Liu-chüan riding on horseback, as if about to make a long journey. After a little friendly conversation, the latter said to him, "Your time is up, and the warrant for your arrest is already issued; but I have ordered the constables to delay awhile, and you can now spend three days in preparing for death, at the expiration of which I will come and fetch you. I have purchased a small appointment for you in the realms below,[2] by which you will be more comfortable." So Hou went home and told his wife and children; and after collecting his friends and relatives, and making all necessary preparations, on the evening of the fourth day he cried out, "Liu-Ch'üan has come!" and, getting into his coffin,[3] lay down and died.

---

[2] As the Chinese believe that their disembodied spirits proceed to a world organised on much the same model as the one they know, so do they think that there will be social distinctions of rank and emolument proportioned to the merits of each.

[3] A dying man is almost always moved into his coffin to die; and aged persons frequently take to sleeping regularly in the coffins provided against the inevitable hour by the pious thoughtfulness of a loving son. Even in middle life Chinese like to see their coffins ready for them, and store them sometimes on their own premises, sometimes in the outhouses of a neighbouring temple.

CLXIII.

ANOTHER SOLOMON.

At T'ai-yüan there lived a middle-aged woman with her widowed daughter-in-law. The former was on terms of too great intimacy with a notably bad character of the neighbourhood; and the latter, who objected very strongly to this, did her best to keep the man from the house. The elder woman accordingly tried to send the other back to her family, but she would not go; and at length things came to such a pass that the mother-in-law actually went to the mandarin of the place and charged her daughter-in-law with the offence she herself was committing. When the mandarin inquired the name of the man concerned, she said she had only seen him in the dark and didn't know who he was, referring him for information to the accused. The latter, on being summoned, gave the man's name, but retorted the charge on her mother-in-law; and when the man was confronted with them, he promptly declared both their stories to be false. The mandarin, however, said there was a *primâ facie* case against him, and ordered him to be severely beaten, whereupon he confessed that it was the daughter-in-law whom he went to visit. This the woman herself flatly denied, even under torture; and on being released, appealed to a higher court, with a very similar result. Thus the case dragged on, until a Mr. Sun, who was well-known for his judicial acumen, was appointed district magistrate at that place. Calling the parties before him, he bade his lictors prepare stones and knives, at which they were much exercised in their minds, the severest tortures allowed by law being merely gyves and fetters.[1] However, everything was got ready, and the next day Mr. Sun proceeded with his investigation. After hearing all that each one of the three had to say, he delivered the following judgment:— "The case is a simple one; for although I cannot say which of you two women is the guilty one, there is no doubt about the man, who has evidently been the means of bringing discredit on a virtuous family. Take those stones and knives there and put him to death. I will be responsible" Thereupon the two women began to stone the man, especially the younger one, who seized the biggest stones she could see and threw them at him with all the might of her pent-up anger; while the mother-in-law chose small stones and struck him on non-vital parts.[2] So with the knives: the daughter-in-law

---

[1] See No. LXXIII., note 2.

[2] The Chinese distinguish sixteen vital spots on the front of the body and six on the back, with thirty-six and twenty non-vital spots in similar positions, respectively. They allow, however, that a severe blow on a non-vital spot might cause death, and *vice versâ*.

would have killed him at the first blow, had not the mandarin stopped her, and said, "Hold! I now know who is the guilty woman." The mother-in-law was then tortured until she confessed, and the case was thus terminated.

CLXIV.

THE INCORRUPT OFFICIAL.

MR. WU, Sub-prefect of Chi-nan, was an upright man, and would have no share in the bribery and corruption which was extensively carried on, and at which the higher authorities connived, and in the proceeds of which they actually shared. The Prefect tried to bully him into adopting a similar plan, and went so far as to abuse him in violent language ; upon which Mr. Wu fired up and exclaimed, "Though I am but a subordinate official, you should impeach me for anything you have against me in the regular way ; you have not the right to abuse me thus. Die I may, but I will never consent to degrade my office and turn aside the course of justice for the sake of filthy lucre." At this outbreak the Prefect changed his tone, and tried to soothe him . . . . . [How dare people accuse the age of being corrupt, when it is themselves who will not walk in the straight path.] One day after this a certain fox-medium[1] came

---

[1] Certain classes of soothsayers are believed by the Chinese to be possessed by foxes, which animals have the power of looking into the future, &c., &c.

to the Prefect's yamên just as a feast was in full swing, and was thus addressed by a guest :—"You who pretend to know everything, say how many officials there are in this Prefecture." "*One,*" replied the medium ; at which the company laughed heartily, until the medium continued, "There are really seventy-two holders of office, but Mr. Sub-prefect Wu is the only one who can justly be called an official."

APPENDIX A.

VISITORS to Chinese temples of the Taoist persuasion usually make at once for what is popularly known amongst foreigners as the "Chamber of Horrors." These belong specially to Taoism, or the ethics of Right in the abstract, as opposed to abstract Wrong, and are not found in temples consecrated to the religion of Buddha. Modern Taoism, however, once a purely metaphysical system, is now so leavened with the superstitions of Buddhism, and has borrowed so much material from its younger rival, that an ordinary Chinaman can hardly tell one from the other, and generally regards them as to all intents and purposes the same. These rightly-named Chambers of Horrors—for Madame Tussaud has nothing more ghastly to show in the whole of her wonderful collection—represent the Ten Courts of Purgatory, through some or all of which erring souls must pass before they are suffered to be born again into the world under another form, or transferred to the eternal bliss reserved for the righteous alone. As a description of these Ten Courts may not be uninteresting to some of my readers, and as the subject has a direct bearing upon many of the stories in the previous collection, I hereto append my translation of a well-known Taoist work[1] which is circulated gratuitously all over the Chinese Empire by people who are anxious to lay up a store of good works against the day of reckoning to come. Those who are acquainted with Dante's *Divine Comedy* will recollect that the poet's idea of a Christian Purgatory was a series of nine lessening circles arranged one above the other, so as to form a cone. The Taoist believes that his Purgatory consists of Ten Courts of Justice situated in different positions at the bottom of a great ocean which lies down in

---

[1] The *Yü Li* or *Divine Panorama*.

the depths of the earth.   These are sub-divided into special wards, different forms of torture being inflicted in each.   A perusal of this work will shew what punishments the wicked Chinaman has to expect in the unseen world, and by what means he may hope to obtain a partial or complete remission of his sins.

The " Divine Panorama," published by the Mercy of Yü Ti,[2] *that Men and Women may repent them of their Faults and make Atonement for their Crimes.*

On the birthday of the Saviour P'u-sa,[3] as the spirits of Purgatory were thronging round to offer their congratulations, the ruler of the Infernal Regions spake as follows :—" My wish is to release all souls, and every moon as this day comes round I would wholly or partially remit the punishment of erring shades, and give them life once more in one of the Six Paths.[4]   But alas ! the wicked are many and the virtuous few.   Nevertheless, the punishments in the dark region are too severe, and require some modification.   Any wicked soul that repents and induces one or two others to do likewise shall be allowed to set this off against the punishments which should be inflicted."   The Judges of the Ten Courts of Purgatory then agreed that all who led virtuous lives from their youth upwards shall be escorted at their death to the land of the Immortals ; that all whose balance of good and evil is exact shall escape the bitterness of the Three States,[5] and be born again among men ; that those who have repaid their debts of gratitude and friendship, and fulfilled their destiny, yet have a balance of evil against them, shall pass through the various Courts of Purgatory and then be born again amongst men, rich, poor, old, young, diseased or crippled, to be put a second time upon trial.   Then, if they behave well they may enter into some happy state ; but if badly, they will be dragged by horrid devils through all the Courts, suffering bitterly as they go, and will again be born, to endure in life the uttermost of poverty and wretchedness, in death the everlasting tortures of hell.   Those who are disloyal, unfilial, who commit suicide, take life, or disbelieve the doctrine of Cause and Effect,[6] saying to themselves that when a

---

[2] The Divine Ruler, immediately below God himself.
[3] See No. XXVI., note 5.
[4] See *Author's Own Record* (in *Introduction*), note 26.
[5] The three worst of the Six Paths.
[6] That the state of one life is the result of behaviour in a previous existence.

man dies there is an end of him, that when he has lost his skin[7] he has already suffered the worst that can befall him, that living men can be tortured, but no one ever saw a man's ghost in the pillory, that after death all is unknown, etc., etc.,—truly these men do not know that the body alone perishes but the soul lives for ever and ever ; and that whatsoever evil they do in this life, the same will be done unto them in the life to come. All who commit such crimes are handed over to the everlasting tortures of hell ; for alas ! in spite of the teachings of the Three Systems[8] some will persist in regarding these warnings as vain and empty talk. Lightly they speak of Divine mercy, and knowingly commit many crimes, not more than one in a hundred ever coming to repentance. Therefore the punishments of Purgatory were strictly carried out and the tortures dreadfully severe. But now it has been mercifully ordained that any man or woman, young, old, weak or strong, who may have sinned in any way, shall be permitted to obtain remission of the same by keeping his or her thoughts constantly fixed on P'u-sa and on the birthdays of the Judges of the Ten Courts, by fasting and prayer, and by vows never to sin again. Or for every good work done in life they shall be allowed to escape one ward in the Courts below. From this rule to be excepted disloyal ministers, unfilial sons, suicides, those who plot in secret against good people, those who are struck by lightning (*lit.* thunder), those who perish by flood or fire, by wild animals or poisonous reptiles[9]—these to pass through all the Courts and be punished according to their deserts. All other sinners to be allowed to claim their good works as a set-off against evil, thus partly escaping the agonies of hell and receiving some reward for their virtuous deeds.

This account of man's wickedness on the earth and the punishments in store for him was written in language intelligible to every man and woman, and was submitted for the approval of P'u-sa, the intention being to wait the return[10] of some virtuous soul among the sons of men, and by these means publish it all over the earth. When P'u-sa saw what had been done, he said it was good ; and on the

---

[7] *Lit.*—the skin purse (of his bones).

[8] Buddhism, Taoism, and Confucianism.

[9] Violent deaths are regarded with horror by the Chinese. They hold that a truly virtuous man always dies either of illness or old age.

[10] Good people go to Purgatory in the flesh, and are at once passed up to Heaven without suffering any torture, or are sent back to earth again.

3rd of 8th moon proceeded with the ten Judges of Purgatory to lay this book before God.[11]

Then God said "Good indeed! Good indeed! henceforth let all spirits take note of any mortal who vows to lead a virtuous life and, repenting, promises to sin no more. Two punishments shall be remitted him. And if, in addition to this, he succeeds in doing five virtuous acts, then he shall escape all punishment and be born again in some happy state—if a woman she shall be born as a man. But more than five virtuous acts shall enable such a soul to obtain the salvation of others, and redeem wife and family from the tortures of hell. Let these regulations be published in the *Divine Panorama* and circulated on earth by the spirits of the City Guardian.[12] In fear and trembling obey this decree and carry it reverently into effect."

THE FIRST. COURT.

His Infernal Majesty Ch'in Kuang is specially in charge of the register of life and death both for old and young, and presides at the judgment-seat in the lower regions. His court is situated in the great Ocean, away beyond the Wu-chiao rock,[13] far to the west near the murky road which leads to the Yellow Springs.[14] Every man and woman dying in old age whose fate it is to be born again into the world, if their tale of good and evil works is equally balanced, are sent to the First Court, and thence transferred back to Life, male becoming female, female male, rich poor, and poor rich, according to their several deserts. But those whose good deeds are outnumbered by their bad are sent to a terrace on the right of the Court, called the Terrace of the Mirror of Sin, ten feet in height. The mirror is about fifty feet [15] in circumference and hangs towards the east. Above are seven characters written horizontally :—"Sin Mirror Terrace upon no good men." There the wicked souls are able to see the naughtiness of their own hearts

---

[11] The Supreme Ruler.
[12] See No. I., note 1.
[13] Supposed to be the gate of the Infernal Regions.
[14] Hades.
[15] Literally, "ten armfuls."

while they were among the living, and the danger of death and hell. Then do they realize the proverb,—

"Ten thousand taels of yellow gold cannot be brought away:
But every crime will tell its tale upon the judgment day."

When the souls have been to the Terrace and seen their wickednesses, they are forwarded into the Second Court, where they are tortured and dismissed to the proper hell.

Should there be any one enjoying life without reflecting that Heaven and Earth produce mortals, that father and mother bring the child to maturity—truly no easy matter ; and, ignoring the four obligations,[16] before receiving the summons, lightly sever the thread of their own existence by cutting their throats, hanging, poisoning, or drowning themselves :—then such suicides, if the deed was not done out of loyalty, filial piety, chastity, or friendship, for which they would go to Heaven, but in a trivial burst of rage, or fearing the consequences of a crime which would not amount to death, or in the hope of falsely injuring a fellow-creature—then such suicides, when the last breath has left their bodies, shall be escorted to this Court by the Spirits of the Threshold and of the Hearth. They shall be placed in the Hunger and Thirst Section, and every day from 7 till 11 o'clock they will resume their mortal coil, and suffer again the pain and bitterness of death. After seventy days, or one or two years as the case may be, they will be conducted back to the scene of their suicide, but will not be permitted to taste the funeral meats, or avail themselves of the usual offerings to the dead. Bitterly will they repent, unable as they will be to render themselves visible and frighten people,[17] vainly striving to procure a substitute.[18] For when the substitute shall have been harmlessly entrapped, the Spirits of the Threshold and Hearth will reconduct the erring soul back to this Court, whence it will be sent on to the Second Court, where its balance of good and evil will be struck,

---

[16] To Heaven, Earth, sovereign, and relatives.

[17] Held to be a great relief to the spirits of the dead.

[18] It is commonly believed that if the spirit of a murdered man can secure the violent death of some other person he returns to earth again as if nothing had happened, the spirit of his victim passing into the world below and suffering all the misery of a disembodied soul in his stead. See No. XLV., note 8.

and dreadful tortures applied, being finally passed on through the various Courts to the utter misery of hell. Should any one have such intention of suicide and thus threaten a fellow creature, even though he does not commit the act but continues to live not without virtue, yet shall it not be permitted in any way to remit his punishment. Any soul which after suicide shall not remain invisible, but shall frighten people to death, will be seized by black-faced long-tusked devils and tortured in the various hells, to be finally thrust into the great Gehenna, for ever to remain hung up in chains, and not permitted to be born again.

Every Buddhist or Taoist priest who receives money for prayers and liturgies, but skips over words and misses out sentences, on arriving at this, the First Court, will be sent to the section for the Completion of Prayer, and there in a small dark room he shall pick out such passages as he has omitted, and make good the deficiency as best he can, by the uncertain light of an infinitesimal wick burning in a gallon of oil. Even good and virtuous priests must also repair any omissions they may have (accidentally) made, and so must every man or woman who in private devotion may have omitted or wrongly repeated any part of the sacred writings from over-earnestness, their attention not being properly fixed on the actual words they repeat. The same applies to female priests. A dispensation from Buddha to remit such punishment is put in force on the first day of each month when the names are entered in the register of the virtuous.

O ye dwellers upon earth, on the 1st day of the 2nd moon, fasting turn to the north and make oath to abstain from evil and fix your thoughts on good, that ye may escape hell ! The precepts of Buddha are circulated over the whole world to warn mankind to believe and repent, that when the last hour comes their spirits may be escorted by dark-robed boys to realms of bliss and happiness in the west.

THE SECOND COURT.

His Infernal Majesty, Ch'u Ching, reigns at the bottom of the great Ocean. Away to the south, below the Wu-chiao rocks, he has a vast hell, many leagues in extent, and subdivided into sixteen wards, as follows :—

In the first, nothing but black clouds and constant sand-storms. In the second, mud and filth. In the third, *chevaux de frise*. In the fourth, gnawing hunger. In the fifth, burning thirst. In the sixth, blood and pus. In the seventh, the shades are plunged into a brazen cauldron (of boiling water). In the eighth, the same punishment is repeated many times. In the ninth, they are put into iron clothes. In the tenth, they are stretched on a rack to regulation length. In the eleventh, they are pecked by fowls. In the twelfth, they have only rivers of lime to drink. In the thirteenth, they are hacked to pieces. In the fourteenth, the leaves of the trees are as sharp as sword-points. In the fifteenth they are pursued by foxes and wolves. In the sixteenth, all is ice and snow.

Those who lead astray young boys and girls, and then escape punishment by cutting off their hair and entering the priesthood; [19] those who filch letters, pictures, books, etc. entrusted to their care, and then pretend to have lost them; those who injure a fellow-creature's ear, eye, hand, foot, fingers, or toes; those who practise as doctors without any knowledge of the medical art; those who will not ransom grown-up slave-girls; [20] those who, contracting marriage for the sake of gain, falsely state their ages; or those who in cases of betrothal, before actual marriage, find out that one of the con-tracting parties is a bad character, and yet do not come forward to say so, but inflict an irreparable wrong on the innocent one;— such offenders, when their quota of crime has been cast up, their youth or age and the consequences of their acts taken into con-sideration, will be seized by horrid red-faced devils and thrust into the great Hell, and thence despatched to the particular ward in which they are to be tormented. When their time of suffering there has expired, they will be moved into the Third Hall, there to be tortured and passed on to Gehenna.

---

[19] A very common trick in China. The drunken bully Lu Ta in the celebrated novel *Shui-Hu* saved himself by these means, and I have heard that the Mandarin who in the war of 1842 spent a large sum in constructing a paddle-wheel steamer to be worked by men, hoping thereby to match the wheel-ships of the Outer Barbarians, is now expiating his failure at a monastery in Fukien. *Apropos* of which, it may not be generally known that at this moment there are small paddle-wheel boats for Chinese passengers, plying up and down the Canton river, the wheels of which are turned by gangs of coolies who perform a movement precisely similar to that required on the treadmill.

[20] In order that their marriage destiny may not be interfered with. It is con-sidered disgraceful not to accept the ransom of a slave girl of 15 or 16 years of age. See No. XXVI., note 8.

O ye men and women of the world, take this book and warn all sinners, or copy it out and circulate it for general information ! If you see people sick and ill, give medicine to heal them. If you see people poor and hungry, feed them. If you see people in difficulties, give money to save them. Repent your past errors, and you will be allowed to cancel that evil by future good, so that when the hour arrives you will pass at once into the Tenth Hall, and thence return again to existence on earth.

Let such as love all creatures endowed with life, and do not recklessly cut and slay, but teach their children not to harm small animals and insects—let these, on the 1st of the 3rd moon, register an oath not to take life, but to aid in preserving it. Thus they will avoid passing through Purgatory, and will also enter at once the Tenth Hall, to be born again in some happy state.

THE THIRD COURT.

His Infernal Majesty Sung Ti reigns at the bottom of the great Ocean, away to the south-east, below the Wu-chiao rock, in the Gehenna of Black Ropes. This Hall is many leagues wide, and is subdivided into sixteen wards, as follows :—

In the first everything is Salt ; above, below, and all round, the eye rests upon Salt alone. The shades feed upon it, and suffer horrid torments in consequence. When the fit has passed away they return to it once again, and suffer agonies more unutterable than before. In the second, the erring shades are bound with cords and carry heavily-weighted *cangues*. In the third, they are perpetually pierced through the ribs. In the fourth, their faces are scraped with iron and copper knives. In the fifth, their fat is scraped away from their bodies. In the sixth, their hearts and livers are squeezed with pincers. In the seventh, their eyes are gouged. In the eighth, they are flayed. In the ninth, their feet are cut off. In the tenth, their finger-nails and toe-nails are pulled out. In the eleventh their blood is sucked. In the twelfth, they are hung up head downwards. In the thirteenth, their shoulder-bones are split. In the fourteenth, they are tormented by insects and reptiles. In the fifteenth, they are beaten on the thighs. In the sixteenth, their hearts are scratched.

Those who enjoy the light of day without reflecting on the

Imperial bounty;[21] officers of State who revel in large emoluments without reciprocating their sovereign's goodness; private individuals who do not repay the debt of water and earth;[22] wives and concubines who slight their marital lords; those who fail in their duties as acting sons,[23] or such as reap what advantages there are and then go off to their own homes; slaves who disregard their masters; official underlings who are ungrateful to their superiors; working partners who behave badly to the moneyed partner; culprits who escape from prison or abscond from their place of banishment; those who break their bail and get others into trouble; and those infatuated ones who have long omitted to pray and repent —all these, even though they have a set-off of good deeds, must pass through the misery of every ward. Those who interfere with another man's Fêng-Shui; those who obstruct funeral obsequies or the completion of graves; those who in digging come on a coffin and do not immediately cover it up, but injure the bones; those who steal or avoid paying up their quota of grain;[24] those who lose all record of the site of their family burying-place; those who incite others to commit crimes; those who promote litigation; those who write anonymous placards; those who repudiate a betrothal; those who forge deeds and other documents; those who receive payment of a debt without signing a receipt or giving up the I O U; those who counterfeit signatures and seals; those who alter bills; those who injure posterity in any way—all these, and similar offenders, shall be punished according to the gravity of each offence. Devils with big knives will seize the erring ones and thrust them into the great Gehenna; besides which they shall expiate their sins in the proper number of wards, and shall then be forwarded to the Fourth Court where they shall be tortured and dismissed to the general Gehenna.

O ye sons of men, on the 8th day of the 2nd moon, register an

---

[21] The soil of China belongs, every inch of it, to the Emperor. Consequently, the people owe him a debt of gratitude for permitting them to live upon it.

[22] Do their duty as men and women.

[23] A Chinaman may have three kinds of fathers; (1) his real father, (2) an adopted father, such as an uncle without children to whom he has been given as heir, and (3) the man his widowed mother may marry. The first two are to all intents and purposes equal; the third is entitled only to one year's mourning instead of the usual three.

[24] As taxes.

oath that ye will do no evil. Thus you may escape the bitterness of these hells.

THE FOURTH COURT.

The Lord of the Five Senses reigns at the bottom of the great Ocean, away to the east below the Wu-chiao rock. His Court is many leagues wide, and is subdivided into sixteen wards, as follows :—

In the first, the wicked shades are hung up and water is continually poured over them. In the second, they are made to kneel on chains and pieces of split bamboo. In the third, their hands are scalded with boiling water. In the fourth, their hands swell and stream with perspiration. In the fifth, their muscles are cut and their bones pulled out. In the sixth, their shoulders are pricked with a trident and the skin rubbed with a hard brush. In the seventh, holes are bored into their flesh. In the eighth, they are made to sit on spikes. In the ninth, they wear iron clothes. In the tenth, they are placed under heavy pieces of wood, stone, earth, or tiles. In the eleventh, their eyes are put out. In the twelfth, their mouths are choked with dust. In the thirteenth, they are perpetually dosed with nasty medicines. In the fourteenth, it is so slippery they are always falling down. In the fifteenth, their mouths are painfully pricked. In the sixteenth, their bodies are buried under broken stones, &c., the head alone being left out.

Those who cheat the customs and evade taxes ; those who repudiate their rent, use weighted scales, sell sham medicines, water their rice,[25] utter base coin, get deeply in debt, sell doctored[26] silks and satins, scrape[27] or add size to linen cloth ; those who do not make way for the cripples, old and young ; those who encroach upon petty trade rights[28] of old or young ; those who delay in

---

[25] Visitors to Peking may often see the junkmen at T'ung-chow pouring water by the bucketful on to newly-arrived cargoes of Imperial rice in order to make up the right weight and conceal the amount they have filched on the way.

[26] That is, with a false gloss on them.

[27] In order to raise to nap and give an appearance of strength and goodness.

[28] Costermongers and others acquire certain rights to doorsteps or snug corners in Chinese cities which are not usually infringed by competitors in the same line of business. Chair-coolies, carrying-coolies, ferrymen, &c., also claim

delivering letters entrusted to them; steal bricks from walls as they pass by, or oil and candles from lamps;[29] poor people who do not behave properly and rich people who are not compassionate to the poor; those who promise a loan and go back on their word: those who see people suffering from illness, yet cannot bring themselves to part with certain useful drugs they may have in their possession; those who know good prescriptions but keep them secret; those who throw vessels which have contained medicine or broken cups and bottles into the street; those who allow their mules and ponies to be a nuisance to other people; those who destroy their neighbour's crops or his walls and fences; those who try to bewitch their enemies,[30] and those who try to frighten people in any way,—all these shall be punished according to the gravity of their offences, and shall be thrust by the devils into the great Gehenna until their time arrives for passing into the Fifth Court.

O ye children of this world, if on the 18th day of the 2nd moon you register an oath to sin no more, then you may escape the various wards of this Hall; and if to this book you add examples of rewards and punishments following upon virtues and crimes, and hand them down to posterity for the good of the human race, so that all who read may repent them of their wickednesses—then they will be without sin, and you not without merit !

THE FIFTH COURT.

His Infernal Majesty, Yen Lo,[31] said,—"Our proper place is in the First Court; but, pitying those who die by foul means, and should be sent back to earth to have their wrongs redressed, we

---

whole districts as their particular field of operations and are very jealous of any interference. I know of a case in which the right of "scavengering" a town had been in the same family for generations, and no one dreamt of trying to take it out of their hands.

[29] Chiefly alluding to small temples where some pious spirit may have lighted a lamp or candle to the glory of his favourite P'u-sa.

[30] This is done either by making a figure of the person to be injured and burning it in a slow fire, like the old practice of the wax figure in English history; or by obtaining his nativity characters, writing them out on a piece of paper and burning them in a candle, muttering all the time whatsoever mischief it is hoped will befall him.

[31] Popularly known as the Chinese Pluto. The Indian *Yama*.

have moved our judgment-seat to the great hell at the bottom of
the Ocean, away to the north-east below the Wu-chiao rock, and
have subdivided this hell into sixteen wards for the torment of
souls.   All those shades who come before us have already suffered
long tortures in the previous four Courts, whence, if they are
hardened sinners, they are passed on after seven days to this Court,
where if again found to be utterly hardened, corruption will overtake them by the fifth or seventh day.   All shades cry out either
that they have left some vow unfulfilled, or that they wish to build'
a temple or a bridge, make a road, clean out a river or well,
publish some book teaching people to be virtuous, that they have
not released their due number of lives, that they have filial duties
or funeral obsequies to perform, some act of kindness to repay, &c.,
&c.   For these reasons they pray to be allowed to return once more
to the light of day, and are always ready to make oath that henceforth they will lead most exemplary lives.   We, hearing this, reply,
—In days gone by ye openly worked evil, but now that your boat
has reached the midstream, ye bethink yourselves of caulking the
leak.   For although P'u-sa in his great mercy decreed that there
should be a modification of torture, and that good works might be
set off against evil, the same being submitted to God and ratified by
Divine Decree, to be further published in the realms below and in
the Infernal City—yet we Judges of the Ten Courts have not yet
received one single virtuous man amongst us, who, coming in the
flesh, might carry this *Divine Panorama* back with him to the light
of day.   Truly those who suffer in hell and on earth cannot complain, and virtuous men are rare !   But now ye have come to my
Court, having beheld your own wickedness in the mirror of sin.
No more—bull-headed, horse-faced devils, away with them to the
Terrace [32] that they may once more gaze upon their lost homes !' "
     This Terrace is curved in front like a bow; it looks east, west,
and south.   It is eighty-one *li* from one extreme to the other.   The
back part is like the string of the bow; it is enclosed by a wall of
sharp swords.   It is 490 feet high; its sides are knife-blades; and
the whole is in sixty-three storeys.   No good shade comes to this
Terrace; neither do those whose balance of good and evil is exact.
Wicked souls alone behold their homes close by and can see and
hear what is going on.   They hear old and young talking together;

---

[32] The celebrated " See-one's-home Terrace."

they see their last wishes disregarded and their instructions disobeyed. Everything seems to have undergone a change. The property they scraped together with so much trouble is dissipated and gone. The husband thinks of taking another wife; the widow meditates second nuptials.[33] Strangers are in possession of the old estate; there is nothing to divide amongst the children. Debts long since paid are brought again for settlement, and the survivors are called upon to acknowledge claims upon the departed. Debts owed are lost for want of evidence, with endless recriminations, abuse, and general confusion, all of which falls upon the three families[34] of the deceased. They in their anger speak ill of him that is gone. He sees his children become corrupt, and his friends fall away. Some, perhaps, for the sake of bygone times, may stroke the coffin and let fall a tear, departing quickly with a cold smile. Worse than that, the wife sees her husband tortured in the yamên; the husband sees his wife victim to some horrible disease, lands gone, houses destroyed by flood or fire, and everything in unutterable confusion—the reward of former sins.[35] All souls, after the misery of the Terrace, will be thrust into the great Gehenna, and, when the amount of wickedness of each has been ascertained, they will be passed through the sixteen wards for the punishment of evil hearts. In the Gehenna they will be buried under wooden pillars, bound with copper snakes, crushed by iron dogs, tied tightly hand and foot, be ripped open and have their hearts torn out, minced up and given to snakes, their entrails being thrown to dogs. Then, when their time is up, the pain will cease and their bodies become whole once more, preparatory to being passed through the sixteen wards.

In the first are non-worshippers and sceptics. In the second, those who have destroyed or hurt living creatures. In the third, those who do not fulfil their vows. In the fourth, believers in false doctrines, magicians, and sorcerers. In the fifth, those who

---

[33] Regarded by the Chinese with intense disgust.

[34] Father's, mother's, and wife's families.

[35] I know of few more pathetic passages throughout all the exquisite imagery of the Divine Comedy than this in which the guilty soul is supposed to look back to the home he has but lately left and gaze in bitter anguish on his desolate hearth and broken household gods. For once the gross tortures of Chinese Purgatory give place to as refined and as dreadful a punishment as human ingenuity could well devise.

tyrannize over the weak but cringe to the strong; also those who openly wish for another's death. In the sixth, those who try to put their misfortunes on to other people's shoulders. In the seventh, those who lead immoral lives. In the eighth, those who injure others to benefit themselves. In the ninth, those who are parsimonious and will not help people in trouble. In the tenth, those who steal and involve the innocent. In the eleventh, those who forget kindness or seek revenge. In the twelfth, those who by pernicious drugs stir up others to quarrel, keeping themselves out of harm's way. In the thirteenth, those who deceive or spread false reports. In the fourteenth, those who love brawling and implicate others. In the fifteenth, those who envy the virtuous and wise. In the sixteenth, those who are lost in vice, evil-speakers, slanderers, and such like.

All who disbelieve the doctrine of Cause and Effect, who obstruct good works, make a pretence of piety, talk of other people's sins, burn or injure religious books, omit to fast when praying for the sick, interfere with the adoration of Buddha, slander the priesthood, or, if scholars, abstain from instructing women and children; those who dig up graves and obliterate all traces thereof, set light to woods and forests, allow their servants to be careless in handling fire and thus endanger their neighbours' property; those who wantonly discharge arrows and bolts, who try their strength against the sick or weak, throw potsherds over a wall, poison fish, let off guns, catch birds either with net, sticky pole,[36] or trap; those who throw down salt to kill plants, who do not bury dead cats and venomous snakes deep in the ground, who dig out corpses, who break the soil or alter their walls and stoves at wrong seasons,[37] who encroach on the public road or take possession of other people's land, who fill up wells and drains, &c., &c.,—all these, when they return from the Terrace, shall first be tortured in the great Gehenna, and then such as are to have their hearts minced shall be passed into the sixteen wards, thence to be sent on to the Sixth Court for the punishment of other crimes. Those who in life have not been guilty of the above sins, or, having sinned, did on

---

[36] A long pole tipped with a kind of birdlime is cautiously inserted between the branches of a tree, and then suddenly dabbed on to some unsuspecting sparrow.

[37] If this is done in Winter or Spring the Spirits of the Hearth and Threshold are liable to catch cold.

the 8th day of the 1st moon, fasting, register a vow to sin no more, shall not only escape the punishments of this Court, but shall also gain some further remission of torture in the Sixth Court. Those, however, who are guilty of taking life, of gross immorality, of stealing and implicating the innocent, of ingratitude and revenge, of infatuated vice which no warnings can turn from its course,— these shall not escape one jot of their punishments.

THE SIXTH COURT.

This Court is situated at the bottom of the great Ocean, due north of the Wu-chiao rock. It is a vast, noisy Gehenna, many leagues in extent, and around it are sixteen wards.

In the first, the souls are made to kneel for long periods on iron shot. In the second, they are placed up to their necks in filth. In the third, they are pounded till the blood runs out. In the fourth, their mouths are opened with iron pincers and filled full of needles. In the fifth, they are bitten by rats. In the sixth, they are enclosed in a net of thorns and nipped by locusts. In the seventh, they are crushed to a jelly. In the eighth, their skin is lacerated and they are beaten on the raw. In the ninth, their mouths are filled with fire. In the tenth, they are licked by flames. In the eleventh, they are subjected to noisome smells. In the twelfth, they are butted by oxen and trampled on by horses. In the thirteenth, their hearts are scratched. In the fourteenth, their heads are rubbed till their skulls come off. In the fifteenth, they are chopped in two at the waist. In the sixteenth, their skin is taken off and rolled up into spills.

Those discontented ones who rail against Heaven and revile Earth, who are always finding fault either with the wind, thunder, heat, cold, fine weather or rain; those who let their tears fall towards the north;[38] who steal the gold from the inside[39] or scrape the gilding from the outside of images; those who take holy names in vain, who shew no respect for written paper, who throw down dirt and rubbish near pagodas or temples, who use dirty cook-

---

[38] I presume because God sits with his face to the south.
[39] Pious and wealthy people often give orders for an image of a certain P'u-sa to be made with an ounce or so of gold inside.

houses and stoves for preparing the sacrificial meats, who do not abstain from eating beef and dog-flesh;[40] those who have in their possession blasphemous or obscene books and do not destroy them, who obliterate or tear books which teach man to be good, who carve on common articles of household use the symbol of the origin of all things,[41] the Sun and Moon and Seven Stars, the Royal Mother and the God of Longevity on the same article,[42] or representations of any of the Immortals; those who embroider the Svastika[43] on fancy work, or mark characters on silk, satin, or cloth, on banners, beds, chairs, tables, or any kind of utensil; those who secretly wear clothes adorned with the dragon and the phœnix[44] only to be trampled under foot, who buy up grain and hold until the price is exorbitantly high—all these shall be thrust into the great and noisy Gehenna, there to be examined as to their misdeeds and passed accordingly into one of the sixteen wards, whence, at the expiration of their time, they will be sent for further questioning on to the Seventh Court.

All dwellers upon earth who on the 8th day of the 3rd moon, fasting, register a vow from that date to sin no more, and, on the 14th and 15th of the 5th moon, the 3rd of the 8th moon, and the 10th of the 10th moon, to practise abstinence, vowing moreover to exert themselves to convert others,—these shall escape the bitterness of all the above-mentioned wards.

THE SEVENTH COURT.

His Infernal Majesty, T'ai Shan, reigns at the bottom of the great Ocean, away to the north-west, below the Wu-Chiao rock.

---

[40] Primarily, because no living thing should be killed for food. The ox and the dog are specified because of their kindly services to man in tilling the earth and guarding his home.

[41] The symbol of the Yin and the Yang, so ably and so poetically explained by Mr. Alabaster in his pamphlet on the Doctrine of the Ch'i.

[42] One being male and the other being female. This calls to mind the extreme modesty of a celebrated French lady, who would not put books by male and female authors on the same shelf.

[43] The symbol on Buddha's heart; more commonly known to the western world as Thor's Hammer.

[44] Emblems of Imperial dignity.

His is a vast, noisy Court, measuring many leagues in circumference and subdivided into sixteen wards, as follows :—

In the first, the wicked souls are made to swallow their own blood. In the second, their legs are pierced and thrust into a fiery pit. In the third, their chests are cut open. In the fourth, their hair is torn out with iron combs. In the fifth, they are gnawed by dogs. In the sixth, great stones are placed on their heads. In the seventh, their skulls are pierced. In the eighth, they wear fiery clothes. In the ninth, their skin is torn and pulled by pigs. In the tenth, they are pecked by huge birds. In the eleventh, they are hung up and beaten on the feet. In the twelfth, their tongues are pulled out and their jaws bored. In the thirteenth, they are disembowelled. In the fourteenth, they are trampled on by mules and bitten by badgers. In the fifteenth, their fingers are ironed with hot irons. In the sixteenth, they are boiled in oil.

All mortals who practise eating red lead [45] and certain other nauseous articles, [46] who spend more than they should upon wine, who kidnap human beings for sale, who steal clothes and ornaments from coffins, who break up dead men's bones for medicine, who separate people from their relatives, who sell the girl brought up in the house to be their son's wife, who allow their wives [47] to drown female children, who stifle their illegitimate offspring, who unite to cheat another in gambling, who act as tutors without being properly strict, and thus wrong their pupils, who beat and injure their slaves without estimating the punishment by the fault, who regard districts entrusted to their charge in the light of so much spoil, who disobey their elders, who talk at random and go back on their word, who stir up others to quarrel and fight—all these shall, upon verification of their sins, be taken from the great Gehenna and passed through the proper wards, to be forwarded when their time has expired to the Eighth Court, again to be tortured according to their deserts.

All things may not be used as drugs. It is bad enough to slay birds, beasts, reptiles, and fishes, in order to prepare medicine for the sick ; but to use red lead and many of the filthy messes in

---

[45] Supposed to confer immortality.

[46] Unfit for translation.

[47] This is ingeniously expressed, as if *mothers* were the prime movers in such unnatural acts.

vogue is beyond all bounds of decency, and those who foul their mouths with these nasty mixtures, no matter how virtuous they may otherwise be, will not only derive no benefit from saying their prayers, but will be punished for so doing without mercy.

Ye who hear these words make haste to repent! From to-day forbear to take life, buy many birds and animals in order to set them free,[48] and every morning when you wash your teeth mutter a prayer to Buddha. Thus, when your last hour comes, a good angel will stand by your side and purify you of your former sins.

Some steal the bones of people who have been burnt to death or the bodies of illegitimate children, for the purpose of compounding medicines; others steal skulls and bones (from graves) with the same object. Worst of all are those who carry off bones by the basketful, using the hard ones for making various articles and grinding down the soft ones for the manufacture of pottery.[49] These, no matter what may have been their good works on earth, will not obtain thereby any remission of punishment; but when they are brought down below, the Ruler of the Infernal Regions will first pass them from the great Gehenna into the proper wards, and will send instructions to the Tenth Court that when they are born again on earth it shall be either without ears, or eyes, hand, foot, mouth, lips, or nose, or maimed in some way or other. Yet such as have thus sinned may still avoid this punishment, if only they are willing to pray and repent, vowing never to sin again. Or if they buy coffins for the poor and persuade others to do likewise, by these means giving a decent burial to many corpses—then, when the death-summons comes, the Spirits of the Home and Hearth will make a black mark upon the warrant, and punishment will be remitted.

Sometimes, when there is a famine, people have nothing to eat and die of hunger, and wicked men, almost before the breath is out of their bodies, cut them up and sell their flesh to others for food—a horrid crime indeed. Those who are guilty of such practices will, on arrival in the lower regions, be tortured in the

---

[48] On fête days at temples it is not uncommon to see cages full of birds hawked about among the holiday-makers, that those who feel twinges of conscience may purchase a sparrow or two and relieve themselves from anxiety by the simple means of setting them at liberty.

[49] Bones are used in glazing porcelain, to give a higher finish.

various Courts for the space of forty-nine [50] days, and then the judge of the Tenth Court will be instructed to notify the judge of the First Court to put them down in his register for a new birth,—if among men, as hungry famished outcasts, and if among animals as loathing the food that falls to their lot, and by-and-by perishing of hunger. Such is their reward. Besides the above, those who have eaten what is unfit for food and willingly continue to do so, will be punished either among men or animals according to their deserts. Their throats will swell, and though devoured by hunger they will be unable to swallow, and thus die. Those who do not err a second time may be forgiven as they deserve; but those who in times of distress subscribe money for the sufferers, prepare gruel, give away rice to the needy, or distribute ginger tea [51] and soup in the open street, and thus sustain life a little longer and do real good to their fellow creatures—all these shall not only obtain remission of their sins, but carry on a balance of good to their account which shall ensure them a happy old age in the life to come. [52]

Of the above three clauses, two were proposed by the officials attached to this Seventh Court, the third by the Chief Justice of the great Gehenna, and the whole submitted together for the approval of God, the following Rescript being obtained :—" Let it be as proposed ; let the three clauses be copied into the *Divine Panorama,* and let the officials concerned be promoted or rewarded. Also, in case of crimes other than those already provided for, let such be punished according to the statutes of the Rulers of the Four Continents on earth, and let any evasion of punishment and implication of innocent people be at once reported by the proper officials for our consideration. This from the Throne ! Obey ! "

O ye sons and daughters of men, if on the 27th of the 3rd moon, fasting and turned towards the north, ye register a vow to pray and repent, and to publish the whole of the *Divine Panorama* for the enlightenment of mankind, then ye may escape the bitterness of this Seventh Court.

---

[50] The seven periods of seven days each which occur immediately after a death and at which the departed shade is appeased with food and offerings of various kinds.

[51] To warm them.

[52] When they are born again on earth.

THE EIGHTH COURT.

His Infernal Majesty, Tu Shih, reigns at the bottom of the great Ocean, due east below the Wu-chiao rock, in a vast noisy Court many leagues in extent, subdivided into sixteen wards as follows :—

In the first, the wicked souls are rolled down mountains in carts. In the second, they are shut up in huge saucepans. In the third, they are minced.   In the fourth, their noses, eyes, mouths, &c. are stopped up.   In the fifth, their uvulas are cut off.   In the sixth, they are exposed to all kinds of filth.   In the seventh, their extremities are cut off.   In the eighth, their viscera[53] are fried.   In the ninth, their marrow is cauterized.   In the tenth, their bowels are scratched.   In the eleventh, they are inwardly burned with fire. In the twelfth, they are disembowelled.   In the thirteenth, their chests are torn open.   In the fourteenth, their skulls are split and their teeth dragged out.   In the fifteenth, they are hacked and gashed.   In the sixteenth, they are pricked with steel prongs.

Those who are unfilial, who do not nourish their relatives while alive or bury them when dead, who subject their parents to fright, sorrow, or anxiety—if they do not quickly repent them of their former sins, the spirit of the Hearth will report their misdoings and gradually deprive them of what prosperity they may be enjoying. Those who indulge in magic and sorcery will, after death, when they have been tortured in the other Courts, be brought here to this Court, and dragged backwards by bull-headed horse-faced devils to be thrust into the great Gehenna.   Then when they have been tortured in the various wards they will be passed on to the Tenth Court, whence at the expiration of a *kalpa*[54] they will be sent back to earth with changed heads and faces for ever to find their place amongst the brute creation.   But those who believe in the *Divine Panorama*, and on the 1st of the 4th moon make a vow of repentance, repeating the same every night and morning to the Spirit of the Hearth, shall, by virtue of one of three characters, *obedient, acquiescent*, or *repentant*, to be traced on their foreheads at

---

[53] Heart, lungs, spleen, liver, and kidneys.
[54] Many millions of years.

death by the Spirit of the Hearth, escape half the punishments from the first to the Seventh Court inclusive, and escape this Eighth Court altogether, being passed on to the Ninth Court, where cases of arson and poisoning are investigated, and finally born again from the Tenth Court among mankind as before.

To this God added, "Whosoever may circulate the *Divine Panorama* for the information of the world at large shall escape all punishment from the First to the Eighth Court inclusive. Passing through the Ninth and Tenth Courts, they shall be born again amongst men in some happy state.

THE NINTH COURT.

His Infernal Majesty, P'ing Têng, reigns at the bottom of the great Ocean, away to the south-west, below the Wu-chiao rock. His is the vast, circular hell of A-pi, many leagues in breadth, jealously enclosed by an iron net, and subdivided into sixteen wards, as follows:—

In the first, the wicked souls have their bones beaten and their bodies scorched. In the second, their muscles are drawn out and their bones rapped. In the third, ducks eat their heart and liver. In the fourth, dogs eat their intestines and lungs. In the fifth, they are splashed with hot oil. In the sixth, their heads are crushed in a frame, and their tongues and teeth are drawn out. In the seventh, their brains are taken out and their skulls filled with hedge-hogs. In the eighth, their heads are steamed and their brains scraped. In the ninth, they are dragged about by sheep till they drop to pieces. In the tenth, they are squeezed in a wooden press and pricked on the head. In the eleventh, their hearts are ground in a mill. In the twelfth, boiling water drips on to their bodies. In the thirteenth, they are stung by wasps. In the fourteenth, they are tortured by ants and maggots; they are then stewed, and finally wrung out (like clothes). In the fifteenth, they are stung by scorpions. In the sixteenth, they are tortured by venomous snakes, crimson and scarlet.

All who on earth have committed one of the ten great crimes, and have deserved either the lingering death, decapitation, strangulation, or other punishment, shall, after passing through the tortures of the previous Courts, be brought to this Court, together

with those guilty of arson, of making *ku* poison,[55] bad books,
stupefying drugs, and many other disgraceful acts. Then, if it be
found that, hearkening to the words of the *Divine Panorama*, they
subsequently destroyed the blocks of these books, burnt their
prescriptions, and ceased practising the magical art, they shall
escape the punishments of this Court and be passed on to the Tenth
Court, thence to be born again amongst the sons of men. But if,
having heard the warnings of the *Divine Panorama*, they still
continue to sin, from the Second to the Eighth Court their tortures
shall be increased. They shall be bound on to a hollow copper
pillar, clasping it round with their hands and feet. Then the pillar
shall be filled with fierce fire, so as to burn into their heart and
liver; and afterwards their feet shall be plunged into the great
Gehenna of A-pi, knives shall be thrust into their lungs, they shall
bite their own hearts, and gradually sink to the uttermost depths of
hell, there to endure excruciating torments until the victims of their
wickedness have either recovered the property out of which they
were cheated, or the life that was taken away from them, and until
every trace of book, prescription, picture, &c. formerly used by
these wicked souls has disappeared from the face of the earth.
Then, and only then, may they pass into the Tenth Court to be born
again in one of the Six States of existence.

O ye who have committed such crimes as these, on the 8th of the
4th moon, or the 1st or 15th (of any moon), fasting swear that you
will buy up all bad books and magical pamphlets and utterly destroy
them with fire; or that you will circulate copies of the *Divine
Panorama* to be a warning to others! Then, when your last
moment is at hand, the Spirit of the Hearth will write on your
forehead the two words *He obeyed*, and from the Second up to the
Ninth Court your good deeds will be rewarded by a diminution of
such punishments as you have incurred. People in the higher ranks
of life who secure incendiaries or murderers, who destroy the
blocks of bad books, or publish notices warning others, and offer
rewards for the production of such books, will be rewarded by the
success of their sons and grandsons at the public examinations.

---

[55] The following recipe for this deadly poison is given in the well-known
Chinese work *Instructions to Coroners*:—"Take a quantity of insects of all
kinds and throw them into a vessel of any kind; cover them up, and let a year
pass away before you look at them again. The insects will have killed and eaten
each other, until there is only one survivor, and this one is *K'u*."

Poor people who, by a great effort, manage to have the *Divine Panorama* circulated for the benefit of mankind, will be forwarded at once to the Tenth Court, and thence be born again in some happy state on earth.

THE TENTH COURT.

His Infernal Majesty, Chuan Lun,[56] reigns in the Dark Land, due east, away below the Wu-chiao rock, just opposite the Wu-cho of this world. There he has six bridges, of gold, silver, jade, stone, wood, and planks, over which all souls must pass. He examines the shades that are sent from the other courts, and, according to their deserts, sends them back to earth as men, women, old, young, high, low, rich, or poor, forwarding monthly a list of their names to the judge of the First Court for transmission to Fêng-tu.[57] The regulations provide that all beasts, birds, fishes, and insects, whether biped, quadruped, or otherwise, shall after death become *chien*,[58] to be born again for long and short lives alternately. But such as may possibly have taken life, and such as must necessarily have taken life, will pass through a revolution of the Wheel, and then, when their sins have been examined, they will be sent up on earth to receive the proper retribution. At the end of every year a report will be forwarded to Fêng-tu. Those scholars who study the Book of Changes, or priests who chant their liturgies, cannot be tortured in the Ten Courts for the sins they have committed. When they come to this Court their names and features are taken down in a book kept for the purpose, and they are forwarded to Mother Mêng, who drives them on to the Terrace of Oblivion and doses them with the draught of forgetfulness. Then they are born again in the world for a day, a week, or it may be a year, when they die once more; and now, having forgotten the holy words of the Three Religions,[59] they are carried off

---

[56] He who "turns the wheel;" a *chakravartti raja.*

[57] The capital city of the Infernal Regions.

[58] The ghosts of dead people are believed to be liable to death. The ghost of a ghost is called *chien.*

[59] On the "Three Systems." See Note 8. *Appendix.*

by devils to the various Courts, and are properly punished for their former crimes.

All souls whose balance of good and evil is exact, whose period, or whose crimes are many and good deeds few, as soon as their future state has been decided,—man, woman, beautiful, ugly, comfort, toil, wealth, or poverty, as the case may be,—must pass through the Terrace of Oblivion.

Amongst those shades, on their way to be born again in the world of human beings, there are often to be found women who cry out that they have some old and bitter wrong to avenge,[60] and that rather than be born again amongst men they would prefer to enter the ranks of hungry devils.[61] On examining them more closely it generally comes out that they are the virtuous victims of some wicked student, who may perhaps have an eye to their money, and accordingly dresses himself out to entrap them, or promises marriage when sometimes he has a wife already, or offers to take care of an aged mother or a late husband's children. Thus the foolish women are beguiled, and put their property in the wicked man's hands. By-and-by he turns round upon and reviles them, and, losing face in the eyes of their relatives and friends, with no one to redress their wrong, they are driven to commit suicide. Then, hearing[62] that their seducer is likely to succeed at the examination, they beg and implore to be allowed to go back and compass his death. Now, although what they urge is true enough, yet that man's destiny may not be worked out, or the transmitted effects of his ancestors' virtue may not have passed away;[63] therefore, as a compromise, these injured shades are allowed to send a spirit to the Examination Hall to hinder and confuse him in the preparation of his paper, or to change the names on the published list of successful candidates; and finally, when his hour arrives, to proceed with the spirit who carries the death-summons, seize him, and bring him to the First Court of judgment.

Ye who on the 17th of the 4th moon swear to carry out the precepts of the *Divine Panorama*, and frequently make these words the

---

[60] Women are considered in China to be far more revengeful than men.

[61] See *Author's Own Record* (in *Introduction*), note 26.

[62] While in Purgatory.

[63] It was mentioned above that the rewards for virtue would be continued to a man's sons and grandsons.

subject of your conversation, may in the life to come be born again amongst men and escape official punishments, fire, flood, and all accidents to the body.

The place where the Wheel of Fate goes round is many leagues in extent, enclosed on all sides by an iron palisade. Within are eighty-one subdivisions, each of which has its proper officers and magisterial appointments. Beyond the palisade there is a labyrinth of 108,000 paths leading by direct and circuitous routes back to earth. Inside it is as dark as pitch, and through it pass the spirits of priest and layman alike. But to one who looks from the outside everything is seen as clear as crystal, and the attendants who guard the place all have the faces and features they had at their birth. These attendants are chosen from virtuous people who in life were noted for filial piety, friendship, or respect for life, and are sent here to look after the working of the Wheel and such duties. If for a space of five years they make no mistakes they are promoted to a higher office; but if found to be lazy or careless they are reported to the Throne for punishment.

Those who in life have been unfilial or have destroyed much life, when they have been tortured in the various Courts are brought here and beaten to death with peach twigs. They then become *chien*, and with changed heads and altered faces are turned out into the labyrinth to proceed by the path which ends in the brute creation.

Birds, beasts, fishes and insects, may ·after many myriads of *kalpas* again resume their original shapes; and if there are any that during three existences do not destroy life, they may be born amongst human beings as a reward, a record being made and their names forwarded to the First Court for approval. But all shades of men and women must proceed to the Terrace of Oblivion.

Mother Mêng was born in the Earlier Han Dynasty. In her childhood she studied books of the Confucian school; when she grew up she chanted the liturgies of Buddha. Of the past and the future she had no care, but occupied herself in exhorting mankind to desist from taking life and become vegetarians. At eighty-one years of age her hair was white and her complexion like a child's. She lived and died a virgin, calling herself simply Mêng; but men called her Mother Mêng. She retired to the hills and lived as a *religieuse* until the Later Han. Then, because certain evil-doers, relying on their knowledge of the past, used to

beguile women by pretending to have been their husbands in a
former life, God commissioned Mother Mêng to build the Terrace of
Oblivion, and appointed her as guardian, with devils to wait upon
her and execute her commands. It was arranged that all shades
who had been sentenced in the Ten Courts to return in various
conditions to earth should first be dosed by her with a decoction of
herbs, sweet, bitter, acrid, sour or salt. Thus they forgot everything that has previously happened to them, and carry away with
them to earth some slight weaknesses such as the mouth watering at
the thought (of something nice), laughter inducing perspiration, fear
inducing tears, anger inducing sobs, or spitting from nervousness.
Good spirits who go back into the world will have their senses of
sight, hearing, smell, and taste very much increased in power, and
their physical strength and constitution generally will be much
bettered. But evil spirits will experience the exact contrary of this,
as a reward for previous sins and as a warning to others to pray and
repent.

The Terrace is situated in front of the Ten Courts, outside the
six bridges. It is square, measuring ten (Chinese) feet every way,
and surrounded by 108 small rooms. To the east there is a raised
path, one foot four inches in breadth, and in the rooms above-
mentioned are prepared cups of forgetfulness ready for the arrival of
the shades. Whether they swallow much or little it matters not; but
sometimes there are perverse devils who altogether refuse to drink.
Then beneath their feet sharp blades start up, and a copper tube
is forced down their throats, by which means they are compelled
to swallow some. When they have drunk, they are raised by the
attendants and escorted back by the same path. They are next
pushed on to the Bitter Bamboo floating bridge, with torrents of
rushing red water on either side. Half way across they perceive
written in large characters on a red cliff on the opposite side the
following lines:—

" To be a man is easy, but to act up to one's responsibilities as such is hard.
    Yet to be a man once again is harder still.

    For those who would be born again in some happy state there is no great
        difficulty;
    It is only necessary to keep mouth and heart in harmony."

When the shades have read these words they try to jump on shore,
but are beaten back into the water by two huge devils. One has
on a black official hat and embroidered clothes; in his hand he

holds a paper pencil, and over his shoulder he carries a sharp sword. Instruments of torture hang at his waist, fiercely he glares out of his large round eyes and laughs a horrid laugh. His name is *Short Life*. The other has a dirty face smeared with blood ; he has on a white coat, an abacus in his hand and a rice sack over his shoulder. Round his neck hangs a string of paper money ; his brow contracts hideously, and he utters long sighs. His name is *They have their reward*, and his duty is to push the shades into the red water. The wicked and foolish rejoice at the prospect of being born once more as human beings; but the better shades weep and mourn that in life they did not lay up a store of virtuous acts, and thus pass away from the state of mortals for ever.[64] Yet they all rush on to birth like an infatuated or drunken crowd ; and again, in their early childhood, hanker after the forbidden flavours.[65] Then, regardless of consequences, they begin to destroy life, and thus forfeit all claims to the mercy and compassion of God. They take no thought as to the end that must overtake them ; and finally, they bring themselves once more to the same horrid plight.

---

[64] That is, go to heaven.
[65] Of meat, wine, &c.

C C 2

APPENDIX B.

ANCESTRAL WORSHIP.

"The rudimentary form of all religion is the propitiation of dead ancestors, who are supposed to be still existing, and to be capable of working good or evil to their descendants."—SPENCER'S ESSAYS. Vol. iii., p. 102.—*The Origin of Animal Worship.*

BILOCATION.

"As a general rule, people are apt to consider it impossible for a man to be in two places at once, and indeed a saying to that effect has become a popular saw. But the rule is so far from being universally accepted, that the word 'bilocation' has been invented to express the miraculous faculty possessed by certain saints of the Roman Church, of being in two places at once ; like St. Alfonso di Liguori, who had the useful power of preaching his sermon in church while he was confessing penitents at home."—TYLOR'S *Primitive Culture.* Vol. i., p. 447.

BURIAL RITES.

"Hence the various burial rites—the placing of weapons and valuables along with the body, the daily bringing of food to it, &c. I hope hereafter, to show that with such knowledge of facts as he has, this interpretation is the most reasonable the savage can arrive at."—SPENCER'S ESSAYS. Vol. iii., p. 104.—*The Origin of Animal Worship.*

DREAMS.

"The distinction so easily made by us between our life in dreams and our real life, is one which the savage recognises in but a vague way; and he cannot express even that distinction which he perceives. When he awakes, and to those who have seen him lying quietly asleep, describes where he has been, and what he has done, his rude language fails to state the difference between seeing and dreaming that he saw, doing and dreaming that he did. From this inadequacy of his language it not only results that he cannot truly represent this difference to others, but also that he cannot truly represent it to himself."—SPENCER'S ESSAYS. Vol. iii., pp. 103,104.

SHADE OR SHADOW.

"The ghost or phantasm seen by the dreamer or the visionary is an unsubstantial form, like a shadow, and thus the familiar term of the *shade* comes in to express the soul. Thus the Tasmanian word for the shadow is also that for the spirit; the Algonquin Indians describe a man's soul as *otahchuk*, 'his shadow;' the Quiché language uses *natub* for 'shadow, soul;' the Arawac *ueja* means 'shadow, soul, image;" the Abipones made the one word *lodkal* serve for 'shadow, soul, echo, image."—TYLOR'S *Primitive Culture.* Vol. i., p. 430.

SHADOW.

"Thus the dead in Purgatory knew that Dante was alive when they saw that, unlike theirs, his figure cast a shadow on the ground."—TYLOR'S *Primitive Culture.* Vol. i., p. 431.

THE SOUL.

"The savage, conceiving a corpse to be deserted by the active personality who dwelt in it, conceives this active personality to be still existing, and his feelings and ideas concerning it form the basis of his superstitions.—SPENCER'S ESSAYS. Vol. iii., p. 103.—*The Origin of Animal Worship.*

TRANSMIGRATION.

"Whether the Buddhists receive the full Hindu doctrine of the migration of the individual soul from birth to birth, or whether they refine away into metaphysical subtleties the notion of continued personality, they do consistently and systematically hold that a man's life in former existences is the cause of his now being what he is, while at this moment he is accumulating merit or demerit whose result will determine his fate in future lives."—TYLOR's *Primitive Culture*. Vol. ii., p. 12.

TRANSMIGRATION.

"Memory, it is true, fails generally to recall these past births, but memory, as we know, stops short of the beginning even of this present life."—TYLOR's *Primitive Culture*. Vol. ii., p. 12.

TRANSMIGRATION.

"As for believers, savage or civilised, in the great doctrine of metempsychosis, these not only consider that an animal may have a soul, but that this soul may have inhabited a human being, and thus the creature may be in fact their own ancestor or once familiar friend."—TYLOR's *Primitive Culture*. Vol. i., p. 469.

TREE-SOULS.

"Orthodox Buddhism decided against the tree-souls, and consequently against the scruple to harm them, declaring trees to have no mind nor sentient principle, though admitting that certain dewas or spirits do reside in the body of trees, and speak from within them."—TYLOR's *Primitive Culture*. Vol. i., p. 475.

THOS. DE LA RUE AND CO., PRINTERS, BUNHILL ROW, LONDON.

INDEX TO THE NOTES.